SHADOW WALKER

L A BANKS

Publisher

Leslie Esdaile Banks, LLC
P.O. Box 42225
Philadelphia, PA 19101

www.LeslieEsdaileBanks.com
Email with Inquiries to: Leslie@LeslieEsdaileBanks.com

Edition: December 2010

DEDICATION

As always, my greatest thanks goes to the Creator and all the angels who shepherd my steps through this journey called life, as well as to the ancestors who whisper in my ear about the people and things they think I should write about (and they keep me busy!).

But there are also certain people—earth angels as I like to call them—who make the process of being on this journey, which feels like a mission or quest sometimes, not just bearable but fun, funny, crazy and absolutely a joy. So I have to thank Lissa, Gretta and Sesvalah who held me up in prayer through the arduous process of getting this particular baby born. They were the true earthly midwives of this process to make *Shadow Walker* manifest. Then of course there are always the eager readers and the staunch street team (who forever has my back). I so deeply appreciate your enthusiasm and positive encouragement—you all bring the Light! At points you cheered me on and made me push, and gave me that extra coaching needed to muscle through the labor pains—even when it seemed like it might be a breeched birth. But no matter what, the book made it to come wailing into the world. Ha! We did it as a team. For that, I THANK YOU and LOVE YOU right on back!

SPECIAL ACKNOWLEDGMENTS

No dedication is right without acknowledging the folks who lent their special talent, skill and sheer force of nature to make this happen, therefore special thanks goes to Lissa Woodson, who hung through the darkest times; to JL Woodson and Barron Steward, who made the website pop; to Leslie Wainger who edited this book back to life after it had suffered so many abuses; to Sara Crowe, who believed it back to life when all seemed lost; to Joe Konrath, the mad scientist who had alternative treatments for the patient that worked miracles (I love you, Joe—you are my hero!); to "52 novels" Rob Siders, Carl Graves and Cheryl Perez who made it do what it do, helped it get up and walk; and to my long-time editor and friend Chandra Sparks Taylor who put the finishing polish on this project; and the uber dedicated Dr. J. MenaqAmurr Neferkhar-Menzise, Ph.D., N.D., C.H., who actually went through the book after the first printing and put his EXPERT eye on each line of each page and caught things that none of the rest of us saw (and corrected them!)—bless you all!

Look for book 2, *Shadow Seekers*, sometime in 2011…

www.NeteruAcademy.com

PART ONE
AWAKENING

"May I look upon my soul and my shadow."

—The Egyptian Book of the Dead

Chapter 1

The Compound

Sixteen years after the Armageddon

The demon was so close now that she could feel its icy breath on her neck. Sarah Rivera swung her bedroom lamp at it as she lurched toward the door, yanked it open and dashed into the dark hallway. The corridor was longer than it had ever been, as though something unnatural had drawn it out before her so that she could never reach the end of it to get to safety.

Running hard, she focused with all her might on the tiny emergency exit light that now seemed miles away. That beacon was the only source of illumination in what had otherwise become pitch blackness. Shadows loomed and stretched around the faraway light as though mocking it, mocking *her,* dimming its effectiveness as she reached out toward it.

Then, as if the air around her had become molasses, her legs suddenly felt heavy and mired in a sticky goo of atmosphere, making her struggle just to put one foot before the other. She tried to scream, even to call for her mother or father, but no sound came out.

Pure panic gripped her as she saw her best friend's bedroom door ajar. Tami would help her. They could fight this beast together.

Sarah slogged through the density that clung to her legs and thrust her way through Tami's open door. Tami was standing in the darkened room, hands on hips, face wearing her usual smart-ass smile. But her friend's eyes weren't right. They weren't Tami's eyes. They were the eyes of the demon!

The bedroom door slammed behind Sarah with a loud bang. Instantly the entire room went pitch black. Not even moonlight shone through the window. Sarah's scream began in the pit of her stomach but never reached her throat. Her heart slammed against her breastbone. She could hear things moving in the dark, circling her, stirring the air.

In the next second, she was awake.

Sarah sat up quickly in the dark, panting. She immediately reached for her nightstand lamp and clicked it on, covering her heart with a hand. A slight sheen of perspiration made her tank top and panties cling to her body. The sheets around her were in a tangle about her legs, and she flung them off her. The pillows were gone from the bed, cast to the floor during the nightmare.

Almost in tears, she leaned forward and rubbed her temples, feeling like her bedroom was closing in on her. Her head ached in a strumming throb. This was the third nightmare in a week. She was tired of trying to convince her mom and dad that the dreams had nothing to do with the stress of taking placement tests for school. Each time the demon in her dreams got closer. Tonight it had gotten too damned close. That had to mean something. It all felt too real.

But it annoyed her to no end that her parents were always so preoccupied with their own lives and problems that they could never seem to make time to really listen to her or to take her seriously. Other people had problems, too. They weren't the only ones in the world going through hell.

If she were psychic, like they were, and had a daughter who was slowly coming into her extrasensory powers, like they did, she would make the time to listen. She was sure of that. But they didn't. Sarah frowned. They claimed she had performance anxiety and then blew her off. Maybe it was easier for them that way. Who wanted to deal with a kid who had issues when you had more important stuff to address?

Sarah let out a forlorn sigh. She could hear her father's voice booming inside her brain like low, rolling thunder. She leaned forward and clasped her hands on either side of her head. Yes, she could hear them. They were somewhere in the compound...Were her parents *fighting*?

She threw back the covers to completely untangle herself and easily navigated her way through her semi-darkened bedroom to yank on some sweatpants and her sneakers.

Their words were hard to make out, but the urgency in her father's tone was unmistakable. Never in her life had she heard her dad sound like that; never had she experienced hearing someone so clearly inside her head. She needed to get closer.

She slipped out of her bedroom and quietly made her way down the hall, still jittery from the all-too-recent nightmare, barely noticing the blood-red moon outside her window.

She had only gone twenty-five feet when she saw her brother, Alejandro, sneaking out of his own bedroom.

"Pssst," Sarah said.

Al gave a quick start and whirled around to face her. His surprised expression turned into his normal glower once he saw it was her.

"Don't do that," he whispered furiously. "What's your problem?"

"Did you hear it?" Normally she only had biting comments for her irritating twin brother, but not tonight. She was glad he was there with her.

"You heard Mom's voice inside your head, too?" he asked, still frowning.

Sarah shook her head. "Just Dad…what's up?"

"They're fighting," Al said, stating the obvious. "Never heard 'em go at it like that before, though. This isn't one of their normal arguments." He glanced down the hall. "I'll let you know if I find out anything."

They stared at each other for a moment. For once she wished her brother would just drop his defenses and be on her side. He was a telepath just like her. If they teamed up, they could find out what was wrong faster. Most times Al didn't seem to be able to do that. But this was so much bigger than who was supposedly their parents' favorite or who was demonstrating special abilities first, or any of that other craziness. Sarah briefly closed her eyes and bit her bottom lip, trying to find a way to reach her twin. When she finally looked at him, she could feel the wall Al always kept between them beginning to crumble.

"Please, Al…can't we do this together? I'm really worried." She held her brother's gaze until he looked away.

"What if they're breaking up or something?" she finally whispered, hugging herself. "I didn't hear what Dad was saying…I *felt* it."

Al ran a hand through his hair. "When I heard Mom's voice, it was like glass shattering inside my chest. I need to get closer so I can hear what's going on."

"You mean so you can eavesdrop," Sarah said dryly, and as soon as she said it, she wished she hadn't.

"Yeah, well, then why are you out here?"

"I know. You're right. I'm sorry. I'm just used to sparring with you, but tonight…"

"Exactly. And that's why I don't wanna be around you," he said, folding his arms over his chest. "You judge people, Sarah. But whatever is going on with Mom and Dad is more important than whatever you think."

Al smirked when she had nothing to say in response. Sarah scowled as he turned and began creeping down the hall again, then sighed and followed. It was better than nothing.

She and Al had long since learned all the back service corridors and stairwells of the old hotel that their parents had converted into a mountain safe house for their family sixteen years ago. In fact, all the Neteru Guardian team members lived there as one big crazy combination of blood relatives mixed in with warrior friends for life that shared no actual blood ties—uncles and aunts were more titles than real biological links. But it didn't matter. They were still considered family. All the kids grew up like brothers and sisters or functioned like cousins under the same roof. All of them had long since learned their way around the property, unbeknownst to the often battle-distracted adults, and had spent hours of play going through the secret passageways of the old hotel.

So, getting to the war room unnoticed—where they suspected their parents were—would be a piece of cake. Or would have been—until Tami opened her bedroom door and joined them in the hallway.

"What's up?" Tami said after a brief yawn, looking at them with a curious smile.

It always amazed Sarah how Tami's great figure could make even a pair of cut-off sweats, a rumpled tank and a bed-head ponytail look good. Her best friend stretched, yanked the scrunchie off her long, dark-brown hair and tugged it into a tighter updo, and then put her hand on her hip. Her curious hazel eyes were lit with mischief, and that, combined with the hypnotic stare that she'd inherited from her once-vampire mom, always made resisting her questions a hard thing to do. "C'mon, guys, spill."

"This is family business," Al muttered. "You should go back to bed."

Sarah glanced at her brother. It was odd how even when he was being snarky toward Tami, his tone softened.

Oblivious, Tami just looked at him for a moment as if he had lost his mind. "My BFF here mentally called me, so don't you tell me to—"

"I didn't call you," Sarah said quickly.

"Sure you did," Tami replied. "Here." She tapped her temple with a finger and gave Sarah a wink.

Yeah, Sarah thought. Ever since her cool older cousin Ayana—or Yaya, as she was always called—who was nineteen years old to her fifteen, had gone off to school, she and Tami had been soul-linked like that. If she was ever in trouble, Tami would know it and vice versa. That was how it had been with her and Yaya. If ever she felt bad, down or blue, Yaya just knew it and came to her with all the right words and a well-timed hug. Sarah swallowed hard, trying to hold back the emotions that might make her voice quaver.

Now she and Tami were connected just like she and Yaya had once been, which was more like twins than she and Al. They'd said one day Yaya would be her mother-seer in a battle compound. But Tami was so different from Yaya. And Tami was also different from Sarah herself, even though in all truth, Sarah had to admit that Tami was her best friend. Still…Tami had an attitude with an edge; Yaya had a soothing gentleness that wrapped around any wound you brought her to inspect.

Her parents fighting downstairs made the ache for Yaya blossom within Sarah's chest. She missed Yaya so much. She wished things between her and Al were different, too. But it was what it was. Sarah looked at Tami, silently begging her to just leave things alone.

"T," Sarah said, exhaling heavily, "our parents are fighting…and it sounds bad. We're going to find out what's going on." She glanced at her brother, who'd already started down the hall. "I'll be back."

Tami looked concerned but just gave her a quick hug and then made the call me sign. She slipped back into her room while Sarah hurried after Al.

They took the back way, which ran behind what was now the war room before heading down two flights of stairs. Sarah tried her best to ignore the forms cavorting in the dark corners. The shadows seemed especially playful tonight. Actually, she called them playful, but she had never bothered to find out what they wanted. Her mom and grandma said they were harmless and that being able to see what was really in the shadows was all a part of her second sight. *Some gift*. But since no one else in the house could see them, she didn't really want to know what these eerily stretching shapes meant.

Right now, she stayed close to Al as she hurried past them and ignored the fact that they seemed to be laughing at her.

She and Al stopped outside the war room and splayed their hands against the wall for better reception.

"They didn't even seal the room," Sarah said in awe. She turned and looked at her brother. "It's wide open to a telepathic siphon."

"More than that, I bet if we try hard enough we can get an image to come into our minds," he said, closing his eyes. "They must be really pissed to leave themselves vulnerable like that."

Her brother's comment chilled her. Sarah closed her eyes, straining to hear.

The twins fell silent once more, losing themselves as they tuned in to the voices just beyond their reach. Sarah felt her hands almost become one with the paint on the service corridor exit walls, her awareness drowning out the sound of her heartbeat and that of her brother's. Muddied voices soon gave way to clarity. She could feel the impact of the emotions like a gut punch first, and then the sound came after it, like a Doppler effect.

"I don't give a rat's ass, Damali!" her father shouted. "I don't want those kids going to the Academy until we find out who or what is snatching bodies! Some agent of evil is kidnapping students, snatching these kids out of thin freakin' air! We forced the Armageddon, Damali, and made it come early. So now who knows what the real timeline is for the return of the ultimate evil? What about that ain't clear?"

Sarah's and Al's heads snapped around, and they stared at each other, eyes wide in shock. Their father was no longer speaking to their mother in his normal controlled diction. He'd lapsed into hard slang and his Spanish accent was now getting thicker by the second the more upset he became. That always happened when her dad went ballistic.

"Bodies?" Al mouthed. "Kidnapping students!"

Sarah shook her head frantically. She didn't want to know what they were talking about. Her father had said someone—or maybe it was actually something—was out there kidnapping people from school. Snatching bodies? Where, how, how many kids were missing? It was so horrible she wanted to just turn away from the telepathic eavesdropping. This had been a bad idea. But curiosity won out as Al pointed to the wall and they both went back to listening.

"You have to have faith…and they aren't babies any more, Carlos," her mother was saying, her tone firm but calm. "Sooner or later the kids have to learn to battle the same things, if not worse, than we fought."

"What? They're only fifteen years old. All of 'em—every kid in this compound! That thing we chased back to Hell during the Armageddon was not supposed to surface for twenty-one years! Every telepath we know said so. And now—"

"We don't know that's what it is, Carlos. It doesn't have to be the ultimate evil, it could be—"

"They aren't ready, D!"

"You mean *you* aren't ready, Carlos. And that's why they *have to* go to the Academy—to learn how to fight what will be coming for them a few short years from now."

"They don't have to go while the school is in crisis, Damali. That's all I'm saying."

"That's all you've been saying since they hit puberty and started presenting their talents. I told you then it was time for them to go into intensive training with the others, but you wouldn't listen to me. Now they're—"

"You and I both know these kids are special, D. They aren't like the kids from other Guardian compounds—they're from *the Neteru squad* and need a few more years of individualized attention."

"Just stop it, Carlos. It's now or never. I'm just as worried about them as you are, and I love them just as much as you do. But as their mother, I know we can't take them to the next level as parents. To keep them here is to handicap them, and I won't allow that. Not with what they're facing as their destiny. They have to get the intensive talent training, all day, every day, plus all the regular stuff, like history, technology, math, science—everything that we don't have time to teach. How are we supposed to do that while we're out in the world battling everything that goes bump in the night? The closer it gets to the return of the Unnamed, the more we're seeing demon raids on innocent humans. Am I wrong? So when will we be here at the compound to keep them safe, huh? When will we be able to take time to keep them sharp on how to slay vampires, how to take down a werewolf or how to behead any number of hellhole vermin without getting nicked? When you figure that part out, Carlos Rivera, you let me know. Until then, they're going to the Academy."

There were two beats of silence, and she imagined her father standing there, his face getting a little red, eyes slowly turning silver, and fangs lowering, which happened whenever he got annoyed—tonight he sounded way more than annoyed.

"And what?" her father finally said. "I'm not ready to have my only baby girl and my only son snatched down a damned demon hole!" His voice was rising again. "Is that wrong? Am I out of line for feeling parental concern?"

Sarah nearly gasped aloud when the strong surge of her father's anger, frustration and, to a lesser degree, his fear pulsed through her. All of a sudden her mind's eye snapped completely open in a way it never had before. Suddenly she could see the inside of the war room. She and Al must have gotten in sync and now were concentrating together so hard that their powers had combined to show them what was going on beyond the wall. Never in her life had a vision exploded inside her head like this one did.

Her father was walking in a tight circle, gathering ammunition, picking up shells and a shotgun, as well as stuffing his vest with grenades. Her mother was at the door, arms folded, blocking his exit. They weren't breaking up. They were having a standoff. But it was clear that he was going demon hunting tonight no matter what her mother said to him.

Her father was in rare form. Tall, muscular, caramel colored, with short dark hair and dark eyes that were flashing fire. Although they were arguing, she could see the look of appreciation in her mother's expression as she watched him pace angrily around the room. But her dad was no pretty boy, handsome as he was. Beneath his normal city street charm as her uncles called it, there was no mistaking that demon-killer instinct lurking just beneath his surface. Something had detonated that in him tonight. She just wished she knew what it was. Bodies were missing? Whose? What had grabbed them? No wonder he was flipping out. Plus, the reminder about her own and her brother's destiny to fight evil made her weak in the knees. She didn't want to be a demon hunter! Not now, *not ever.*

Her dad was a warrior, merciless when protecting his own. Vampires were, by nature and reputation, ruthless—and her dad used to be a vamp before he went into the Light. That was no secret. Everybody in the family knew it, all the other Guardians knew it, and it was the thing that gave him a little extra street cred when he told people he had a bad feeling about something. She just wondered why her mom wasn't listening to him about something as important as this.

Puzzled, her palms moist against the wall, Sarah strained harder to hear. It just didn't make sense. If her dad wanted to defend them all against something terrible, then what was her mom's problem? Legend had it that her dad had taken the word *ruthless* to a whole new level while in the Dark Realms. She'd seen the vamp trait of being ice cold when it came to revenge in both Al and Tami, but the ruthless gene seemed to have skipped her entirely. Sarah let out a soft sigh. She definitely took after her mother and was more prone to diplomacy rather than brute force.

Well, at least Dad hadn't totally dropped fangs yet, she thought. Even though her Mom had told her long ago that, technically he wasn't a Vampire any longer, at least not since he'd been pardoned by the Light, some things were still fused in his DNA. His fangs were one of those leftover things from his past, like his temper. When her father's fangs started showing at full length, it was a sure sign he was about to blow.

"Then let's do a sweep, me and you—as Neterus," her mother finally said, tucking a Glock nine-millimeter in the waistband of her fatigues. "If we can shut down any demon portals that have opened up near the school, then they go. But we cannot home-school these kids forever until all evil in the world is vanquished. That just isn't a part of their destiny."

Sarah and Al glanced at each other once again. They had long gotten used to hearing about their "destiny" and the war they would inherit as their parents' children.

It was common compound knowledge that, sixteen years ago, just before she and Al had been born, the world as everyone knew it had come to an end. To hear their parents tell it, everything had changed big time. It was hard to imagine a world different from the one they now lived in, but within all their lessons and as a regular part of the conversations around the compound, everybody referred to the secret war that had gone on for centuries between The Light and the Dark Realms. Then all of a sudden the battle had come to a head because their parents chased the darkness into the depths of hell, and the Armageddon—the last battle—hit the streets, where normal humans finally saw what had gone unseen for eons. Governments fell, economies crashed...She could feel Al's question forming in his head just like it was forming in hers—was it happening all over again, but this time earlier than the prophecies foretold?

Back then, pockets of humanity had eventually returned. But if another huge war like that broke out, what would people do? Food was already scarce, disease was rampant, people fought like animals for clean water and anything that would make life bearable. Her family said that living in the world as it was now was like living in a nightmare. For months now, leading up to her planned departure for the Academy, she'd been having horrible nightmares…the kind her mother and Nana said would pass, but their eyes told her differently. They knew something was wrong, too.

Just like she'd always been able to feel things a little deeper than the others could, right now the hairs were standing up on her arms. What if their destiny was here now? What if evil wasn't going to wait until they were twenty-one? That was what nobody else in the compound seemed to get. Sarah covered her heart with one palm and squeezed her eyes shut tighter. Her heart felt like it was slamming a path out of her chest. This whole destiny concept wasn't going to be fun—it would be bloody and terrifying, as far as she could tell. Besides, what if the evil that missed them the first time was now on a rampage, snatching kids from school in search of the Neteru compound brood? They were *so* not ready to go to war, to be any kind of heroes, much less to save the world.

But then again, what was she going to do, stay home alone while her parents were off fighting demons and the other kids were at school? At least at the Academy there'd be safety in numbers. Sarah said a silent prayer. *Please, please, God, don't let the Armageddon be happening again.*

Most of the survivors of the Armageddon lived in colonies established by the new world leader, who her parents said was an agent of the Antichrist. It was forbidden to mention his name, because according to Nana Marlene, words and names had power, especially when spoken by those with supernatural strength. Regardless, those colonies were strictly governed and fiercely protected. But not everyone chose to live there. Not everyone trusted that new leadership. Her parents clearly didn't.

But what could be going on outside their little oasis, if her parents and aunts and uncles had driven evil back to the Dark Realms years ago? Where had the students and staff gone missing from—in the little-town colonies around the compound? At the Academy itself? It was all too bizarre.

It didn't seem likely they could be attacked here. Sarah repeated the facts to calm herself now, the same way she would when she had bad dreams. She had to relax; she was just freaking herself out.

Her dad had used his powers to relocate them to the Greenbrier Hotel deep in the Appalachian Mountains. It was well-hidden and inaccessible except by air or by energy transport. All the roads leading to it had been destroyed in the war. It was from here that all the adults in the family continued to fight against any remnants of the Dark Realms, alongside other guerrilla Guardian colonies around the world. But here, *home,* was supposed to be safe. It was. *It was.* It really, really *was.*

An uneasiness crept through Sarah as her brother turned away to continue listening. Her parents weren't just regular Guardians of the Light—they were Neterus, the highest level of warrior, chosen as the leaders by all other Guardians. And their children's destiny training was supposed to begin at the Academy, the secret, exclusive school set up to train the best warriors of the Light. How could the place that housed kids from all the Guardian teams all over the world not be safe?

But from her parents' argument, it was clear that trouble was brewing at the Academy. Bodies. They had mentioned bodies. If that was true, then maybe she and Al weren't going to get the chance to learn slowly or to get a little older before taking on the Dark Realm, or even get to meet other Guardian kids their own age. Maybe it meant they would get thrown right into combat or something equally bad. All her life she'd dreamt of just having a chance to be normal, not to have to live in hiding…maybe be around other people besides her relatives. Now it seemed like maybe none of that would happen.

That sucked.

Sarah glanced at her brother. Al would jump at a chance to carry weapons and blast demons. She could feel the excitement coursing through him, and it made her sad. Even if they didn't like each other very much, she still loved him and didn't want to see him dead. Resigned, Sarah closed her eyes again and touched the wall.

"Okay," her father was saying when she tuned back into her parents' conversation. "We do a sweep tonight, then. My main concern is that the Morrigan could be involved. If that's true, we're screwed."

"If we've gone up against the Unnamed One and the entire Vampire Council," her mother argued, "then I'm not afraid of the Morrigan."

Sarah gasped, and Al cut her a sharp look to be quiet. But didn't he get it? The legends they'd always heard about, the history they had been taught over and over, was coming to life!

The Morrigan might be involved in this…fallen Guardians who used their talents for the dark side. They were as bad as Vampires, as far as she was concerned. From everything she'd ever been told, the Morrigan would do anything for favors, extra human comforts, and for power to lord it over people who were stuck in controlled colonies. Sarah jerked her attention back to her parents, both hearing them and seeing them in her mind's eye. Now she really had to know what was going on.

"I never said anything about *fearing* the Morrigan," her father snarled, his fangs cresting in anger. "I said we're screwed because they know our ways, knew our defenses before they fell…know about the Academy. They can hurt our children, Damali."

Her father paced away from the munitions tables and raked his fingers through his hair. "Now kids are missing, Guardians are being picked off one-by-one. If we don't find this bastard now or find out who's actually doing his dirty work and how…"

History and legend were coming to life right before her eyes as their parents prepared for a night raid. Al and Sarah glanced at each other again, knowing that their dad was now talking about Zaphon, although nobody used that name for him anymore. All Guardians knew that Zaphon was still a threat, but they were always told he wouldn't surface until they were at least twenty-one years old. Her parents had breeched Hell to drive him back where he belonged and had badly injured him, which was what kicked off the Armageddon early when his dad found out.

But what if the Dark Realm had discovered a way to heal him early? What if, because her parents had forced the Armageddon early, this was the real time when it had been meant to happen—well before she and Al were ready to deal with their so-called destiny to fight in it?

Horrifying thoughts took flight inside Sarah's head. Panic made it hard for her to breathe.

"Carlos," her mother said, her voice soothing, and Sarah wondered how her mom managed to sound so calm. "I know you wanted to smoke the beast's heir before he claimed power over the world, but you just might have to accept the fact that maybe it's our children's destiny to handle that, not ours."

Sarah felt like she was about to pass out for a second. It could not be her and her brother's destiny to go up against Zaphon. She didn't care what they'd been told all their lives about destiny. She'd never thought that meant Zaphon. No, no, no, no, no.

"I'm not accepting that philosophical bullshit, Damali!" her father shouted, pointing at her mother. "It's my job as their father to give them a leg up and a safer world!"

You tell her, Dad, Sarah whispered inside her mind, squeezing her eyes shut tighter.

"You *did*. *We* did," her mother said firmly. "But we are not God, not by a long shot."

Her father stopped pacing, placed his hands on his hips and let his head drop forward wearily. It was a while before he looked up at her mother again. When he did, his expression was softer, and there was a different kind of intensity in his eyes. Sarah let out a short breath of frustration. This was the way all their fights seemed to end—her mom just broke her dad down with relentless, tenderly stated facts, and he wound up kissing her. It was the most inexplicable magic she'd ever witnessed. But she was conflicted that her mother had employed the tactic tonight. Feeling torn, half of her emotions wanted to go to school, the other half wanted to wall up in the safety of the compound until whatever was kidnapping students was found. But who wanted to be stuck at home when there'd be a chance to meet other kids her own age, regardless of the danger?

Tomorrow they were supposed to be leaving to start their first year at the Academy. Left to their father's opinion on the matter, none of the kids in the compound would ever leave home—especially not her and Al.

"You are my angel," her dad said softly, going to her mom.

Al let out a huff of breath and shook his head. "Aw, man, here they go," he muttered in a hard whisper. "Skip all that and get to what's kidnapping people, will ya?"

"Technically, Dad is right," Sarah fussed under her breath, giving Al a sidelong glance. "She's part seraphim, part Powers level angel."

"You are so stupid. That's *not* what he meant." Al turned away from her, shutting his eyes tighter. "Geeze, where did they get you from?"

Their father slid his arms around their mother's waist and pulled her in tight, then buried his face against her neck.

Sarah pulled back from the wall. "This is private, Al…we shouldn't—"

"Shut up and listen," he said between his teeth. "If you'll be quiet, maybe we'll learn where they're going."

Tentatively Sarah leaned closer to the wall, not sure she wanted to see the depth of her parents' affection for each other. It was enough for her to know that the argument wasn't leading to a breakup, but seeing them kiss was not something she felt comfortable with. To her relief, they were just hugging each other. Her mom's arms were draped around her dad's neck as though he could solve all the problems in the universe. And if her mom believed that, she sure did. Sarah could feel herself relaxing as her father's voice rumbled low and deep and calm.

"I just wanna be sure my family is safe, baby," he murmured against her mother's hair.

"It'll be all right, Carlos," she told him.

"We'll take a few Hunter and Warrior class Guardians. Big Mike, Rider and Yonnie. In and out."

"In and out," her mother echoed in a more relaxed tone as she stroked his back.

"I'm going, too," Al whispered, suddenly turning toward Sarah and breaking her trance.

"Are you crazy?"

"Look, I wanna know what bodies they're talking about. If it's happening at the school, that must be why Dad is so bent."

Al turned to leave, and Sarah caught his arm.

"Bent. *Bent*? Do you want to see Dad drop fang when he finds out you snuck out after them? Have you *completely* lost your mind, Al?"

Al shrugged out of her hold. "You're just chicken shit, Sarah. Afraid of the dark. Admit it. But if they think fallen Guardians could be in on this, plus kids are missing at school and Guardians are getting snatched…I'm in. This is my chance to see some real live action. I'm not like you, satisfied with sitting on the sidelines and afraid of my own shadow. Mom and Dad left themselves open enough psychically for us to put a light tracer on them—that never happens, okay. This is a once-in-a-lifetime opportunity. Stay here if you want, but I'm going."

Sarah cursed silently to herself as he strode off. Al was always such a hothead! Always wanting to jump in feet first, no matter what the consequences. He never appreciated the fact that she could always, ever since they were little, feel whenever something terrible was going to happen to him. That was a burden. Didn't he understand that? To know as sure as you knew your own name that something tragic was looming over someone you loved—but not knowing what to do about it—was crazy-making. Telling him only seemed to make him bolder. Telling her parents only made him resent her when they insisted he be careful or revoked his grounds privileges. And tonight…She had such a bad feeling about tonight that it put gooseflesh on her arms.

Dammit, she could feel her own incisors lengthening. Her brother always knew how to push her buttons. Why did she have to inherit fangs from her dad instead of her Mom's angel wings!

Calling her chicken shit and afraid of the dark was definitely one way to send her to Def-con 5—mainly because it was true. Her stupid brother had no idea how much she was afraid of both the dark and her destiny or the very valid reasons why. They'd all said that when she was born, she was the one who'd come out crying and fighting mad with her fists balled up, and he was the calm one. Go figure. But that all changed when the shadows started scaring her as a toddler. Al didn't see the stuff she could see lurking in the darkness. So, yeah, the last freakin' thing in the world she wanted to be was some demon hunter. She hated working in the dark, night-vision capability notwithstanding. She'd seen enough by fifteen years old—had seen things in her sleep that haunted her with all the lights on. It didn't matter that Nana Marlene said it would pass. But she'd never give Al the satisfaction of saying all that tonight.

"You've never flown at night by yourself, jerk!" Sarah finally said between her teeth, jogging to catch up to her brother's long strides. "And they are so gonna kick your dumb ass."

Smirking, Al gave her a casual shrug as he walked away. "I'm not gonna fly alone. Uncle Yonnie is going, so by rights, me and my best hombre, Valencio, got this."

Panic raced through Sarah as her brother bound up the steps and disappeared.

Missing Guardians, the Morrigan, a midnight mission—and now her brother was running off into the night like he was crazy to watch her parents fight demons or possibly their worst enemy. This night was going from bad to worst.

And unfortunately, she had to do something about it.

CHAPTER 2

Sarah ran back up the stairs and down the hall to Tami's room. She needed reinforcements. None of them were ready. They needed training. And now her brother was leaving the compound with their cousin Valencio on an unauthorized run like he'd lost his damned mind!

Tami opened her bedroom door and waved Sarah in before she'd even reached it.

"What gives?" Tami said, looking at Sarah with wide-eyed concern. "You're seriously stressed out. I could feel you ever since you hit the bottom of the stairs. Are your folks really headed toward splitsville?"

Sarah shook her head and pushed her hair up off her neck. "They were arguing about letting us go to the Academy."

"What?" Tami asked, stunned.

"Apparently there've been kidnappings at or around the school, and some rogue Guardians have gone missing."

Tami's jaw dropped. "Get. Out."

"Yeah, and my parents are going to investigate new demon portals near the school, and my stupid brother and Val are going to follow them!"

"Are you serious?" Tami said, grabbing Sarah by both arms. "That is *so* cool! I'm in."

"Wha—No that is *not cool*. It's the stupidest thing I've ever heard in my life!" Sarah said, struggling out of her best friend's hold. "Our parents are going to go down a freakin' demon hole to bust things up!"

"But think of it, Sarah…what a *rush*," Tami said, looking like she was in rapture from the idea alone. "And since we can't fly because we didn't get blessed with wings like the guys did, we can be Al and Val's navigators."

Sarah slumped in defeat. There was no arguing with Tami when she got like this. Her mother had been a vampire for forty years, they said, before she got her life and soul back. Add to that, Uncle Jack Rider's wild personality and you got a kid as crazy as Tami. So much for being the voice of reason and stopping Al from doing something dumb.

"All we have to do is get beyond the compound energy safeguards so we can mind-link with them. You link to Al, I'll link to Val. It'll be insane!"

Sarah folded her arms over her chest. "Yeah. It *is* insane. One problem. Al will never let us tag along." It rankled her to no end that her brother had thrown out the challenge that she was too chicken to go knowing that she really was, and yet if she tried to go, she knew he'd tell her she couldn't. It would serve him right if she did force the point and showed up with Tami.

Tami folded her arms over her chest. "He has no choice. It's called extortion. Either we go with them, or we blow the whistle on the whole mission."

Sarah smiled slowly. Having something to hold over her brother's head did have a certain charm to it.

"He'll be so pissed," Sarah said, grinning.

"Uh-huh," Tami said, going to the door, her answering grin saying she knew she had hooked Sarah with the one thing she couldn't resist. "So we all go or nobody goes." She held the door open. "After you."

..*

"This is complete bullshit!" Al said through his fangs as he yanked his black t-shirt over his head.

He *so* got on her nerves. What a jerk. Why all the compound guys wanted to be like him and all the girls had wanted him at one point or another was beyond her. Her brother was cocky, arrogant and a royal pain in the behind. He got in trouble and stayed there. So what if he was tall, lean and muscular? Who cared if his skin looked like gold under the blood-red moon? Good looks and ability weren't everything. It sure didn't beat brains at a time like this.

She watched her brother run his fingers through his thick, soot-colored curls like he didn't have a care in the world. He glared at her, his dark eyes an intense replica of her father's—like that mattered. He wasn't her dad and couldn't tell her what to do!

He flexed his shoulder blades and forced out huge, pristine white wings, his eyes going silver in the process. It just wasn't fair. Al had gotten the good looks and the wings to go along with the superior telepathic ability and fearlessness. He was the perfect combination of their father's vampire and mother's angel DNA. Her twin brother had clearly robbed her in the womb, leaving her with an unruly mop of brown curly hair, a flat chest, a complete lack of curves that her mother claimed was an athletic build, mediocre telepathic ability and fangs that only popped out when she was angry. Oh, yeah, plus there was some freaky attraction between her and stuff in the dark. But at least she'd come away with all the common sense.

And since, as her dad always said, "fair exchange was no robbery," it was her recurring mission to keep her out-of-control brother in check. Tonight was definitely one of those times. She was not going to stand by and let him kill himself and take Val out right along with him. If she did, without at least putting up a fight, she'd never forgive herself. But why did she always have to make sure Al didn't do something stupid? Maybe the better question was, why did everyone in the compound, especially her mom and dad, always expect her to look after her brother like it was her job or something?

But more than she was furious at her brother right now for putting her in this position, she hated that he'd lured her over to the other side of the light barriers that kept the compound safe and into the dark. She *never* went out at night.

"You all are not coming," Al said, pointing at her as he walked closer to the edge of the cliff. Then he issued Tami a sexy vamp stare. "Tell my sister to stand down and get out of my face."

Tami's response was a smirk, which only seemed to piss Al off even more. Tami was the only one who didn't fall at his feet when he turned on the macho charm. She was more likely to kickbox him instead. There was no one who could get under his skin more. *Yes!*

Anger flared in her brother's eyes. "I'm not kidding!"

Tami held up her hand. "Save it, fly boy. We're coming."

Al clenched his teeth and turned to his best friend, who merely casually yanked his white t-shirt over his head with a shrug. It was clear that Val was taking a neutral position; as the peacemaker, he always did.

"Man, why don't we just chill and let them navigate? What could it hurt?"

"Whatever, man," Al said, giving in, and looked out over the edge of the cliff, waiting for Val to step up beside him.

Sarah stared at Val, pleased when he gave her a secretive wink that her brother didn't catch. Val was always on her side, a private victory to be savored. Any lingering resentment she had for her brother fled when Valencio flexed his shoulders and spread his own wings. They stretched six feet on either side and were a gorgeous amber that glistened under the moonlight. He was part vampire from his father's side and part Valkyrie, courtesy of his mother. The combination was awesome. If there was any guy who could challenge the great Alejandro Rivera in the looks and body department, it was Valencio. And he also seemed to have one additional thing that her brother didn't, and that was brains.

He was as tall as Al, but with exotically dark brown skin and a deep, mellow voice. His eyes reminded her of rich milk chocolate, and his smile was...wow. A little hint of fang added a pearl-white gleam. One dimple always peeked out on the left side of his cheek when he gave her one of his heart-stopping half-smiles. A huge, wild afro crowned his head, but it was his easygoing personality that she loved the most.

Just like all of the kids in the compound, they had been raised together like brother and sister, but though they called each other cousins, there were no blood ties between any of them except her and Al. She was secretly glad of that, and suspected she wasn't the only one who felt that way. Sarah looked down toward the ground, suddenly feeling too exposed by her lingering glances at Val's fabulous physique. Every adult was called Aunt or Uncle, Nana or Baba, was simply given that title out of love, respect, deference to age and familiarity, because their parents were comrades in arms, a band of brother and sister demon-hunting rebels. But it was nice to know that it was possible to have a secret crush in the house without it being weird.

"Okay, tell us when you've got a lock," Al snapped over his shoulder, clearly resentful of having to wait until they did.

Leave it to her brother to ruin the moment. Sarah just stared at him with a frown.

"Sheesh, give us a second," Tami muttered, rubbing her temples.

"I've already got a lock on my parents," Al said to Val, ignoring Tami. "They're heading toward the border town at the base of the mountain."

Val nodded, clearly as eager to get going as Al was. "Hey, if you're not up to the task, ladies, we'll catch you on the rebound."

Al laughed, exchanged a fist pound with Val, and then suddenly nose-dived off the cliff.

Val jogged backward, glanced at Sarah and offered her another dashing smile. "What can I say?" Then, in a running leap, laughing, he took flight and glanced back at her. "It's cool—I've got his back."

"You guys were supposed to wait for the mind-lock!" Sarah shouted as she watched them fly away. "I knew they'd pull this crap," she grumbled.

Tami chuckled. "Yeah…as soon as the shirts came off and the wings came out, truthfully, I was done. I kinda forgot about navigating for a second."

Sarah closed her eyes with a groan.

Tami held both hands up in front of her, laughing. "Lighten up, Sarah. You have to admit they're both fine, even though I would never tell them that." She gave Sarah a friendly shove, presumably to stave off the objection she knew was coming. "You don't have to say it. You're right. There are more important things going on, like all that stuff with your parents. But Val is responsible. He's not gonna let your brother get hurt, you know."

"They should have waited for us to lock with them, though," Sarah muttered.

"Yeah, well, what would have been nice is if they'd let us view the action with them…so when they get back I'm gonna give 'em hell. Trust me." Tami flopped down, sat crossed-legged on the ground and shrugged. "But we still have leverage—if they don't spill, we can threaten to tell."

"Yeah, right. My brother knows we won't snitch, and so does Val. Since when have any of us done that since we were babies?"

"Okay, point taken. I guess we'll have to find some other way to find out what's going on." Tami looked up at Sarah and raised her eyebrows. "I bet Val would let you into his thoughts. And while we wait, I could give you some creative pointers on what to think that would blow his mind."

"Will you be serious for once, Tami?"

"Okay, suit yourself, Miss Doom and Gloom." Tami hadn't lost her smile or her good cheer.

"I have a really bad feeling about everything that's happening. They shouldn't be out there alone without backup." Sarah tore her gaze from Tami's to look out toward the vast stretch of dark night beyond the cliffs, suddenly taking in panicked, shallow breaths. "We should go back inside…maybe get Aunt Inez or—"

"Face it, Sarah, no offense—and you know you're my best friend and compound sister, so I'm saying this to you with pure love—but you *always* have a bad feeling about *every* frickin' thing. Life isn't perfect. Shit happens. But do you actually wanna be sitting on the sidelines forever, scared to death that something terrible might happen? You gotta live." Tami yanked on Sarah's sweatpant leg while looking up at her with a big smile. "Sit down. Take a load off. Breathe deep and relax. Pretend you're in one of Nana Marlene's meditation classes."

Sarah sat down hard, trying to talk herself out of pitching herself over the edge of the cliff. Instead, she picked up tiny pebbles and hurled them over the side in frustration as Tami gave her a sidelong glance.

"C'mon…by tomorrow, when we all get to the Academy, none of this will matter. We'll be able to go on real adventures. We won't be treated like babies and sheltered from everything that's going on. Like Yaya told us the last time she was home on break, we'll get a chance to see real live combat situations on mentored demon hunts."

Sarah just stared at her friend for a long moment.

"Think about it, Sarah. That's why Al and Valencio are so antsy. Can you really blame 'em? All of us are ready to embrace our destiny, but who can do that with over-protective parents hanging around? And *I* think all this drama at school and whatever is scary crazy exciting. Around here, everything is boring."

"Exciting?" Sarah could only shake her head. Tami had no idea how bad a demon attack could be. Tami had never dreamt of them in vivid detail the way she had. The stories the adults told at dinner or during combat classes at the compound only seemed to make Tami and the gang more curious and more eager for an encounter, but for her, those stories were haunting.

"Yes, exciting," Tami said with conviction. "Plus, there'll be guys. Not just corny compound brothers. I'm talking about real ascended masters of the talents from the Upper Spheres. Can you imagine what they're like?"

Tami elbowed Sarah, who smiled despite her foul mood.

"There'll be students from all over the world. C'mon, Sarah, get with the program. By tomorrow morning we're sprung. No more hovering parents and only, say…maybe fifty instructors to three-hundred-plus students. How much supervision do you think they can have? Not much. We are home free, girl!"

"Yeah, I can't wait to get out of here," Sarah said as she stared off into the darkness. Agreeing with Tami right now was the only way to get her to drop the subject. Her brother and Val were nowhere in sight, and the small lights from the valley towns were miles and miles away. If she could just get her friend to abandon this crazy mission of sitting outside in the dark tonight. Leaving Tami to be outside alone wasn't an option. The guys had each other. Compound rule number one was never leave a friend alone and unarmed in the dark.

With a sigh, Sarah pushed herself up and extended a hand toward Tami, who only looked at it with a question in her eyes. Sarah's mind raced as she thought of a way to make it look like leaving made sense. "C'mon. They're long gone. No sense in sitting out here like a couple of losers. Knowing them, they lied and never even followed the Warrior squad. I bet they're back in the house, raiding the fridge. C'mon back and I'll fill you in on what Al and I heard our mom and dad talking about."

"I'm game," Tami finally said, allowing herself to be pulled to her feet. She dusted off dirt and gravel from her jeans, then smiled and shook her head as they walked back toward the compound. "You really don't like being outside the light barriers, do you?"

Sarah didn't glance at her friend as her gaze continued to sweep the area. "No. I really don't."

"Is it because you remember things from before you were born…like how Nana Marlene would do those in-water telepathic exercises with us, trying to figure out if we'd been emotionally traumatized in the womb because all our moms were fighting while they were preggers? Maybe that's why you're scared of the dark."

"Listen, I'm not scared of the dark. It's more like what's *in* the dark," Sarah said. "I just respect it…and no, I'm not suffering from post-traumatic womb syndrome or whatever."

Sure, she'd had nightmares as a kid, but that didn't mean anything.

"But maybe you did get psychically scarred or something, you know? Maybe that's why you always feel a sense of doom." Tami shrugged. "Like, I've been thinking about this for a long time. What if because your mom was the one the Dark Realm was really looking for, they went after her harder than the other Guardians? I'm not saying you're…well…just think about it, Sarah."

"Then how do you account for Al?" Sarah said, becoming defensive. Now her best friend thought she was over-exaggerating her fears? The offensive concept burrowed down inside her and made her stomach churn.

"Hey," Tami said, totally oblivious to Sarah's darkening mood. "He's a guy. When they're scared, a lot of times they get more macho. They go over the top. If you ask me, that's what happened, and that's why Al acts like he does. I'm no shrink, but I think you went nerd scared and Al went über macho—all because the dark side was primarily focused on your mom while she was carrying you guys."

"Is that what you think? Is that what you all think? That my mom—"

"Hey, hey, hey," Tami said, jogging to catch up to Sarah, who'd begun walking faster. "I'm not talking smack about anybody's mom, least of all yours. You know how much I love Aunt D. It's just that…well…a lot of us have always wondered why you're always afraid of stuff when your parents are the freakin' compound generals. They're the Neterus, you know? So, sometimes, just in trying to figure it out, we've tossed around some theories—out of love. Never dogging you behind your back or anything."

"Gee, thanks," Sarah said quietly, feeling hurt and anger collide within her chest. She couldn't believe Tami was saying this stuff or that she'd been discussed by the others in the compound. Now she really felt like a freak. Yeah, maybe it *was* time to leave her so-called home to be around new people who didn't know her so well. People who wouldn't judge her.

"Look," Tami said, still half-jogging, half-walking to keep up with Sarah's angry pace, "forget I said anything. It doesn't matter. What's important is we're best friends. When our moms were pregnant and all our parents were battling the—"

"Don't say the name of the unspoken out here on the far side of the light barriers," Sarah said, and stopped walking to quickly clamp her hand over her friend's mouth.

"Okay, okay, I forgot," Tami said the moment Sarah removed her hand, slinging an arm over Sarah's shoulder and giving her a quick hug. "BFFs?"

Sarah nodded and started walking. It was impossible to stay angry at Tami. What she'd said was probably true. She *was* different. Had known that within her soul all her life—no matter what her mom or nana said. It just sucked hearing it said out loud, and by her best friend. Tami's words reconfirmed every fear she'd ever had, and she so didn't need that on the night before she was presumably headed to the Academy.

But the undeniable fact remained; the dark side had attacked her mother more viciously than it had gone after the other warriors of Light. The entire Vampire Council had a bounty on her parents' heads at one point. Probably still did. The devil and his wife, Lilith, had hunted for her mom and dad in particular. If they destroyed her parents, then the dark side would have broken the back of the Light rebel forces. So maybe Nana Marlene was wrong. Maybe there was something instinctive that was locked away inside her and Al's DNA. Maybe the fear that haunted her wasn't a phase, and maybe she was really, truly different.

"You okay?"

"Yeah," Sarah said flatly.

"You don't sound okay."

"I'm fine," Sarah said, and kept walking. But when she suddenly stopped walking, Tami came to an abrupt halt as well.

"What?" Tami whispered.

"Something doesn't feel right." Sarah turned in a slow circle and then grabbed her girlfriend's hand. "Run!"

She could sense it before she saw it, complete blackness coming for her like a yawning, gaping mouth ready to swallow her whole—exactly the way it had been in her dreams as a kid. As she and Tami ran away from the edge of the cliff back toward the compound, she heard it breaking brambles and scattering dried grass. Felt the sting of its icy winds against her skin, sucking her into it as it entered her pores.

And this time it wasn't a dream.

Suddenly Tami's hand slipped out of hers as if she'd been snatched away. Sarah came to a skidding halt as she turned, frantically searching the darkness for her friend while shouting her name. In the distance she heard Tami's scream, heard her own as an out-of-body cry. From out of nowhere a pair of green glowing eyes and saliva-slicked fangs lunged at her. The demon moved so quickly that she couldn't get a good look at it. She stumbled back, screaming as her foot caught on a root, and then she was going down with a smelly, slime-rotted demon on top of her. Green scaly skin, jagged yellowed teeth and hooked talons were coming at her. A spade-shaped tail bullwhipped behind the agile creature, which was now airborne, lunging like a pouncing tiger.

Eyes shut tightly, she realized she was going to die as demon bait. There were so many things she'd never done, and now her life was over! Then, like a vacuum sump pump, all sound and sensation was gone…but she was falling.

Her arms and legs flailed, awkward and useless. Slow-motion vertigo stabbed into her mind as she opened her eyes, the nausea of judging the distance she was falling and waiting for the horrendous impact blurring her vision with tears. The world of nothingness suddenly exploded as she hit a thick carpet of dark grass with an *oomph.* The scent of rich earth and plants stung her nose, and when she tentatively moved, she was surprised to find that no bones were broken. Then she looked around her and froze. God help her, she'd been here before.

She got up, gingerly testing her sore limbs, and started walking while trying to remember where she'd seen all this before. Sarah bit her lip to keep in a sob of relief that she wasn't dead. Then instinct and all her former training at the compound immediately kicked in. A demon had been on her tail, and she had to find a hiding place, had to find a weapon. Soon she found herself running with her hands out in front of her as though she were blind, trying to feel her environment. Trying to remember what had saved her before in her sleep.

A glowing copse of trees revealed itself over the edge of the dark horizon, and Sarah skidded to a halt, not ready to fall again.

However, light was light, and she'd been taught that that was the one illusion demons couldn't cast. Testing the ground quickly, she dashed for the lit tree line. As she neared it, she saw a being standing in front of a large Baobab tree and shining with so much brilliance that for a few seconds she couldn't tell if it was male or female. She hesitated for a moment. Maybe it was the same one that always managed to save her in her nightmares. *Please, God, let it be the same one.*

Instant recognition made tears stream down Sarah's face as she drew closer, running without looking back. The entity showed herself as a female holding a long golden staff. Colors moved beneath her skin like a kaleidoscope of shimmering lights, changing in hue from milky almond brown to copper to deep ebony with every subtle shade in between. She wore a luminescent white robe that moved in shimmering pastel hues as she opened her arms, and her eyes were wide and beautiful, reminding Sarah of the Kemetian Queens she'd learned of as a child.

The unfathomable being's presence calmed her, and Sarah simply hugged herself as she came to a stop only a few feet away, bathed in the entity's light.

She didn't move as the entity walked up to her and gently reached out to hold her chin. There were so many questions bubbling inside her, but as she stared at the strangely beautiful being, Sarah found herself unable to form words. The being examined her for a moment, then gave a nod, her exotic eyes containing what seemed like approval. Before Sarah could utter a word, the entity leaned forward and kissed her on the forehead, and then placed a finger between her brows and said, "Nexse," with a calm smile. Then she pushed, and Sarah felt herself falling again.

Instantly, she was sprawled back on the plateau by the cliff where she'd been before. She scrabbled quickly away from the edge. The demon that had been chasing her lay at her feet, burning, parts of it already turned to ash. The stench of sulfur choked her, and she covered her nose with her hand as she stumbled to her feet and began to run back to the compound. Her only goal was to make it to the safe zone behind the light barriers. She pitched forward as she willed herself there. Blinded by tears and terror, she tripped over a stone but caught her balance, still running headlong back toward safety. But in her peripheral vision she saw movement. Her heart was pounding as she whipped her head around to see how far away the threat was.

Two small dark shadows that moved like stretchy amoebas were heading toward her, coming quickly, as though they were playing leap frog with each other. They weren't demons; she knew that because they looked exactly like the hallway shadows that always teased her in the compound. Her parents had assured her that no demons could get past Nana Mar's spiritual barriers, so the shadows had to be…something else. But tonight that knowledge brought no comfort. The fact that they were out here right after a demon attack was totally unnerving.

"In the name of the Light, get thee behind me!" she shouted, hoping that would be enough to send the shadows away.

Strangely, her mention of the Light just seemed to make them bolder, and they leaped over each other faster to get closer. When she screamed, they simply blinked out with a soft puff sound, only to reappear in front of her, closer than they'd ever been before. Sarah skidded to a stop, made a zigzag move and skirted around them to begin running toward the compound again. But she knew she wasn't going to get away before they were on her.

"No, stop!" she cried out as she glanced over her shoulder, still running with all her might.

Relief tore through her when she heard Tami, Al and Val calling for her. She threw another quick glance behind her and saw nothing. Still, she kept pressing steadily forward until friendly hands drew her past the lights that meant safety and strong arms surrounded her.

"Oh, my God, what happened?" Tami said, hugging her tightly.

"It was a demon," Sarah gasped, wondering how Tami got back before her when Tami was actually snatched away first. A stitch stabbed her side from running so fast, so hard, as she tried to catch her breath. "Just came out of nowhere. It's dead, but we've gotta keep moving."

"It grabbed me then dropped me, just flung me aside like it was…I don't know. Looking for someone else," Tami said, glancing around nervously.

Sarah squeezed her eyes shut tightly for a moment and kept her voice low. "It wanted me."

"A demon?" Val said, touching Sarah's back and breathing hard from the recent exertion of running to get back to her and Tami. "Did it draw blood?"

"Yeah, did it cut or scratch you? Did you get bitten? Tell me you didn't get nicked," Al said, his gaze filled with rare concern.

Sarah shook her head, ashamed that tears brimmed and fell against Tami's shoulder as she continued to cling to her friend. "No, but can we get out of here and figure all that out later?"

"Damn, sis…you sure you're okay?" Al's voice came in bursts between deep breaths. Like Val, he'd also obviously been running.

For some reason, Al's question only made more tears fall. If he was worried, then even he thought she really could have died.

Her brother pulled her away from Tami's hug and held her at arms' length to inspect her. "It's gonna be all right…we were looking all over for you." He gripped her hand for a moment. "You're safe, Sarah. Now chill and tell me what happened."

It helped that Tami and Val were right beside her when her brother let go of her hand, but her stomach was still doing hard flip-flops. The actual compound was close, and all she wanted to do was get inside. She hated standing in the courtyard—stuff could still happen.

"I fell into a demon hole or something," Sarah finally said, when it was clear that nobody around her was going to move. She wiped at her tears quickly with dirty hands. She didn't care if any of the adults overheard them or saw them out here, where they weren't supposed to be after dark. Getting grounded was better than getting eaten.

She also didn't care that she was probably leaving mud streaks on her face. She didn't care if they got busted by their parents. Right now none of that mattered. She just wanted to be inside where it was safe. "Can we just get out of here?"

"We're inside the barrier, honey. It's gonna be all right," Tami said, slinging an arm over Sarah's shoulder.

Al and Val shared a look.

"You actually went down a demon hole?" Val said in awe. "Righteous."

"We only got as far as the outskirt of the battle," Al said, still breathing hard, sweat pouring down him. "But T sent us a hard mental telepathy shot to the head with a screaming SOS message."

"That wasn't me," Tami said, looking at Sarah as they began a slow jog toward the compound. "I'm not that strong. Had to be you. I told the guys that one minute you were beside me, the next I got flung away and you were gone—and I saw a demon go down a black hole with you, and then get regurgitated up as flaming ash!"

"What? Are you sure?" Sarah said, picking up the pace, driving the others harder until they reached a flat-out run.

"We got back as soon as we could," Val said, sucking in a huge gulp of air. Sweat still poured down his chest and dripped from his chin. "We got the SOS, but by then the team was already down a demon portal, which is why we were the only ones to head back."

As soon as they made it into what had once been the hotel lobby, the foursome collapsed on the overstuffed chairs and sofas. Sarah plopped down next to Tami, who hugged her again. That only made Sarah start crying all over again. It was purely a relief reflex. The fact that she'd been so scared and now was letting the guys see her cry really kicked her butt. But there was no way to hide it. Her entire body was shaking.

"Seriously…You okay, sis?" Al asked again, as though he hadn't believed her the first time. He got up and came over to inspect her for demon wounds and contagion.

Sarah nodded but didn't let go of Tami. "Yeah. I told you I'm okay," she said with a sniff, wiping her dirty face with the backs of her hands. "It never had a chance to cut me."

With the overhead light as an added help, her brother checked her neck and her exposed arms again, making her realize how stupid it had been to go out in just a tank top and sweats. She didn't even have a weapon!

"Did you really off a demon?"

For the first time in her life, she heard what sounded like awe in Alejandro's voice.

"I don't know," she told him honestly, not sure what had smoked the demon and really not caring, as long as it was dead.

"Figures," Al said, without disguising his disappointment. "We do the flight and get out on the actual battlefield, and then the girls get all the action on the hillside, just sitting in the dark." Al flung down his t-shirt and stormed up the stairs, not waiting for the elevator.

Sarah and Tami just stared after him.

Val shrugged. "Don't mind him…you know how Al is. The Guardians went down a demon hole and we couldn't follow. He just wanted to get his first demon kill claim, you know?" He smiled, showing a little hint of fang that made his wild afro look even wilder. "Me, I'm good with just knowing we all got back in one piece. Besides, if we'd lost you ladies, your dads and mine would have had a cow."

But his expression became more serious as he stooped down in front of Sarah and took her hands. "For real…if anything had happened to you, none of us would have been right after that…especially me." After a moment he released her hands and stood slowly. "I'm glad you're okay." Then he loped away.

"My suggestion is that we don't discuss any of this till we get to school," Tami said, staring at her nervously. "Like, if your parents and mine are already spooked, they might tell us we can't go until next semester, which would really suck."

Too weary to comment, Sarah just let Tami babble on as she leaned her head back on the sofa and closed her eyes.

"But you've gotta tell me what happened when you went down that hole," Tami said, dropping her voice to a conspiratorial murmur. "More important, how the hell did you get out?"

Sarah cringed at the word *hell,* and Tami gave her hand a squeeze.

"My bad…wrong choice of words. Look, why don't you stay in my room tonight? You shouldn't be alone, and I know you aren't a fan of the dark. I'll keep the lights on, too, I promise. Because after what just happened, I'm not really feeling all that brave myself. 'Kay?"

Sarah just nodded, too numb to do anything else but so glad that Tami shared her fear for once. There was no doubt that she was going to sit up all night in Tami's room, giving her the blow-by-blow details, but there was so much she really didn't understand. Maybe there had been some light-powered trip wire out there, a booby trap set by seasoned Neteru Guardians that the demon had rolled onto and exterminated itself as it dragged her into the demon hole. Or maybe it was something else? Who knew, and who cared? There was only one thing for sure: She didn't care if she never saw another demon or dark forest again in her life.

CHAPTER 3

Sleep had, as predicted, been impossible once they'd gone to Tami's room. Sarah was too wired from her near miss with the demon, and with the whole night left to sit up and talk about it, she'd taken advantage. Plus, her girlfriend apparently had more vamp in her than she did, but even so, staying up all night was a ritual that they'd definitely have to break once they got to school. Now they were paying the price of not sleeping. Dawn had come with a vengeance.

The only saving grace was that Tami was as snake-bite mean in the morning as she was, so she didn't have to make nice like she would have had to if she'd been hanging out in Hyacinth's or Allie's room. Those two took Miss Merry Sunshine to a whole different level.

The smell of pancakes drew Sarah and Tami out of bed, but it was still a painful process.

"Meetcha downstairs," Tami muttered, staking her territorial claim on the bathroom.

"Yeah. Thanks for staying up with me," Sarah said, dragging herself to the door with a yawn.

"De nada," Tami replied with a wave of her hand, and then stopped, squinted and stared at Sarah full on.

"What?" Sarah quickly looked down at her body and then felt her neck. Had she been nicked by the demon after all?

"You are gonna be so pissed. There's a huge zit at twelve-o'clock right between the ole eyebrows. Kinda Cyclopean, if you ask me."

Horrified, Sarah gasped, and her hand flew up to her forehead. Sure enough, a very tender, volcanolike mound had formed right where the glowing being had touched her. What was her savior doing handing out zits? Weren't goddesses or angels or whatever she was supposed to do good things for the people they saved?

Sarah groaned aloud. Why was it that other girls walked away from their fairy godmothers with dresses, cool shoes, a fly ride—even a handsome boyfriend—and all she got was acne?

"That thing is about to erupt," Tami said, making a face. "Put a hot compress on it and squeeze it before you come down to breakfast. It's disgusting."

"Sure," Sara muttered, and then slipped into the hall. What else were best friends for, other than to tell you the brutal truth?

Hurrying to her bedroom, Sarah rushed in and ran straight for the bathroom. A mini snow-capped mountain had formed in the center of her forehead, just like Tami had said. Sarah leaned on the sink with both hands and let her head drop forward. Why did something like this have to happen on the first day of school?

The first day of Upper Spheres.

The first day of uniforms.

The first day of dreaded talent divisions.

Then again, if she were lucky and if the stars aligned properly, maybe the trip to school would be indefinitely delayed—at least long enough for the zit to heal. But luck was rarely on her side.

Sarah groaned. They'd been taught all the basics at home, and now it was time for the Upper Sphere training away from home, and she looked like an alien. Every kid in the compound had already been sorted into a different talent division based on their extrasensory gift. Solid seers, like Hyacinth, were going into the clairvoyant talent division—just like Yaya had. It wasn't fair that 'Cinth got to be with Ayana who was now a college-level mentor in the very senior level, and she didn't.

Allie would be able to channel all her kinetic, electro-static energy into classes in the Tactical division. The cool jock division. Al, plus her compound brothers Miguel and Val, would be in the top talent division, Specials—and they even had a chance to further move up into the elite division called Shadows. And here she not only had a zit in the center of her forehead, but she would also be showcasing it for the entire school—though at least she'd be with lovable geek Donnie and her BFF, Tami—all of them still hanging together in the scrap-heap division for kids with questionable powers. Blends.

Life sucked.

She thought about locking herself in her bathroom all day and refusing to even go to the Academy, but it would be just like her dad to simply energy whirl her there regardless. So the only rational thing to do was to emerge from the sanctuary of her room and go down to breakfast.

* * *

Chaos greeted her in the main dining room, and she slipped past all the bustling bodies to go hide in the kitchen. At least there she would find her aunt Inez, compound chef extraordinaire. Her aunt's rule was simple: If you helped, you could stay, *and* you got first dibs on what came off the stove.

"Hey, baby," her aunt said with a wide grin. "Come gimme some sugah this morning. You all ready for school?"

"No." Sarah jogged over to fill the loving, meaty arms that had opened to her. She bent with a smile and pressed her cheek against her aunt's warm brown neck.

"Well, we ain't ready for you to go, either. It was bad enough when Ayana left, now y'all? What are we gonna do without you?" Inez said with a sigh. "But I guess we've gotta let you go sometime." She released Sarah from her embrace and dabbed the corners of her eyes before she picked up a spatula again and then turned back to the huge industrial-sized stove. "You give your momma and daddy lots of hugs before you head out, and look for your cousin when you get to school. Some of those girls up there can be mean, Yaya tells me, but you've got plenty of family going with you, understand?"

Sarah nodded, and she could feel her aunt smile.

Then Inez turned and gave her a wink. "You're getting good, baby. You picked up my smile, didn't you?"

"That's because you were helping," Sarah said, secretly pleased.

"No, you did that all on your own. Pretty soon you're gonna be a rock-solid compound seer. I promise you."

Sarah went to a large tray loaded down with sausages, bacon and steaks. "Then how come I got stuck in the Blends?"

"You take that platter in there to your uncles. Can't get 'em off the meat, especially after they've been out huntin' all night," her aunt said, turning with a frown. It was obvious that the subject was a sore one for her. It was all in the way her microbraids bounced as she used the pancake spatula to accent her talking points in the air while one hand rested on her thick hip. "Then you come back in here and get the tofu scrambler and seitan sausage for your momma and them…and then we'll talk. I swear, I think your mother's dragon pearl done lost her mind. She used to be such a good oracle, but now…Counselor Zehiradangra has issues, honey…we have to be gentle with her, but I told your momma as well as your gran that wasn't right. But what do I know? I'm just a house seer. Nana Marlene told me to leave it alone, so if that's what your grandmother said to do, then who am I to disobey?"

"Thanks, Auntie," Sarah said, grabbing the platter and heading toward the dining room.

Then Sarah hesitated, feeling the answer to her question so close to the surface of her aunt's mind that she couldn't leave. It was right there. Her aunt was going to let her into her thoughts and tell her without words, so it wouldn't be like she'd actually broken a confidence and spilled the beans. What was going on in the house? It was linked with what was happening at school. Linked with her destiny. For a second their eyes met. Her aunt nodded ever so slightly as a thin sheen became visible on her forehead. Something dark flitted through her aunt's thoughts, and Sarah whirled to avoid it. Terrified of what she might see, she rushed toward the door, still clutching the platter.

"Sarah, baby, wait. Try again. Stay with it."

But her uncle Mike met her at the swinging metal door.

"Hey, hey, where's the fire?" He placed a broad palm on top of Sarah's head.

"Auntie said to get this to you in a hurry."

"Auntie was right," her uncle said, laughing. "Why you think I'm standing here in the door? Think I don't know my wife can cook?"

"Stop sweating my pots, Mike," her aunt called out, both good nature and a hint of disappointment ringing in her voice. "Baby, you come back in a little bit and I'll have some more for you…for the trays, all right?"

"Okay, thank you," Sarah replied softly, knowing her aunt was speaking to her in code. Her Aunt Inez had left an opening for them to speak privately as soon as she got rid of her Uncle Mike, then she could really open up and discuss what was on her mind. "I'll be more careful next time."

"You do that. I'm expecting that from you, all right?"

Her uncle gave her aunt a quizzical glance. “She ain’t dropped nothing, ‘Nez. Stop giving the girl a hard way to go.”

“Both of y’all get out of my kitchen,” Inez said, and then went back to the stove.

Sarah looked up at her uncle’s six-foot-eight hulking frame as he blocked the doorway. He had to be somewhere between 280 to 320 pounds, as a conservative guesstimate. Uncle Mike made it seem as though midnight had eclipsed the entire doorframe, but there wasn’t a mean bone in his body—unless you were a demon he was after. And of all the uncles, he was the only one who seemed to greet mornings with an upbeat attitude after a hunt. There was something about his huge bulk and the deep sound of his voice that always made her feel special.

She held up the platter to him with a grin, already feeling much improved just from a dose of family.

“Thanks, baby—now a man can eat.” He kissed the top of her head, accepted the platter and called over his shoulder with a wink, “You and the ladies can eat all that tofu mess, if ya wanna.”

“Cholesterol’s gonna kill you, Mike,” one of Sarah’s other aunts called from the dining room.

“After chasing vampires, werewolves and ever’thing else, do I look like I’m scared of some sausage, girl?”

Sarah had to laugh as she dashed back into the kitchen, hungry for some more of her aunt Inez’s good cheer and clandestine advice. But Tami’s dad came in just as she was trying to angle her body up on a stool.

“Mornin’,” he muttered, scratching the blond and gray stubble on his chin. “I’m getting too old for this bull, ’Nez. Where’s the coffee?”

“In the big pot in the dining room—where it always is,” she said over her shoulder.

He lifted his mug toward her. “Then I guess I meant the sweetener.”

"Jack Rider, it is too early in the danged morning to be putting Jack Daniels in—"

"Shhhh," he said, squinting. "C'mon, now, Inez. I've been up all night. Gotta drop my daughter off at school, which is only a cesspool of horny teenage boys—I need a drink. And I'd appreciate it if you kept your voice down so my wife doesn't start up." He gave Sarah a meaningful look. "Good morning, darlin'. You know how your aunt Tara is…well, once a vampire, always got a mean streak and can hold a nasty grudge. She doesn't understand what it's like for us dads."

Sarah made the sign of a zipper across her lips. The legends said that Tami's mom, Val's dad and her own were the only vampires who had been granted amnesty by the Light for helping humans. But just because they were now mortal and technically human, they still had all their vampire ways and powers, which meant they hated mornings. She often wondered how her mother, her uncle Jack and her aunt Val could deal with their spouses' morning-vamp bad mood. The last thing she was going to do was tell on her cool uncle Jack.

He gave her an appreciative nod and lifted his coffee mug to her. "Thanks, kiddo. Knew you'd understand after years of dealing with your old man's morning fangs."

"Far cabinet to the left, behind the flour," Inez said, shaking her head. "And don't be making that girl an accomplice to your bad habits. Sarah doesn't have to keep any secrets around here. If your wife finds out, it's your fault, not hers."

"Bless you, 'Nez. You're a saint," he said, finding the bottle and pouring a healthy shot into his coffee. After taking a long slurp he closed his eyes and sighed, then kissed Sarah on the top of her head as he passed her. "Tami's looking for you out there. I'll tell her that instead of back-talking her mom and me, she should be in here helping get breakfast on, like you are."

Sarah slid off the stool. Her conversation with her aunt had now been officially derailed, and any chance for sneak telepathy was a thing of the past. She and her aunt shared a look.

"It's gonna be all right, baby. I promise you. I can get the rest of this food out. You go eat. Just don't be letting them make you feel bad up there at school. You hear me?"

"I won't. Thanks, Aunt 'Nez." Sarah's shoulders slumped as she grabbed two pitchers of fresh-squeezed orange juice and headed out the swinging door.

There was definitely something comforting in the chaos of compound life. She glanced around as she set down the pitchers at the end of the buffet. The food had clearly already been blessed, because plates were piled high, and the boys were plowing through it as though there was a new famine. The last thing she was prepared for was Val heading in her direction.

She turned her back to him and poured herself some juice.

"Hey, can I get some?" he asked, and she could feel his wide grin.

She handed him a glass and turned away.

"Uh, good morning," he said, tapping her shoulder playfully.

"Good morning," she said quickly.

"Are you okay?" He grabbed her arm and turned her around, then stared at her forehead.

Sarah closed her eyes. "Go ahead. Say whatever you've gotta say."

Val offered her a casual shrug when she peeped open one eye. "It'll go away in a couple of days. So what?"

She opened both eyes.

"I'm just glad that's all that happened,. It's good to see you enjoying the sunshine, know what I mean?" He knocked his juice glass against hers with a wink and loped away.

Her gaze followed his retreating form for a moment before she caught herself and began fixing a plate. She glanced around at everyone, hoping no one had seen her looking at Val the way she had been. Yeah, she did know what he meant. Last night she could have been demon bait, which would have meant that this morning—if she'd lived—she'd have a serious aversion to sunlight and pancakes. No one needed to know they'd broken at least a half-dozen house rules, and in a couple of hours, they'd be home free, so to speak, at the Academy. It was a nice secret to share with Val, and she was grateful he hadn't teased her about her pimple.

Allie was the first one to push away from the table and rush over. Allie was hopeless at stealth, no matter how hard she was trying to act like she was just coming over to get some juice. Allie's mom and dad—Aunt Heather and Uncle Dan—looked like they were going to a funeral, but her Bubbie Stella and Pop Pop Frank were all smiles. They were dorm wardens at the school and would be getting Allie full time.

Her friend's tiny button nose was a red bulb, her tea-and-milk complexion was streaked with dried salt lines, and her normally crystal-clear gray eyes were puffy, like she'd been crying. What had happened? This wasn't Allie's regular allergy-season look. She was truly upset. Her shoulders were sagging, and she kept twisting an overused tissue around in her hands.

Allie threaded her arm around Sarah's waist, dipped her head low and said in a quietly frantic tone, "They're making me nuts. Make them go away. I'll be the laughingstock of the entire school if everyone finds out that my grandparents run the Upper Sphere dorms. They promised before that they wouldn't let people know, but now they want to come with me to see me settled in? No!"

"It's gonna be okay, seriously." Sarah gave her friend a supportive hug. But they both knew the truth, the poor girl was doomed. Upper Sphere students hated rules and regulations imposed on them by the dorm monitors, and the moment they found out Allie's grandparents were the enforcers, Allie would have hell to pay.

Trying to figure out anything positive she could say, Sarah pressed on. "Ayana's Grandma Delores and Pop Pop Monte run the kitchen and maintenance services over there, and she lived, right?" Sarah added, searching for something positive to cling to. "Plus, Hyacinth's and Donnie's grands run the lower dorms. So don't worry. The kids at school can't hold that against you."

Tami had come over to where they were standing to pour more black coffee in her mug, and from the surly way she did it, it was clear that her morning mood hadn't improved. "Yeah, they can," she muttered now. "Nobody else's grands came to orientation to totally embarrass them in front of the whole school." She flung her long brown hair over her shoulder, hazel eyes glinting with mischief. "You gotta work it to your advantage. Lotta kids in the Upper Spheres wanna get out, wanna go down the mountain with the Regulars. You have influence with the people giving out demerits. So, you know, one hand washes the other. Make 'em think you have the power to screw up their day passes if they mess with you. I'd make 'em be *real* nice to me." She smiled, using what Sarah liked to call her vamp smirk, then she took a sip of her coffee and closed her eyes. "Damn, I hate mornings."

"How do you think this stuff up?" Allie sniffed and glanced up at Tami.

"My mom passed a little political savvy to me. Glad I didn't get my dad's schnozz, though. Woulda sucked, puking up my guts all of first year. I would hate to be an Olfactor like him."

Sarah had to silently agree. Freshmen Olfactors, otherwise known as Ollies, were infamous for their reaction to first-year training. Every new smell set them off.

"Just as long as they don't split us up in the dorm—you think they'd actually do that? It's bad enough the talent classes are going to be separate tracks," Allie whispered. Her voice was tense, and she sniffed again.

"I told you what Ayana said. No. We'll all be together in the dorm, so stop stressing before you start giving everybody static cling again." Sarah glanced over to her uncle Jack and aunt Tara.

"Okay, okay," Allie said, hugging herself as the girls headed back to the main table.

"You'd just better hope they're gonna let us get out of this joint to even experience school," Tami muttered under her breath.

Sarah cut Tami a warning look to knock it off and then nervously glanced around at the adults. Yeah, something was still wrong—big time. Her mother's private warning to her dad last night, coupled with her own senses, told her there was a silent undercurrent of worry running through the group, and it went beyond general separation anxiety.

Tamara's parents looked as worried as hers did; the only difference was that her aunt Tara had a cool, vampire reserve, her gaze slowly traveling over each of the compound kids, whereas her uncle Jack looked like he was ready to have a nervous breakdown. Whatever they'd seen on the hunt last night could not have been good. Later she'd have to pull Tami to the side so they could dissect the problem even further.

But Tami was right about one thing: They had to get out of the compound before one of the nervous parents changed their minds. Last night Sarah had been dreading going to school, today she was dreading staying at home. Just looking at the adults' faces instantly clinched the decision for her. Going to the Academy with the whole gang was better than being left alone at home on twenty-four-seven lockdown with a bunch of freaked-out parents. Being able to be with Ayana again would be great...and maybe there'd also be someone else at the Academy like her—a blend of everything and master of nothing.

Sarah released a quiet sigh. At the Academy, maybe she could finally do something to make her parents proud—or make herself proud. She clearly wasn't ever going to overachieve here. Maybe she could go away, train hard and come back awesome and filled out and beautiful. There was a hopeful thought.

As Sarah looked around, it was easy to tell who'd been out all night on the mission. Her dad was gripping a mug of coffee between his palms as though it was the only thing keeping his head from hitting his plate. His eyes were closed, he hadn't shaved and a dark five o'clock shadow covered his jaw. Her mom yawned, picking at her fruit, and every now and then she wrapped her white silk robe around herself more tightly.

Uncle Yonnie's wild afro looked like someone had been pulling his hair, and every few minutes his head would loll forward until he'd catch himself with a hard jerk, open his eyes and then go back to nodding. His daywalker fangs were down, like he just didn't have the energy to retract them. She swallowed a laugh when her aunt Valkyrie stretched out a long, graceful amber wing and reached past aunt Jasmine to give her husband a shove to get him to stop snoring at the table.

"Morning, everybody," Sarah said quickly, receiving a round of good mornings in return. Her uncle Jose just gave her the thumbs-up, his mouth was so full. But she made it a point to keep her back to the boys at the far end of the room, where her brother was sitting, suddenly remembering the zit.

There was an open seat, as always, next to Tami, and after helping herself to pancakes and fruit, she slid into it. Anybody with any sense avoided Tami's morning snipes. Tami had clearly gotten her ex-vampire mother's aversion to morning and could be crazy-wicked verbally if you got on her nerves. If very slightly provoked, she'd also fight and go round for round, pound for pound at the drop of a hat. This morning, Sarah truly wished she could sit anywhere but next to Tami, who was no doubt going to start in on the whole zit issue. However, if she elected not to sit by Tami, that would start a whole hot mess.

But somehow, because her aunt Inez was blind to any flaw in anyone she loved, despite being a great psychic, and because her normally sarcastic uncle Jack hadn't said a word about it, nor had her lovable uncle Mike—not to mention Val had been so cool about it—the Everest-sized thing protruding from her forehead had momentarily slipped her mind.

That is until Tami brought her back to harsh reality.

"No progress, I see," she muttered, spearing a sausage.

"I tried the compress," Sarah whispered through her teeth, keeping her head down low close to her plate. "It didn't work."

"Understatement. I think it made it worse."

Allie put her hand on Sarah's back and stared at her with big gray eyes. "It's okay, Sarah. Nobody will notice." Her red curls accidentally spilled over her shoulder and into the syrup on her plate. "Oh…no…" High-strung and beginning to spark at the fingertips, Allie unsuccessfully tried to rescue her hair.

"It's okay, it's okay," Sarah said quickly, pressing down Allie's silverware, which was beginning to levitate. She caught her friend's juice glass before the electromagnetic charge around it toppled it and created a mess.

The static outburst was common enough that nobody at the table paid them any attention. But at school, something like this would be a disaster.

Sarah let out a sigh as she quickly grabbed both of Allie's hands, feeling the charge ripple up her arms. She looked down at the delicate tea-and-milk hued fingers that held hers tightly and then glanced at Allie's parents, wondering how Aunt Heather, a Scottish Druid stoneworker, and Uncle Dan, a Tactical Guardian, two relatively serene individuals, had wound up with a kid who sparked at the least provocation.

"I'm so sorry, Sarah," Allie said, dripping syrup onto her pink robe.

"It's okay. We're all just nervous about going to school this morning—day one jitters," Sarah said, feeling the charge beginning to wane.

It had taken everything in her parents' powers to get Allie to calm down enough while taking the school placement tests that she could be put in the tactical division. It was a real coup, and it had the side benefit of being the talent division that had all the good-looking jocks. T-Rexes. That was where the true athletes were, the guys who could do the heavy lifting with just magnetic force alone, but poor Allie was far from a kinetic athlete, and the girl was a nervous wreck.

"Look at my hair," Allie wailed softly. "There's not enough time this morning to get it back to how I had it. I got up extra early this morning so I—"

"That's what you get for lying to Sarah about that volcano on her face," Tami muttered over a sip of coffee, but then her head flew back as her mother yanked her ponytail.

"Ow! Mom!"

"Ease up," her mom said, flashing fang. "Leave the poor girl alone."

Tami stuck out her tongue at her mother's back, while Sarah grabbed a napkin and tried to dab syrup out of Allie's hair.

"I'll help you blow dry it after you wash it again—don't panic," Hyacinth said, her wide blue eyes focused on Sarah's forehead. Hyacinth's voice was as soothing as her hypnotic stare. Her gentle smile, framed by her pretty heart-shaped face and long, onyx hair, seemed to summon calm if anyone just looked at her. "Listen…we have to all stick together, especially when we get to the Academy." Then she leaned in closer and dropped her voice to a whisper. "Especially with *everything* that's going on."

"Later," Sarah murmured, and then she motioned subtly toward the adult end of the table. Just great, Hyacinth had picked up on stuff floating around in the ether, but the girl obviously didn't have the good sense not to try to talk about it around Ascended Masters!

"Yeah," Tami said in a sullen tone and then gave Hyacinth a look to shut her up. "It's bad enough that they've already separated us," she pressed on more loudly and off topic, as a cover for Hyacinth's carelessness. "You're going to the clairvoyant division, and me, Donnie and Sarah will be with the slow kids in Blends. All we need is a static outburst by a kid from our compound at the lunchroom table."

"C'mon," Sarah said, giving Tami a look. "She said she was sorry." Sarah threw an arm over Allie's shoulders as she glared at Hyacinth, warning her to play along.

"Thanks, Sarah," Allie said, lifting her chin. "But at least we'll all be rooming together." She looked around the table at her other girls. "OMG, what if you're wrong and they actually do change their minds and split me and Hyacinth up after all? That would be horrible. Tragic!"

"They won't split us up. We won't let them." Hyacinth grabbed one of Allie's hands. "Stop obsessing. Let's go fix your hair, okay?"

"They so get on my last nerve," Tami grumbled under her breath as Hyacinth and Allie took their plates and left the table. "I can't stand that much sugar in the morning. The sweetness is sickening," she said with a shudder, and then took another sip of her black coffee.

"Give 'em a break," Sarah said, picking at her food. "You know how they are…they're really not that bad and—"

"They're sickening," Tami said with a frustrated snort.

"*And* they are our compound sisters," Sarah said, giving Tami the eye.

"Do we have to be responsible for them at the Academy? Please tell me no."

"Yes," Sarah said flatly. She glanced at Allie's parents and then at Hyacinth's, and then leaned in toward Tami, dropping her voice low. "Do you want to be the one to tell Uncle Dan and Aunt Heather how you dissed Allie at school because her powers were coming in wobbly? Or could you actually look in Aunt Jasmine's face and break her heart by telling her you didn't have Hyacinth's back because she got picked to be in the hot clairvoyant talent division? It's not her fault she made it into the Clavs. Uncle Bobby would be crushed. It's not 'Cinth's fault that her mom is the best dragon painter in the world and can make tapestries of dragons she's painted come to life or her dad is a wizard. So she got picked to be in one of the most talented groups—don't hate."

"I'm not hating," Tami said with a scowl. "It's just hard enough to fit in somewhere new without adding a klutz and a goody-goody nerd to the equation."

"Or a best friend with a gigantic zit." Sarah looked at Tami hard.

"Well, now that you mention it—call me shallow…but I love you anyway."

"Just great."

"I'm just joking." Tami shook her head and wolfed down her breakfast, now smiling.

Sarah sat back and stabbed her pancakes with a fork. Arguing with Tami when she dug in her heels on a subject was futile.

Voices drifted around her as she ate, snippets of conversation in a textured collage of sound. Aunt Krissy was at the far end of the table twirling a long blond lock around her finger, fretting about how Donnie was going to make out in school, while Donnie's dad remained calm and just ate. Obviously Uncle JL didn't want to discuss it. The old Ninja Tactical just calmly sipped his green tea and asked his wife to keep her voice down. Aunt Tara was clearly pissed at Uncle Jack again. She must have figured out that he'd snuck booze into his coffee. The slight hint of fang was a dead giveaway during their tense but quiet exchange. No wonder Tami was in such a foul mood—who wanted to deal with their parents bickering at the breakfast table?

Aunt Juanita's voice sounded worried beneath the din of the boys' rowdy banter halfway across the room. It was hardly more than a whisper and was all but drowned out by Al, Miguel, Val and Donnie's raucous conversation.

Sarah cast her aunt a discreet sidelong glance. It was odd how Aunt Juanita looked like a younger version of Aunt Tara, although there was no blood relationship. Both women were almond-hued and curvaceous, but Tami's mom was of Native American extraction, with darker eyes and hair, whereas Miguel's mom was Latina, with long auburn hair. Uncle Jose, Miguel's dad, looked like her own father's younger brother, but again, like everyone in the house, they weren't related by blood, just by battle. Uncle Jose was leaning toward her dad, and Sarah strained to listen.

"The perimeter here and at the school is secure? You're positive?"

Sarah watched her father's expression as a little silver flickered around the edges of his irises before he answered.

"Would I let my kids go if it wasn't?" Her father sat back and stared at Uncle Jose hard. "Marlene added extra spiritual lines of defense in both places, awright?"

Uncle Jose held up his hands in front of his chest and kept his voice low. "If you like it, I love it, hombre."

"I *don't* like it," her father said, cutting a glance at her mother, "but I don't have a choice."

"We've been over this already, Carlos," her mother said in a quiet but firm tone.

The back of Sarah's chair bumped suddenly and broke into her eavesdropping. As she spun around quickly, she saw her brother coming from the buffet with a fresh stack of pancakes and bacon.

"I was gonna ask you how you were doing, but I see your third eye is trying to pop out of your forehead. Damn, that's a beaut," Al said laughing, and then jumped back as she tried to elbow him. He sloshed his milk, but shot a tactical charge at it before it could hit the ground, returning it to his cup. "I got skills, sis, so you've gotta do better than that."

Sarah was out of her chair with the intention of shoving him hard, but her father snapped his head up from his conversation, eyes beginning to turn silver.

"I'm not in the mood this morning, Al. Leave your sister alone."

It wasn't a comment, it was a command, and it rolled across the table and paralyzed her brother like a rush of instant thunder.

"She pushed me!" Al argued, trying to save face.

"I did not!" Sarah yelled. "He's always got something smart to say—I can't stand him!"

Sarah watched her father take a very slow sip of his coffee, fangs beginning to lengthen.

"What did I say?" her father asked slowly, dropping each word with perfect diction. His silver gaze was fixed on Al. No one spoke, no one moved, all conversation had ceased. The general had spoken. "I swear to you, if I have to get up…"

Her mother let out a huff of breath and tossed her napkin onto the table. "All of you kids need to hurry up and finish eating, then get ready for your first day at the Academy, so stop horsing around."

Just like a hard, clean rain, the tension was broken, and uncles and aunts began eating again. Damn, Sarah thought. Her mother had averted a potential confrontation that she'd so wanted to see. Would it have been so bad to have Al get vamp-snatched by the scruff of his neck? But, no, her mom always had to save her dumb brother's hide!

Al walked away with some of his dignity still intact, and Sarah stuck her tongue out at him as she cleared away her plate.

"He's stupid, you know that," Tami said a few minutes later, as they scraped their dishes and put them in the dishwasher.

"He's no different than the hundreds of other kids who are going to see Mount Everest on my forehead this morning," Sarah said, dejected. "I gotta go get dressed."

* * *

Once breakfast was behind her, it felt like it had taken forever to get away from everybody and reach her room. Once inside, she did something she rarely did. She locked the door. She didn't want to deal with Tami bursting in with more sarcastic comments, or Allie's fretting or Hyacinth's too cheery view of the world. This morning sucked. Her position at the Academy sucked.

Sarah snatched the letter off her dresser and reread it, hoping the contents had changed since her last reading.

Dear Mr. and Mrs. Rivera,

Per our conversation two days ago, this letter is to confirm that your daughter, Sarah Rivera, will be placed in the Blends talent division at the start of the school year. Again, I apologize that it was necessary to test Sarah three separate times. We certainly never expected to receive three completely different yet inconclusive results. Since she has demonstrated such an unusual mixture of talents, we feel that the Blends division is the right place for her at this time.

We will also be happy to continue to watch her development throughout the school year and will be more than willing to retest her at a later date. We expect that, given her parentage, Sarah will quickly place in one of the more refined talents division—perhaps the Specials, along with your son, Alejandro.

How dare that crazy old dragon mention that idiot in her letter!

If you have any questions at all, I am more than happy to set up a time to talk to you via PirateNet, or we can arrange an in-person meeting at the Academy. In the meantime, we humbly welcome Sarah and Alejandro to our institution, and look forward to shaping them into fine Guardians and more.

Sincerely,

Ms. Zehiradangra, Guidance Counselor

Dragon Pearl Oracle of the Highest Order

Nothing had changed. Same crappy letter. Sarah practically shook as she crumpled it up and tossed it in the trash. Washed-up old broad. What did Ms. Z know anyway? Everyone knew the woman was half crazy—and yet she got to test kids and determine their fates. Where was the logic in that?

Sarah stomped back over to the mirror with a handful of her clothes to get dressed. She was already showered, and if she went back into the bathroom she'd be tempted to try to lance the huge zit, which would only leave a scar.

The whole talent division process grated her. Why did they have to have placement tests, anyway? Some people just didn't test well, and she was one of them. Here in the compound all her aunts and uncles and both her parents were thrown together as family in one big pot. Nobody cared that Uncle Jack and Uncle Jose were noses—the best Olfactors and trackers around. Aunt Inez was a great seer, and she was married to Uncle Big Mike—Ayana's stepdad, who could hear demons like a danged hunting dog. Who was gonna tell the big audio he couldn't sit wherever he wanted at the breakfast table?

Uncle Dan and Uncle JL could practically levitate whole buildings, as veteran Tacticals…and then there were the family members with special talents. Aunt Jasmine could draw stuff on the walls and make it come alive. Aunt Krissy and her brother, Uncle Bobby, were white-lighters, wizards whose lineage went all the way back to Merlin's time. Heck, her Aunt Valkyrie was a battlefield flier, and there were maybe only a handful of those left in the world now. Hyacinth's grandparents were healers. But nobody was separating her family and saying those team members couldn't work as a group. Compounds didn't function according to talent divisions in the real world, so why did kids have to go through this at school? It wasn't realistic, wasn't practical. Not that her opinion mattered.

But someone had made up a stupid rule that every Guardian had to have a talent, an extra sensory ability that they were born with, and people with the basic skill-sets got split up into four groups at the Academy: Olfactors,

Audios, Tacticals and Clairvoyants. Those who excelled at everything were dubbed Specials.

But she had the misfortune of falling into the dreaded category of kids whose talents hadn't presented fully yet, despite puberty, despite age, despite parental lineage. In short, they were the duds. Weapons that didn't fire, like a bum grenade. The division you got put in determined whether or not you were marked for success or had to endure teasing, possibly for your whole life. She would never forgive Ms. Z for this.

There was no getting around the fact that her dad had been so proud when he'd heard that Alejandro had been tapped for the Specials division. It had been written all over his face…followed by the worried look he gave her when he learned she'd tested into Blends. Sure, he'd given her a hug, the one that said she was still his baby girl, but that only made her feel worse.

Sarah struggled with getting her red sweater over the white blouse and tugged on her khaki skirt—her uniform for the next year until she moved up a level. She blew out a breath. Leave it to the headmistress, her grandmother Marlene, to color code the freakin' uniforms by the chakra system. First years, the lowest level, got red. Great. Just great.

Sarah looked in the mirror and cringed. *Oh no! Allie!* What she saw wasn't some new talent emerging—it was static cling, courtesy of Allie's first-day nerves. Working frantically, she tried to ground herself and dispel it by touching her wooden dresser with one free hand. No luck. Every time she brushed her sweater down with the other hand, a blue haze of static crackled over it and made it emphasize her lack of curves in an even less flattering way. Even her red socks were crackling, and the laces of her sneakers were standing straight up in the air. When she felt her ponytail begin to lift off her neck, she almost screamed in frustration.

Her father's bellow for them to hurry up made Sarah hug herself and close her eyes. At the light knock at the door she let out a long sigh. She knew who was on the other side of the door and was so not ready to deal wi that situation on top of everything else.

Chapter 4

"You okay?"

Sarah turned around and looked at her mom as she came into her bedroom. "Yeah." What was the purpose of locks if your mom had tactical ability to just turn the tumbler and come in anyway? But she really couldn't be angry. Her mom never barged into her room, and she had just mentally screamed...Maybe she had called her hard in her head without meaning to, because if anybody could fix what was wrong, it would be her. Sarah just hated having to ask.

The two of them regarded each other for a long moment, quietly searching for a way to begin the conversation that needed to be had. In that moment Sarah knew why her dad had fallen in love with her mother. Who wouldn't have? She had goddess written all over her. Perfect cinnamon brown skin, even at her age. Not a wrinkle on her face. Thick, long, amber-hued dreadlocks. A body that would make all the Upper Sphere boys' jaws drop when she showed up in Kemetian robes. But that was better than having her mom show up in leather battle gear—they'd have to pass around smelling salts for the guys, if she did that.

"You don't sound so okay," her mother finally said, then waited, leaning on the doorframe as she closed the door behind her.

It was always the same way. Her mom would make a comment, then wait as silence slipped into the quiet space between them to answer the question for her. Sarah watched the angle of her mother's gaze go first to her forehead and then to her clothes before it lingered on the trash can and then came back to her eyes.

"I'll be fine."

The last thing she needed was to worry her mother about a pimple and static cling. At least that was what everyone always told her: Don't bother your mother, don't trouble your father, your parents have enough on their minds.

But her mother crossed the room and enfolded her in a warm pair of arms anyway, and the gentle breath against her scalp made the tears Sarah had been holding back hard to fight.

"I remember my first day of high school," her mom said, kissing the crown of Sarah's head. "I was scared to death I wouldn't fit in."

"Not fair," Sarah said, stiffening. "You're supposed to ask before reading my mind. House rules for all clairvoyants, even mothers."

"I didn't read your mind, just your eyes, honey. I wouldn't do that to you without your permission."

"Yeah, okay, thanks. Sorry." Sarah let her breath out in a hard rush, frustration claiming her as she pulled away to collect her suitcase. Distance helped keep the tears in check. "But you stood out because you were the pretty one, the one who had extra powers—not because you were the opposite."

Her mother dragged her graceful fingers through her dreadlocks and tried to look serene. "It's always hard being different, honey…and you're not the opposite."

"Face it, Mom, I'm not you. I didn't get the superpowers, didn't get the looks—didn't get any of the stuff you had going on when you went to school. Al got that, not me. And I hate that everyone is always telling me to watch out for my brother, when I'm the last person he listens to."

"Sarah…I know how you—"

"Don't say you know how I feel, Mom—because you don't." Sarah turned away and hugged herself, wanting to both scream and cry at the same time, and not completely sure why. "Times are different. Why can't you accept that? Just like I'm different. They didn't even have schools like this back in your day, just regular high school for normal human kids without special stuff. All the kids in this school have gifts or at least way more cool gifts than anything I've got. To be going to a school like…like almost a normal human is like…" Sarah looked away. "It's like being a reject. The worst part is, all my best friends will still be in different divisions once I bomb out on my tests again, and I'll be all by myself with a bunch of new people I don't even know or like."

"Tami will be with you, honey, and so will Donnie."

"Tami is gorgeous and fits in wherever she is. She may be crazy, but she's crazy in a cool kinda way that'll make her fit in with the bad-ass girls, who are always in the cool club." Sarah glanced at her mom, realizing she'd let a curse word slip. "Sorry, Mom, but you know what I'm saying. Anyway, chances are Tami will come into her vamp powers real soon and will be out of Blends quicker than you can blink." Sarah's shoulders slumped as the magnitude of it all weighed on her. "And as much as I love Donnie, as far as fitting in with the cool group, he's a social and talent disaster—like me. Great friend, loveable guy, but a geek. Period."

She could literally feel her mother cringe at her words, and it only made the tears she'd been battling finally fall. So she was right. That was how her mom saw her, too. Non-talented.

"Sorry I disappointed you and Dad. I know me placing in Specials like Al would have meant a lot to you both, especially Dad." Sarah sniffed hard and wiped her nose with the back of her wrist.

"Oh, Sarah…The last thing you are is a disappointment, honey. You are beautiful, smart…Your gifts will come in. Mine came in stages and—"

"And you're an angel, Mom," Sarah said quietly, looking in the mirror and realizing that after her mother had hugged her, both the pimple and the static cling were gone.

"I wasn't always." Her mother issued a brilliant smile and arched an eyebrow. "You have no idea."

Yeah, right. Her mom was the epitome of poise, grace and beauty. "Be serious, Mom," she finally said.

"One of these days I'll tell you some stories," her mother said, laughing and shaking her head. "Oh, boy—but not today. Just know that no matter what, you'll always be special to me."

There was no arguing with the woman. Her mom said the kind of thing moms were supposed to say when giving you a pep talk—as if you didn't realize that she was supposed to say that stuff, so it really didn't make you feel better after all.

But Sarah tried one last time to get through.

"I'm your kid, so I know you'll probably always think good things about me…but what happens when you're not around?"

"I'll be thinking good things about you when I'm gone and when you're away at school, just like I always do when I'm here. That will never change. The world could blow up tomorrow and that still wouldn't change, sweetheart. I love you."

Sarah sighed hard, finally giving up. "Love you, too, Mom."

It was a standoff; her mother would not be swayed from her state of denial. Her children were perfect; world peace was possible, hope sprang eternal and love could conquer all. This from a woman who blew demons to smithereens, beheaded vampires, and took out werewolves and zombies. Go figure.

In true Neteru form, her mother retained her regal presence, lifted her chin, folded her arms over her chest and smiled with a queen's knowing gaze. Yet, even for all her mother's stateswomanship, for once she seemed helpless to fix a problem, even though it wasn't hers to bear. Sarah knew that had to be making her mom crazy. But rather than give in to defeat and just accept that her kid was semi-powerless, her mother lifted her chin, eyes shining with unshed tears, and set her jaw with determination, as though confident that one day things would change.

"I had another bad dream last night," Sarah said quietly, looking away. It was an opening offered for her mother to step through, an invitation into her personal mental abyss, where she could disclose her experience with the demon without even admitting even to herself that she had ratted out the misbegotten mission from the night before. But it was clear from her mother's pleasant, dismissive wave of her hand that she wasn't taking the bait.

"Sarah, honey, anxiety on your big day is normal…natural. But by tonight you'll be sitting up in the dorm, gabbing away with all your friends from home and a bunch of new friends, too, I bet. You'll be having so much fun and staying up so late that you won't even have time for bad dreams."

"*Mom*." It was a final one-word plea.

"*Sarah*." It was the only word to trump her own.

Her mother was cheating, trying to break through her foul mood by going for the smile that fought its way free. The whole thing was so hopeless that Sarah suddenly wanted to laugh.

"I'm gonna miss you, honey."

"Gonna miss you, too," Sarah admitted. "Besides, who's gonna be there to clear up my acne?"

"If you aren't dipping into grown folks' business, as your grandmother would say, you won't have third-eye acne."

Sarah felt her face get hot.

"Uh-huh," Her mother chuckled. "This time I'll let it slide, but stay out of your father's and my conversations. Understood?"

"Sorry," Sarah said quietly. "We heard you guys arguing and just got worried."

"Your father and I are fine. Whatever you overheard has been addressed."

"So if I mind my business, no more acne?" Sarah said, trying to make her mother smile. Although her mother was too diplomatic to outright bust her for eavesdropping, and probably knew where the zit came from, she was glad her mother didn't say I told you so. "So, if I mess up and get nosy without permission at the Academy, can you come to school and get rid of the zits?"

Sarah smiled as her mother lost composure and laughed. She knew then that an immediate truce had been made.

"You're just like your father—trying to make me laugh when I ought to be mad." Her mother shook her head. "I bet after a month or so at school you'll be able to clear up your own acne, especially with Nana Marlene giving you herbs."

"You mean Headmistress Stone," Sarah corrected, doubtful any new healing talents would sprout within her that soon, but glad that her mother wasn't going to throw a fit about the eavesdropping incident.

"Ah, yes…Headmistress Stone," her mother repeated, taking Sarah's suitcase from her. "But we'd better hurry up. You know how your father is."

"Yeah, I know the general is wondering what's taking so long."

Her mother waved her hand dismissively. "Today, he can wait. I'm not in any big hurry to turn my children over to the Academy."

"It'll be fine, Mom."

Sarah looked at the strain on her mother's face. This *was* a really big deal for her mom, even though she was trying to act like it wasn't. She could also imagine the quiet war her mother had waged to get her father to relent and let them all go, even after last night's successful mission. The spontaneous hug her mother gave her just then confirmed it. She set the heavy bag down quickly and drew Sarah into her arms as though she'd never see her again. All her mother's misgivings were immediately telegraphed right into Sarah's skin.

"Lord, Lord, Lord, take care of my child," her mother whispered into Sarah's hair, hugging her so tightly she almost couldn't breathe. "I love you so much, Sarah. Don't you do anything crazy that will make me have to kill anybody or anything."

Whaaaat?

Sarah just hugged her mother back. "I won't."

Her mother released her, sniffed and quickly wiped at a tear, then forced herself to smile. "You'd better not. Do you have any idea how much we wanted to have you?"

Sarah stared at her mother with raised eyebrows. They'd never spoken like this before, and the fact that her mom, who'd always been pretty tough, was crying, was making her own eyes moist. Wide eyed, all she could do was stare at her mother, this woman of so many dimensions. When her mother's smile suddenly faded, Sarah knew something had changed.

"Well, we did," her mother said quietly, touching Sarah's cheek. "I never told you, but I'd lost a child before you and Al…and I wanted kids so badly. So did your father. Losing that baby almost killed him. So if *anything* happens to you guys at school, we won't be able to…I can't even think like that. So you listen to your teachers and to Nana Mar, you hear me? You do not go into the forbidden zones on any stupid dares or whatever…and you make sure your brother knows I'll kill him twice over if *he* does. I've already told him not to play with me on this issue." She looked at Sarah for a long time, a warning in her stare. "I talked to Al about that this morning. Now I'm telling you. People have recently gotten hurt, but it's nothing for you kids to concern yourselves with if you stay on campus and follow the rules. So promise me."

"Yeah, Mom, sure." A frown creased Sarah's brow as she shrugged and gently extricated herself from her mother's embrace. Fear was something she'd never seen in her warrior queen mother's eyes or heard in her mother's voice. Somehow, in these few moments of interaction, the tables had turned and her mother was now the one who needed reassurance.

"Promise me," her mother repeated in a whisper, her gaze boring into Sarah, "so I can sleep at night."

Her mother had to know they'd snuck out last night but was being cool enough not to rat on them.

"I promise," Sarah said again, lifting her chin. "And I'll kick Al's butt if he does something dumb."

Her mother nodded. "You're the one I can always count on—my go-to girl. Thank you."

Her mother's shoulders relaxed. Sarah swallowed a smile, unwilling to reveal how good that small compliment made her feel, knowing that she was the dependable one, the rational one, even if she wasn't the more spectacular and gifted one. It was something all her own.

Another one of her father's bellows made them look at each other. Smiles of understanding banished their somber mood.

Her mother was out the door first, carrying the suitcase, hustling down the hallway yelling, "All right, all right, Carlos!" Her voice echoed along the corridor in amused annoyance. "Five minutes won't change the course of destiny! Give us a break."

Sarah tried to keep stride with her mother's athletic pace. When they finally got downstairs, the entire team and all the cousins were gathered, and her father's eyes were blazing silver. He was clearly tense this morning, too.

But poor Donnie, Sarah thought as she glanced over at her brother and the other guys from the compound. Donnie not only had Neteru Guardian parents to worry about—Uncle JL was the best martial arts tactical on the squad, and Aunt Krissy was a white-lighter—but he also had grandparents,

Uncle Richard and Aunt Marj, who were wardens of the Lower Sphere dorms, and the poor guy didn't even have his first power starting to show. Worse yet, the school administrators had to put him in the Blends with her and Tami, which was only going to make him the target of extra teasing, since everybody knew that Blends division was the dumping ground for kids with spotty skills.

"I know," Hyacinth said, moving to Sarah's side.

"Oh, man, I wish you wouldn't do that," Sarah said with a groan. "Get outta my head."

"Sorry," Hyacinth replied in a rush. "It's hard to control when I'm excited."

"As long as you tell us what the hotties are thinking, your Clair-V skills are okay by me," Tami said with a wink.

Sarah dragged her fingers through her hair with a groan. It was always like this. Always.

"How can you even begin to think about hot bods at a time like this—they are going to shun us, Tamara." Allie wrapped her arms around herself and hung her head.

"Yeah…if you look like *that* they will. But if you go in there with attitude…"

"We can't," Hyacinth whispered, glancing quickly at her parents. "The popular girls will hate us on sight."

"Is that a real Clair-V prognostication or just a lousy gut hunch?" Tami shook her head. "Me, doing retro-Goth with this body, they'll hate, and I'll give 'em good reason. You…cute, petite, sweet as pie, smart and wouldn't hurt a fly—what's to hate?"

"Don't tease her, Tam, come on," Allie whispered, her gaze darting around the lobby.

Sarah landed a firm hand on Tami's shoulder. "Let up—just till we get to school, okay?" She gave Tami a meaningful look. "There's more important stuff to talk about—later."

"Fine, fine, my bad," Tami said in a huff, and then smiled a mischievous half-smile.

Poor 'Cinth—what would make her try to argue with Tami? Sarah stared at Hyacinth's wide, startling blue eyes and heart-shaped face. She was the perfect blend of her mom and dad. She had Aunt Jasmine's gorgeous Philippine looks and onyx hair and Uncle Bobby's blue eyes, and her clairvoyance came from her father's side of the family, too. If you didn't know her, she was easy to hate for being so perfect.

Standing in the middle of gleaming green-and-white marble floor with polished mahogany all around, big, comfortable sofas and chairs, sunlight streaming in the windows where lush ferns and elephant plants turned their leaves to the warm rays…yeah, they had grown up in the lap of luxury. That alone was enough to inspire resentment, even outright hatred. The stories that had come back from Ayana during her school breaks—stories about how some kids had survived, how they'd lost parents, everything they'd endured—were enough to turn anybody's hair white.

But was it their fault that her mom and dad, as the world's Neterus, had found this forgotten sanctuary? Their parents had a standing offer to all the Guardian teams worldwide to take in any and all children—gifted or not—so it was up to the parents to decide whether they wanted to send their kid to the compound to grow up or even send them to the Academy early, or keep them at home to love for as long as possible. Nothing about the situation was her family's fault. People made choices, so how come it was all so complicated?

The dark side had released the demons, zombie walkers, the viruses and all kinds of contagions, so why the resentment of her family? How her older cousin had endured that all alone was beyond her. In her mind, Ayana was her own brand of superhero, because Sarah knew that if she'd had to put up with that all by herself, she probably would have caved. At least she'd be going to the Academy with all her friends. Even if they got split up for talent specialty classes, they'd still have basic ed classes together, and they'd be in the same first-year dorm wing. But she still worried about the times when they'd be separated. Ayana had told her how students got bullied, and in a school where everybody had more impressive superpowers than you, that was like a living nightmare.

Nothing got her blood boiling like bullying. She might not fight for herself all the time, but seeing some weaker kid being picked on made her snap and go ballistic.

The sight of her brother walking toward her, the other guys trailing behind, put Sarah on guard. Al had a smirk on his face that told her he'd come over to pick on her, now that he knew she was in the clear when it came to demon contagion.

"I see Mom must have cleared up that zit on your face—guess that's what took you so long to get down here." Al shook his head. "Next time ask her to work on your morning attitude while she's at it."

Sarah felt her fangs extend. Why couldn't he just let the breakfast incident go?

She saw Miguel laugh, while Valencio looked down and Donnie looked away.

"Yeah, your mom went to help Sarah right after she mowed your back hair," Tami said with a sneer and flipped him the bird.

But to Sarah's horror, rather than a quick comeback, her brother turned on the oozing charm.

"Any time, Tamara," he said with a wicked half-smile, allowing his fangs to crest as he glanced at her middle finger. His smile widened as Tami yanked back her hand and folded her arms over her chest.

"In your dreams," Tami said with a glare, sudden fury making her cheeks rosy.

"No, in yours, baby—I've been there every night, remember?"

Tami lunged, but Sarah caught her around the waist, knowing that her brother wasn't above retaliating—and then Tamara might drop fang and try to rip out Alejandro's throat, and that would be disaster any day, much less today.

"Save it for the bored Upper Sphere chicks," Sarah grumbled toward her brother.

"C'mon, man," Val said, getting between Al and Tami. "Chill."

"Okay, guys, break it up."

The group went still as Carlos Rivera's voice rolled across them. Her father's voice was definitely like thunder this morning. It had been the same last night, an actual vibration that she could feel in her chest. Sarah let out an exasperated breath as her father strode over to their group.

"Gather 'round, everybody. One last squad meeting before we move out."

Sarah lifted her chin as her father slung his strong arm over her shoulder, and her brother backed off. Her father didn't yell, just spoke in a low, almost warning growl—all vamp. Yeah, her brother would never be him. Standing next to the reassuring solidity of her father gave her confidence. She met Alejandro's eyes. The sibling animosity was mutual. Good.

"Listen up, all of you," her dad said, making the full compound team, warriors and students, draw closer to hear what he had to say. "This is a big day," he said, his steely silver gaze roving over the group, then singling out each of the kids. "We won't be there in school with you to break up any squabbles. You're on your own till you come back here on break. But while you're there, you've gotta stick together as a team and watch one another's backs. I'm expecting that from each and every one of you."

Sarah suddenly felt so small, so silly—and wished so badly that she had the vamp ability to disappear in a fold of mist. But she was stuck there with her dad's iron arm over her shoulder while he warned the group against infighting.

"You represent the best of the best warriors in the world, The Neteru Guardians—we are the Warriors of Light. We kill demons, and the rest of the world's Guardians look up to us as an example. Our battles are legendary, but there is still a lot of history left to go, and you will be the ones who will make that history. So while you're at school, your job is to learn, to come into your own powers and to put away childish behavior so that when you graduate, you'll be ready to die for one another, if you have to. You have to be ready to walk straight into hellfire for your teammates, which means all the bull's gotta cease and desist once I energy whirl you into the Great Hall of the Academy. You will *not* embarrass your parents with undisciplined bickering and arguing. And, my two," he said with added emphasis in his voice, "you know I don't go for that. We clear?"

Yes, she would die of embarrassment before she even got to school. She was sure of it. But perhaps not before her twin did. And had she noticed a slight tremor of worry in her father's voice?

As she glanced around at her fellow compound-mates, the thought of dying for them really hit home. What would she have done if Tami had been snatched into that demon hole last night? For all her sassy bravado, Tami's scream in the dark had hit a note that could have shattered glass. Or what if it was Hyacinth or Allie? If it was poor Donnie…or even irritating Miguel…or, God forbid, Val? Damn…what if it was her brother? The thought was as sobering as her father's gaze roving the group in silence. It was effective, the combination of silence and his silver stare.

Apparently Alejandro hadn't answered the great Carlos Rivera fast enough. Her father's arm slowly shifted from her shoulders the same way a huge, muscular anaconda might unfurl itself from a tree limb. She could feel a vamp-snatch in the offing. It would be lightning quick, like a cobra's strike, lifting Al off his feet by the front of his shirt before he could even draw a breath.

Oh, yeah, her dad was seconds from going there. She saw it in the way her mother's eyes telegraphed a flicker of horror that said, *Please, honey, don't embarrass your son.* It was also in the static electricity that crackled in the air as her dad tilted his head like a hunting dog listening to a distant sound. The feeling of imminent doom was magnified when Al stepped back in anticipation, but he was wise enough to cough out the right answer in time to salvage his dignity.

"Yes, sir—one team."

Her father relaxed and nodded, and then looked at her, that signature silver stare now somewhat gentler but no less authoritative.

"One team, Papi," she said in her sweetest voice, and then watched her father's eyes go from a metallic blaze to a warm, normal brown.

Whew...

"That's my girl," he finally said, giving her a slow half-smile. "You knock 'em dead in school—and you let 'em know who your father is, if anybody gives you a hard time. But behave yourself. Don't make me have to come up there and hurt one of those boys, either."

"Oh...my...God, Dad."

"I mean it."

Before she could find words of protest, her father had turned to her brother.

"That's your job while I'm not there—all of you gentlemen. Got it? You make sure that your compound sisters are all right, hear?"

Too bad they won't let 'em have firearms up there," Uncle Jack said. "Could solve a lot of problems."

"Gentlemen," Sarah's mother said, stepping forward, "can we just whirl these kids to school without the drama?"

CHAPTER 5

Until this moment, Sarah hadn't realized the similarity between the sensation of falling into the demon hole the night before and stepping into her father's energy whirl. The difference was, his was filled with blinding white light and didn't inspire instant terror. Instead she felt a comforting weightlessness after the initial high velocity that sucked her in, and then she was out. But as she and the others were emerging, something shadowy flashed past her peripheral vision. Had to be vertigo…or maybe eye floaters caused by the speed.

A massive Mayanlike stepped pyramid loomed before them, its capstone—taken from the Great Pyramid at Giza—almost blotting out the sun. It was everything Ayana had described to them on her trips home for the holidays. But the capstone wasn't attached to the building. Instead it floated eerily above the platform on what appeared to be a thick plume of mist, almost as though a huge cumulus cloud separated the pyramid's platform from the actual capstone. When the giant eye carved into the capstone slowly blinked, Sarah almost screamed!

Sarah's heart pounded. Everything was so new and surreal. Still somewhat disoriented from the trip, it took her a few seconds to get her legs to stop wobbling. Then she looked around, saw all the wide-eyed stares, and froze. A loud gong was sounding, and for a second she couldn't tell if it was coming from the pyramid or if it was inside her head. Then a huge being stepped out onto the edge of the pyramid's platform and announced, "The arrival of the Neterus has commenced!"

For several seconds Sarah gawked at the being's sheer size. He was amber hued and wearing what looked like a leather and brass skirt with sandals laced up to his knees. His chiseled chest was bare, but he held a large bronze shield and wore a helmet that made it impossible to see his face. Then the sun glinted off his armor and he was gone.

The entire school—everyone who had already arrived, anyway—was apparently gathered in the courtyard, she realized. They had all come to witness the arrival of the Neteru Guardian kids.

To make matters worse, her uncles were strapped and looked like they were ready to rumble. They had enough weapons on them to march off to war. She knew they always traveled through the energy whirls like that, but still, it now made her uneasy with everyone staring at them. It also made her even more aware of just how dangerous the world beyond the compound truly was. Ever since they'd been old enough to remember, all the kids in her compound were told how they had to be vigilant because of all the kids on the planet, evil wanted the ones who came from the Neteru compound the most. Sarah closed her eyes. Just great.

With a sigh she opened her eyes, then jumped when she saw something scamper into the shadows. The little thing had skittered around the far edge of the pyramid's base before disappearing. Sarah scanned the courtyard quickly. It was at least two or three times the size of the football field their dad had created in what used to be the parking lot behind the old hotel they lived in.

Suddenly that eerie feeling of being watched from the shadows swamped her again. She no longer begrudged Uncle Mike his shoulder cannon and Uncle Jack his crossbow and sawed-off shotgun. Still, the last thing she planned to do was worry her parents by telling them about the little shadowy things she had been seeing all her life and that now seemed to have followed her here. Especially not when her parents were already tense enough about whatever was going on at the Academy. Besides, she didn't want to look like a lunatic in front of the entire school.

"Hey, did you see anything strange while we were in the whirl?" she whispered to Tami.

"You kidding?" Tami scoffed. "I blinked and we were here. By the way, your dad sure knows how to make an entrance."

"I know," Sarah mumbled, aware that every eye was on them. "I feel like a bug under a microscope."

"Yeah, well, your dad definitely doesn't do low key," Tami muttered under her breath. Then she looked at her own father. "On second thought, wanna trade?"

Sarah glanced at Uncle Jack and sighed.

"Didn't think so," Tami said. "Coin toss for whose dad is the absolute most embarrassing."

"At least none of them wore SWAT gear this time, like they did when they took Ayana to school," Allie whispered.

"Shhhh," Hyacinth said in an urgent whisper. "You know Uncle Mike can hear everything. You'll hurt his feelings."

Val just smiled like he was amused at everything, and Miguel seemed like he was having the time of his life. Donnie looked positively nauseous. And of course Al looked like he loved it all. Fawning females were already giving him *the look*.

Just then Ayana came bounding forward from the group of students gathered in the courtyard and ran toward Big Mike with a laugh. Excitement thrummed through Sarah. Her older cousin was everything she wanted to be. Ayana was the highest caliber seer there was. Yaya was destined to one day lead a Guardian team as their mother-seer the way Nana Mar had led their compound. Plus, her cousin was tall, had a great figure, beautiful brown skin and always wore the latest hairstyles. Today she had on an Upper Sphere indigo sweater with her khaki skirt, and she somehow managed to make even a uniform look cool. Her long micro-braids were swept up in a swinging ponytail, and all eyes were on her as her stepdad beamed, tossed his shoulder cannon to Uncle Jose and then opened his arms for her.

Big Mike swept her up in one huge arm, bicep bulging. "Hey, baby, gimme some sugah," he said, laughing, too.

Ayana kissed his cheek, then smiled up at him. When he didn't set her back down immediately, she laughed harder. "Uh, Dad, can you put me down so I can hug Mom, too?" She waved at her mother, and then turned to look at Sarah and the others from the compound. "Hey, guys!"

"Hey, Yaya!" Sarah called out in harmony with the others, so excited she could burst. There was a friendly face here; maybe day one wasn't going to be so bad after all.

"Mike, put my child down, please. You're embarrassing her in front of her friends," Aunt Inez fussed, laughing herself.

Her aunt looked like a shorter, plumper version of Ayana; her braids were twisted into a dignified bun, but the warm smile was the same.

"Aw, 'Nez…she's my baby, too, you know."

But her uncle grudgingly complied, and as soon as Ayana was on her feet, her mother squeezed her in a breathless hug.

"Hush," Aunt Inez said when Ayana protested. "I can embarrass you. I'm your momma."

"I need to bring in the rest of the students," Carlos said to Yonnie, his top lieutenant. "Since the Academy isn't accessible by normal roads, I'm energy-dragging them from pre-designated meet points along the way, so they'll be white light whirling in fully loaded—that way when I send the parents back, their vehicles will be clear of any demon booby traps and they'll have safe transport back to their compounds."

"Okay, you guys fall back. Convoys in heavy vehicles—gotta make room," Uncle Yonnie called out. "Incoming!"

Slowly a dense, horizontal funnel cloud formed as Sarah's father stretched out his arms and opened his hands. Muscles in his forearms and biceps strained, and a deep V of sweat formed on the back of his fatigue shirt. Students huddled close to the base of the pyramid as dust and small stones and tiny twigs swirled around.

Her aunt Valkyrie went airborne, causing students to murmur in awe as she spread her beautiful amber wings and took a position above the mouth of the energy funnel with silver arrows drawn. Other Neteru compound warriors aimed their weapons at the mouth of the whirl, and that was when Sarah became truly aware of just how dangerous a transport could be.

Or maybe it was just this time, because of what they'd found out last night.

New fear gripped Sarah as it became obvious that the Guardians were prepared to blast anything unusual that came through the vortex with the teams that her dad was bringing through the dimensions. Maybe she should have mentioned that she might have seen something scamper into the shelter of the pyramid out of the corner of her eye, but she told herself what she had seen was probably the same as the little shadows that danced around the compound, eerie but not actively dangerous. And anyway, her parents had enough on their minds. Maybe Tami was right, and she just needed to relax and go with the flow.

"There are no roads in and out of here—your dad put the school on a mountaintop with only this cliff landing area for maximum security," Ayana said, indicating the courtyard rimmed by marble balustrades.

Ayana's voice startled her. She'd been so consumed by her own thoughts that she'd almost forgotten her cousin was beside her.

"This place is awesome," Ayana said with pride. "You'll get a tour later." Then she leaned in toward Sarah and whispered in her ear, "We need to talk. They've never been armed like this for a transport before. Understand?"

Sarah nodded and hugged herself, glad Ayana was there. The other students seemed to know what to do, as though they'd already been told to stand clear of the energy whirl. Sarah and her crew numbly grabbed their bags and followed the crowd, not sure what to expect.

Tami, Allie and Hyacinth gathered closer to Sarah and Ayana, while the boys stood in their own huddle. The rest of the students fanned out close to the massive building, while the administrators and compound warriors fanned out near the marble guard railing. The small, horizontal funnel cloud kept kicking up more dust and high winds that made everyone squint. The first thing that came through the whirling dust was a fully loaded military Humvee, complete with ultraviolet rack lights, bladed rims and a silver-stake-spiked grill.

"Awesome," a girl behind them cooed.

Sarah turned at the sound of the voice, and her gaze locked on a pair of hard but gorgeous hazel-green eyes. The other girl had the kind of beauty that made one stare for a moment, as well as being tall, with supermodel build. She caught Sarah looking at her and raised one perfect eyebrow, looking her up and down with disdain before flinging her long, perfectly glossy black hair over her shoulder and linking arms with two other equally striking girls.

"Watch out for that crew," Ayana muttered, indicating the threesome. "Frickin' witches right out of *Macbeth.*"

Sarah and Tami shared a look with Hyacinth and Allie. Pure venom had been in the mystery girl's eyes when she'd looked at Sarah, but the girl's attitude didn't make sense. The way Sarah saw it, the green-eyed girl had it all over her—height, beauty, curves and, apparently, social standing, because as she passed through the crowd, the guys around her stepped aside with wide smiles and enthusiastic greetings.

Which was how Sarah learned her name. After five, "Hey, Melissa," callouts, how could she not? She learned the other girls' names the same way. The petite blonde with the mean crystal-blue eyes was apparently Angelica, and the curly haired brunette with the body that could stop traffic was Amy. And if her brother and her compound brothers didn't stop drooling over those hateful females, she was going to lose her mind. Why were guys so blind? she wondered.

She was about to nudge Tami and make a comment when she suddenly realized that, just that fast, Tami had strayed from their group and was fully engaged in watching the vehicles come in. "Tam …" Sarah called, trying to get her friend's attention.

Ayana rested a hand on Sarah's shoulder and leaned in to speak privately in her ear. "Let it ride, li'l sis. It'll be a couple of years before you can take them on. That's Melissa Gray, Angelica Roberts and Amy Feingold—real stank Clavs. Don't let 'em in your head. They practically grew up here, and they all came from the same besieged compound up north—Boston area. I don't even mess with them." Ayana gave a swift nod toward another girl, just as beautiful, who was hanging back. "That's Melissa's older sister, Patty."

The girl that Ayana had pointed out was almost a head taller than her sister, with long auburn hair and cat-green eyes. But there was a gentleness about Patty Gray that the "witches" definitely didn't possess.

"She's in my division. Patty's all right, but her younger sister is a true bitch. So are all the rest of her little bad-girl terror squad. Watch your back in here, boo. I won't be around all the time. Hip your crew."

Ayana didn't have to tell her twice. Sarah allowed her eyes to follow Patty as the last car came bouncing in. Other students were watching the procession of Jeeps, Bradlees, armored cars and Humvees.

With her older cousin nearby, Sarah relaxed and turned her focus to the cars as students started stepping forward, friends and family recognizing each other. Though it was something she'd always known, of course, it had never before struck her how odd it was that unlike the students coming from other compounds, all her compound siblings had been born in the same year and around the same month as she had been—all except Ayana, who was five years their senior and in the top division of Clairvoyants in the Upper Spheres.

Complete chaos filled the courtyard as students rushed about, reuniting. Her own compound sisters were in the midst of the fray, urged forward by Tami to see the new incoming male prospects. The guys from their compound were also lost in the throng, heads pivoting as they ogled the new array of girls.

All of a sudden the sounds, the smells, the brightness, the mind-chatter, seemed too much. Sarah walked a few paces away from Ayana and stepped into a cool shadow cast by the edge of the building. Only then did she feel like she could truly breathe. That was when she looked up, fully focused and finally seeing the totality of the grand structure. *This is what my parents built*, she thought.

Ayana came over and gave Sarah's hand a little squeeze, and stared up at the pyramid with her.

"He brought it in from Egypt when I was little," Ayana said. "Moved an entire pyramid for your mom, and then Atlantis-light cloaked it with the help of all the moms. They'd battled in the Middle East, and your mom was having a fit about the destruction and desecration of the old Kemetian temples and pyramids, so he gave it to her as a present just before she had you guys. Your dad really is a softy inside, Sarah. He adores your mom and you guys."

Sarah glanced over her shoulder at the man who was barking orders and sorting out chaos a hundred yards away, and then looked back up so far that she thought she'd fall flat on her behind. "I know we learned about this, saw the drawings, but…"

"Seeing it is way different, huh?" Ayana said, then kissed her cheek and left her gaping to go off and find her friends.

"I'll say," Sarah murmured, speaking to herself, not Ayana, who was now long gone.

One-hundred-and-twenty-foot-tall Anubis guard statues stood on either side of the monolithic structure, bearing war axes and scythes. She could see alabaster sphinxes poised at the top of what had to be a thousand steps, each facing a cardinal direction. The sheer scale of it was mind-blowing, and Yaya was right, seeing it was way different from being told about it.

Sarah stared up in awe, now that she was closer to the impressive structure. Just like the picture on the ancient dollar bill her father kept in his wallet from before the war, the pyramid was definitely split. Three quarters of it was on the ground, with doors and warrior statues, but the upper capstone really did float on a thick mist or clouds. It was almost impossible to really tell until she got up close to the structure. An all-seeing Egyptian eye practically covered the stones and she stepped back with a short gasp as it blinked again but this time slowly rolled to stare down at her.

"Sarah!" Tami said, grabbing her arm and causing her to jump. "Girl, you are missing everything." Her girlfriend pulled her away from the building. "What the hell is wrong with you, staring up at some old stone building when you can see pure stone-cut bods getting out of the cars—Oh my God!"

There was nothing to do but laugh as Tami maneuvered them over to an excellent vantage point. Their parents had begun to mill about and talk to the other newly arriving parents, while she and Tami watched with their mouths hanging open as carload after carload of cute boys emerged from her dad's energy whirl. Finally Sarah saw her father shake out his arms and collapse the funnel, then stretch his back before he rejoined her mother and several of the other Guardians.

"I am going to have to stop talking bad about Uncle Carlos," Tami said, setting her sights on one particularly cute boy with long, dark dreadlocks.

Sarah laughed. “I might give my dad a free pass myself,” she said, admiring several cute options as they were unloading their luggage. But her mirth faded when she saw Melissa Gray introducing herself to her parents.

This time it was Sarah who grabbed her friend, leaving the rest of the compound crew behind, and then jogged forward just in time to catch Melissa mid-sentence.

“Mr. and Mrs. Rivera, it’s an honor to meet the two Neterus in person. We’ve all heard so much about you and your legendary battles. It must be so exciting to travel around the world. I’ve been here practically all my life, being prepared to become a true Guardian,” Melissa said in a too-charming voice. “And I just want you to know that if there’s anything I can do to assist any of the students from your compound, I’d be only too glad to help.”

Sarah’s eyes narrowed. Not ten minutes ago this chick had given her a look that told her she’d drop her down a demon hole if she ever had the chance, and now she was trying to play Miss Sweetness in front of her parents? No, Sarah knew a deceiver when she saw one. Melissa was beyond fake. Tami cut Sarah a sidelong glance. Apparently her best friend knew a fake when she saw one, too.

“Thank you. We’ll keep that in mind,” Sarah’s mother said coolly.

Her mother gave the girl a civil smile, but it was not lost on Sarah that for the first time that she’d ever witnessed, her mother’s smile contained no warmth. Good. Obviously Mom knew the deal the moment Melissa opened her mouth. Her father smiled, too, but it never reached his eyes.

Suddenly Sarah could see the little shadows that had been hanging back behind the building beginning to slip between the legs of people in the crowd as though trying to get closer to her, yet not too near. The way the sun hit them, she could see they had open mouths and serrated teeth, like a jack o’lantern, and they waved stubby amoebalike arms that stretched and boinged in weird shapes. She almost jumped back, but then she noticed that they seemed to be making faces at Melissa. Whoa…

The most bizarre part of it all was no one else seemed to see a thing. Then again, she'd lived with the phenomenon all her life, so why should today be any different? The little shadows creeped her out, but didn't scare her badly with everyone all around her. But it was the first time she'd seen her little shadow buddies seem to take offense at someone. They'd never behaved like that when they'd appeared to her at the compound. Yet another sign that Melissa was bad news.

From the corner of her eye Sarah saw her brother headed her way. He was ten yards ahead of the rest of their compound crew. Certain that Al was only coming over to try to talk to Melissa, Sarah body blocked him subtly, so the only place for him to stand was behind her. But before she gave Al her back, she saw how his tongue was practically dragging on the ground. She wanted to kick him, then gave in to the impulse.

"Yo," Al said, jumping back. "What's your problem?"

"I need help with my bags," she lied when her mother raised an eyebrow.

"Then next time ask like a normal person." Al dusted off his pants leg with a scowl.

"Help your sister," their father said calmly. It was obvious he was being cool so he wouldn't embarrass his son.

Tami folded her arms, cocked her head to the side and simply glared at Melissa as Allie and Hyacinth caught up to the group. Al's boys hung back but stayed near him, watching.

"You must be Sarah," Melissa said, extending a well-manicured hand. "Welcome to the Academy. You don't have to worry about the bags—there's help for that." She gave Sarah a dismissive smile after she shook her hand and almost laughed in Tami's face before she turned back to Sarah's parents, her voice dripping with honey. "It was so nice to meet you, Mr. and Mrs. Rivera. Thank you again for providing us with this haven." Then she turned and beamed at Alejandro.

If he'd had a tail, it would have been wagging.

"I'm Melissa," she said with a smile.

Sarah watched her parents exchange a look as their uncle Mike came over.

"Alejandro…but my friends call me Al."

"Oh, brother," Sarah muttered.

Melissa looked away shyly. "Then…see you later in assembly, Al."

With a giggle and a wave, Melissa ran off to rejoin her group. Sarah just shook her head. Her brother practically needed smelling salts to keep from passing out.

"Butt kisser," Tami muttered.

Sarah just rolled her eyes.

"Daaaayum…" Al said, meeting Miguel's fist with his own, making Val laugh.

"Whateva," Tami grumbled.

Sarah's mother just threw a look heavenward.

"Straight barracuda. That'll trip you up, son," her dad said quietly, shaking his head.

"I'll trip over that any day," Al said, laughing, and jogged back toward the pack of students who were already beginning to climb the pyramid steps. His compound brothers followed him, laughing and cuffing his shoulder.

"You need to say that louder, Dad," Sarah muttered under her breath, "so he can get it through his thick head."

"Yeah, you do, man," Uncle Mike said to her father and gave him a wink. "You know how you used to roll, G. There must be something you can tell the boy."

"Not a damned thing," her father said, and then let out a weary breath. He gave Sarah a sidelong glance. "Stay out of your brother's business, but don't let him get played too hard, all right?"

Sarah just stared at her father. Stay out of his business, but don't let him get played? Be serious. Instant resentment shot through her. The double standard hit her hard, fired her up and made her ears ring. If some boy had come up to her in the yard, her father would have had a fit. But because it was some girl fawning all over his son, it was okay? It wasn't right. Why did Al get more respect—not to mention leeway—than she did when it came to stuff like this?

She was about to protest the inequity of it all when her mother stepped between them.

"Carlos, leave those kids alone," her mother said with a wide smile, this time containing its normal radiant warmth. "They have to work through things themselves—it's called life."

"Carlos Rivera, as I live and breathe!" a loud, booming male voice called out.

Sarah and Tami turned to look, as Hyacinth and Allie drew closer. A tall, deeply tanned, broad-shouldered man jogged over from one of the newly arrived cars, dropped a designer knapsack on the ground and then confidently strode up to her father. He had on a beige linen suit, a cranberry collarless shirt, and soft leather slip-on shoes. Nothing about him said warrior. His thick salt-and-pepper hair looked freshly barbered, and there was an expression of smug satisfaction in his haughty blue eyes.

But even though the man had hailed her dad like he was a friend, Sarah noticed her father only stepped forward a little. The men were eye-to-eye in seconds, clasping each other by their right forearms in a warrior's handshake.

"Long time," her father said, but, oddly, he didn't smile. He released the man's arm and stood a little taller.

"Long time, Rivera. You and your lovely wife have to visit Italy soon." He beamed at Sarah's mother. "I know we no longer use the old names for the places that once were, but some habits die hard."

Sarah's mother offered him a cautious smile in return. "I understand and hate using the new city names too. It seems to give in to their illegitimate power to have restructured the world."

"Yes, and that's why we're all still fighting." He offered her a slight bow with an even wider grin before looking at Sarah's father again. "The Mediterranean is beautiful this time of year. Vatican City is almost rebuilt. Resources are plentiful. Way better than the water-logged, burned-out place in that Massachusetts-Connecticut complex I used to own." Without waiting for her father's reply, he turned to her mother again, but this time took up her hand. "And of course we'd love to host the legendary huntress. As always, I am honored."

So this guy was a fake Italian imported from the US mainland? No wonder her father wasn't feeling him at all. Sarah could sense her father's energy bristle as she spied the man's expensive watch, and she looked at the soft leather slip-on shoes and fine linen suit again. What kind of warrior wore that kind of get-up? One thing for sure, the man had airs and was getting under her father's skin.

"Thank you," her mother said with an arched eyebrow, and then calmly extracted her hand. "I hear your boy is coming this year."

"Yes," the man boasted, sticking out his barrel chest farther. "Wil placed right in on the Varsity track team plus tested strong in dual talent divisions—Tactical and Specials—so the old water dragon finally made up her mind, recognized the boy's genius and put him in Specials. Then she looked at his scores again and put him right in the Shadows corps."

"Counselor Zehiradangra," her mother corrected with a narrowed gaze, ignoring all of the man's prattle about his son's accomplishments. "Not 'the old water dragon.'"

"*Perdonarlo,* lovely Neteru, I forgot that you are still close to your oracle. I meant no harm, but she is a bit...*pazzesco*."

"This is our daughter, Sarah," her mother said, allowing the slight against her old friend to pass without further comment. "And this is my niece Tami— Jack Rider and Tara's girl—you've met them—and my nieces Hyacinth and Allie. This is Mr. Archer."

The girls muttered hello, waved with the tips of their fingers and gave the man tight smiles.

"*Bella, bella,* pleased to meet you, young ladies." He smiled at her mother again, and then turned away to glance toward the cars. "As soon as Wil gets his gear, I'll have to introduce you to my boy. Nothing like a son, right, Rivera?"

Sarah almost thought she heard her father growl. As she glanced across the courtyard, trying to figure out which kid could possibly be Mr. Archer's son, she saw her uncles frowning. Her uncle Jack was chewing a stick the way he always did when he wanted a cigarette in the worst way. Uncle Yonnie's fangs were showing, and Uncle Mike was rolling his shoulders like he was loosening them up for a heavyweight bout. The rest of her aunts and uncles were passing dirty looks between them. Apparently there was bad blood between this Mr. Archer and her family.

"So, what's going on with the Rogue-class Guardians who've gone missing around town?" Mr. Archer asked. "We all have a right to know, given that there have never been disappearances like this so close to the school. Plus, I heard two students bought it? I also heard that there's a countrywide dragnet out, since some witches and Fae are missing, too. It's as if—"

"Michael," her mother interrupted, glancing around at the girls, "this is a discussion for a sealed area."

"Right—not in front of the kids," he said, with an awkward shrug. "But sooner or later they're going to have to learn to hunt, and that tragedy is just a part of life. Can't shield them forever. I would have taken Wil on a demon excursion if I had a lead on where it came from. I take my boy hunting with me all the time. Hell, your kids should be veterans of at least one demon hunt by now, given that they grew up in the Neteru compound."

"What risks you take with your kid is your business," her father said through his teeth, eyes changing. "Meanwhile, the situation is under investigation, and we're coordinating with Guardian teams across the globe." He gave Archer a pointed look. "We're not ruling anything out—including Morrigan involvement."

"Whoa…Morrigan? That's big," Archer said. "So does that mean the missing are presumed dead?"

Sarah stopped breathing as she felt her parents' fears snake through her. Kids had died. They were only looking for bodies now, not the missing. Oh, God! No wonder her parents had been so freaked out at breakfast this morning.

"Now you know exactly why you don't take untrained kids on a mission like that," her mother said coolly, without answering his question, and then glanced at the girls. "You don't take them hunting when you aren't sure what predator you're after. As my husband said, it's still under investigation."

Archer allowed a smug half-smile to creep onto his face before he cast a look of pity in Sarah's direction. "Understandable why you wouldn't take your child on a hunt. My apologies. Again, *perdonarlo*."

Quiet tension strangled the group for a few seconds.

"So how's the rest of your team?" her mother finally interjected.

Archer swept up her mother's hand and kissed the back of it. "*Grazie* for asking."

Sarah's silent prayer was simple: *Dad, don't start…not here. Even if the guy* is *a complete jerk.* Sarah's attention bounced between her father, her mother and the interloper who too slowly dropped her mother's hand. Who was this dude, putting the moves on her mother and grating her father's nerves? There was definitely some history here.

"There's my boy," Michael Archer announced with obvious pride.

The father might have been a self-important windbag, but the son…*Oh…my…God,* Sarah thought. She couldn't have looked away if she'd tried.

"Hey, I'm Wil," he said, striding up to the group and extending his hand toward Sarah first. "You new this year, too?"

She just nodded and shook his hand, loving the feel of it as she stared up into his sea-green eyes. Something about the warm slide of his palm against hers stopped her breath. A perfect jawline made a cleft in his chin, and it was clear that plenty of sunshine and exercise had added a beautiful copper glaze to his olive-toned skin. A thicket of black hair framed his handsome face, and his chiseled body reminded her of a Roman warrior.

"Come meet the Riveras and some of the kids from their compound," Wil's father boomed. "We fought together some time back when New York first got invaded. Our teams from Connecticut and Massachusetts reinforced their squads before the East Coast just got too bad."

Carlos put two fingers in his mouth and whistled for Al and the boys to join them. Archer turned to greet the boys, and Carlos stepped closer to his wife. "That was a *long* time ago, and from all the Italian he's dishing, you'd think he'd never been stateside," Sarah's father said, leaning down and muttering in her mother's ear.

"This is Mr. Archer," her mother said, employing diplomacy. She quickly introduced Al and the other boys. "And this is his son, Wil."

Nervous energy finally made Sarah draw her hand out of Wil's hold.

"This is my family," Sarah said to Wil, feeling awkward.

"Nice to meet you," he said in a pleasant tone, and then they shook hands all around.

"Is your daughter in Wil's group?" Mr. Archer asked in his too-loud voice.

"No…not this year," her mother said carefully.

"Well, what talent division do they have you in? Ah, wait, let me guess, Clairvoyant, I bet, like your beautiful mother?"

Humiliation tore at Sarah. "No, sir, actually, I'm a Blend."

"No..." Mr. Archer said, recoiling, and then released a dramatic sigh as he turned to her dad. "Well. We can't all be...special, can we, Rivera? Maybe some talent will evolve, but I would have thought for sure—"

"She's still in the process of being tested, Archer." Her dad's eyes were turning silver at the edges, beginning to spark at the rims of his irises.

"It's cool," Wil said, giving his dad a quick frown before turning back to Sarah.

Her face felt warm. If she could just disappear...Then, to make matters worse, her brother slapped Wil five.

"Yo, man, I hear you're in Specials division, too—can't wait to see what you've got." Al stood back and rubbed his chin with a wide grin on his face.

"Likewise, dude," Wil said. "Heard you have a crazy flight pattern that nobody can touch."

"I do a li'l something," Al said, clearly pleased and nodding toward his friends. "Val's not bad on the wind, either." His smile grew wider as he nodded over at some girls he'd just been talking to. "Word travels fast, bro. Heard you were in the same compound with them for a while before Boston fell and that you have some serious tactical game yourself." Although Al smiled, it was obvious in his tone he hadn't expected to encounter a kid that could best him. Her brother drew himself up a little taller before delivering a compliment. "Enough to land you in Shadows."

"Not too shabby." Wil smiled and gave his dad a warrior's handshake, then waved good-bye to the rest of them, his gaze remaining on Sarah for a moment. "Nice to meet you. See you inside."

Wil's smile lingered in her mind even after he'd turned away. It was a nice smile, a genuine one, just like his voice. It was so clear that he was nothing like his rich, boastful father. She watched him bound across the courtyard, her brother and the guys from their compound following in his wake, but felt her heart sink a little when she saw him quickly surrounded by Melissa Gray and her treacherous crew.

"Have they done medical tests to see what's wrong with the girl?" Mr. Archer asked with false concern.

Her father was about to explode, she could tell, but her mom came to the rescue before her father could draw a breath—maybe before he could draw blood.

"Michael," her mother diplomatically interrupted, "we really must get all these kids settled before they put us parents out. And as you can imagine, we'd like to spend as much time with them as possible. Please tell the members of your compound that we said hello."

Sarah just stared after her mother for a moment as she turned on her heels and headed inside the Great Hall, sure that she wanted to get away from Wil's father but not so sure what would be waiting for her at school.

CHAPTER 6

Sarah, Tami and the rest of the gang crossed the huge courtyard and began the climb up the steps that led to the Great Hall. A gazillion thoughts pinged through Sarah's brain as she made her way up the steep incline. They had already learned that students were missing, not just Guardians. But now they also knew that some of those students had died. Wil Archer's dad had spilled the beans, and she could tell that her parents were as pissed off about that as they were about his airs. She couldn't wait to get somewhere private so she and the girls could talk. But Wil…A quick stumble pulled Sarah's focus back to the narrow incline, lest she miss a step and really fall.

The scene was at best organized chaos. Parents were trying to keep up, some much more agile than others. Inside the Great Hall at last, Sarah's attention ricocheted from three hundred extremely curious and excited students to the strange beings sorting the students' luggage according to dormitories.

Petite Panlike creatures held clipboards in their dainty hands, as their small, shiny hooves rang against the highly polished stone floors. Tiny faeries in rainbow hues double-checked luggage tags, while short, muscular elves kept a luggage assemblyline going out through a passageway.

Sarah and Tami shared a look. Their aunt Valkyrie was hovering about, smiling and excited as she reunited with old friends on the luggage detail. They'd all heard her speak of the Land of Nod—another dimension that existed alongside theirs—but they'd never actually seen a being from there.

They'd just learned in home-school history that the veil between Nod and their own dimension had been torn in one of the bigger battles between the Light and Dark realms. Her mother had given sanctuary to many who once lived in Nod, and according to her parents, that was how Aunt Val met Uncle Yonnie—a Valkyrie and a Vampire, go figure. The bizarrely beautiful combination had made Valencio.

Ayana had told them a lot about what they could expect, but hearing about it and actually seeing it with her own eyes were two entirely different things. There was simply no way she could have prepared her mind for beings that seemed as though they'd stepped right out of the pages of an ancient mythology textbook.

Sarah glanced toward the hall entrance, where light poured in, wondering what other types of creatures her mother had given sanctuary to once the shielded dimension of Nod had imploded. It was so strange how all of the stories she had once blown off now had meaning, now had life. No one had really listened to Aunt Val's tales about Nod before. Who wanted to sit around listening to a bunch of adults rehash the past? All the kids in the compound were always in a rush to do their own thing. But this…This was like watching fairy tale creatures magically come to life.

"Don't stare—and they are *not* 'creatures,'" Hyacinth whispered, reaching around Allie and Tamara to squeeze Sarah's elbow—hard. "They like to be called *beings*. They're no more creatures than our Aunt Valkyrie is, so don't even think of them that way. It's rude."

Sarah simply nodded, too overwhelmed to protest as she stared around the Great Hall. Massive stone walls surrounded them, polished until they shone like glass. Fast-moving gold- and silver-etched hieroglyphics told a story that she could only intuit in fits and starts, each wall and column bearing a different language from antiquity. Some she knew, but the quick rate at which the meanings went by made her temples throb.

Large gold and silver embroidered tapestries with the world's old, pre-One World Order national flags emblazoned on them in monochrome stretched from mahogany rods and were suspended from the ceiling by thick satin ropes. But the longer she stared, the more she came to see that the entire suspension mechanism was made from the fluid, interconnected movements of living dragon art.

Flames from broad iron wall torches licked a path up the stone until it practically glowed. Dragons guarded opened stone skylights with slow, undulating movements full of threat. Aunt Jasmine gave her a quick wink. Her aunt's specialty was drawing things to life, and she'd obviously taken great care to draw to life the protectors of the Great Hall. Aunt Jasmine loved dragons—believed they were good luck. Maybe they were. Or maybe there was a reason why all the uncles and aunts had brought weapons. If the dragons were the good guys, then what did the demons that were threatening the school look like? Maybe none of what Ayana had told her was embellishment. One thing for sure, the thing that had attacked her last night had been bad enough that she didn't want to meet anything worse.

Atlantean, Kemetic-Egyptian, Cuneiform, Aramaic, Coptic, Chinese, Greek, Hebrew, Latin, Rune, mound-dweller wall art, Aztec…they all scrolled by at a dizzying pace. Then a word stuck out: *Nexse.* Within a second it was gone again. Sarah froze. That was the same word the Light being in the darkness had used. As soon as she had seen the word, it was as though she could hear the being speaking it in her head. Sarah glanced around, but no one else was paying attention.

She stared at the columns intensely, but the word didn't appear again. What did it mean? Then she was jostled from behind and snapped back to the present, and she hurried after Tami, Hyacinth and Allie.

Thick plumes of frankincense and myrrh tickled her nose and made her eyes water as her gaze haphazardly wandered. The Great Hall was pure sensory overload. In addition to the grand splendor of the building and the strange moving words, she'd also noticed Wil again. It was a long shot to think he'd ever notice her, with all the pretty girls at school. She tried to stop staring at him, but that was next to impossible, even though he was way out of her league.

Without consulting her brain, her gaze remained on Wil. He looked away from his conversation with her brother and Val and gave her a smile. Problem was, he was standing close to Melissa and company. The moment he glanced in Sarah's direction, Melissa caught it and whispered to one of her friends, and they all laughed.

Sarah's face burned, and she quickly looked away.

"Dare to dream," Hyacinth whispered, making Tami giggle.

Sarah reached around Allie and pinched Hyacinth, who squealed. "I'm warning you, quit barging into my private thoughts."

"Did you see the Uppers," Allie whispered, squeezing her eyes shut for a second. "Ohmigod, ohmigod, oh, my *gawd*."

"Did I see the Uppers?" Tami murmured, her gaze slowly roving the students surrounding them. "You mean did I see the pure eye candy in every delicious flavor from semi-sweet dark chocolate to amaretto to pure blond macaroon hunk?"

"If you don't keep your voice down, I swear I will never speak to you again, Tamara Rider!" Hyacinth snapped.

Allie's nervous gaze darted through the crowd before returning to Tami. "And what about the Upper Sphere girls, huh? They'll probably kick our butts for even looking."

"Just for looking?" Sarah let out a hard sigh. "Be serious, Allie. I think you're overreacting. The seniors aren't worried about us. We're no competition. Just look at them."

"*Spell casters*," Tami said with a smirk, moving toward the seats arranged in semi-circular rows on the far side of the hall. "I'm not scared of those bitches, and I'm pretty sure I could give any one of them a beat-down they'd never forget."

"Do something with her, Sarah," Allie lamented, stepping closer to Sarah to distance herself from Tami.

"You know you can't do a thing with Tami but love her and give her a tissue when she gets her nose bloodied and the snot beat out of her." Sarah shook her head.

"All right, all right," Tami whispered back, laughing. "Chill out. Geeze Louise, don't get your panties in a knot. But just look at all the available trouble on two legs."

Sarah followed Tami's line of vision, much to Allie's and Hyacinth's horror, and checked out the rows of students settling themselves on intricately carved, gleaming ebony Ashanti stools, grouped according to division colors. Suddenly it hit her. Every female student's stool had a Sankofa bird on it, the same tattoo her mother had on her lower back. All the male students' stools had the same tattoo that her father had been given years ago to cover the Vampire bite on his throat at his jugular vein. It was the *Nkyin kyin* symbol that was carved into the boys' seats.

As her gaze lingered, she instantly spotted Ayana sitting in the first color band with the fourth-year students. Sarah was about to wave, but Ayana gave her a shake of her head, then turned away. She could understand that Ayana wanted to separate herself now that she was with her classmates, but it still stung. Sarah faced forward, feeling disappointed. Then the hair began to rise on the back of her neck. She glanced around and saw Melissa Gray giving her the evil eye. She turned to look at Ayana again, but her cousin seemed lost in her own conversation.

Faculty members stood at the ends of the rows, guiding the new students toward the correct section, while the students who'd been there before already knew the drill and quickly took their places. Most parents sat in the very back, but hers were headed toward the stage area.

Suddenly Ayana got a message through to her. *Your mom and dad built this. Don't let those hater witches make you forget who you are.*

Sarah nodded as she looked over her shoulder toward her cousin. Ayana's eyes were angry, and that gave her confidence to turn around and return her attention to the goings-on. Somebody had her back. The disappointment she'd felt faded. Ayana hadn't abandoned her. But she was still conflicted. Wil was only a few rows away, and his gaze was fastened to the female splendor that surrounded him. And Melissa and her crew were still whispering and sending visual daggers in her direction.

Then everything hit her all at once. This was all so new, and she was so unprepared. Her parents had built monuments, and that was a lot for a kid with mediocre powers to live up to—and being hated on sight by a bunch of mean girls didn't help.

Just look at this place, Yaya, Sarah mentally shot back.

Yeah, I know, but what are you gonna do? Ayana shrugged.

A slight shudder of awareness ran through Sarah. In reality, Ayana had been conservative in her descriptions about what it was like at the Academy. There had been no yeast in her story to make it rise into a full-blown whopper. If anything, that would have made Sarah feel better—because that also would have meant that Ayana had probably exaggerated her stories about school and about her senior training battles on the road. But Yaya hadn't exaggerated a thing, which also meant that her parents' exploits might have been way more dangerous than they'd ever let on.

As she looked around, a dozen plaques in the Great Hall were dedicated to the significant battles her parents and the other Neteru Guardians had fought.

Sarah spotted eight empty stools at the end of the closest row, where other Lower Sphere students had already taken their seats. At a subtle nod from her mother and after a bit of shuffling, she and her compound siblings were seated on the appropriately carved stools.

Front and center, her grandmother stared down from her seat on the dais. Sarah counted thirty-three stone steps up to the platform where her nana, now Headmistress Stone, and Baba, now Headmaster Shabazz, sat on silversmith-created versions of the student stools.

Never in her life had she seen her stand-in grandparents look so regal—or so serious. She was glad they'd taken over for her real grandparents, who had died fighting vampires. She wondered what they would have been like if they'd lived. As she stared up at the platform, she saw kindness in her nana's eyes but also unwavering authority. Quiet pride filled Sarah, chasing away the dread for a moment.

Elegant. Today, Nana Marlene was elegant. She wore long, finely embroidered, iridescent purple robe with gold embroidery. Her ancient white dreadlocks were swept away from her dark brown face, and her head was covered in the same heavy fabric, but tied in such a striking way that the headdress seemed almost like an exotic bird. To her left sat her husband, the school's head of security and defense training. Baba wore a golden grand Boubou African robe with pantaloons that had deep purple embroidery—the reverse color pattern as Nana's—his small square cap of the same rich fabric, his graying dreadlocks flowing down his back.

Unlike Nana, Baba didn't study any of the compound students—never made eye contact, not even with her. Today he was clearly the enforcer, while Nana was responsible for spiritual and educational pursuits. Beside them were golden stools etched with symbols from the Akan and from Kemet, symbols that she had seen in the fabrics and art gracing the compound all her life. Semi-circular rows of stools behind the headmasters were filled with a very strange collection of warriors and beings seated with proud postures. Teachers? Had to be the weird faculty Ayana told them funny stories about.

Staring at Sarah, her grandmother suddenly stood. It was such a swift motion that all murmuring fell silent. Her grandmother lifted the thick ebony walking stick that she always carried, grasped it tightly in her right hand and brought it down with a loud crack against the floor. Immediately the etchings along the surface of the wood were lit from some preternatural source within. All the students in the Upper Spheres quickly got to their feet, so she and all the other new students quickly scrambled to their feet, as well. From the corner of her eye, Sarah could see her parents and the rest of the compound parents forming pairs along the purple runner that led to the bottom of the steps, which led to the platform.

At another crack of her great walking stick, the flames in the Great Hall sputtered as Headmistress Marlene began to speak.

"*Anetch hrak atef mut Neter, ita em, amen tua en Hetep*. We ask for ancestral knowledge and permission to begin."

"Ashe," rang out from the faculty and Upper Sphere students in unison.

Her grandmother's voice was loud, majestic and strong. A male faculty member in white brocade stood, holding a water-filled gourd and walked forward, as a female faculty member in matching traditional ceremonial robes brought forward a small fern. The woman positioned the plant at Headmistress Stone's feet, and then the man handed the gourd to her. With an agile flip of her wrist, a clear stream of water spilled over the lip of the gourd as she continued speaking, her voice echoing through the hall.

"Supplant unknowing with wisdom, supplant education with knowledge, keep these the last children of a generation of Guardians safe. Keep their hearts pure. *Ashe*."

Again the word *Ashe* rang out in response. But this time the parents were on the move, walking to the front and heading up the steps single file. Her mother and father were leading the group of Neteru Guardians.

Thunderous applause followed them, causing Sarah and crew to look at one another with questioning stares. As the Neteru Guardians stood before their stools, whatever they had on slowly dissolved into white and silver traditional ceremonial robes. Sarah's jaw went slack as the students behind them whooped and cheered, stomping the floor in three-beat stanzas, until Headmistress Stone lifted her walking stick.

"They have brought the Light. They have conquered the darkness. Now you must conquer the darkness within your own minds and be hungry for true knowledge—that is your job here until it is your time to battle." She glanced around the massive hall and then nodded to her husband.

Headmaster Shabazz accepted her walking stick and raised it high in the air, then slammed it down against the stone floor, sending out a sudden white light that rippled down the steps, flowed over the floor like translucent lava and crawled up the walls, making the dragons roar. Students gasped. Her nana's eyes glowed white. Within seconds, the metallic tapestries were illuminated, and soon scenes of battles moved across them, as though they all made up one continuous high-definition television screen. It was amazing.

"Every year, to educate our new students and to refresh the memories of our already inducted Spheres, we review the sacrifice. This is what your parents faced, what the Neteru Guardians faced. Many have sacrificed for your education. Many brave warriors did not survive. This—education, time to learn and grow and become whoever you are destined to be, in a safe haven—is a privilege. You must never forget that."

Using the walking stick as a pointer, Headmaster Shabazz motioned beyond the horrific scenes playing out on the tapestries toward the hieroglyphics. "These walls tell the stories of great human civilizations that came to be and devolved to dust thousands of years ago. You do not have the luxury of thousands of years or many lifetimes, many incarnations. The last Guardian children that we know of are all assembled in this Great Hall. If there are to be more, then they will be *your* children—but that will happen only if you survive and create a place for them to thrive."

Mesmerized, the students stared up at the epic battles being played out in living color. Sarah had never in her life seen her mother as she appeared in that moving spectacle. It was all so real, so much larger than life, that she could almost taste the dirt and smell the sulfur. Her heart was practically beating a path out of her chest. Sweat covered her body as she watched, adrenaline racing through her veins. Demon splatter suddenly hit the screen, causing students to cover their faces and groan as the creature's head fell with a thud at the bottom of the screen. Sarah peered through her fingers. *That* was her *mom* and her *dad*?

Sure, she'd seen the silver glare when her dad was annoyed. Had seen him get a little toothy…but in full battle mode? Transfixed, she watched as a multi-eyed demon came up behind her mother, who'd just beheaded two zombie walkers. Her father spun out of an energy whirl to rip out the demon's innards with his bare hands, and then called a blade into his grip as her mother took flight with her aunt Valkyrie.

Valencio glanced down the row at her, his expression as dumbfounded as hers.

They turned back to the tapestries to see Val's mother, who was all warrior rage in the air, firing silver-tipped arrows into a cloud of circling, gargoylelike Harpies. His dad was in full daywalker mode, sending black charges into a cloud of demon bats, fangs glistening with the blood of battle.

They'd never seen their parents like this. They had thought that all the stories told around the dinner table and at holiday meals were inflated by memory with a little dash of ego for seasoning.

All around them the students were going wild. Cheering and shouting as Uncle Mike lowered a shoulder cannon and took out a charging werewolf squad with a hallowed-earth-packed rocket, then threw down his spent weapon, hurtled over two Amanthra serpent demons and full-on tackled a werewolf, snapping its neck. Before the thing could recover to attack again, her father was at her uncle's side to behead the creature with one furious strike.

Sarah's attention bounced between the crowd and the tapestry screen, but then she saw her grandmother in the mix and thought she'd pass out.

"Nana…?" Her voice came out as a disbelieving croak. Eyes wide, Sarah sat with her mouth open, staring up, watching her nana Marlene gore two fast-moving vampires with her walking stick and then explode them into burning embers with a white-light discharge from the same staff.

But when her baba Shabazz shed his clothes to transform into a huge, muscular black jaguar, she felt for Allie to help hold her up. Baba was a shape-shifter, not just a Tactical? Oh. My. God!

Allie practically started hyperventilating as she kept her gaze glued to the images, staring in disbelief as her parents fought back-to-back, her mother charging stones with white light as her father hurled them into a thundering demon cavalry. Demon slime clung to her father's blond hair, while her mother's red hair rose from her shoulders in an angry static charge.

"My-my-my mom and dad…" Allie stammered in a shocked whisper.

"Un-*frickin*-believable," Tami whispered in awe. "Uncle Dan always seemed so…so…regular." Then she stopped speaking for a moment as her own father jumped on a Harley, pump shotgun cocked, and rode into a demon whirl of Harpies shouting obscenities while he unloaded hallowed-earth-packed shells.

Tami's whoop joined that of the entire Great Hall when her dad rode out of a rain of cinders and her mom dropped out of a vampire fold-away onto the back of his bike wearing black leather and sporting fangs. Hyacinth practically froze on her stool as she watched her grandfather open a vein so her mother could finger-paint a dragon on the side of a building with his blood. Hyacinth's mouth fell open when the monster came off the bricks to assist her dad, who was whirling like a white-light Merlin.

Yeah, okay, everybody knew Aunt Jasmine drew living art…but damn. And everybody knew Uncle Bobby was a wizard, had seen him do cool parlor tricks…but watching him ride a dragon, sending lightning bolts into a flying demon air squadron, was something to behold. The man had no fear.

The cheering reached a deafening level as her uncle Jose mowed down everything in his path, and then Aunt Inez pulled the pin on a grenade, lobbed it toward a water tower and blew back half a unit of demon infantry when the blessed water fanned out like napalm.

This is what the Neteru Guardian team did when they weren't home?

This is what she and the rest of the compound gang had to live up to?

Sarah felt light-headed. The queasiness was back with a vengeance. She clasped her hands together to keep them from trembling and stared at the floor.

Riveted, she couldn't have stopped watching the images careening across the tapestries if she'd wanted to. Two seconds staring at the floor had been too long. The dragon anchors holding the tapestries were agitated, as though reliving parts of the battle, snapping at the air at what they thought were demon morsels flying off the screens.

Suddenly the demons on the screens began retreating. Students cheered, but the looks on the warriors' faces seemed anything but victorious.

In the careening images, Sarah's mother and Uncle Richard broke away from the battleground first. Her mother's voice carried throughout the Great Hall as she shouted, "Medic!" and Uncle Richard followed. That was when the entire Great Hall witnessed what was so callously called "collateral damage" on the Council Group News Network.

Sarah's eyes filled as she saw her mother pull a victim from the rubble of an apartment building, then clasp the young woman to her breast, trying to save her. The girl looked no older than Ayana, and she coughed, clawing at Sarah's mother's wings, and then hiccupped blood as her mother rocked her, trying to staunch the pain and stop the hemorrhaging.

Chaos prevailed. Her parents had won the battle but were clearly losing the war. On the tapestries above, Guardians fanned out, Sarah's dad trying to extinguish conflagrations set by the demons during their retreat. She watched silver tears fill her dad's eyes as a woman knelt beside her young son, caught beneath a collapsed building, and begged her father to save him. But it was obvious to anyone that the teenager had been ravaged by vampires. His eyes were already glowing red, and the rubble that had trapped him soon wouldn't be enough to hold him as he hissed at the approaching dawn.

All her dad said was, "Ma'am, I'm so sorry. May his soul rest in peace." Her father's bicep flexed, his grip tightened on his blade handle. The woman screamed, "No!" Her father moved so swiftly that it was a blur, and the only sound that followed was a dull thud drenched by the mother's screams. The woman flew at her father, calling him names, punching him, kicking him, clawing at him as he held her and told her over and over in a gentle voice, "I know. I'm sorry. I know."

The images slowed to a haze as Headmistress Stone's eyes returned from a glowing white to their normal, ancient, wise brown. With a wave of her staff, she motioned for everyone to pay attention.

"That is the hardest part of the battle," Sarah's father said in a strong voice, walking to the edge of the platform and holding the audience in thrall. "Never forget why we do this. It is for those who cannot fight, those who are vulnerable. Every civilian you cannot save haunts you for the rest of your life...So save as many as you can. They are why we need you to bring the light and humanity back to the world. The easy part is killing demons. The worst of it is burying the human dead…or the undead."

He pointed at the now quiet tapestries as the anchor dragons grumbled and resettled themselves. "Don't get caught up in the hype. The battle is only fun when you watch a Clair-V vision replay of it, like Headmistress Stone's vivid recall—but while you're there, it's anything but fun. And if you think burying a civilian is hard, or beheading one so he doesn't get up to harm his own family…try having to behead a comrade—a fellow Guardian who you've lived with, who you love, who's like your blood brother or sister. *That's* why you need to listen to your instructors."

An eerie silence fell over the room. Sarah watched her mother step forward to stand beside her nana. Her father stood beside her grandfather. Slowly her mother allowed her wings to unfurl, sliding out of her shoulder blades and through the open slits in the back of her white robe. It was a majestic sight to behold.

Murmurs of awe and appreciation hummed through the crowd as her mother spread her pristine white wings to their massive six-foot width and then called her Madame Isis blade into her grip, making it materialize out of thin air in her hand. In this place, under these circumstances, a strange awareness began to overtake Sarah. It didn't matter what she had been told over the years. Here, in this hall, it finally sank in and she realized what it meant that her parents weren't just normal Guardians. They were the Neterus.

Her Baba Shabazz was the strongest Tactical Guardian on the planet, and she stared up at him now as his eyes glowed gold, as if the jaguar spirit within was looking out at her. His upper and lower canines were extended, and after watching the tapestries, she understood why no one in the school wanted to tangle with him. Until today, she'd never seen him change. He would always threaten the compound boys, especially Al, not to bring out the bad cat in him, but he'd never done it around any of them. He was the last of a breed, a carryover from the old days. There were no more shape-shifters like him left, not that she'd heard of.

But her mother's wings…It was something she'd only witnessed a few times in her life, yet each time it always stole her breath. Then her father stepped forward and snapped her mind back to the immediate. Now, after the visionscape on the tapestries, he seemed taller, looked thicker, more muscular, his fangs sharper, as he called his weapon—the glowing Blade of Ausar—into his fist.

"We knew your parents." Her father's voice thundered through the hall, speaking to all the students present. "Some we unfortunately watched give their lives."

"And some," her mother said more moderately, "we were able to heal. Some still fight on to this day."

"But the mantle is being passed." Her father looked at her mother and then lifted his chin. "We will do everything we can, till the last man and woman fall, to keep the demon incursion at bay, but you must apply yourselves. There is still a lot of work to do."

Her mother spoke again. "We came today despite great risk...The forbidden zones are widening, the astral plane is teeming, and the point *beyond the edge of Light* is growing. During your first days here you'll be instructed in the parameters past which you must not venture. Study them well. Heed the advice of your instructors, and respect this faculty and staff." Her gaze went to Alejandro and remained there until he looked away.

She continued speaking. "There are many spies, the Morrigan, not to mention demons and human helpers, searching for this enclave, as you well know. We've thwarted them for years as we have protected the children, you, our future. Do not be so eager to battle the unseen just yet. Off campus is off limits until Headmistress Stone and Headmaster Shabazz say you're ready. I know the towns at the base of the mountains seem exotic, and curiosity is a big lure—but you also saw what can happen to a town if they know Guardian children are there. We need each and every one of you. If we lose even one of you, our hearts will shatter." Her mother's voice wavered with passion as she lifted her Isis blade. "You are the future."

"My wife is always so diplomatic," Sarah's father said, his silver gaze scanning the Great Hall. "I've been to Hell—used to run that joint for a while, at least in the Vampire Council. If it weren't for my wife, whose plea won me amnesty from the Light, I wouldn't be standing here." He waited theatrically as gasps and murmurs rippled through the hall. "Yeah, that's right. I know every warrior thinks he's a badass—until he gets captured. But let me tell you, the Dark Realms will do whatever it takes to break you. And the things they can think up to do will haunt your dreams for the rest of your life—if they let you live. You must become stronger, not only here," he said, tapping his temple, "but also here." He raised the fist clutching the blade to his heart.

Headmaster Shabazz stepped forward to speak. "As you know, some students stay here year-round and don't go home on break. All new students start in September. But before this semester began, at the last full moon a month ago," he said, rubbing the tension away from his neck, "we had a couple of unfortunate incidents locally. I'm sure you've all heard the rumors on PirateNet about the loss of Guardians from several North American compounds, as well as some students and faculty here at the Academy. It's true. We have experienced some recent and devastating losses. We've found the bodies of Peter Matthews and Gregory Duncan, but there are still some students and faculty we haven't found. So now is not the time for pranks or sneaking off campus."

"It wasn't a rescue mission when we went looking for two missing Valkyrie fliers," her father said flatly, looking particularly hard at the compound students. "It was a *recovery* mission."

Headmaster Shabazz's gaze hardened as it traveled around the Great Hall. His jaguar was peeking out again. "The students who died in the forbidden forest were simply victims of the forest itself. But the others had violated curfew and were on the grounds when they went missing, just as the instructors were. We haven't found them—yet. We are still in search-and-rescue mode as we look for them. That's why, when we lay down rules and tell you that certain areas are off limits or set a curfew, it's with good reason. So don't make me to have to shape-shift to come down the side of that mountain looking for you. Trust me, you really do not want that."

"Or to have to have the school send in aerial support," Sarah's mother said, gaining a nod from Aunt Valkyrie.

Nodding as the awareness that *all* the faculty members were also warriors overtook the new students, Headmistress Stone continued. "The brave people in the border towns would rather risk the threat of demons, dark creatures and even the occasional walker that comes out of the woods than deal with the repressions taking place under the One World martial law system or the madness of corruption and crime in the dense population zones. Our mountain town neighbors don't know about us, and we like to keep it that way. They are simple people who live off the land as best they can, because if you go into the cities, you can't buy or sell or move about without the central number and ID. But just because these folks have bucked the system, don't think they can't be infiltrated by evil. As Neteru Damali Richards-Rivera said, there are spies everywhere. Sanctions for putting yourself or your fellow students and the faculty at risk are severe. This isn't a game."

Sarah stared at her mother, catching her eye, seeing extra moisture there. It was the same look she'd given her earlier. Her mother was scared, and rightfully so. Something had happened inside the walls of the school. What did they think had abducted the students and teachers? There, information was still not being shared.

Her grandmother's voice rang out, distracting her from her thoughts almost as if on purpose.

"That said, we are blessed." Headmistress Stone opened her arms wide. "We are not going to let the dark side steal our joy or frighten us into paralysis or apathy. We will conduct classes, educate you and even throw in a party or two in order to maintain all the normalcy we can muster. Losses are devastating, but the living must continue living, or those who have perished will have died in vain. Neteru Rivera salvaged part of this monument from the ravages of the eruption of Popocatepetl and combined it with what he could salvage from Egypt. When that great volcano erupted in the end of days, lava threatened this Mayan landmark, and he brought it here—camouflaging it as one of the mountains and then adorning it was the capstone from Khufu, because even out of the rubble, something good can be salvaged."

Gracious applause from the older students and faculty rang out. Wil leaned in slightly, his voice low and gravelly as he spoke to Alejandro in a private murmur, but Sarah heard it—moreover, she felt it.

"Yo, man, your dad even relowed a pyramid? Holy shit."

"Yeah," Al said with pride. "Crazy, huh? Wish he'd relocate my pain-in-the-ass sister, though." He gave Sarah a look that told her to stop eavesdropping.

Wil smiled and shook his head and Val gave her a quizzical look as she shot her brother the evil eye. He gave her the finger in return, but held his hand down low and shielded it with his other hand so he couldn't be seen by the adults.

"Floating above us is the capstone salvaged from the post-battle wreckage that took place in Egypt at the Valley of the Kings. This is where our Upper Sphere Tehuti Akashic Records Library of astral truths and sacred texts is held, thanks to our Neterus. Students accessing these records must be able to either transport themselves there or do their studies via telepathy and astral travel."

Ayana had told her that the library was nicknamed the dollar bill.

Headmistress Stone pointed above her head. "Note that there is a full three floors of nothing but pure ether between our dragon-protected ceiling and the library entry. But Lower Sphere students need not fear. We have a more traditional library located along one of the normal underground corridors."

Intermittent chuckles threaded through the Great Hall from both adept Upper Sphere students and faculty as Headmistress Stone offered a brilliant smile. But it faded after a moment as she directed her gaze around the hall.

"A library is a privilege in this era, students. You have no idea what it took to save all the texts and manuscripts that we have here. After the New World Order commenced and then evolved into the One World System, every dissenting book and film was burned. Music deemed revolutionary or unfit was eradicated. All religious texts were confiscated. Sacred scrolls, ancient hieroglyphics, codicils, you name it, were burned. Much of what is stored in the Tehuti Library was sent to us via astral projection from the Neteru Queens and Kings Councils, and angel hierarchies…so some of the more obscure texts are only in that ethereal form while our diligent scribes from the Land of Nod work on the restoration effort. But you will have the next seven years of Tree of Life Sphere ascension to learn about these things. Patience and a firm dedication to your studies is the key."

Seven years. But the horror they were facing, the thing that everyone was telling them was their destiny, was coming six years from now—unless it was already here. They didn't have seven years to learn all that they needed to know!

Sarah felt like the bottom had dropped out of her stomach. This was only day one, and she was already scared, confused and mentally exhausted. But her nana seemed excited, even while casting a stern warning. How did a woman her age have so much energy?

"Now that you've heard and seen a brief history, as well as a sobering update from our wise security council," Headmistress Stone said with a warm smile, "let us meet our new incoming students according to talent division, so that they may be properly inducted into our fine institution."

Again applause thundered through the hall. And again that sick feeling returned to overtake Sarah until she shuddered.

CHAPTER 7

Questions swirled in Sarah's mind, even though the dread of public talent divisioning was upon her. Having partial information about the dead and missing was almost worse than being kept in the dark. She wanted to know more than just the names of the students who had died. Just how had they been killed by the forest? Where on the grounds had the abductees been when they went missing? What were their names, ages and talents? Did they have families who would grieve for them? What security measures had been put in place to make sure it wouldn't happen again?

Sarah's mother stepped forward and stood next to her nana Marlene, jerking Sarah away from her darkening thoughts. Her mother turned one palm up and one palm down, mirroring the Egyptian hieroglyphics on a nearby pillar. Her grandmother matched her mother's stance, her hands turned in the opposite directions, as though one woman was sending something invisible and the other was receiving it. They were only separated by a few feet, but soon their body auras became visible, golden light bathing each woman in a shimmering glow.

Murmurs of hushed awe filtered through the audience, and Sarah had to admit that her mother and grandmother looked like the gorgeous queens of old. Within seconds the space between their hands seemed to draw in the light from their energy fields, the golden beam splintering into the full color spectrum before flaring into a white light that drew audible gasps of pleasure from the students. Then suddenly that light condensed into a single solid beam that focused on the largest of the dragon anchors until the eyes of the huge creature began to glow. Unlike the others, this huge one was a massive water dragon that looked as though her aunt Jasmine had painted him in water color hues from the jewel blue deep.

"Whoa…" Alejandro murmured, his voice a low rush of respect that blended in with the mesmerized responses of the other students.

The huge Asian water dragon closed its gold glowing eyes for a moment, its antennae twitching. Suddenly it seemed as though the light that had once escaped through its huge irises imploded, to light it from the inside out, turning its multi-hued, iridescent scales a kaleidoscope of shimmering color as it broke away from the wall to stream its large body up and out through the skylight.

The students craned their necks, their eyes trained on the opening in the ceiling, watching the watercolor-hued dragon spiral toward the capstone that hovered over the Great Hall.

As quickly as it had risen, it returned in a nose dive that made some students duck and cover their heads. But rather than crash against the students or the stone floor, it undulated down the main aisle with what looked like a giant completely round snow globe in its mouth.

Her mother and grandmother gave each other an amused glance as the dragon rolled over on its back a few times like a playful Labrador and then released a rumbling growl of delight.

"Mojo, you can play with Zehiradangra later," Headmistress Stone said, barely concealing her smile. "She has work to do right now."

The dragon frowned and let out a huff of annoyance, then righted himself. Sarah's mother looked away for a moment, looking as though she might break out into laughter as the recalcitrant dragon lowered his head, still holding the globe in his massive jaws, and backed away from Headmistress Stone in sheer defiance.

"Drop it," Sarah's father demanded, making the dragon growl.

"You oughta let him out more," Uncle Jack commented from the sidelines, but a quick glare from his wife was enough to silence him.

"Pearl," Sarah's mother crooned with a smile, speaking to the globe and using the oracle's pet name. "Will you explain to Mojo that we have students here this morning, sooo…uhm, we need his cooperation."

Tiny bubbles created a strobe effect inside the globe as it changed from translucent to varying and deeper shades of pink. Clearly unhappy about whatever had transpired in secret dragon language, Mojo moved to the platform with a scowl and gently placed the globe on the light bridge extending between Sarah's mother's and grandmother's palms. Grumbling all the way back down the aisle and as he returned to his ceiling perch, the dragon turned away from her mother as she tried to console him with a "Thank you, Mojo" that fell on deaf ears.

It was almost comical as the huge dragon shunned the two women who had taken his prize. Mojo wouldn't even look at the riser that held amused faculty. He just turned away and covered his head in the coil of his tail.

Mother's and grandmother's hands and backlit by the white light, Sarah could see that the globe was filled with water and had a sugar-sand bottom that cushioned a magnificent pearl—the most perfect, iridescent pearl that she could ever have imagined, magnified by the water to appear many times its real size.

"This oracle was a gift from the Neteru Council of Queens during my journey of self-discovery," Sarah's mother said with love in her voice, her gaze leaving the students to focus on the globe for a moment. "My queens sent me on a mission, and along my path of enlightenment, I—we," she amended, glancing over to her husband, "met Zehiradangra, a water dragon of the highest order from the Land of Nod."

Applause rang out from the faculty, who stood. The Upper Sphere students followed suit, while the rest simply looked around, bewildered.

"Ze—uh, Counselor Zehiradangra," Sarah's father said, once the applause had died down, "is special to us all."

His comment drew an angry growl from Mojo, and the globe released a stream of tiny bubbles that made the dragon resettle himself with a disgruntled huff. Headmistress Stone looked away and seemed to be biting her lip, and Sarah's mother couldn't conceal a wide smile as she resumed her speech. Oh, yeah, Sarah was sure there was a story there, but there was no time to figure all that out now.

"Counselor Zehiradangra is someone every student should respect, and it is a blessing that we have her on our faculty. She is a water dragon who gave up her incarnation as a free swimming being to become a dragon pearl oracle to the Neterus during one of the most crucial chapters in our history. I wore her throughout the battles of the Armageddon and affectionately call her Pearl, and I am—as we all are—forever indebted to her for her selfless sacrifice, constantly radiant good nature, guidance and, ultimately, her wisdom. She will not steer you wrong, for she listens with a good heart, then magnifies the divine voice that speaks to your soul in a soft whisper until you are ready to hear it."

The Great Hall fell completely silent as the light brightened around the globe, and then suddenly the tapestries lit up again. The anchor dragons resumed their slow, undulating dance, and Mojo began to weave between them as though somehow orchestrating their movements.

"Welcome, students," a watery, disembodied voice murmured. "I am honored to be here with you on this auspicious day." There was a slight pause as the lighting on the tapestries began to run the gamut of rainbow hues. "Hello, Damali…I've missed you so. Carlos, as always, it is a pure pleasure to see you." When the large dragon stopped moving and stared at Sarah's father, the oracle sighed. "Now, Mojo, do *not* start. We have been through this a hundred times, if once."

Sarah glanced at Tami, who whispered, "Tell me that old lady pearl is not flirting with your dad!"

"Not now," Sarah said, blushing. She was going to die. Oh yes, she was absolutely going to die.

"Today," the oracle went on, undaunted, "we will all be embarking upon a most glorious adventure. Once a month I will meet with each of the thirty new students, and with the Upper Spheres once a quarter, to chart your progress. Determining destiny is not an exact science. It is more of an art…because you are the variable. Destiny is based upon your choices—and it is always your choice, for you have free will—of the various options along your personal path. So I want each of you to remember that where you find yourself today is not necessarily where you will be six months from now, much less a lifetime. What matters most is how you envision yourself. Just ask Neteru Damali Richards Rivera—she is so different now than she was when she and I first encountered each oth—"

"Ahem, yes," Headmistress Stone said with a chuckle. "But perhaps that is a longer story for another day?"

"Perhaps so," the oracle cooed with a giggle, causing Sarah's mother to blush. "Then let the talent divisioning begin."

Silence filled the Hall, and students turned in their seats and looked up the aisles.

"What's happening?" Sarah asked. Tami shrugged, and they turned around, too.

At first it didn't seem like anything was happening, until Allie grabbed Sarah's arm and said, "Look!"

Thick black smoke began rolling down the aisles. It spilled into the rows and down to the very front of the Great Hall. It undulated around their ankles and began to rise.

"What the hell?" Al said, jumping to his feet.

Sarah was about to stand, as well, when the older students broke out into wild cheers and began clapping, then finally stood themselves.

The black smoke began to climb the walls until it reached the ceiling, and it was as if they were surrounded by a cage of black pulsing smoke.

"Somebody better tell me what is going on real fast!" Tami said, looking a little panicked.

All of a sudden there was a whoosh of sound, and all the black smoke rushed toward the center of the ceiling, then came plummeting down. Many students screamed and ducked, including Sarah, who, felt a strong cool and somehow familiar wind rush by her, powerful enough to tug at her clothes and hair. She looked around frantically to see where the next attack was coming from. The black smoke whipped about the room and then dove toward the ground at the front of the Hall. It slammed into the floor, and when it cleared, a tall dark-haired boy was standing there, holding a gold-and-black flag, and behind him stood four other students, one of whom was Wil.

Sarah whipped around, and sure enough, Wil was no longer in his seat. She turned back around and stared wide-eyed.

"Shadows!" someone yelled, and the Great Hall exploded in whoops and yells.

From the response of the students and from the smiling faces among the faculty, this clearly was how the Shadows made their entrance during the talent divisions. Couldn't someone have warned them before she died of heart failure? She looked at Tami, whose eyes were glowing with excitement—now that she knew they weren't being attacked.

"Oh, that was awesome!" she said, and Sarah laughed.

"We welcome our new Shadows—the most talented members of the Specials division," Counselor Z said, and the applause rose once again.

Next the sound of trumpets filled the Hall, and six large flags dropped from the ceiling. Each was a different color or combination of colors and bore a different symbol. The red-and-white flag with a gold crown represented the Specials; the purple flag with the image of an eye represented the Clairvoyants; the yellow flag with a lightning bolt down the middle represented the Tacticals; the orange flag with the image of an open lotus blossom represented the Olfactors; the blue flag with the image of an Akan war horn represented the Audios; and the green flag with an Akan war drum represented the Blends.

Six flag bearers appeared and began to walk down the aisles. Cheers went up around the room as the students cheered for their divisions.

"Who is that? Tami asked, staring.

Sarah followed her line of vision and immediately saw who she was talking about. It was the Specials flag bearer.

He was tall and dark-haired, and his intense gray eyes held a hypnotic quality. His gaze almost seemed intrusive; Sarah wanted to look away but couldn't. It was hard to tell what he was. Part vampire, maybe?

"Hybrid, you think?" Allie whispered in a rush. "Like some kinda telepath…but he also gives off something else, something that scares me."

"Whatever he is, he's sexy as hell," Tami murmured.

Sarah just shrugged, her eyes still following the boy with the hypnotic gray eyes. Allie was right; there was something frightening about his vibe. She tried to shake off her uneasy response to him, reasoning that if an ancient oracle, plus her mom and Nana, had allowed him to enter the Academy, then he couldn't be genuinely dangerous.

Once the flag bearers got to the front, they turned and faced the assembly.

"You have each received your letters, now please take your place behind your division's flag," Counselor Z said. "Come, come now," she continued, when no one leaped to their feet. "Get behind the flag of your talent."

Sarah looked around in confusion and was horrified to realize that all eyes were fastened on the Neteru Guardian kids. This was the moment they had all been waiting for, and no one was moving until they saw what divisions the Neteru crew had placed in.

Sarah wanted to die. There went her slender hopes of slipping into her division unnoticed. She'd known all along that it had been a pointless fantasy, but still…

The rest of the compound girls sat there, frozen, looking at Sarah to make the first move. Why were they looking at her? She was going to sit there all day if she had to.

Of course, Al had no qualms about rising to the occasion. He shone in moments like this, and why wouldn't he? He wasn't a Blend and hadn't shamed his parents. Her brother stood, shoulders thrown back proudly, and walked calmly and confidently to the Specials flag bearer and stood behind him. Cheers erupted all over the Great Hall, clearly from other Specials. They had scored big, getting one of the Neteru kids in their section. When Val got up and joined her brother, more cheers rose.

Miguel stepped out and walked over to the Audio section. Cheers went up just as he was about to step behind the flag bearer when Counselor Zehiradangra said, "Wait."

The Hall fell silent.

They watched Miguel lift his chin and straighten defensively. His parents, along with Aunt Juanita and Uncle Jose, leaned forward apprehensively, trying unsuccessfully to seem neutral. There was a heated discussion going on up on the dais that made Sarah and the others crane their necks.

"Young man, you are in the wrong section," Counselor Zehiradangra told him. "Your placement has been re-evaluated. You will be with the Specials starting today." Miguel's face lit up. "But note," she added. "From those to whom much is given, much is required…"

Ignoring the implicit warning in the oracle's words, the Specials broke out into a collective chant. "Special Forces, hoorah!"

Whoops and cheers rang out as Miguel ran over to bump fists with Alejandro and Valencio, laughing. And Uncle Jose's joy was uncontained as he shouted, "Yes! That's my boy!"

When things settled down again, all eyes turned back to the remaining Neteru kids.

Allie had started to spark. Hyacinth took her hand, but she looked at Sarah with sad eyes and shook her head. *I don't want to,* she said in Sarah's mind. *I don't want to be separated from you guys.*

You have to, Sarah mentally told her and smiled a little.

"Oh, what the hell?" Tami said, standing abruptly, breaking into Sarah's thoughts. Her friends stared as she marched over and stood behind the Blend flag bearer, lifting her chin defiantly.

At first no one said anything, and then confused murmurs rose throughout the Hall. Even the Blend flag bearer looked like he didn't understand what was going on until a few scattered but puzzled cheers gave way to more enthusiastic ones, as if the Blends were slowly realizing that Tami standing behind their flag wasn't a joke. But Sarah heard comments like, "One of them is a Blend?" and "Are you serious?"

She leaned forward and whispered , "Hyacinth, Allie, just go."

"No, I—"

"*Go,*" Sarah said, her tone leaving no room for argument. "Now."

Hyacinth's shoulders slumped. Allie bit her lip as though she were about to cry. But both of them reluctantly got up and walked across the Great Hall, and then Hyacinth stood behind the Clairvoyant flag, while Allie went to stand with the Tactical division. Wild cheers went up around the Hall, and someone yelled out, "Now that's more like it!"

Sarah noticed that Melissa Gray and her two friends clapped apathetically. She looked meaningfully at her stressed-out compound brother, Donnie.

He nodded, but he looked like he was about to puke.

Sarah took a deep breath and then stood up.

A hush fell over the crowd again. She refused to look at her parents' expressions and imagined they had to be dying a thousand deaths, just like she was now. If she'd looked and seen pity in their eyes, she might have bolted for the door. Instead, she kept her gaze focused on the flag bearers.

Sarah began to walk down the aisle, aware that Donnie was following her. She felt the weight of everyone's gaze on her and raised her eyes to meet Tami's, which were locked on hers in moral support. Her best friend gave her an encouraging nod, though Tami hardly looked like she was enjoying herself. Maybe the old saying was true and misery *did* love company. Sarah was halfway to her destiny when Counselor Zehiradangra called out to her.

"Sarah."

Startled, she stopped in her tracks and looked up.

Her mother and grandmother looked mildly surprised, as well. Her father took a step forward, suddenly tense.

"Latent talent is often the most powerful force," Counselor Z said calmly. "There are many gifts competing within you for dominance, and I predict that in a very short time you'll be a force to be reckoned with."

Now what in the world did that mean?

Sarah saw her mother smile, while her father continued to frown. Had he hoped that Counselor Z would place *her* in the Specials at the last minute, too?

"You may join your division."

No last-minute save, and in front of the whole school. Hushed snickers followed her. Damn…why couldn't she have caught a break like Miguel had?

Sarah walked the rest of the distance and stepped behind the Blends flag bearer, then listened as the Great Hall exploded in a cacophony of voices—both scandalized and unbelieving. The fact that one of the Neterus was a Blend was obviously bad enough, but also the daughter of the Riveras, plus a third from the Neteru compound…? The school seemed to be in a complete uproar. Sarah closed her eyes, wishing the floor would just open up and swallow her whole.

"Now will everyone please join their divisions?" Counselor Z called out in exasperation.

The rest of the students jumped to their feet and scrambled to line up behind the appropriate flags. When they had all gathered with their divisions, Headmistress Stone stepped forward once again. She raised her hands.

"Hope is the future. Hope is our students," she called out. "Hope is that one day, we will all be free!"

The dragons shifted, their inner illumination lighting the tapestries, which displayed images of all the Guardian teams from around the world, whether they had children at the Academy or not.

Multicolored lights danced within leaping, spiraling, twining dragon bodies. The sound of Kalimbas and African, Asian and Latin drums filled the air from the edges of the Great Hall, as Nod beings created a fusion of world music, adding in didgeridoos, bagpipes, lyres, gourd shakers, cow bells and harps.

"Your life-changing journey begins right now," Headmistress Stone said, excitement and pride brimming in her eyes. *"Ashe."*

Sarah looked over at Ayana, who smiled and gave her a thumbs-up.

The talent divisions were finally over.

* * *

Pandemonium broke out as the ceremony came to a close and the students said their good-byes to their parents. Thirty tapestries were lit, each one bearing an incoming student's larger-than-life smiling image, along with the flag from their country of origin, which gleamed as brightly as their smiles. The images shifted to include the parents. There were proud couples, cheering single mothers and happy single fathers, even grandparents and other surrogates. Some were just shimmering images of the dead. The complex variety of what made up a family was as wonderfully assorted as all the new faces that Sarah had encountered since her arrival.

She watched as her mom and dad spent time with the other new students, especially those who had no parents. Her mother produced tiny items from her pockets to hand to each one. Some got a small charm for their hair, or a bracelet, some a tiny ring. Each student got something from her as a token of remembrance, but what they seemed to crave most was her mother's hug.

And her mother didn't rush those angel-winged embraces.

Her mother held each student until they were ready to let her go. Then she said something to them, something private and nice, that made that student nod and stand up taller or outright promise her they'd never forget what she'd said. Her mother had that effect on people. It was surely something from the divine. What was odd was seeing the same support being offered by her dad…a steady hand on a shoulder, a deep, introspective word, a pep talk such as only he could deliver, and then a hug followed by a fist bump that left even the eldest, most confident guys in the hall starstruck.

Maybe it was then, for the first time in her life, that she truly understood just what she'd had. Her grandmother's words and the stories that Ayana had brought home from school now made her realize how afraid she'd been all these years…just how scared she was that, one day, when they left home, her parents might not come back. When her mother faced her, Sarah barreled into her arms. Humiliation singed her; she wasn't supposed to act like a big baby in front of all these people.

Willing herself not to cry, she inhaled deeply as her mother stroked her back.

"I'm gonna miss you, too," her mother said in her ear. "You know you are my favorite girl, and you know I believe in you. Grow. Learn. Make friends. Now it's your turn. That's all you have to do in order to make your dad and me proud, all right?"

Sarah nodded quickly, her face still hidden as she sniffed hard, those glorious wings of her mother's surrounding her with downy warmth.

"I know you're scared," her mother whispered. "So am I. I've never done this before, either."

Sarah looked up into her mother's shimmering eyes and took in her soft smile.

"Never have I left my babies away from home. This is new for me. You be the strong one for me today, all right?"

Sarah smiled and sniffed hard as her father came over and broke into their hug.

"Hey, doesn't Dad get some love?"

He pulled her away from her mother and into his arms. "I was always *papi*. Now…I guess you're too big for me to be hugging you in front of all your new friends, huh? But I don't care, I'm gonna do it anyway, even if I embarrass both of us."

Sarah laughed as she laid her head against her father's chest and allowed two big tears to roll down the bridge of her nose. "You'll always be my *papi*," she said through another hard sniff.

Her dad hugged her tighter and spoke into her hair. "Good. You let all these good-looking knuckleheads in here know your father has fangs, too. You call me."

She laughed and stared up at him. "Daddy, we've been through this already—like a couple of hours ago."

He let her go with a wide grin. "Yeah, I know, I know, I'm sounding like a broken record."

Sarah frowned and tilted her head in curiosity.

"You're dating yourself, honey," her mother said, smiling hard.

Her father slapped his forehead and gave her a lopsided grin. "What am I gonna do, boo? Answer me that. Somewhere along the way I lost track of time and got old. How in the hell that happened, I don't know."

"Goes like that," Uncle Mike said, lifting Sarah off her feet for a hug, and making her laugh as he passed her off to her uncle Jack. "All these kids are growing up so fast. Look at my Ayana."

"It happened in your sleep, dude," Uncle Jack said, laughing and hugging her as he moved between the students. "It snuck up on ya. The passage of time is a weapon from the dark side, man—ask me how I know!"

Her father laughed as her aunts fought to get a hug in between her uncles' attentions, as everybody's children became anybody's in a jumble of extended family.

Then her father's gregarious smile eased into a gentler expression, one so tender that it made Sarah glance away. He put his finger under her chin to make her look up at him.

"Doesn't matter. I can get to be a hundred and fifty years old and you can get to be a hundred and ten, you're always gonna be my baby girl. Always gonna be my pride and joy—so you do good in school, and don't you worry about nothing else, all right? I'm very proud of you, Sarah. Been waiting for this day all your life, and then it was your old man who wasn't ready. I love you."

He gave her one last hug and then walked away. Her mother's calm smile confirmed it—her dad was two seconds away from public tears, something he'd never allow. Her father was upset in a way that she'd never seen him before. Sarah glanced at Alejandro, and he gave her a nod, a rare brother-to-sister "yeah, I know" kind of look.

Her mom and dad had gone to her brother first, after they'd made the rounds of all the new kids. But it was the moment between her and her dad that made him leave the hall with his head up, shoulders back, posture straight—and a deep well of emotions he hid from the world.

As the wall torches dimmed, her mother whispered softly in her ear, "He fights with you the most because you touch him more deeply than anyone else on this planet."

Sarah's gaze softened as she took in her mother's words. It was true. Her dad always had something to say about whatever she was doing, but when it came to Al, he only challenged her brother when he was doing something particularly dangerous or stupid. But when she and her dad fought, it was almost always over some principle of fairness, equity in the compound or justice. Heck, they argued about practically everything to the point where sometimes it made her crazy…and yet, her dad always seemed to trust her more than he did her brother. Until her mother said what she did, she could never fully understand why.

"You're his little girl," her mother pressed on softly, touching Sarah's cheek. "Be advised. He's not as tough on the inside as he seems on the outside. It took me a few years to learn that, and it's now *our* secret."

Sarah stared up at the ceiling, unblinking. What was she supposed to do with information like that? What did it mean? Why had her mother told her this?

Suddenly his double standard, his chauvinism, the unfairness of his treatment of her and Al, and who got to do what, had just gone right out the skylight with the dragons.

CHAPTER 8

Her parents were gone. She heard students chattering away—the new students waiting to be shown to their dorms and the others just socializing. Sarah caught snatches of gossip and gathered that the Neteru kids were going to be the topic of conversation for a while. She let out a sigh.

Right then and there she made up her mind that she wasn't going to listen to any of it. She refused to allow any reference to her deficiency to kill what was left of her already fragile self-esteem. She would ignore the juicy tidbits of scandal that she overheard. Instead, she would focus on what her mother had told her.

When she felt a hard bump to her back, she turned around, ready to apologize for being in the way. The apology died on her lips when she saw who it was.

"Sorry, but you need to watch it, B-D," Melissa said with a sneer, her cohorts standing behind her and sneering. "Maybe you would have seen that coming if you had some real Clav skills."

B-D! Did that witch just say B-D, as in beadie? Sarah's gaze narrowed. Her cousin Ayana had told her about all the school slang for losers. Now some girl that she didn't even know had not only nearly knocked her down but had also called her by the dreaded term that made anyone in the Blends division cringe. Those were fighting words.

Anger rose fast in Sarah, and she could feel her fangs beginning to come down. "What's your problem?"

"Oh, look, she has fangs," Amy said, with a giggle, pointing at Sarah.

"How cute, in an ugly sort of way," Angelica cooed, and then laughed along with Amy and Melissa.

"And they work," Sarah said. She stepped forward and felt a small stab of satisfaction when Amy took a step back.

Melissa glared at Amy in annoyance, then turned back to Sarah. "Well, it's obvious that the fruit fell very far from the tree that bore it. Listen, Neteru brat, don't think you're anything here just because of who your parents are." Her gaze narrowed. "I run this school, and should you forget that, just know that a lot of things can happen when nobody's looking. And you'd better tell your flunky to watch *her* back, too."

"No, skank," Tami said, materializing from the crowd. "*You'd* better watch *yours*." Tami eyed the other girl's long hair. "Think twice before you threaten Sarah again. I would hate to see you hanging by your wig from a back stairwell one dark and lonely night."

"Hey, what's the problem?" Al said, catching up to the group.

Melissa smirked. "Your sister and her pit bull just violated rule number one here at the Academy —threatening another student," she told him.

"You did what?" Al asked.

"Mind your own business, Al," Tami said. "You tag it, we'll bag it—you know the compound motto."

"What?" Melissa asked frowning.

"I think she told you to watch out," Sarah said with raised eyebrows, then inhaled sharply when Melissa's eyes darkened dangerously.

Alejandro rubbed his palms down his face, obviously fighting a combination of embarrassment and rage.

"Why'd you threaten her, Sarah?" Al finally said as he threw his shoulders back, clearly posturing for the new girl.

Sarah saw a small smile of amusement on Melissa's lips. "I didn't," Sarah said through her teeth.

"I bumped into her by accident and she got all huffy," Melissa said, tossing her glossy hair over her shoulder.

"Is that all?" Al said, stepping in front of Melissa as if to shield her from Sarah. "Are you nuts?"

Sarah stared at him as if he had lost his mind.

"C'mon, guys, ease up," Wil said, making his way over to the scene. His gaze shot past Melissa and landed on Sarah. "If you don't stop, you'll get kicked out on your first day."

Sarah almost choked on her disappointment and outrage. Wil thought she had started this stupid scene, too?

Melissa smiled at him. "Well, if it isn't our new warrior. Congratulations on placing in the Shadows, Wil."

Al scowled, clearly feeling upstaged just by Wil's presence.

Wil shrugged humbly, but Sarah could see that he was proud. "Thanks."

"Yes, congratulations, Wil," a quiet, feminine voice said.

Sarah immediately turned to see who'd spoken. At some point during the argument, Patty Gray had joined the group. Now she walked up to Wil and gently kissed him on the cheek.

Wil cleared his throat awkwardly and said, "Thanks, Patty."

Melissa gave Sarah an evil smile, then turned to Patty and said, "Hi, sis."

Sarah looked at the stunning Upper Sphere girl and suddenly felt like she had dirt under her fingernails and spinach between her teeth.

Don't start to dream too big, loser.

Sarah jumped at the sound of Melissa's voice in her head. Then her eyes narrowed in fury. Melissa had riffled through her private thoughts! But she'd also left her more information than she'd planned. Obviously Melissa had miscalculated and underestimated her opponent, her anger making her sloppy. The one thing that Nana Marlene had always taught them was that when you went into someone else's thoughts, they could pull out information, too. The most pressing question that had been on Sarah's mind when Melissa went into it was, why was the girl messing with her? The answer came back now like a slow slingshot of information: Stefan. Town. Him getting close to Tami and spoiling a secret. Okay, who the hell was Stefan? Not that it mattered at the moment. What infuriated Sarah was Melissa getting up in her face and, worse yet, inside her head without permission.

Sarah stepped toward Melissa. "You had no right—"

Suddenly a strong hand landed on Sarah's shoulder.

"Is there a problem, ladies and gentlemen?"

It was her grandmother.

"No, ma'am." The words came out of everyone's mouth in a disgruntled mutter at the same time.

"Good. Don't let there be," Headmistress Stone said, eyeing the group. "Melissa, the new Clairvoyants are ready for their tour. Please don't keep them waiting."

"Yes, Headmistress Stone."

Sarah stared at Melissa with a frown. The girl didn't strike her as the type who would volunteer to show new students around.

The headmistress didn't wait to hear any more, she simply reinserted herself into the throng, saying good-byes and speaking to parents like the elder stateswoman she was.

"I don't know what's wrong with you, but why don't you go cool off?" Al said to Sarah, then headed off to catch up to Melissa.

"You cool off," Sarah muttered to his retreating back, folding her arms over her chest. She was just glad the rest of the compound brothers hadn't come over with Al to gang up on her, too.

"Sit with us at lunch, Al?" Melissa said, loudly enough to be overheard, leaning into him flirtatiously as they walked toward the waiting Clairvoyants. "That way we can *really* show you and your friends around later on."

Furious, Sarah watched her brother walk away with Melissa and her two lackeys. Patty had disappeared as silently as she had appeared. Unbelievable—how could Al be *that* stupid? She was about to make a snide comment when she glimpsed Wil out of the corner of her eye. He was standing off to her side, looking very awkward. If anything diffused her rage a little, it was seeing Wil still standing there. She took quiet pleasure in the fact that he hadn't followed Al and Melissa and her too-rude crew. He also hadn't followed Patty, the real stunner.

It was a small victory, but she couldn't deny that it still felt good, though she wasn't altogether ready to forgive him for semi-siding with Melissa just yet.

Tami gave Wil the evil eye. "Friend or foe, dude? Decide now, because as you can see, war just got declared."

Sarah elbowed Tami.

"What?" Tami protested, frowning. "It's true. You saw how she treated us."

"They really aren't that bad once you get to know them," Wil said.

He burst out laughing at their highly skeptical expressions. Sarah and Tami glanced at each other, then had to laugh themselves when they realized how they must have looked.

Sarah liked the sound of Wil's laugh. It was rich and deep and genuine, and it made her feel warm and tingly all over. And his smile was positively gorgeous. She loved how he got little crinkles in the corners of his sea-green eyes.

Would it be so wrong to forgive the poor guy for one teeny little mistake?

"Okay, okay, so maybe they *can* be like the Macbeth's witches," Wil said, still laughing.

"You pulled that out of my head, didn't you?" Sarah said, laughing harder.

"Guilty," Wil said sheepishly, and raked his hair with his fingers. Then his smile faded, and he shoved his hands into his pockets. "We grew up together. So even though they're not always the nicest people, it's…force of habit, I guess."

"Well, that's cozy," Tami snapped.

"No, it's not like that. It just is what it is…history, family, what can I say?"

Both Sarah and Tami stared at him.

"Long story," he said, smiling at Sarah.

"We've got time," Tami said, wiggling her eyebrows.

"Look, I've gotta go catch up with my division and get my stuff into my room." He turned to go.

"Hey," Sarah said, and he turned back around. "Congratulations."

Wil gave her one of his full-blown gorgeous smiles. "Thanks. See you later. He gave them a wave and jogged off in the direction of the black-and-gold flag bearer.

Sarah spun on Tami the moment Wil merged into the crowd and shot her a hard look.

"What?" Tami put up her hands, laughing. "If you had let me dig harder, I would have gotten the vital intel you need to know before you plunge headlong—"

Sarah clamped her hand over her friend's mouth. "Would you *please* be quiet?"

"You're smothering me," Tami mumbled through her laughter. Once Sarah removed her hand, Tami took a huge, theatrical breath. "I'm just looking out for you."

"I sure wish you'd look out for me," a deep male voice said, giving both girls a start.

The red-and-white flag bearer was no longer holding his division colors. He was leaning against a pillar with his long legs crossed at the ankles, arms folded over his broad chest, and his electrifying gray eyes were eating Tami alive.

Sarah opened and closed her mouth in disbelief when her girlfriend giggled and then blushed.

"I see you don't mind mixing it up," he said, looking Tami up and down. "I like that…a chick who won't get all girlie and scream and fall when the monster comes."

"I do all right," Tami said, smiling wider, but speaking in the most bashful voice that Sarah had ever heard from her.

Could this really be *Tami*?

"That's good to know. Can't have a woman who can't hold her own, you know what I mean? Anybody with sense would want a girl who looks good enough to eat but won't wind up demon bait." He licked his lips sensually and then pushed away from the pillar. "See you around, Tamara." He winked, and in the next instance had rounded the pillar and was gone.

"Did you see that?" Tami whispered, squeezing Sarah's arm.

"Yeah, I saw it," Sarah said, worried.

"Ohmigod, he's got *vamp* stealth!"

"Yeah, but—"

"I have to find out his name," Tami gushed. "Ohmigod, *he* knows my name!"

"Listen, Tami, that guy—"

Just then a voice interrupted.

"Hi, I'm Jessica Porter," a thick-bodied girl wearing Upper Sphere colors said. She had an honest smile that seemed to light up her warm, cocoa-brown face. Her dreadlocks were thick, dark and caterpillar fuzzy, and they hung down to her shoulders, bouncing as she spoke. Jessica's voice embodied that same lyrical quality that Sarah's Uncle Monte, who was from the Caribbean, had. The new girl's friendly, inviting eyes accentuated the warmth of her voice. Sarah recognized her as an older Blend from after the ceremony when all the students grouped around their division's flag. "I see you've met our self-proclaimed queen."

"I guess you could say that," Tami said dryly, knowing the other girl was referring to Melissa Gray.

Jessica shook her head. "Yeah, we knew she wouldn't like you."

Sarah and Tami glanced at each other, not sure how to take that.

"I'm Bebitta Mettullus," a new girl said, walking over to stand next to Jessica and waving. "Ethiopian by way of London."

Sarah gazed up at the tall, agile beauty with huge, dark eyes rimmed in the thickest, most luxurious lashes she'd ever seen. Bebitta wore a long fall of braids that spilled over her Upper Sphere sweater.

"That's Andrea Goodwin," Jessica said, pointing out another girl. "And that's Ernest Scheeler." She indicated the tall, lanky flag bearer for the Blends.

Jessica put her hands on her hips and smiled. "Well, everyone ready for the grand tour?"

Sarah wasn't sure if she'd ever be ready, but what was the point in saying so?

CHAPTER 9

There were so many names, faces and feelings to sort through that Sarah's head was spinning. But it was good to be walking. She needed to move. Donnie and the other boys had gone off with Ernie Schneeler. The girls were left in a tight, nervous huddle to stand with Jessica and company.

Student groups were splitting off from one another, each taking a different exit to avoid overlapping narratives as their student guides showed them the ropes.

"Okay, look, we're going to do this tour a little differently," Jessica said, leading them down a hallway. She stopped and faced them. "We all know some crazy stuff has been happening, and we think there are some things you should know in order to protect yourselves. The other kids are getting some of this on their tours, but we're going to show you some things that they aren't being shown."

"But we're at school," Sarah said nervously. "Nothing should be able to happen to us here, right? Did the missing students wander off campus or something…? I mean, the actual school is safe, right?"

"That's what Arthur and Casey thought, too, I'm sure," Jessica replied, looking grim. "So did the two faculty members and the couple of Upper Sphere fliers from the Spec division who went out to try to save them."

Tami and Sarah glanced at each other, horrified, but hanging on Jessica's every word.

"How well did you know them?" Sarah finally asked.

"We all know each other pretty well," Jessica said, rubbing a hand over the back of her neck. "As you saw, there aren't that many Blends in the school. With you three we're twenty-one total. So we tend to stick together. But we were especially close to Casey."

"What happened?" Tami asked.

"Come on," Jessica said, turning around. "Let's walk and talk. I'll tell you what I can along the way."

"Hey, guys, wait up," Ayana called out, running to join the group. She gave Jessica, Bebitta and Andrea a quick hug. "Okay, if I take the newbs for a private family tour?"

"Oh, so now you're poaching our new Blends?" Jessica said with a big grin.

The older girls laughed and gave each other affectionate shoves.

"They're all right with me," Ayana said to Sarah and her friends with a smile. "They made life here bearable while those who shall remain nameless gave me the blues." Ayana and Jessica exchanged a meaningful glance.

"We'll go keep an eye on your other two younger sisters from the Net-pound," Bebitta said.

"Yeah, especially the one all by herself with the Clavs. She seems sweet and we'll do what we can," Andrea said, hustling off with Jessica and Bebitta.

"Okay, the rest of you Blends, follow me," Jessica announced.

Jessica then turned to Sarah and Tami. "You'll be in good hands with Ayana. For a Clav, she's a good egg."

"Thanks," Ayana said as the other Blends waved and left, and then she turned back to Sarah and Tami. "C'mon, guys, I have so much to fill you in on that it's ridiculous."

Sarah couldn't force her mind away from the questions tumbling around in her head as they walked. She barely noticed where Ayana was taking them.

"See, here's the thing," Ayana said, lowering her voice to a conspiratorial whisper. "The two kids who've gone missing, Arthur and Casey, weren't rule breakers. Those two were straight arrows and would have rather given their eye-teeth than get in trouble for sneaking into town or anything like that. They were the last people I would have thought would go out after curfew, for cryin' out loud."

Ayana stopped walking and pulled the girls into an alcove, drawing them in closer and dropping her voice. "Art was a science whiz—one of the best in the school—with an ace nose and second sight that allowed him to replicate any formula or spell batch if he'd sniffed it once. That guy was studying for advanced class placement tests when he went missing, so why would he sneak out after curfew and blow a chance at moving up? Same with Casey," Ayana added, leaning in closer. "She was a solid intuitive with a photographic memory, and word had it that she was being considered for Shadows division, so none of this makes any sense. They wouldn't risk doing something stupid. It just wasn't in their nature."

"Do you think someone forced them to leave the school?" Sarah asked with raised eyebrows, worry lacing every word. "Or lured them out somehow?"

Ayana stared at Sarah and Tami with a puzzled gaze. "That's the problem, nobody really knows. But around here, anything is possible."

"What's that supposed to mean?" Tami whispered nervously.

"Listen, there's a lot of stuff that happens here that even the instructors don't know about."

Silence momentarily strangled their conversation.

"You're gonna hear all sorts of speculation, okay," Ayana warned. "Stuff like, what if somebody drugged them and kidnapped them from campus…or planted a hypnotic suggestion that made them leave school on their own—something they normally wouldn't have done." She glanced around to make sure no one else was around to overhear them. "Everybody is so paranoid now, it isn't even funny. But the rumor mill is right, anything could have happened."

Sarah's eyes widened as Tami's mouth dropped open.

Ayana put her arms around them in a quick three-way hug. "But, look…seriously, if someone was actually coming into the school to snatch kids, this place would have been shut down faster than you could say your own name. Don't worry, guys. But also don't be stupid, all right? If some guy asks you to sneak out of school and take a trip to town or to go make out somewhere, just say no, okay?"

Make out? Sarah just stared at her cousin. It was the first time Yaya had even broached the subject of sex beyond saying there were cute guys at school. Now that they were at the Academy, it seemed as though her relationship with Yaya, and the kind of information her cousin was willing to divulge was about to reach a new level. But right now Yaya just gave her a look that said, not now, wait until it's just me and you.

Tami frowned, missing the silent exchange completely. "But why them? Why Arthur and Casey?"

Ayana shook her head and gave them a sad shrug. "We don't know. That's just one of the things driving us crazy about this whole thing." Frustration had crept into her voice. "It just doesn't make sense."

Sarah slid a supportive arm around Ayana's shoulders. Ayana smiled at her and then seemed to pull herself together. The threesome began walking again, this time a little more slowly.

"Okay, first thing." Ayana pointed to the symbols carved into the granite above a doorway and echoed on the floor. "Every passage has a series of protective symbols surrounding it, in case our school is breeched by the dark side. Watch." She walked over the threshold into an inner chamber.

"Cool," Tami murmured, clearly impressed when white light filled the lettering.

"If something is chasing you, cross a threshold," Ayana said. "Whatever's on your heels will fry. Just like the barriers Nana set up at home, with added prayer power."

"These thresholds won't react if you're under hypnotic suggestion," Ayana said, "but they'll definitely get anything else."

"But nothing's ever actually come in here, right?" Sarah asked nervously, looking around.

"They had a breech once, in the old days, I heard." Ayana glanced around as another group of girls passed them, brand-new students following their tour guide like little ducklings, waiting until they were out of earshot to speak again. "First day is hard enough, but the Neteru compound crew needs to know."

"Yeah," Tami said, looking at Ayana. "If something's up, we definitely wanna know, Yaya. Seriously."

"What happened?" Sarah said, rounding on Ayana and putting a hand on her arm. "If something got in here once, maybe it got in here again and abducted Art and Casey. It's possible."

"Okay, I'm going to tell you, but if Nana asks, you didn't hear it from me, all right?" Ayana said on a weary sigh.

"We'll probably hear it all in the lunchroom anyway," Tami pointed out.

"And we'd rather get the straight story from you," Sarah said in a pleading tone.

Ayana glanced around again, making sure no one was eavesdropping. "Well, when they first set this place up, a couple of walkers made it past the blackened forest…their noses led them. They could smell human flesh, human blood, even though they couldn't see it. The school founders—our parents—hadn't counted on that part. They had only put in safeguards for stuff that could fly and the more common entities, like werewolves, vamps and your basic demons, whatever. Word has it that they didn't have the dragons up then, or even the telepathic tapestries—the place was still under construction. But there were already students in the lower chambers. A couple of faculty got torn to pieces, and a few even turned into the undead right in the Great Hall. They led the other walkers down into the student quarters, and the place was nearly overrun. Baba Shabazz put himself between the fleeing students and told Nana Marlene to stay with them until backup came. He didn't want her to get the walker virus, and he couldn't get it on account of being a shape-shifter."

"Oh, my God! So what happened?" Sarah asked, her gaze ricocheting from Ayana to and Tami.

"There are a lot of different theories," Ayana said. "Nana won't talk about it—she says it just keeps negative energy swirling, and we should focus on our studies—but some say the Neterus—your mom and dad, Sarah—drove them back into the beyond the edge of the light. I couldn't even pry it out of my mom. So all I can tell you is that because some of the faculty turned, there's always the chance they could come back, and since they know the ins and outs of this place, if something is on your ass, cross a threshold."

All Sarah could do was stare at her cousin. She'd had no idea….

"C'mon," Ayana said after a moment. "So far, no student's gotten eaten. Let's go down to the bunker."

Sarah and Tami didn't move.

"It's safe, I promise," Ayana added, glancing over her shoulder and waiting until they began to follow her along the hall and then down what seemed like an unending spiral of stairs. "You remember how Aunt Marjorie taught conspiracy theories and American history at home?"

"Yeah," Sarah said, glad to be off the subject of walker invasions.

"Well, this is the Project Greek Island she used to quiz us on, created long, long ago under American President Eisenhower. Remember how she told us that he'd built a bunker to withstand a potential nuclear war?"

"It's hard to believe regular humans actually built this," Tami said with amazement in her tone. She trailed her fingers along the walls as they walked, eyes wide.

"Yep, Regulars built this," Ayana said with an authoritative nod, and then pressed on. "This bunker was supposed to be a safe haven for the legislative branch of the American government." Ayana shook her head with a smile. "All that stuff they taught you at home wasn't just theory, guys. They taught it for a reason."

"I remember," Sarah said softly. "This place was only five hours from Washington, DC, where the Armageddon began. This place was kept a secret for decades. Regulars dug out eighteen thousand feet of tunnels a hundred feet underground, then hid them behind twenty-eight-ton steel doors."

"Right," Ayana said with a clearly pleased smile. "We're going down beneath what used to be the Greenbrier Hotel—our compound. We're just on the other side of it here, and the Great Hall is on the opposite side of the mountain from it." Ayana frowned and placed a finger to her lips. "The other kids think the old hotel is all boarded up and demolished, that it got overrun by the dark powers years ago. Nobody is ever supposed to know where the Neteru compound headquarters is located, so you keep that under serious lock, got it?"

Both girls nodded, stunned mute.

"Good. Keep it that way." Ayana let out a breath of relief and then pressed on. "This place is so cool. The Regulars were preparing for what they considered the worst possible event, a nuclear holocaust, not realizing what was *really* coming when they put eighteen dorms in here that slept sixty people each. They were trying to save the government and wound up saving the worldwide Guardian teams' kids. And we lucked out because the whole place was built on white sulfur springs for healing, something that the dark side really hates. You'll see when you get downstairs." Ayana continued with enthusiasm. "This place even has a five hundred seat auditorium, fully stocked library, broadcast-ready television and radio stations, medical and dental labs, a catacomb of offices on the second level, riot gear and weapons, along with decontamination showers and an incinerator for anyone who died."

"Okay, you really are scaring me now," Sarah warned.

"Nobody that we know of has been incinerated, all right?" Ayana glanced at both girls and urged them forward.

"What about the bodies they found?" Sarah asked, leaning on the wall for a moment to let everything she'd just heard sink in.

"They did find those two flier kids who went down in the forbidden zone…which is why I'm telling you to act like you know. We clear?"

Sarah and Tami exchanged a worried look as Ayana began walking again. None of the kids in the compound had ever heard a thing about what existed just below the Greenbrier Hotel. Until today, Sarah had always thought Ayana was being unnecessarily vague about where the Academy was located. But it had just become crystal clear why they were never allowed to leave their side of the mountain. If they had, they could have tipped off the whole school about where the Neteru headquarters were.

But in addition to all the terrible things her cousin had disclosed, Ayana had also mentioned the location of the library the Lowers were allowed to access. It struck her that she might finally be able to find out what the word *nexse* meant.

"Hey, Yaya," Sarah said, jogging forward to catch up with her cousin's purposeful strides. "Can anybody go into the library at any time?"

Ayana smiled. "Spoken like a true Net-pound geek. Yeah. Sure. As long as you don't have class or something."

"Have you ever heard the word *nexse*?"

Ayana shook her head.

"Nope. Seen it on the walls in the Great Hall, but couldn't tell you what it means. That's def what the library is for. But you'll get a lot of archaic language work in ancient scrolls class, not to worry."

"Thanks," Sarah said, making a mental note to be sure to find the library as soon as she could after they got settled in the dorm.

She and Tami filed down a long corridor in silence behind Ayana, eyes darting toward the huge ceilings covered in hieroglyphs delineating ancient prayers. When they came to two large twelve-foot-high doors that were etched with gold and silver symbols, Ayana stopped.

"This is the gateway," she said. "Like I told you, back in the 1950s, regular people dug this cavern out and blocked it with twenty-eight-ton steel doors. There's a small city behind them, but nobody can stand to be underground like that indefinitely. Although this is the main door, the Neteru team added other exits that will put you in hidden courtyards and plazas, so you can get some fresh air and keep from going stir crazy. For security purposes, each one requires a special opening-of-the-way incantation to get in or out, and I guess you can understand why. So it's really important to remember communication protocols, to travel in pairs, to make sure someone knows where you are at all times…and most importantly, to know how to get back in before sundown."

Ayana spoke the words to open the doors, and long tile corridors stretched before them in what felt, as they traversed it, like an unending labyrinth, a human-created honeycomb of halls. The only thing that made the maze seem less foreboding was that it had been modified from its previous nuclear war functionality by grand murals painted by students and faculty to make the place seem less like the bomb shelter it really was.

Beautiful scenes of outdoor majesty and environmental splendor helped cue Sarah to where she was along the unending route. And just like the stream of arcane words in the Great Hall, the art moved, seemed to come to life on the walls, but when you touched it, the scene became inanimate again.

"This is *so* freaky," Tami said, laughing, pressing her hands against the butterflies in the meadow scene that had been drawn outside the cafeteria.

Sarah tried to smell the wildflowers near them and bumped her nose on the wall.

"It changes at night, too," Ayana said, giggling. "Fireflies come out, and the sun in the mural actually sets. It's really cool. You can tell true time by it. Our Upper Sphere life-art gifted students did a lot of this with Aunt Jasmine. They've been working on it for years. Every semester they add new elements to it…keeps it interesting."

"Whoa…Hyacinth's mom coordinated all this?" Tami said, wide-eyed.

"Yeah. And listen. Don't drop any trash in the hallways or bathrooms," Ayana warned. "Hybrid beings, Fae and mythicals maintain the facilities, and they hate any destruction of property. They take it as a personal affront, probably because this is their new home now, after Nod got overrun by demons."

The three of them began walking again, and Sarah took in the surreal quality of the section of the mural that depicted marine life. There were leaping dolphins, slow-moving whales and graceful stingrays beside schools of fish, many of which were created by bits of glass and mirrors and rocks, to add depth and texture to the art. The pool and gym were in this area, followed by calming scenes of lush greenery, where the nurse's office, medical and dental facilities and instructors' offices were located..

"There's a full hospital down here," Ayana announced, waving her arm as Sarah and Tami came to a stop. "Even got a bunch of medical personnel who were relocated from their Guardian field commands to be here, plus a dentist and school nurse for basic stuff. Plus, the teachers' offices are on this row. This is where you'll have to show up if you need extra help or get in trouble, because you *do not* want to have to go up into the administrative area to see Nana and Baba if you can help it."

"You don't have to tell us," Sarah said, thinking back on the firm discipline her grandmother wielded when at home.

"Oh, I am so not trying to get into trouble with them," Tami said fervently. "Try being grounded until, like, forever."

"Right," Ayana replied, waving them on. "They've got really gruesome chores for you to do if you get demerits. And, trust me, Nana is harder on those of us from the Net-pound than the other kids, just to set an example for being crazy enough to piss her off when we're supposed to know better." Ayana smiled. "And don't ask me how I know."

Sarah and Tami exchanged a meaningful look.

Ayana hustled the girls along, making them follow her like a bunch of normal human third graders on a field trip. The only thing Ayana didn't do was tell them to hold hands. "Classrooms are in the purple zone," she said, stopping just long enough for them to peer down one long corridor that was bisected by another. "The Lower Sphere library is that way, and down at the other end are the common study areas."

Sarah's eyes remained fixed on the library's entrance for a long moment before she began walking again. A thick marble door frame held huge oak doors with smoked, etched-glass windows and a massive brass plate marked *Library.* That was all she could see of the place that she so badly wanted to enter. Something within that sanctuary of books was drawing her, something eerie that made the hair stand up on her arms. Something dark. She shook off the chill and closed the gap between herself and the others. As soon as she got a chance, she was going back there to look up the word that was haunting her.

Hues ranging from the palest lilac to the deepest midnight amethyst covered the walls to depict the expanding universe as a mesmerizing fractal mosaic of cells splitting, molecular attraction, scrolls and books moving as rings around slowly rotating planets and DNA strands. It was so impressively hypnotic that Sarah barely heard Ayana's breakdown of the different departmental wings by subject matter or her explanation of where the student lockers were located.

"Students did some of this?" Sarah hadn't even realized she was going to speak until the words were already hanging in the air. It was as though she'd entered a whole new world, and she couldn't help herself.

"Adding to it is part of the Upper Sphere senior project every year," Ayana said proudly. "If you stand in one area long enough, you'll notice that each section of the mural's gradually moving with the rotation of the earth. Each color zone is set up to give you a sense of the flora and fauna of a region...what it used to look like before the war, anyway. In the green zone today, you're seeing what parts of New Zealand were like. Come back a week from now and it may be rotating through the Amazon rainforest or Ireland—same color schematic, just different flora and fauna."

"Now that is *way* cool," Sarah said quietly as she scanned the walls.

"It's also for your protection," Ayana added.

"Protection?" Tami wrinkled her nose with the question.

"That's right." Ayana looked at Sarah and Tami, and then let out a sigh. "While each area is there to remind you of the beauty of the earth and all living things, those living things can be called off the walls to help protect an endangered student. The dorms are in the yellow zone, for instance," she said, beginning to pace. "That covers the grasslands of Africa, various world deserts, a lot of regions. The instructors' dormitories are over in the orange zone, where you'll see murals of the Grand Canyon, Sedona and the auditorium, broadcast studios and science labs are all in the red zone with lava murals, Ayers Rock in Australia, things like that. So if a walker got in here, or a werewolf happened to be on the loose, wouldn't you want a pride of lions from the yellow zone to have your back?" Ayana folded her arms. "Or, say, scorpions to burst out of the desert scenes—maybe a mess of rattlesnakes that could overrun an attacker?" She made a face. "Okay, snakes, not so much. But you get the idea. A rhino could come storming out of the Savannah on your behalf. The students were put near the most prodigious color band, in terms of wildlife."

"And the green area, where the medical center is, is also really well guarded," Sarah added, catching on to the way the school was themed. "So, like, if you're laid up with the flu or have a broken leg, and something was to get in the building, you would be seriously safe."

"Yeah, you could have a Bengal tiger or an Amazon jaguar come out of a green jungle on an assist," Ayana said, nodding.

"Not trying to be funny, though," Tami said, looking around with obvious concern. "But what happens if one of them *accidentally* gets out of the mural?"

"That's why you don't get taught how to do any of that until you have the discipline to handle living art in a life-or-death battle," Ayana replied flatly. "You don't do it to play a prank on some kid—you could get somebody killed. By the same token, you don't get to waltz around the halls by yourself as a Lower Sphere student, anyway, so if something were to be chasing you, you'd have an older student guide who could help defend the both of you."

Sarah just stared at Ayana. The information didn't help calm her worries in the least, but she vowed not to ask another question until her head stopped spinning.

"And…uh…we are going to get a book of all the rules, right? Because there seem to be a whole lotta ways to screw up around here big time." Tami hugged herself tightly, waiting for an answer.

"Most definitely," Ayana said with a smile. "You're gonna get a rule book, class schedule, locker, keys, passwords to open the big doors to the Great Hall, all of that—if you let me get you to your room."

The older girl chuckled, turned on her heels and began walking at a brisk pace. There was nothing to do but follow Ayana through the maze of hallways and try to keep up.

As they passed through brightly hued sunflower fields, the girls' section of the dormitory was a welcome sight. An endless procession of boys was flowing to the right, and Ayana, Sarah, Tami and the other girls they'd run into in the hallway joined the crowd heading to the left.

Colorful doors with corkboards and erasable note boards lined the corridor. Laughter and girls' voices rang out as the new-student tours came together and broke down into sheer pandemonium.

Sarah peered into the room that Ayana indicated and glanced around at their waiting luggage, lively yellow frescos, twin bunk beds, four desks, four dressers and four wardrobes. Again she and Tami shared a look that held an unspoken question—who would be the third and fourth roommates, and would they all get along?

"Don't worry. They didn't separate you guys," Ayana said with an easy smile. "They don't do that here. Guess they figure the kids coming in have been through enough traumas and have lost enough familiarity along the way. Hyacinth and Allie will be joining you guys soon."

Sarah smiled. She was so glad that Ayana had been the one to give them the tour and not someone they didn't know—even though Jessica and her friends seemed nice. Sudden emotion drove her to give Ayana a spontaneous hug, which Tami immediately joined in.

"Thanks, Yaya," Sarah said, laying her head on her cousin's shoulder.

"For real," Tami said, squeezing Ayana hard.

"It's gonna be okay. I told you, I've got your backs, all right?"

Both girls nodded and finally let Ayana go.

"Okay, I'm peeling off," Ayana said, waving to some girls in the hall. "Catch you at lunch."

Sarah's stomach growled. It would be a late lunch, and she just now realized how hungry she was. Sarah looked after her cousin as she disappeared down the hall and tried not to let her body slump with relief. She didn't want to seem like a baby, but it meant the world to her that their foursome wasn't getting split up here in the dorm, even if talent divisioning had separated them in other ways. Just knowing that was enough to return the smile to her face and lift the invisible weight that had been bearing down on her entire body.

"Hey, where's the bathroom in this joint?" Tami called out before Ayana disappeared, making both Sarah and Ayana laugh.

Ayana waved for them to follow her. "C'mon. This way. Can't believe I almost forgot the most important place around here."

Sarah and Tami followed Ayana until she came to a halt in front of a wide doorway covered in opaque stained glass. The designs were of water dragons in peach and golden hues.

"Say hello to Rama and Sita," Ayana said, laughing. She waved at the large serpentlike forms that slowly patrolled the door's glass, and Sarah gasped when they nodded in reply. "They keep the guys out of the girl's locker room, bathroom and shower. Down by the gym, there's another pair, Harry and Sally, plus the orcas—and don't get me started about the dolphins. Complete gossips," she added with a wink, and then pushed through to the bathroom.

Ultraviolet light combined with overhead fluorescents cast a glow that kept large potted ferns alive. It was the strangest combination Sarah had ever seen. On the one hand the bathroom was fully functional, military style, with rows of sinks and mirrors, as well as stalls, yet the wall art and the hanging plants made it seem almost spalike. Several groups of students were huddled in the locker and shower area behind a marble half-wall, and everything there looked just as pristine. And spotting Hyacinth and Allie made Sarah smile.

Soon they could go to their room and take a break, however brief, from all this craziness.

But the haunted look in Hyacinth's eyes gave Sarah pause. Something wasn't right. Hyacinth was standing alone, apart from the crowd, a little hunched over, as if something was hurting her. Melissa Gray was giving some final little speech to the group of new Clavs, while her girlfriends hung in the back, whispering and laughing. Their laughter seemed to be directed at Hyacinth. But she noticed that one of Jessica's friends, Bebitta, seemed to be standing close to Hyacinth, glaring at Melissa and crew. Andrea had a supportive arm over Allie's shoulder, and she gave Ayana a meaningful look. Something had gone down foul. Sarah could feel it.

Just then Melissa looked over at Sarah from the corner of her eye and shot her a nasty glance. Remembering what had happened in the Great Hall, Sarah quickly said a prayer to shield her thoughts, calling down the white light to shield her mind.

Sarah's eyes narrowed as she continued looking at her desperately unhappy friend. She wasn't one to start a fight, but she would have no problem finishing this one. Hyacinth was a gentle soul who wouldn't hurt a fly—someone who was the same to her as a sister. An elbow in her ribs from Tami confirmed that she wasn't the only one who'd caught the bad vibrations coming from Melissa's group. Ayana nodded and then sent Sarah a mental message. *You need to pick your battles around here. This one is minor and not worth it.*

Sarah shot Tami a look that said *later*, promising herself that "later" was coming soon.

CHAPTER 10

Sarah, Tami and Allie were waiting as soon as Hyacinth walked through the door. They stared in disbelief at the scrapes and bruises on her arms and legs. She looked like she had been in a fight and lost.

"Hyacinth, what happened to you?" Sarah said, dashing forward. She took her friend by the arm and led her to one of the lower bunks.

Hyacinth sniffed and burst into tears. "Ohmigod, that was so horrible!" she said in a quiet, intense rush. "Two Upper Sphere Clair-Vs kept making me trip down the hall, fall up the stairs and bump into archways. The messed up my depth perception, so I would see the floor as higher or lower than it really was and stumble like a clumsy idiot all over the place! Bebitta came by and saw what was happening, and she tried to stop them, but because she's a Blend, she wasn't strong enough." Two big tears slid down Hyacinth's nose.

"It was that bitch Melissa Gray, wasn't it?" Tami said, furious.

Hyacinth shook her head. "Melissa didn't actually do anything. It was her two friends, Amy Feingold and Angelica Roberts." She wiped her cheeks and drew a shuddering breath. "But Melissa didn't do anything to stop it." She looked up at Sarah. "She wants to get you kicked out, Sarah. She's using me as bait."

"What?" Sarah asked shocked.

"You know how it is. No matter how strong a Clairvoyant you are, you can't be in someone else's mind without them sensing something about *you*, too. Well, Amy and Angelica are strong, but I picked that much up from both of them. Melissa wants you out of here, and she's going to try and make you get yourself in trouble—the kind of trouble that can get you expelled."

Sarah placed her hands on her hips. "Like messing with my compound sister so I'll kick her butt kind of trouble, I bet." She glanced at Tami. "First she started by bumping me in the hall and had some axe to grind with Tami, now she's picking on you. It's only a matter of time before she comes for Allie."

Tami frowned. "Of all the dirty, rotten, low down—"

"That's horrible," Allie said, talking with her hands. "Tami can take care of herself, and I don't care what she tries to do to me, I'll zap her. But we've gotta do something to help 'Cinth, stuck in the Clair-V division with that crazy chick. Ayana is in Upper Spheres, so she won't be around to protect her. We can't just let that beyotch torture poor 'Cynth. We could—"

"Beat her ass down in a dark hallway when nobody else is around?" Tami said, narrowing her gaze and resting her hands on her hips.

"Well…" Sarah said. "We could, but…isn't that a bit…?"

"Extreme?" Allie finished for her. "I mean, I don't even understand what started all this in the first place. It's insane. We haven't done anything to her, Sarah!"

"Sarah exists, doesn't she?" Tami said dryly. "I'll tell you what I think is going on, but maybe I'm wrong. If you ask me, Melissa Gray thinks she's the queen around here. It's clear that she doesn't want any Neteru kid messing that up."

"Yeah, you're right."

"You think she made you want to fight her?" Allie asked.

Sarah shook her head. "No, she wasn't manipulating my thoughts or anything like that, but…she set me up. Everybody who saw what happened blamed me for everything."

"When was this?" Hyacinth asked, looking confused. After Sarah explained her encounter with Melissa, Hyacinth nodded and said, "That makes sense."

"I say we kick her ass right now," Tami said, not bothering to lower her voice.

"Shhhh!" Allie whispered.

"Screw them," Tami said, her voice escalating in defiance.

"Tami," Sarah said sharply. "That would mean falling right into their trap, and we're not going to do that. There's gotta be a way to keep this psycho chick off our backs without getting in trouble. Plus, there's something more going on here than her thinking she's queen bee around here. She's got some secrets she's worried about. But just outright kicking her or her friends' butts isn't an option."

"Fine," Tami said. "What do you propose, fearless leader?"

"I don't know yet. But if this chick has secrets, that's always good for possible leverage—my dad taught me that. And stop calling me fearless leader," Sarah said with a frown. She turned to Hyacinth, "Is there anything else you can tell us? Anything else you picked up from Amy or Angelica?"

Hyacinth shook her head. "Just that they're kind of scared of Melissa, too, and they think she's wicked strong."

"Okay, well, we're going to have to protect our thoughts, so white light prayers every morning, all right?" Sarah told them. "Just like Nana taught us."

"That's not going to be enough." Tami said.

"I know," Sarah said, frustrated. "Do you have any suggestions?"

Tami was silent, looking thoughtful. "Well, maybe we can find some strategies in the library."

They all stared at Tami.

"What?" she said defensively.

"You're suggesting that we go to the library?" Allie asked.

"Does anyone have any better ideas?"

They all looked at one another.

"The library it is," Sarah said, and got to her feet.

"Right now?" Tami asked, disbelieving. Hesitating, she opened her duffle bag and took out several sweaters, and then walked over to the bureau she'd instantly claimed. "I know it's my idea and all, but we just got here." A mischievous smile lit her face. "I'd rather do some digging and find out who the guy with the gray eyes is over in Specs," she said, closing her eyes. "Wow."

"He makes me nervous," Allie said.

"Ohmigod, Allie!" Tami threw her sweater into a drawer. "Everything and everybody makes you nervous."

"Tami, we need to focus here," Sarah said. "Plus, isn't anybody the least bit interested in the bigger problem going on here at the school?"

Everyone stopped fidgeting to stare at Sarah.

"Guys," Sarah said, now talking with her hands outstretched, "two students are missing, and two others have died. Doesn't that make you the least bit curious about what's going on—for no other reason than to make sure it doesn't happen to anybody we know? Or to us?" Sarah stopped and looked at her roommates, and then closed her eyes, her hands on top of her head. "Some jealous chick is the least of our worries."

Stony silence made Sarah open her eyes.

Hyacinth's gaze lingered on hers, and then her friend searched the other girls' faces. "You know, Sarah has a point. This insanity with Melissa and her crew really isn't as important as life or death…or some cute guy."

Allie nodded, glancing at Hyacinth. "'Cinth is right. We can go to the library to find out ways to protect ourselves from Melissa, but maybe we should be trying to research how to protect ourselves from whatever evil abducted those kids right from school grounds."

"I can't get the stuff Ayana told us out of my mind," Sarah said, turning her attention to Tami.

"What stuff?" Hyacinth asked, as she and Allie stepped closer.

"Yeah," Allie said. "Spill."

"They'll go over it all in a dark arts protection class or whatever, I'm sure," Tami muttered.

Sarah kept her focus on Tami, ignoring Hyacinth and Allie for the moment. "Do you really wanna wait to figure out how to rig up personal protection? I sure don't." She turned to Allie and Hyacinth. "On the tour, Ayana gave us the inside scoop, stuff I bet only the Upper Sphere students are whispering about. I'll tell you on the way to the library."

"Fine," Tami said. "Let's go to the boooring library." She sighed wistfully. "But, damn, Sarah, for a little while, it was sure nice to dream."

CHAPTER 11

It took several loops through the hallways, but they finally found the library again. Running forward with anticipation, Sarah pushed open the massive oak-and-brass doors, then stopped and for a long moment simply gaped.

Tall, gleaming wooden shelves created perfect alcoves for private conversations between friends, but before taking advantage they glanced up and down the rows for any sign of a librarian, teachers or other students. There were none—the place was completely deserted.

Whoever the librarian was, he or she must have been on break, because the coast was clear. The moment that was confirmed by four extremely anxious pairs of eyes, they launched into an intense whispering session.

Sarah leaned in and dropped her voice. "First of all, we need to find defensive strategies to protect us in the room at night, in case anything gets into the building. I think we'll be okay during the day, in class and in the halls. Safety in numbers, you know?"

"And what about those smuts who keep attacking us? The likelihood of some monster crashing in to drag us from our beds at night is really remote, Sarah. I say let the administration and parents worry about that. Our immediate problem is Melissa and her witchy friends," Tami said, folding her arms over her chest. "'Cinth was in public and they made it look like she tripped by accident. No safety in numbers there."

"Fine," Sarah replied with a frustrated huff. "But we look for defensive strategies only," she said, looking hard at Tami. "We don't wanna get sent home for starting a fight, but if *they* start it and we just protect ourselves…And nothing too complicated. We don't want to do anything that a teacher would have to undo and we'd have to explain. We have to stay off any faculty or administration radar."

Allie smiled. "That's a plan I can get behind."

"Okay, I'm in," Tami said with a half-smile.

"But…" Hyacinth whispered, leaning in. "That stuff Sarah is worrying about is valid. I'm really not as worried about Melissa as I am about what could happen to any of us if…whatever it is gets back in. You guys go look for light defensive arts to use against the witches. I'm going into the stacks to find anything I can on advanced dark arts protections."

Everyone looked at Hyacinth, the team's brain, but no one argued with her. If anybody could figure out a solid demon defense, it would be 'Cinth. Sarah put her hand out, and three hands immediately covered it.

"Then let's get started," Sarah said.

Her three friends gave her a silent thumbs-up and then began to look around.

"There's gotta be a section on easy white-light protections and protocols," Tami said, hunting through the rows. "Something a little more heavy-duty than we were taught at the compound, but not enough to fry anyone."

"Yeah," Sarah said, beginning to figure out how the books were arranged. "Make sure it's only defensive stuff, though."

"Yeah, we heard you the first time," Tami said, but she smiled.

"I'm going to hunt over there," Hyacinth announced, pointing. "Something's calling me—I can feel it. I bet I can find us just what we need."

"Cool," Tami said under her breath, sidling up to Sarah and Allie. "The sooner we can find something and get out of this dead joint, the better."

Allie picked up a book off a shelf, and a fist-sized black-and-white spider scuttled out, squeaking in spider gibberish as Allie dropped the text and screamed. The little mutant creature parachuted off the shelf shaking its tiny fist, then scampered along the floor and disappeared.

A blue static charge rippled around Allie, making her hair frizz out wildly as she clutched her chest. "Did you see how big it was?"

"Was it me, or was that little guy cussing us out?" Tami scratched her head, while Allie peered frantically around her.

"*Little* guy? That thing was huge!" Allie made a face. "*Eeeew.* I hate spiders."

"Is everything okay?" Hyacinth called out from several rows away.

"Yeah, just a big ugly spider!" Sarah yelled back.

"Okay, I'll keep looking," Hyacinth said.

"You know," a large land snail said, sliding out from between two large texts on the opposite shelf. "That was a thoroughly offensive thing to say about someone of such a complex phyla." It left a gleaming trail along the wood as it moved. "Anansi is a renowned cataloguer from the Land of Nod, and a respected member of this bibliophile community, not unlike myself." The voice seemed to indicate that the creature was female. "What are you ladies doing in here at this hour without a hall pass? And do please stop shocking the shelves, young lady," she said to Allie. "Our inhabitants are at risk."

Allie clutched her hands to her chest and murmured contritely, "Sorry."

"We're new," Sarah said after a moment, looking at her friends in utter amazement. "And we had some free time, so we thought we would check this place out."

"Very well, then—I am Miss Tillie, not to be confused with Miss Tittle, your homeroom teacher and a wonderful Phoenix. Anyone who has enough of a yen to read that they would spend their free time here researching is a friend of ours. But do apologize to Mr. Anansi. I am sure he was highly offended by your outburst."

Allie nodded, then cast her gaze around, trying to spot the irate spider, but he was nowhere to be seen. "Umm, Mr. Anansi," she called out. "I'm sorry. Forgive me. I was just…startled. Sorry about the spontaneous zaps, too. I'm still learning how to control my talent."

They only had to wait a few seconds before the huge spider dropped from the ceiling. Allie covered her mouth and dodged behind Tami to keep from screaming again. Sarah stared at him closely, squinting. He was indeed a fascinating little fellow, with a pattern on his thick body that looked like X-Ray art, and he wore a little purple scarf around his short neck. She smiled broadly when she saw that he was wearing tiny round glasses and a tiny purple cap.

Sarah giggled. "Pleased to meet you, Mr. Anansi. Forgive my friend Allie. Are you the librarian?"

Several unintelligible squeaks preceded Miss Tillie's protest.

"Oh, heavens no, child. Mr. Anansi is much too busy spinning new stories to actually maintain interaction with students, just as I am too busy keeping the shelves ship-shape. Mrs. Hogan is responsible for you students, her being a faery godmother, and all...That reminds me. If you'd like a job to earn some class extra credits, this is one of the most fascinating places in the entire academy."

"Thanks, but I'll pass," Tami said, rolling her eyes.

"Ummmm…we really should see what our workload is going to be like before committing," Allie said in a small voice, staying as far away from Mr. Anansi as possible. "But thanks for the offer."

"Dear child, no insult intended," Miss Tillie said, "but I think our library residents would protest unless you were able to control your tactical proclivities. However, if your friend is interested…" Miss Tillie trained her independently moving eyes on Sarah and waited.

Sarah glanced around her. It was indeed the most incredible library she'd ever seen. If she could master this place, maybe she could even get an early pass into the Tehuti Library. Being able to get up into The Dollar Bill would be awesome.

"I'm in…I mean, yes, I'd like to work here, if they have an opening," Sarah said. She paid no mind to Tami's incredulous look.

Allie's eyes were wide, but she nodded, her expression saying *good thinking* without words.

"Wonderful, excellent," Miss Tillie crooned, slowly moving along the edge of the shelf. "I shall inform Mrs. Hogan the moment she returns." She stopped and frowned at the shelf. "Never enough time to fight this on-going battle with the motes…Just write your name and room number in the dust in front of me and I shall relay the message. See, Mr. Anansi, not all of these children are, ahem, daft."

Sarah remembered the other reason why she'd wanted to visit the library. "Ah, ma'am," she said, walking closer to the retreating snail. "I need to look up a word I heard. *Nexse.* Can you tell me where there's an ancient or mystic language translator?"

Miss Tillie stopped and gazed at Sarah with both bulbous eyes. Sarah ignored her friends' quizzical looks and focused on the snail, her heart beginning to beat more quickly.

"Nexse…nexse," Miss Tillie said. "Child, wherever did you hear that?"

"Ummmm…in a dream," Sarah said evasively.

"Oh, then that makes complete sense," Miss Tillie said in a cheerful voice. "It means awaken, wake up, arise and open your eyes in Coptic."

Sarah blinked. "Really? Wow…Okay…thanks."

Awaken? The being of Light had told her to awaken…but awaken to what?

"Come, I'll show you to our translation section," Miss Tillie said.

But before Sarah could accept her offer, Hyacinth's voice rang out.

"Hey, I think I found something," she called out. "This should be the right place, but it's all gray down this aisle, no books and it's getting foggier as I walk. Maybe the books are in a separate room—can one of you guys see if you can hit the lights back here?"

Sarah, Allie and Tami just looked at one another. They'd momentarily forgotten that Hyacinth was off exploring. But before they could call back to her, Mr. Anansi had scurried up a shelf and Miss Tillie released the most alarming squeak.

"No, no, no, child!" Miss Tillie cautioned as loud as one could expect a snail to manage. Her eye stalks flailed in every direction as she tried to propel herself forward more quickly, to no avail. "Call her back!" she said breathlessly. "That poor child is headed down The Shady Path—the astral projection realms for the Upper Spheres! It is the advanced classes section and forbidden to students who haven't taken Mr. Everett's white light barrier course! At her grade level, she must have an instructor or an Upper Sphere student with her, someone who is versed in the way of the path! She could get lost in there—or worse!"

Sarah took off down the aisle, calling Hyacinth's name. Her heart was racing as each of her friends took a different aisle, shouting for Hyacinth at the tops of their lungs. Tiny shadows slipped from the bookshelves and combined to create two yawning stretching shadows that made Sarah gasp and skid to a stop. But the way they were bouncing up and down wasn't wholly threatening.

Something in their urgent motion seemed almost like an appeal for her to follow them. Taking the risk, she followed their lead, even though they were urging her in a different direction, noting how this time she actually heard them squeak and squeal as though in delight.

They led her to a misty aisle, and when she hesitated, she felt something shove her forward and almost screamed. Then one of the shadows seemed to inhale, and instantly the mist began to clear away.

The moment it was gone, Sarah saw the open doorway that said Senior Reference and knew that was where Hyacinth had gone. "'Cinth, you've gotta get out of there!" she called out. "*Now*! It's dangerous!"

One of the long, stretchy shadows rushed to the door, as though urging her to go through it.

"I can't see!" Hyacinth said in a far-away-echo voice.

"Okay," Sarah said, trying not to hyperventilate. "Just stop walking. Tell me when you've stopped walking."

"Okay, but I'm scared, Sarah!" Hyacinth yelled back.

"Think of me. Close your eyes and picture me in your mind. Use your Clav skills. I'm closing my eyes, too, so I can picture you."

One of the shadows tugged on Sarah's sleeve, and she moved gingerly through the door, gaining confidence with each step. The shadows were helping her find her friend. In a place where her ability to see in the dark was severely limited, the shadows were helping her to safely make her way forward like supernatural guide dogs.

"Okay, Sarah," Hyacinth said in a shaky voice, "but it feels like there are other presences in here with me, and I really don't want to close my eyes."

"Bring the white light down around you—remember how Nana Marlene taught us at home? I'm going to think of a golden light around your white light. Then I'm thinking of the sealer we always do…c'mon, say it with me, just like Nana taught us. 'In the name of the Most High of the Light, I am safe in all dimensions of time and space in which I exist on all planes and subplanes, and consciousness time zones.'"

Sarah waited until her friend repeated the words along with her, her voice sounding stronger as she spoke.

"All right. Now, nothing can hurt you, so you can close your eyes."

"Okay, Sarah…I can see you standing by the door. But there's a big spider beside you."

"He's cool—that's Mr. Anansi. It's not a dark side illusion."

"I can see Tami running down the aisle, and Allie is behind her. There's a snail back where you guys were before, and—"

Sarah caught a brief glimpse of a shadow in the shape of a girl, reached out into the mist and pulled hard the minute she connected with something solid. Then Hyacinth was in her arms. She wrapped her own arms tightly around her friend and dragged her away from the open doorway.

When they were far enough away that she felt safe, Sarah allowed them to collapse to the floor, their backs against a bookcase. As soon as they caught their breath, she blurted out, "Ohmigod, 'Cinth—no matter what, don't go through unknown doorways around here by yourself. Are you crazy?"

The shadows that had been in the aisle with her jumped up and down as though they were also fussing, but Sarah couldn't spare any attention for them now.

"I didn't think there could be any danger in a freakin' library, Sarah! I thought I was going to find something that could help us," Hyacinth said, burying her face against Sarah's shoulder. "It was so dark and scary in there."

Tami and Allie bumped into them as the large spider scampered away.

"There's so much we don't know about this place. If anything seems questionable, wait for backup, okay?" Sarah pushed Hyacinth away so she could look her in the eyes. "Safety first. Always."

"We left Miss Tillie screaming on the shelf. We'd better go tell her you're all right before she has a heart attack or pops out of her shell," Tami said, then glanced at Allie, Sarah and Hyacinth, who all just stared at her. "What? I'm just saying."

Suddenly two large figures loomed in the doorway, then moved forward with such velocity that there wasn't even time to scream. In seconds, Tami's mystery man somersaulted to a stop beside them as his blond buddy came sliding out on his backside, laughing. Sarah stared at them both hard, remembering that the blond kid had been sitting close to Ayana during opening ceremonies.

The shadows made scary faces, but then squealed and jumped back into the bookshelves, intermittently peeking out. Sarah glanced up at them once, but she didn't want to draw attention to her connection with them, so she turned away from them quickly. One of her tag-along shadows had actually stuck out its tongue at the two boys.

"Whew, what a rush!" the athletic blond guy said, rolling over and doing a hard pushup off the floor.

"Sweet," Tami's mystery man added, back-flipping up to his feet. He smiled at her. "Long time no see, newbie."

Tami smiled and looked down. He moved toward her, and Sarah's focus was split between the threatening presence she sensed behind the door, Tami and the guy slowly stalking her. Allie and Hyacinth were no help—they were huddled against a bookcase holding each other and looking confused.

The blond Adonis chuckled under his breath as gray eyes lifted Tami's chin with one finger. "You ever take a walk on the dark side, babe?"

"No," Tami said, trying to sound tough.

"If you've got the right tour guide, it can be a lotta fun. I heard you have a little vamp in you." He smiled and then ran his finger down the side of her neck.

Tami gave him a sexy smile and lowered her voice to a husky murmur. "A little bit…on my mother's side."

"A little bit is all I need."

"Hey, you're Ayana's little cousin, aren't you?" the blond guy said, looking at Sarah.

"Yeah," Sarah said uncomfortably.

"Impressive performance earlier—a Neteru kid making it all the way into Blends division, go figure," he said with a smirk, clearly letting her know that he didn't think she'd been impressive at all.

The dislike between them was instant and palpable.

"Hey, Tam, we've gotta get back to our room and, uh…finish doing stuff," Allie said, sounding lame as she tried her best to get them away from obvious trouble.

"In a minute," Tami said, clearly enjoying flirting.

Sarah's stare bored into the guy with the gray eyes, and flashes of Melissa stabbed into her mind. There was a connection there; she just didn't know what it was. She slowly dragged her focus to the door. Behind that door were secrets. But she wasn't strong enough to get more than fragments. It wasn't like when she was at home on familiar ground, listening to unblocked conversations with her brother helping.

That was when it hit her. The Upper Spheres had blocked all eavesdropping and scrying…not just one-on-one, it was such a blackout of information that it had to have been done as a group. So, that was how it was done around here, huh. Groups. And it made sense, if students were sneaking doing stuff they weren't supposed to right under the noses of some of the strongest telepathic teachers on the planet. Okaaay. She'd just learned something valuable, and she would ask Ayana for more details later. Sarah returned her focus to the boys and frowned.

"Why don't you tell your girls you'll catch 'em later?" Gray Eyes murmured in Tami's ear, his body pressed tightly against hers as he gently pressed her against the stacks.

Was this guy seriously going to make out with Tami right in front of them? And was Tami seriously going to let him? What the hell was wrong with Tami when it came to this guy? It was like she fell under some kind of spell that left her stuck on stupid.

"Because we roll as one squad," Sarah said calmly, getting to her feet. She grabbed Tami's arm and looked the guy square in the face. "And we don't know you."

"The name's Stefan, and I'm trying to get to know her better," he said with a chuckle, holding his hands up in front of his chest.

Alarm bells went off in Sarah's head. That was the name she'd picked up from Melissa's mind when they first clashed. "How about you do that another time?" she said, giving him a hard look.

"Sarah…" Tami said in a whiny tone she'd never heard her friend use in her life.

Taken aback, Sarah let go of Tami and stubbornly folded her arms. She was so not leaving her best friend here with only a big spider and a snail to keep her safe.

"I don't want to get into a beef with you, fang girl," Stefan said to Sarah. "I might accidentally have to show you mine." He gave her a slow smile. "And trust me, babe, mine are bigger."

"You sure about that?" Sarah said, lifting her eyebrow.

"Aw, man, leave the newbies alone. You wouldn't want the Neteru twins to call Mommy or Daddy, would you?" the blond guy said, laughing.

"I'm so glad you crack yourself up," Sarah snapped, trying to hide her embarrassment. So that was what everyone thought—the moment any of the kids from the Net-pound had a problem, they'd snitch to their parents?

"Be cool," Tami said, frowning at Sarah. "Forgive my roommate," she said to the boys. "She's just a little overprotective."

Sarah looked at Tami in disbelief. Her best friend had just thrown her under the bus for this slimy Casanova?

Stefan stared at Sarah for a moment with a triumphant smirk. "You and I are cool…I just like your girl," he added, slowly allowing his upper and lower canines to crest.

Sarah just stared back at him for a moment, vaguely aware that Allie and Hyacinth were as dumbstruck as she was. His *were* bigger, and he had a double set, too—like Headmaster Shabazz. *Shit...*

He gave her a wolfish grin, allowed his canines to go back to normal, then leaned in and kissed the side of Tami's neck. It was a slow, sensuous caress that made her blush and giggle.

"Later," he murmured. "We'll get to know each other when you don't have a bodyguard." He backed off and gave his friend a swift nod.

Within moments they had melted into the aisles and were gone.

"You okay?" Sarah said, rushing over to Tami, with Allie and Hyacinth on her heels.

Tami just fanned her face and slid down the shelf. "He's *the one*."

Sarah felt heat flush her entire body. Was Tami out of her mind? She drew a deep breath, ready to launch into an argument, when a shrill voice made all the girls turn around.

"Heavens to mercy! Goodness gracious!" a short, chubby woman with blue hair exclaimed. Erratic sparks flared from the end of the blue marble wand she was waving about, causing Sarah and her friends to duck with each pass.

Sarah realized immediately that this must be the librarian, Mrs. Hogan. It also occurred to her that they had just been found in a forbidden part of the school. Well, hell.

Mr. Anansi dropped from somewhere unseen, his squeaking was an agitated recitation of what had transpired, no doubt.

Mrs. Hogan blinked several times, her small violet eyes shaded by long blue lashes, and her pink cheeks deepening to fuchsia before normalizing to a dusty rose.

"You ladies could have been severely injured!" she fussed, adjusting the powder-blue dress that matched her hair. "Before you go rummaging about in the library, it is vitally important to get a basic orientation." She let out a peeved sigh and tapped her wand against her small plump palm. "I am Mrs. Hogan, and you would be…?"

"I'm Sarah…and we're sorry, ma'am. We didn't know there was an off-limits section."

"Ah, yes! Sarah the brave, my new work-study student," Mrs. Hogan said, rushing in close to hug her. "Wonderful instincts. Mr. Anansi reported it all—but the next time you reach into the Shady Path, you must be doubly sure that what you pull out is truly a friend." She peered at the other girls until Tami finally spoke up.

"I'm Tamara, and these are my friends Allison and Hyacinth."

"These two ladies don't have their own voices?" Mrs. Hogan asked with a droll smile.

"Yes, ma'am," Allie said with a nervous curtsey. "I'm Allison, and she's Hyacinth."

Mrs. Hogan shook her head. "So it is only poor Hyacinth who cannot speak, eh?"

"No, ma'am…I mean, yes, ma'am. That's me, Hyacinth."

"Nervous child, my goodness. But I dare say you have reason to be, although thankfully you're none the worse for the wear." Mrs. Hogan let out a little sigh, and then folded her arms over her ample chest and nodded toward the open door. "Ladies, are you aware of what's behind that Senior Reference sign?"

When none of them answered, Mrs. Hogan clucked her tongue. "That area is for Upper Sphere students. It contains a tear between dimensions. Guardian warriors must learn how to block dark forces from slithering out of such regions."

Mrs. Hogan began pacing, using her wand to draw sparkling images as she spoke. "Only a person who is extremely versed in countering demon attacks and building white light barriers should ever enter there. Those are usually our more senior Clair-V students, and even then, we send them in with another strong student who grounds them from the outside of the chamber, and we have an instructor on standby. It is not a place for the uninitiated, as you can literally feel presences touching you in there, even succumb to a temporary possession—which means we'd have to do an exorcism, yada, yada, yada, not pretty. And with all the recent issues we've had at the school, we do not want students or faculty going in there until the disappearances have been addressed. Understood?"

Hyacinth immediately began to pat down her body with alarm. "Mrs. Hogan, did anything get on me? Can you tell? I'm not possessed, am I?"

The three friends peered at each other nervously. Mrs. Hogan wrinkled her nose and waved her wand over Hyacinth's trembling body.

"Hmmm…hard to tell…let me see. You were in there for how long?"

"Only a few minutes," Sarah said breathlessly.

"Never can tell how long it takes, though," Mrs. Hogan said, rubbing her chin, and then smiled when tears welled in Hyacinth's eyes. "You'll live. But no more shenanigans in my library."

Hyacinth rapidly nodded.

"Good, then be off. And before you ladies explore another thing, open your PIUs and learn about the danger zones, thank you very much."

The girls watched the blue matron float away.

Tami glanced at the others. "Just one question. What the heck is a PIU?"

PART TWO
KNOWING

I have come into the Island of Fire, I have set right in the place of wrong…"

—The Book of Going Forth by Day

CHAPTER 12

They left the library without finding any defensive protections, but at least Sarah felt better now that she'd learned what *nexse* meant, though not why the being had said it to her.

Now they just needed to find their way to the cafeteria, which was turning out to be easier said than done.

They'd made a complete and frustrating circle twice before getting it right. Between having a seer in their group and using Tami's expert tracking skills, they were finally able to figure out that the color grid was laid out like the chakra system. The delicious smell and hubbub of activity greeted them before they actually saw the cafeteria. Then all they had to do was enter the flow of hungry students, following along, and being bumped and shoved like she'd seen on old DVDs of salmon swimming upstream.

The hallway madness dumped them out into the mouth of the cafeteria, where it took a moment to get oriented. Rather than utilitarian tables and glass-shielded vats of mass-produced gunk, like she'd expected, it was more like an endless buffet of gourmet choices.

A loud gong sounded and the older students stood still, causing the new students to freeze where they were.

"*Es*, *Es*, *Hetep,* students!" Headmistress Stone called out in the ancient Kemetian greeting while opening her arms, walking stick held high, and bringing the group to full silence. "We shall ask for a blessing over the food that was prepared for the nourishment and health of your bodies, *Ashe*. We will ask the divine Creator to have mercy over all students, staff and faculty, and to allow you to partake in this wonderful feast with grace, health and thanks, *Ashe*."

"Ashe," rang out in the cafeteria.

"We do this because there are always dark spiritual forces lurking, and also because to cleanse the food before consumption is wisdom, *Ashe*."

"Ashe," the student body responded as one.

The headmistress smiled a wise old smile and lowered her ebony walking stick. "Then, my children, enjoy."

It was as though Headmistress Stone had lifted invisible floodgates. Students grabbed trays and plates and silverware and rushed about in a frenetic ballet. Everyone jockeyed for position to get in line for their favorite food; it was survival of the fittest, pure and simple.

In easy-to-access stations placed around the room, there were salads, breads, hot and cold dishes, make-it-yourself sandwiches and fountains for cold drinks…even a dessert station and ice cream bar near the coffee and tea urns.

But the best thing of all was that her grandmother had not come over to her. They'd simply shared a knowing look. God bless Nana Marlene for staying in character as Headmistress Stone, so that she could be a regular student for now. Later, she would sneak off for a private visit. For now, learning the ropes of the lunchroom without embarrassing oneself was paramount.

As Sarah glanced around she saw multi-armed beings, something like a cross between giant squids and humans, wearing white chef outfits and flipping pans of made-to-order pasta and stir-fry for eagerly waiting students. Must have been some of the Mer come over from Nod, she decided. She tried not to stare, but that was impossible.

Tiny fauns scurried between the tables, wiping down the highly polished wood and keeping order as small Fae sprites made off with crumbs. Nymphs refilled platters, while faeries drizzled nectar and honey over sweet rolls and sticky buns. Burly elves were left to the task of methodically reloading fruit trays on ice and replacing five-gallon drums of juice and water as supplies were devoured by ravenous students.

Faculty had its own clearly designated area in the back, but even in the student section she saw only square tables that seated four and round ones that seated up to ten. But of course there wouldn't be long institutional benches here. This place had been built for the legislative branch of the then-government, so it wouldn't look like a military camp. It made sense that it had cushioned chairs and gleaming wood tables, along with the fancy food stations, even if it had been designed to feed a horde of eighteen hundred. With only about three hundred students, maybe fifty faculty and a hundred or so support staff, there'd be plenty of seating.

"Sarah!" she heard a voice call. It was Ayana. She was seated at a table with two other girls. The blond Adonis was there, as well, along with his sleazy friend. Sarah waved back, noticing that Tami was practically swooning, and then they all hurried away to get their food. Sarah was relieved that they had someone to sit with at lunch—even if she hated having to encounter Stefan again. Worse yet was knowing that she couldn't stand her cousin's friend—maybe boyfriend?—whatever his name was. The guy was a complete jerk, but the last thing she wanted to do was upset Yaya by making a scene.

She filled a plate and started toward Yaya's table, then remembered that Jessica, Bebitta and Andrea had said they could sit together at lunch. Man, the lunchroom politics were already underway, and it was only day one. Glancing around quickly and relieved that she hadn't spotted the Blends crew yet, she kept moving toward Ayana's group. She was just passing Melissa Gray's table when Allie, coming up behind her, lost control of her talent and zapped Sarah's glass of apple juice.

In that split second it was impossible to tell whether Allie had just freaked out at seeing Melissa and her girls snickering at them, or if Melissa had somehow caused the spontaneous energy burst. There was barely even time to react. Sarah jumped back, and the juice, the plate of pasta, her sweet roll and salad all came heading toward her sweater, a huge and embarrassing disaster in the making.

"Reverse!" a voice said, and suddenly everything stopped mid-spill and then righted itself on her tray.

She stared in disbelief and let go of the tray without thinking, but it just hovered there in front of her.

"You gotta hold it," the voice said, and she looked up to see Wil gracing her with a dashing smile.

She quickly reached out and grabbed the tray. "Thanks," she said, turning crimson.

"Spaz," one of the Gray gang muttered.

Sarah didn't care. The most gorgeous guy in the place had just kept her from making a complete fool of herself. She took a quick sip of juice, and then promptly choked on it.

"Hey," Wil said laughing. "Go easy. It's still got a post-spell kick to it."

Sarah blushed even harder and hurried away. She slid into a seat across from Ayana, who reached over and squeezed her hand. Blond Guy didn't look amused.

"These are my compound sisters," Ayana said with a wide smile. "This is Sarah…Allie, Tami and Hyacinth—and these are my BFFs Tina and Darlene."

"So we don't get no love?" Stefan said in a sexy rumble, looking at Tami like he could eat her alive.

"Stefan, right?" Sarah replied before Ayana could say anything, giving him the evil eye. "I just never caught your friend's name."

"When did you two meet?" Ayana said, then turned to the blond guy, who was looking totally bored, and beamed. "This is Brent."

Yup, boyfriend, Sarah thought.

"Yeah…whatever," he said, taking a slurp of lemonade. "We already met in the library. But here's the question, Yaya—why do they have to sit here? I thought we decided to keep our table off limits to newbies?"

"Brent…" Ayana said, her tone soft and pleading. "Come on. They're family."

Sarah was speechless. Her adored cousin was *pleading* with this guy? She couldn't believe it.

Tina smiled at Sarah and her friends, and then cut a withering glance in Brent's direction. "The newbies won't get in the way of your zombie bopping, so leave 'em alone, okay?"

"Yeah, Brent, come on," Darlene said with a slight frown.

"Fine, let 'em stay," Brent replied in a bored tone, and then picked up a slice of whole-wheat pizza and began chomping on it.

"Zombie bopping?" Tami looked from Sarah to Ayana.

"Takes skill, babe," Stefan said with a wide grin. "You ever play?" He leaned closer to her. "Better question is, do you wanna play?"

"Oh, no," Ayana said, laughing nervously. "Back off, bro."

"See, Tam? I keep trying to get to know you, but your bodyguards keep coming out of nowhere at me."

"So what's zombie bobbing?" Sarah said, trying to divert Tami's attention away from Stefan and having completely lost interest in her lunch.

"Get up on the lingo," Stefan said with a low chuckle. "ZBing we called it, and we like to keep the instructors none the wiser, so chill."

"You need a strong seer navigator," Brent said, giving Ayana a sexy wink, "plus an expensive board—skate, snow, surf, doesn't matter, as long as you've got the tactical juice to make it go a hundred miles an hour without losing your balance. Then you bob in and out of the trees like they're the frickin' living dead. The only thing that keeps you from being roadkill at that velocity is some serious athletic ability—and a beautiful mind." He held up his pizza, holding the group enthralled. "Without a good seer, you'll wipe out and look worse than what's on this green pepper and mushroom slice. We used to play up at my dad's compound in Big Sur. I'm legendary on the boards—boards run in my family. Before the floods, my dad was the best surfer dude in Malibu. It's all in the DNA."

Brent bumped Stefan's fist, and both guys laughed.

Okay, so now Sarah knew it was official. Her cousin was dating a rich, privileged jock who had a little bit of charm, but not nearly enough to override the fact that he was a cocky, thrill-seeking jerk. What was wrong with Yaya?

"You play, too?" Tami said, beaming at Stefan.

"Naw, babe—I'm the only one around here fast enough on the ground to keep up with the boards. I'm a ref," Stefan said proudly and received another fist bump from Brent.

"So what was up with you guys coming off the Shady Path?" Tami asked outright, just as bold as ever. "Is that how you sneak out of school to go ZBing? It's more than a rift between dimensions—it's an exit, isn't it?"

Tina and Darlene looked at each other, groaned and shook their heads.

Ayana turned on Brent. "You told me you were going to stop doing that!"

Brent leaned over and kissed her on the lips. "Don't worry, Stefan just wanted to check it out, make sure everything was still cool in case we need to make a quick escape, you know?"

"Leave me out of it," Stefan said, laughing, and then turned his attention to his pasta.

Ayana looked at Brent with a frown. "Brent…" she said in a warning tone, but Sarah could tell that she wasn't really angry with him.

Brent smiled. "I only took Stefan because you wouldn't come with me," he said, his voice low and intimate. Ayana blushed, instantly flustered.

Sarah frowned. "I don't get it. With everything that's going on, students dead and missing, aren't you guys worried that something really bad could happen on the Shady Path? Why the heck would you risk going in there?"

"Well, if you're a thrill-seeker like these two, then that's exactly why you go there—for the danger high," Tina said, and then arched an eyebrow.

"And what a lovely high it is," Brent said with a wide smile.

"Sweet," Stefan said, nodding with a slightly wicked grin.

"And for others…well, let's just say it's a primo make out spot," Darlene said, lowering her voice and giggling. She winked at Tami.

"The Shady Path?" Sarah asked incredulously.

The older students shook their heads and laughed at Sarah. Ayana slung an arm over her shoulder.

"Not yet, guys, okay?" Ayana eyed Stefan with a smile and then stared at Tami warningly. "These are my little sisters."

Tami looked like she was about to protest but began picking at her salad instead. Part of Sarah was glad that Ayana had said what she had, but another part of her hated feeling so naïve and new to everything.

"It seemed really scary," Allie said with a shiver. "I don't ever want to see the place."

"I'll say," Hyacinth added with a shudder.

Stefan smiled, looking directly at Tami. "I'd be glad to show you sometime."

Tami blushed furiously. "Any other forbidden parts of the school we should know about?" she asked with a sexy smile of her own. Her vampire half was clearly coming out to play.

Stefan smiled back. "A few."

Suddenly Al loomed up behind them, breaking the moment—much to Sarah's relief.

"Hey, Tam," he said. "Now that we aren't in the compound anymore, want me to take you up on that offer you made this morning? I believe it was something about, 'in my dreams.'" He waggled his eyebrows at her and gave her one of his most dashing smiles.

"Al, can't you see I'm eating?" Tami said, blowing him off.

"Chickening out? Because I figured after all that trash you were talking earlier, Tamara, you'd want to back it up," Al said, his tone baiting.

"Why don't you leave the lady alone?" Stefan said in a low rumble, making everyone fall quiet. His gray eyes were focused on Al with a deadly expression.

"Yeah, why don't you do that?" Tami said.

Why was she egging Alejandro on? Sarah wondered. Was she really so sure that he wouldn't directly confront an Upper Sphere?

Al stared back at Stefan, their eyes meeting in a silent challenge. "This is between family…just a joke that's been going since home, man."

"Yeah, whatever," Stefan muttered, and then went back to his meal, dismissing Al. "That woman is too fine to be joking with. If she ain't feeling you…" He looked up at Al without blinking, his intense gray eyes pools of mystery. "You feel *me*?"

Brent laughed. "Don't eat the newbie. You know how the young bucks are—gotta come in here and flex."

Tami looked adoringly at Stefan, pointedly ignoring Al. Then she picked up her fork with a rosy grin and way too much flourish as Al walked away, defeated.

Sarah almost felt sorry for her brother.

"You said there were other scary places," Allie said nervously, as if the interpersonal drama hadn't even registered with her. "Like what?"

"Yeah, because I never, ever want to accidentally stumble into a place like the Shady Path again," Hyacinth said, her eyes squeezed tight, as if to shut out the memory.

Stefan and Brent shared knowing looks.

"On that note, we're out," Stefan said, standing.

Allie and Hyacinth stared, blinking and clearly confused. Tami shot them a glare, as if she blamed them for making Stefan leave. Sarah just sat back, watching, taking it all in.

Brent got up and then leaned down to whisper something private in Ayana's ear. He straightened and added, "Later."

"Okay," Ayana said, smiling up at him.

"You said there were other dangerous places," Allie insisted, turning back to the older girls as soon as the guys were gone.

"Oh, you'll hear all about them," Tina said, "when you get one of these bad boys." She took out a small electronic unit with a touch screen and a couple of mysterious push buttons. "This is a PIU—Personal Information Unit."

"The librarian, Mrs. Hogan, mentioned that we'd all be getting them," Allie said.

"It will be your new best friend," Ayana told her. "Don't lose it."

"It's really cool technology," Darlene said. "They took old smart phones that had been outlawed and retrofitted them. Check it out."

They all leaned in, curious and expectant.

"On here," Tina said with a grand gesture, turning her unit on, "you'll get your syllabus, class schedule, school code of conduct and your mailbox digital code. It's also got a GPS chip in it, so if students get lost, instructors can find them."

"Then how come they couldn't find the missing students?" Sarah asked quietly.

"That's the big mystery," Ayana said, looking around the table. "But, listen, don't let that spook you. There's enough day-to-day stuff you need to get under your belts right now. Just focus on that, stay away from restricted areas, and don't let one of the guys around here talk you into doing something crazy, okay?"

"Right," Darlene said, nodding rapidly. "If you've got Miss Tittle for homeroom, which you do, as first years, whatever you do, don't be late. Make sure you learn your rosters. She gives out detentions like she's giving out lunch."

All eyes remained fixed on Tina as she began to slowly scroll through the menu option on her unit. She looked up after a moment and smiled. "Since the war, with cell phones outlawed, it's gotten almost impossible to find any more that can be doctored, so treat yours as a very precious resource, and remember that it belongs to the school, not to you. Each unit has been reinforced by a white-light charged quartz crystal to keep from dark side information intercepts. You'll receive important school broadcasts on these, and you can plug into the PirateNet...we've even resurrected Twitter, not just for student-to-student communications, but so you can be in contact with your families."

"There's also a facility for downloading outlawed music that PirateNet has saved and archived," Darlene added, digging into a slab of chocolate cake.

"Sweet!" Allie said, making the other girls laugh.

"Yeah," Tina said with a smile. "You'll definitely work hard at this institution, but we don't have a complete moratorium on fun." She held up the unit again. "One more thing: This serves as your entry and exit pass—an ID badge—because of the white light and ancient prayers inside it. You'll need to press it against the lock pad panels beside each bunker exit." She held the unit between two fingers. "Note the genuine sterling on the case. Know why?"

"So a demon can't hold it?" Sarah said quickly. "That's awesome."

"Right you are," Tina said, and then moved her finger across the device. "This is your 911 alert button. If you get in trouble—maybe are being pursed—this will alert your Upper Sphere mentor as well as security."

"Tell 'em about security," Ayana said. "Otherwise, if they see Mr. Hubert, they'll pee their pants."

The girls looked warily at one another and then focused on Tina.

"Dude is about seven feet tall, midnight blue, with large bat wings and a long, spade-tipped tail."

"Stop lying," Tami said.

"For real," Tina said, casually munching on a piece of garlic bread. "Dude is so cut, his frickin' hands look like anvils, but he's got hooked claws on the ends. Red eyes, the whole nine yards."

"And they wonder what took those missing students?" Tami said, shocked. "Why the hell would they let something like that run around the campus? Shouldn't they smoke it?"

"Mr. Hubert is cool, came from Nod," Darlene said calmly. "A hybrid, and luckily on our side. His mom was some kind of maiden who got suckered by a gargoyle or whatever. Anywho…Part of your education will be to discern things with your spirit and your mind, not just your eyes. Looks can be deceiving, and prejudices and assumptions can get you hurt."

"Besides, he's really just a spirit," Tina said, handing off her PIU to Sarah while she picked at her salad. "He was lost at the battle of Morales, in Mexico, fighting against the Vampire Council and Cain…but as a warrior hybrid, he wanted to come here and help the Neteru squad guard the students. His wife, Sarina, is a teensy-weensy faery. Cute as a button—I don't know how they do it."

"He's married?" Hyacinth said with a grimace.

"Maybe if they're spirits, they don't do it anymore." Sarah said with a smile.

"But at one time they were alive and probably did." Tami tilted her head to the side and arched her eyebrows. "Just saying."

"Why are we talking about spirits—or anybody—doing it?" Hyacinth asked, closing her eyes. "I swear, Tamara, that's all you think about!"

The three older girls laughed.

"Well none of y'all need to be worrying about *doing it* until you know what you're doing," Darlene said, chuckling and polishing off her dessert.

Tina slapped her five, then turned and looked at Ayana. "That means your boyfriend's ZBing ref can't be taking Tami on one of his little jaunts into town."

"Tina!" Ayana said in a low rush. "I know. I'm not stupid. I'm not going to let any of them get hurt or caught up in something they can't control."

Sarah and Tami glanced at each other.

Just then Wil walked past on his way over to one of the food stations, and it was all eyes on him. Darlene sighed. "That new Shadow can protect me. I'd go anywhere with him and have *no* fear."

Ayana and Darlene laughed, breaking the sudden tension. Sarah had to agree with Darlene on that one. Then she noticed her cousin's laughter fade as Brent strolled back to the table. His brows were knit into an angry frown. All the girls stopped talking and stared at him, and then at Ayana.

"Shadows ain't shit," Brent said with a sneer. "Once inside my head, always there, babe. Don't forget that." He picked up Ayana's glass, throwing back the rest of her juice as if it were a shot of something more potent.

Sarah, Tami, Allie and Hyacinth exchanged meaningful glances. Ayana was mind-locked with Brent like that?

Ayana tossed her braids over her shoulder, clearly flustered, but trying to maintain her composure in front of her friends. "I thought you and Stefan were—"

"If you're finished schooling the kiddies, it's time to go," Brent said, cutting her off. "Come on, let's get out of here. Stefan and I have b-ball practice."

Ayana's cheeks were flushed with embarrassment as she turned to Tina and Darlene. "See you guys later tonight?" They nodded. She turned to Brent. "I'll meet up with you in a little bit. I want to talk to Sarah for a minute."

Brent rolled his eyes and walked off in a huff. Sarah watched him go and saw Stefan waiting by the exit. He shook his head in disgust and slipped out the door.

Jessica caught her eye and waved from across the room, where she was sitting with her fellow Blends. "Sorry," she called over. "Didn't mean to leave you guys high and dry. Forgot to go check who I'll be partnering with on this year's lab project. I want first dibs, because this year there're several cool prizes up for grabs for Upper Sphere students."

"It's cool," Sarah said, feeling a surge of sudden joy. It was nice to have several Upper Spheres looking out for her and her newbie buddies. "Maybe see ya at dinner?"

"K," Jessica said.

Ayana smiled when Sarah returned her attention to the table and said, "Come with me for a minute."

She got up, and Sarah followed, wondering what Yaya wanted to tell her. The scene she'd just witnessed between her cousin and Brent truly bothered her. Yeah, the guy was good-looking, but this wasn't like Ayana at all. Where was her fire, her fight? Sarah wondered, as they sat down a few tables away from everyone else.

"I heard about what happened between you and Melissa, and what happened to Hyacinth. I'm sorry I wasn't there to protect 'Cinth from that witch."

"It's not your fault, Yaya. That bitch has it out for me, so she's going after my friends."

"Tell me everything," Ayana said, looking grim.

"But can you block Melissa from finding out whatever I tell you...I mean, since you and Brett are, uhmmm...you know—mind-locked?"

"Piece of cake," Ayana said, waving her off and then pointing at her temple. "I've got so much white light up here against that skank that she'll fry if she goes in. So *tell* me."

Sarah did, including the quick mental snapshot she'd gleaned from Melissa regarding secrets and Stefan.

"I'm so not surprised," Ayana muttered, glancing toward Melissa. "She's afraid of you guys, as new girls and from the Net-pound, are going to replace her tired, used-up crew...and Stefan is the access man around here. He gets all kinds of contraband in and out of the school by using the Shady Path, so she wants to keep him focused on her. I'm sure she hates the attention Tami is getting, and she's even more pissed because Tami's your best bud. Understand?"

Sarah certainly understood jealousy, even if she thought Melissa had no reason to feel any.

"When Melissa came here two years ago, the first thing she did was establish herself as queen bee," Ayana went on. "Frankly, she didn't have a real tough time. She has the brains, beauty and talent to make herself Miss Number One. She's one of the strongest Clair-Vs in the school."

"Stronger than you?"

"Not anymore. Powers can get stronger over time, especially if you know how to build them. And Melissa gave me plenty of motivation to get stronger."

"She messed with you, too?" Sarah asked surprised.

Ayana gave a short laugh. "I was one of the very first people she went after. I was a Neteru Guardian kid, and if you're going to be the biggest fish in the pond, you either have to get rid of any other big fish or make the big fish act like small fish." Ayana shrugged. "I can't say it was the easiest time, but I got through it. Others didn't. She likes to attack the mind—get into your head and use your own thoughts against you. You got a little taste of that. I'm not bragging or anything, but none of you are as strong now as I was two years ago. But you do have something I didn't have."

Sarah frowned. "What?"

"Each other," Ayana said. She laughed at Sarah's blank look. "You guys can use the power of four."

"The power of four. Isn't that when four beings connect as one and it increases their power? But I thought that was sorta taboo in Nana Mar's book—I mean, when used against people, not entities."

"If a witch is screwing with you and making you fall downstairs, all bets are off." Ayana let out a huff of annoyance. "You didn't hear any of this from me, but calling for strength through the old Adinkra symbols is a completely acceptable defensive strategy. You guys just have to rest up, be unified when you put your collective energies together as you visualize the symbol, and stay in the light. If you look at the symbol, there are four quadrants, and each of you can mentally hold the light in one of them. But don't do it if you guys are tired and bickering with one another," Ayana added, "or it won't work. Let me show you."

Ayana reached into her bag and pulled out a sheet of paper and a pen. "This is called a *damedame*," she said, drawing a symbol.

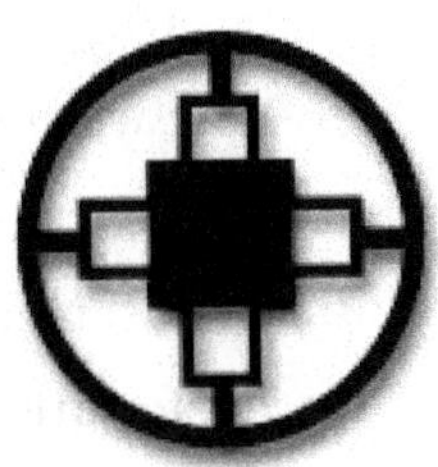

"It's the symbol for craftiness, intelligence, strategy and integrity—and believe me, you're gonna need all of those around here."

"Yeah, I recognize it. Nana kept that in the four corners of all the rooms at home. I thought it only protected spaces, not people."

"Nana knows a lot of stuff that works in multiple ways," Ayana said confidently. "Check this out. This one is called a *dwennimmen.*" She drew four connected spirals.

Ayana tapped the drawing. "The spirals emphasize the unity of the whole, representing the three elements that are essential to one's being—strength of mind, body and spirit—plus the fourth and unseen element of the divine. Actually, this is the one I'd use first, now that I think about it."

"Maaan…I've forgotten so much of what Nana used to talk about at home."

"Nothing you learn at home or in class becomes real until you actually have to use it. That's why they do live-action drills around here, boo, but you shouldn't have to worry about that until next year. Wait till you get to Mr. Everett's class, with battles and mortars whizzing by…geez Louise."

"Are you serious?"

"Yeah, and trust me, it's scary. But when something is chasing you out in the real world? That is *so* not the time to learn."

"Yaya," Sarah said in a whisper. "Last night, at home, some of us broke house rules and went outside the light barriers after dark…and a demon attacked me. So I know what you mean."

"What!" Ayana whispered back, grabbing Sarah's arms. "Were you scratched or…bitten?"

"No," Sarah murmured. "I got lucky, but I was so scared. It must have tripped over one of Nana's hidden barriers and torched on impact. Believe me, I have plenty of respect for what's out there."

"Good," Ayana said, sounding somewhat relieved but still a little skeptical. "You are so lucky Nana was here at school and had no idea what you were doing, and you'd better say a prayer of thanks that your mom and dad didn't catch you."

"You're telling me?" Sarah let out a hard breath. "All I wanna do is go to class, have fun with my friends and stay safe. I really don't want to deal with Melissa and her bull. She can run the school if she wants. I could care less, and the last thing I wanna be is one of Stefan's contraband queens. Puh-lease."

"The problem is, one, Melissa doesn't know that, and two, her freakin' ego won't let her allow you to just concede, because of who you are. She has to make it look like she beat you."

"Oh, gimme a break!" Sarah ran her fingers through her hair and held her head in both hands. "I just want her off our backs."

Ayana shook her head with a smile. "The biggest defense is just being fortified against the drama before it starts…Remember, when a small group comes together in unity, with clear focus and pure intent, they can accomplish anything. They become part of the unity. You four can invoke strength far beyond the sum of your individual powers, and that will give you protection against any attacks from Melissa—any telepathic attacks, at least. I suggest Hyacinth connect with you and Allie, since you two are the…least strong in this area, and Tami can serve as a booster. She's the one with all the fire." Ayana added, laughing, "That girl is a hot mess."

"Yaya, this is great," Sarah said. "This really is a big help, even though I might not sound like I think it is. We were actually trying to find some white light protections in the library."

Ayana laughed. "Well, I just saved you some very long hours of research."

"I can't thank you enough."

Ayana got to her feet with a grin. "No problemo—what's family for, huh? But always send prayers of protection up to the Most High and bring down the white light before you do anything. There's a very thin line between doing a legitimate ward that's coming from a correct, defensive posture, and getting caught spell-casting against another student. You know how Nana feels about that, and you don't wanna get on her bad side—or open up a hot spot in the dorm that she's gotta close."

Sarah just stared at her older cousin for a minute.

"Don't worry, boo. You'll be fine. The main thing is, I've got your back. If they really do something foul, you let me know." Ayana gave Sarah a quick hug and stood. "Now I gotta go."

Sarah jumped up and threw her arms around Ayana. "Thanks, Yaya!"

When Sarah pulled back, Ayana smiled. "Yeah, I'm the best." Then her smile faded and her expression turned serious. "Just one more thing: It's pretty obvious that Tami and Stefan are feeling each other, but tell Tami to watch herself. Stefan's a little bit of a...bad boy. And he and Melissa used to go together, you understand what I mean? She's not just his contraband distributer, they had a thing."

Sarah closed her eyes. *A bit of a bad boy*? Understatement to the fifth power. Was her cousin crazy? That meant that Brent was also really bad news for Yaya, if his close friend was Stefan.

"That's just great," Sarah said, finally looking at Ayana. "Of all the guys Tami could have the hots for, she has to pick the Wicked Witch's ex-boyfriend." She opened her eyes and looked at Ayana. "And let me guess: Melissa still wants him."

Ayana shrugged. "I don't know about that, but she definitely wouldn't want any of you peeing on her tree any more than you already are. Understand?"

"Yeah," Sarah said, suddenly feeling very tired. "I hear you."

CHAPTER 13

The first afternoon of classes was going to be interesting, to say the least. After lunch, all the new students had a one-hour orientation, followed by a crazy, abbreviated schedule of going to all their classes accompanied by other Lower Sphere students who already knew their way around the school, until it was time to break out into talent divisions at the end of the day.

But Headmistress Stone dropped a bombshell on everyone during orientation: There was going to be a Wednesday night mixer, a luau to welcome the new students, and only two days away, taking place on a day of the week that didn't conflict with anyone's Sabbath. That just added another level of stress for the newbies. None of them had been to a real party, one that wasn't just family members and other compound kids. Now, Sarah thought, she would have to really worry about what to wear, how to fix her hair, what the latest dances were. That would mean intensive training from Ayana, but her cousin had a courseload that was crazy tough, so how much free time was she likely to have?

In the meantime, there was the not-so-small matter of learning her way around the school.

Sarah was sure this frenetic test run of finding classes, getting books and figuring out what the instructors were like was designed to torture the new students. Between her interrupted sleep from the night before and the harrowing morning she'd already experienced, all she wanted to do was to pass out on her bed. Thinking about the mixer was destined to give her hives.

But finding somewhere private where she could curl into a little ball and make the world go away wasn't going to happen any time soon.

The minute the end-of-lunch bell rang, the abbreviated afternoon started off with homeroom with the notorious Mrs. Tittle. First period was English—again, with battleaxe Tittle—second period was math, which was then followed by biology, chemistry, lunch—which was skipped, since they'd already had it—gym, then history, and finally what would be a grueling ninety-minute lecture that lasted until 5:00 P.M. once real classes began, where each specialty met to work on honing their gifts. Today talent division classes would only be an hour, but that was still a long time. The vastness of the entire challenge made her head hurt.

What Sarah really couldn't figure out was how in the world was she supposed to squeeze in extracurricular activities like the Night Vision Photog Society, the debate team, theater club, band or student government? With all the papers they had to write, when was there going to be time for writing articles for *The Daily Papyrus* or join the Society of Pirate Networks computer club, let alone play sports or sign up for the Dimensional Explorers Club? Yet the Uppers seemed to find time to do it all, and just thinking about that left her feeling totally inadequate.

All first years had a majority of their classes together, so she, Tami, Allie Hyacinth and all the guys had the same instructors as all the other newbies. However, they did have a couple of advanced classes, thanks to their education at home, so they had Dimensional History-walking and math with the third and fourth Spheres. She was pleased to discover Wil was on the accelerated track, too. Unfortunately, being in advanced classes meant that Sarah and her friends would have to encounter Melissa Gray and her crew daily, which was more of Melissa, Amy and Angelica than she ever wanted to see.

So when Sarah walked into yet another classroom and saw her nemesis sitting there surrounded by her circle of admirers, her eyes narrowed dangerously. Every time they'd run into each other since lunch, Melissa'd had something smart to say. It was always just a snicker or a mutter, followed by an evil glance, before she began whispering to her friends again. Tami was near the explosion point, but poor Allie and Hyacinth looked positively miserable. Then and there Sarah decided, she wasn't going to shrink from this bully. If it was going to be drama, so be it. She and Melissa had some unfinished business where Hyacinth was concerned, anyway. This time Melissa only glanced in Sarah's direction before looking away dismissively as Sarah passed by.

Thankfully, all seating was alphabetical. As a Rivera, that meant Sarah would always be in the rear, near Allie, a Weinstein. But that also meant she had to sit next to her brother in every single flippin' class except talent division.

Now Sarah walked casually to the back of the room and sat down, dropping her book bag at her feet. She crossed her legs, leaned back in her chair, ignoring her brother, and said, "Hey, Melissa!"

Melissa turned around, wondering who was calling her. She raised an eyebrow when she saw that it was Sarah.

Sarah stared into Melissa's eyes. "Next time," she said, "why don't you take up your problem with me, instead of 'Cinth—unless you're afraid that you can't handle me."

Al just shook his head as Melissa glanced at Hyacinth and Allie, then smiled and leaned forward, resting her chin on her hand. "Protective, are we?" she murmured.

Just then their instructor, Mr. Everett, entered the room, and Melissa turned around and faced front.

Mr. Everett walked up to the desk, put his books and briefcase down, and stood facing them.

Though chubby and only four-eleven, he was the stereotypical professor in a white button-down Oxford shirt, a brown tweed jacket with patches on the elbows and tan corduroy pants, and he played with the buttons on his cuffs as he impatiently waited for his students to get settled. The moment they did, he beamed at his class expectantly.

"Walking between dimensions," he said. "We of the Twi people have extensive experience in this." He gestured excitedly as he began to walk up and down the aisles.

"This is the cornerstone to understanding history," he said with great flourish, continuing to talk with his hands. "Not just understanding the past in order to make sense of one's future, but rather identifying with its challenges and triumphs. That is the Sankofa of reason…looking back to chart a course forward that is wiser. Shall we begin?"

Sarah looked up quickly when, to her surprise, Mr. Everett fell silent. She noticed that all the students were glancing around nervously. Their instructor was moving his lips in what seemed like a silent prayer. He pointed to the four corners of the room, then up toward the ceiling.

In awe, she realized that wherever he left his invisible fingerprints in the air, tiny golden sparkles remained. Then each twinkling asterisk spawned a line of golden light, the lines connecting in a giant square over the students' heads.

Murmurs of awe and delight buffeted her senses as Sarah stared up at the translucent golden square that had replaced the ceiling. Mr. Everett stretched out his arms and began to lower the golden light until it became apparent that what had looked like a square was actually the underside of a crystalline, golden tinged pyramid.

He pushed one corner of it with a finger, making it begin to slowly rotate counterclockwise. He released a long, satisfied breath and briefly closed his eyes, smiling.

"Ah…" he murmured. "That is so much better." He opened his eyes and sent his gaze around the room. "So young to have so much negative energy pervading your temples—my goodness, students, your minds, bodies and spirits are wide open to dark influences in this state!" He *tsk*ed, then shuddered as though he'd swallowed something bitter. "We cannot walk between worlds, children, with hearts and spirits so dark and heavy. No, no, no, no, no. That is not of Ma'at." Mr. Everett closed his eyes again. "In a few minutes we will begin. I will wait."

Sarah just nodded as the entire class stared up at the darkening pyramid, which looked as though it was vacuuming up an angry storm. Dense plumes of sooty gray-black energy filled the gleaming crystal like dirty dish water that churned from some inner conflict all its own. Then it dawned on her. Mr. Everett's class cleansings were sucking the students' residual dark-consciousness energy up into the pyramid! She bit her lip. Mr. Everett opened his eyes and clapped hard, and suddenly the structure was gone.

"Yo!" Miguel shouted. "That's crazy!"

Pandemonium broke out but quickly settled as Mr. Everett repeated the process. The second time, the pyramid only seemed to be able to vacuum up stray plumes of light gray.

"Good enough for day one," he said calmly. "I have to do this every class," he added with a weary sigh. "Maybe, before this semester is over, we'll have an opalescent day. One must remain ever hopeful." He looked at the class and tilted his head. "This is why we cannot do the history of the dark side until you all learn to carry your own inner light more capably. That realm—the dark side—doesn't do theoretical. To use a very outdated term, it likes to *keep it real*, as they used to say, and sometimes the dark powers break through the veil between, and a simulation is no longer a simulation—very unfortunate circumstances for unprepared students. Therefore, for this semester, we will look at history from the perspective of the light."

He walked over to his desk and hoisted his chubby little body up to sit on it, leaning forward eagerly and talking with his hands again. Sarah found herself worried for his safety as he edged closer and closer to toppling over, yet he never did.

"We live inside an energy-plasma, multidimensional grid with choices of selves replicated out to at least the twenty-fifth plane."

Blank stares greeted Mr. Everett's bold statement, and he simply smiled.

"Twenty-five reduces to the number seven. In other words, two plus five equals seven. And seven is the supreme number, the number of the Creator and creation. And in creation, everything replicates in sevens and threes…but I'll leave that for Professor Watson, who will be teaching you cosmic math. What is important for you to take away from this class is that there are twenty-five potential yous out there in the cosmic grid. You've become the one you are now as a result of the choices you've selected from that grid. There's a brave you and a not so brave you, a more physical you and the converse of that…there's a nerdy you," he said, looking at Alejandro with a wide grin, "and a heroic you," he added, giving Donnie a jaunty wink.

"So. Who will you be?" Mr. Everett looked around. "What energy will you magnetize from the grid to maximize your potential? We can all be better than we've heretofore dreamed…our potential is unlimited, as long as we're light beings and not functioning from the negative."

He opened his arms wide, and a blue-white, sparking grid overlaid the classroom, to the awed admiration of the students. Sarah could actually hear the hum of electromagnetic charge thrumming through each axis line and square.

"The universe is a vibrant, pulsing, living organism, as are the earth and every planet and creature, down to the very last cell and atom. This is the source from which our *Tacticals* draw their wonderfully elegant charges. This is the source of white Light that our stoneworkers and white-lighters gather their *juice* from, as you kids say. It is this grid that our seers enter to mentally race along an energy line to see past, present or future, and it's the site from which our telepaths can draw down thoughts, using it almost like a chat room or a three-way cell phone call."

Hyacinth reached out, mouth open with fascination, and let her fingers delicately trace a visible line. “I’ve never seen it, could just intuit it,” she said quietly.

Even Melissa Gray, for all her haughty snobbery, was clearly impressed.

Lisa Chapman touched a line and then squealed with delight. “There are murmurs on the lines!”

“Yes,” Mr. Everett said, beginning to rock where he sat. “For my *Audios*, this is where those murmurs are captured…those whispers that are too faint for the average person to hear.”

“But what about us *Ollies*, Mr. Everett?” Akiba, one of the new girls who had been placed in the Olfactory division, called out.

“I am so glad you asked that, child,” the instructor said, clapping his hands and popping off his desk. “Smell, taste, sensation—Blends, you have a combination, so you listen up, too. It’s all in the grid. *All of it.*” He looked around the room, mischief twinkling in his eyes. “Shall we journey, so I can show you?”

“Yeah!”

“Cool!”

Consensus rang out.

“Then let’s go to a historic battle. Hmmm…how about the Battle of Morales? You will experience being there as a point on the grid, but in truth you will be walking *in-between*. You will feel the rush of sensation, smell the gunfire discharge…you might even upchuck or wet your pants. But I want you to feel the past, live a piece of it, so that you’ll understand why your lessons here are not just abstract data points to amuse your teachers’ draconian proclivities, or to fulfill our desire to torture you…but rather a way to prepare you for what you’re going to face once you leave these hallowed halls.”

Almost every student leaned forward—the chance at a field trip too seductive to resist. Not a single student could feign cool boredom as their desks melted away and they found themselves on the battlefield.

Sarah flattened herself to the ground as huge mortars rocked the earth. Charging demon cavalry scaled a wall, and behind them there was a castle under siege. Holy water catapults sent napalm-like fire to scorch the demon-covered earth, and she heard Donnie scream as Al yanked Tami out of the line of a hurling stake that had been released from a crossbow.

"Get down, get down!" Val yelled, yanking Hyacinth and Allie out of the way of Uzi-fire.

A black nightmare stallion bearing a demon warrior swinging a huge spiked mace was heading her way. Sarah had to get out of the way of the massive cloven hooves that thundered toward her. A bolt of white light exploded the rider and sent the horse down hard on its shoulder, skidding rapidly in her direction. Wil yanked her out of the way just in the nick of time. Bullets passed through Akiba, and she fainted. Trying to escape, Melissa ran blindly, and the ground opened up beneath her to reveal camouflaged pikes in a pit trap. Instinctively, Sarah reached out and grabbed her hand.

"Don't let me fall! Don't let me fall!" Melissa screamed, clawing at the muddy earth as it gave way all around her.

Her body began to slide as she kicked the air above a gaping hole filled with sure death. Gargoyle-like Harpies came out of the mud, trying to drag her onto the pikes as Sarah, joined by Wil and Val, held onto Melissa's slippery hands for dear life. Al spread his wings, trying to airlift Tami and another girl behind the castle wall, where it seemed the Guardians were holed up. But a black bolt from the tip of the dark general's sword was headed his way, and he turned just in time to face a huge fanged warrior shouting his name.

“I am Cain, son of Dante. How dare you defile the earth with your presence?”

Al dropped and rolled, pulling his two classmates toward cover. But behind him, Sarah saw their father’s face, dirty, bloodied, the black charge meant for him and not his son.

The divide broke, students huddled in the center of the classroom as several Harley Davidsons suddenly cleared the barrier wall around a fortress-like hacienda, bearing Guardians on kamikaze missions against the demons making an all-out rush against them. It was as if a new reality had poured into their classroom like water bursting through a weakened dam, replacing what had just seconds ago been a normal school room.

Still holding Melissa’s slippery hands with the help of Wil and Val, Sarah glanced up with a grimace, a prayer not to drop her classmate in her heart, only to see her mother go airborne amid mortar fire. Wil began trying to attach a Tactical charge anchor around Melissa’s waist. Then suddenly the ground quaked, and Melissa slipped out of both Val’s grip and hers. Sarah’s scream matched Melissa’s, and she covered her head, not wanting to hear the crunch and gush of her classmate’s death. Val’s elongated “Noooooo!” made Sarah cover her ears, but then another thunderous explosion deafened her to any sound.

Things moved in slow motion as she spat out mud and opened her eyes long enough to see herself caught in the center of a clash between forces wielding huge blades, machetes, semi-automatics…there were even Guardians pulling pins on grenades and lobbing them as they launched themselves into battle. Shadows suddenly fanned out from all around her, covering the students and slashing at the demons. The vortex opened, and she saw scratches being etched into the ground, which for a second flashed in her vision as the classroom floor before once again becoming dirt, made by fingers frantically trying to gain purchase and keep from being dragged in.

Students covered their heads and braced for impact. There was nowhere to run, nowhere to hide. Sweat covered her body. She heard her classmates sobbing. Most seemed to be paralyzed, hyperventilating or barely breathing. Mr. Everett's clap brought them back. The vortex instantly closed at the sound.

The stench of gunfire, mud and death receded. Students sprawled on the floor in a heap, Melissa and Akiba amongst them.

"This is unity," Mr. Everett said simply, appearing very pleased with himself as students wiped tears from their faces.

Several students leaned over and hurled.

"Very good. Get it all out. But I bet you will never forget the battle of Morales, will you?" When they all just looked at him, he laughed. "Oh, this was nothing, just wait until the final exam."

CHAPTER 14

"My brain is leaking out my ear," Tami said as they stopped by their lockers.

They had just come from chemistry, which, they'd heard from some of the other students, was normally taught by the cheerful Ms. Guilliume—but unfortunately she was taking a sick day on account of one of her experiments having gone awry. That meant they had to endure Mr. Peterson as a substitute, and he ran his class like it was a military platoon.

"How do they expect us to keep up with this crazy schedule?" Tami asked.

"You're a Guardian, Rider. Guardians endure," Sarah said, mimicking Mr. Peterson.

Tami saluted sharply, while Sarah, Allie and Hyacinth laughed.

Sarah turned away and was putting her books in her locker when she heard Allie scream.

They all whirled around to see Allie standing there covered in green slime.

"What the—"

Laughter echoed through the halls as Sarah, Tami and Hyacinth stared in disbelief at their slime-covered friend. It quickly became apparent to Sarah what had happened.

"Booby trapped locker," Sarah said through lowered fangs.

"*Melissa*," Tami said, just as furious.

Allie was gasping in despair and sparking all over the place.

Sarah slammed her locker shut. "Let's get her back to the dorms."

Allie was drawing more and more attention, which only caused her to become more and more distressed. But a mid-hall collision knocked the wind out of Sarah as the girls quickly rounded a corner on their way to their room. A pair of unfortunately familiar hazel eyes glared at her.

"Watch it, compound brat." Melissa Gray flipped a silky strand of jet-black hair over her shoulder. "This is the second time you've been in my way. Now, if you'll excuse me, I need to get to my locker."

"I see your girl already found hers," Amy Feingold said, and the witches all laughed.

Tami lunged at Amy suddenly, but Hyacinth grabbed Tami just in time.

"Lemme go!" Tami said, trying to twist out of Hyacinth's hold. "I need a reason to get sent home anyway."

"Oh, please, do let her go," Melissa said coolly. "I'd love to see her get expelled on day one. Maybe she'll learn how to stay away from other people's men then."

"What are you talking about?" Tami said, panting.

That's right, Tami doesn't know, Sarah thought. *I should have found a way to tell her.* But everything had been happening so fast, and there were eavesdroppers everywhere. She'd planned to tell Tami about everything once the four of them were alone.

"Don't play stupid," Melissa told Tami, wrinkling her aristocratic nose as if she found Tami distasteful. "You know that Stefan belongs to me."

"Oh, yeah?" Tami said smirking. "Did you remember to tell *him* that?"

Melissa laughed. "Oh, my God, you have no idea, do you?" she said. "Do you honestly think you can handle someone like Stefan Oaphse?" She looked Tami up and down. " He will eat you alive."

"You really did this because you have a beef over some guy?" Sarah asked. "And why Allie, if your problem is with Tami? Or me?"

"Oh, I didn't do anything," Melissa said, studying her nails. "I think you're just not popular, brat. You or your stupid crew. It's too bad, really." She turned to leave, then tossed a warning over her shoulder. "You know how it is in the world—the weak get picked off first. It's not my fault that Hyacinth and Allie are your weakest links."

Sarah was seething now, so furious that she couldn't even think of a quick comeback. She should have let Melissa drop into the pit in Mr. Everett's class just to see her piss her pants!

Amy smirked. "Might want to keep an eye on your two klutzy friends there. Never know when something bad might happen to them when they're all by themselves."

Sarah wasn't sure how it happened, but as Amy turned to walk away, the pool of shadow where she had been standing suddenly pulsed and she went down as though struck. Her face hit the floor, and she screamed in pain as blood smeared the gleaming marble.

"Oh, my God! Did you see that?" Melissa shouted, going to Amy's side.

"Yo, she just fell," a student in the crowd that had gathered to watch the argument called out.

Amy was sobbing and holding her mouth.

"Ladies, ladies," Mr. Foggerty, the biology prof, said, coming out of his classroom and waving a long, floppy hand. "What seems to be the trouble? Don't you all have classes this afternoon? And, heavens, have you been to the pool already?" he said, motioning to Allie. "Why are you all wet and dripping?" He blinked bulbous eyes behind thick glasses, waiting on a response. Squinting at them all more closely, he drew back with a gasp. "That young lady is bleeding...and green slime? Where did that come from? I demand an answer!"

His Upper Sphere students craned their necks to see what was going on as their instructor blinked several times in obvious annoyance when no one answered his questions, bringing his large caterpillar eyebrows together and adjusting his thick bifocals up the bridge of his humongous nose.

“Then if you are all intent on silence, I suggest some of you get that young woman to the infirmary and the rest of you help your friend to the showers. This is a disgrace! Disperse immediately, before I alert Headmistress Stone. This hallway is not for congregating or settling petty disputes—you are disturbing my students. Hurry off.”

He shooed them away as though they were a cloud of gnats and then stepped back into his classroom with a loud “Harrumph!” before he slammed the door.

It was clear that he hadn’t heard the content of their argument and had only witnessed the result—elevated female voices, a cut and green slime. But a bunch of other students *had* heard it, when they’d stopped to hear the commotion in the hall.

Sarah led her group one way—toward the showers; Melissa led hers in the opposite direction toward the infirmary.

A question kept niggling in Sarah’s head. Had Amy Feingold fallen because she’d moved too quickly on a polished floor…or had something else really happened? Had she really seen what she thought she had? Amy had been standing in shadow, and strange things happened with shadows when Sarah was around. That creepy feeling was back, too, as though something was staring at her. A chill raced down her spine.

The moment they hit their dorm room, Allie dashed to her closet. She was so upset she was sparking and had to keep touching wooden objects to dampen the charge.

“Somebody ground her, would ya?” Tami muttered when a stray spark zapped her.

Hyacinth foolishly grabbed Allie’s hand, then jumped back, silky hair frizzed at the ends. “Ow, watch it!”

"Sorry," Allie said, holding onto a bookshelf and counting to ten, watching dust motes scatter. "But I have to hurry or I'm going to miss the next class—you guys don't have to wait."

"It's just gym, and I'm not going to leave you. I'll wait—Hyacinth and Tami can go, so they don't get in trouble, too. But I'm probably gonna get kicked out, anyway," Sarah said, beginning to pace.

"Get kicked out for what?" Tami put her hands on her hips. "Nobody pushed her. Nobody did jack! She tripped. Maybe she slid on some of that slime bomb they put in Allie's locker. Served her right, and if they tell, we tell—so it's a fair guess that nobody is gonna rat. None of us are leaving Allie, and none of us are getting in trouble. We'll tell the gym teacher that some anonymous person boobytrapped Allie's locker and slimed her, and we went to help her. We've got evidence," Tami added, waving her arms toward Allie's dripping clothes. "And plenty of kids saw what happened. A half-truth is always the most convincing lie, and I'm sure that Allie isn't the first freshman to get pranked by an Upper Sphere, so stop stressing. Melissa's flunky slipped on the slime, so what? We're not responsible."

But Sarah knew in her heart that wasn't what had happened to Amy. She hugged herself and leaned against a desk, trying to calm down. It totally freaked her out that a shadow had come to life and literally attacked a girl, and she was the only one who had seen it.

"I can't go back to the Clair-V's," Hyacinth said. "Why did you have to try to fight that girl, Tami? Why couldn't you try to be nicer to them?"

"Them? *Them*!" Tami shot back, fuming. "Did you hear what that cow said to *me*? And the worst part was you holding me back when I could have ended all of this by opening up a can of whup-ass on Melissa. That girl has had it coming!"

"And then what?" Sarah said, quickly getting between Tami and the others. "You'd be kicked out of school, or maybe we all would—because if you punched her lights out, her friends would have jumped in, and then we would've jumped in, because we wouldn't let them beat you down, no matter what."

Tense silence strangled the group for a moment as Tami turned away, still fuming, but seeming somewhat mollified that Sarah and the others had her back.

Sarah went to her to try to calm her down. This wasn't getting them anywhere, and it was burning precious time. They might have to cut more than gym if Allie didn't get to the showers soon.

"There's so much I have to fill you in on, Tami," Sarah said in a gentler tone, trying to reach beyond Tami's rage. Although now was certainly not the time to mention that Tami needed to back off Stefan—even if her reason wasn't because of Melissa but because he was bad news—she did need to catch her friend up on how they could protect themselves from another hallway attack.

"I talked to Ayana after lunch. She showed me a strong white light defense we can use. I was going to tell you guys once we were where the walls didn't have ears, but the day was going by so fast, everyone was watching us, snickering about us…there just wasn't time and—"

"Who cares about this stupid school?" Tami finally muttered, cutting Sarah off and glaring at her friends.

"Give it up, Tam," Allie said in a rare display of anger. "Tell me that just because of a stupid fight with some jealous hater, you honestly want to go back home where there's nobody left there but parents?" When Tami turned away from her, Allie rounded Tami to get in her face. "And all to maybe get Melissa and her witches sent back to their neighborhood to fight beside their parents without the Academy's extra training and maybe—"

"And that's our problem how?" Tami said, throwing up her hands and beginning to pace. "I hope they *do* get shipped back to their sorry sewer-hole compounds and have to take mortar shells and dodge demon—"

"Because the same thing would happen to us," Allie said pointedly. "Or, more likely, we'd be locked up in the compound, still home-schooled until we were of age. They're not gonna put Neteru team kids on the front line, so if that's what you're hoping would happen, stop dreaming. It'd be six more years at home and not a chance of doing anything interesting, meeting anyone interesting, or going anywhere new. Think about it, Tamara Rider. It would just be the four of *us girls* there for *six years*—no, *seven*, if you count the balance of this year."

Allie nodded when Tami's eyes grew wide with dawning reality. "Yeah. You think about it, Tamara. Watching old DVDs from decades ago…old bands, old cartoons, all the outlawed stuff we've seen over and over again until I could throw up. I want to learn the new dances, the latest slang, the newest styles from out in the world. You heard it in orientation—they're having a dance on Wednesday night. The first real mixer we've ever been to, and I want to go! So don't screw this up, all right?"

When Tami looked away, Allie pressed on with conviction. "I'm pretty sure that I could do the boring time, and probably so could 'Cinth and Sarah, but can *you*? All you've talked about since you got here was this hottie or that hunk—you wanna go back under your dad's watchful eye and sit at home missing *everything*?"

Quiet crackled between the four friends. When Tamara didn't immediately respond, it was obvious the stalemate was over. Sarah stared at Allie in amazement. Of all people, *Allie* had broken through with an argument that *Tami* couldn't beat? The really weird part was, Allie had also broken the code on what was at stake for them all—something she hadn't been able to define until Allie actually said it out loud. There was freedom here, even in its very strange disguise of onerous rules and regulations.

So, as much as she hated the rules and regulations, as much as she hated the lack of time and personal privacy, as much as she hated the girls who had it out for them, it wasn't until she saw a sea of students from all over the world that she'd realized just how isolated they'd been. Curiosity had won out over dread, at least for the moment. With the chance to be around all those kids her own age and older, even the shadows didn't feel as scary—especially since they seemed to be siding with her.

They might not really want to move forward into this scary void called, the Academy, but they also didn't want to be left behind back home, to miss the exciting newness of it all. None of them wanted to blow the opportunity of a lifetime on something stupid, and even though no one in her small group had had the chance yet to listen to the school policies on their PIU's, she was pretty sure that a hallway brawl over some guy they didn't even know would be frowned upon.

"All right," Sarah finally said. "One team—us against them."

"One team," Tami said grudgingly, and they all placed their hands together in an air pile.

"I've gotta show you guys what Ayana showed me this afternoon, so if we're gonna skip a class, let's make it worth our while."

"Can I get a shower first?" Allie said in a forlorn tone.

"Yeah, but hurry back," Sarah said, glancing at the time on her PIU. "I don't trust those chicks, now that one of them got hurt. I bet they'll have an even worse ambush waiting for us now."

CHAPTER 15

To Allie's credit, she was in and out of the shower within ten minutes, and had wound her hair up into a wet bun and was dressing quickly as Sarah produced the symbols Ayana had drawn.

"We have to be united," Sarah warned, looking around at her friends' faces. "We need to call down the white light of protection over each of us individually *and* the group, and then imagine ourselves in a spiral of white light. Close your eyes and make that white light follow you to the center, where all of us meet. Hyacinth can help with the telepathic visuals. Tam, we need your fire of intention, and Allie, we could use your kinetic charge. We put all our hands together, and I'll say the prayer, okay?"

"Let's do this thing," Tami said. "But I sure wish Yaya had given you something to blow them away with."

Sarah let out a hard sigh. "We've been through that a hundred times, Tamara, so quit it. No attacks, school rules. Nobody can fault us for self-defense, but—"

"Okay, okay," Tami fussed. "Let's just do this thing."

"Here's the other thing…Yaya said we shouldn't do this when at odds or mad at—"

"Like that's gonna happen when around here?" Tami just stared at her and Allie and Hyacinth nodded.

"We have to protect ourselves," Hyacinth said in a quiet rush after a moment. "There may not be an optimal time...Tami could be right."

All eyes were on Sarah, and even Allie nodded to agree with the others. Against Sarah's better judgment, she released a long sigh and let her shoulders slump. "Okay, okay, you guys win," she said, glancing around the group. "But don't blame me if anything backfires."

"No one will blame you, Sarah," Allie said softly. "But we have to try."

Sarah nodded. What Allie said was true. They needed protection and sometimes one had to come up with a solution on the fly. Sarah waited a moment until the group settled down and everyone made a pile of hands. She held the symbol above their unified fists and gave Allie a little nod. Slowly Allie's blue-white static charge covered their hands and then began to swirl out from the center of the dwennimmen, spiraling around each girl.

"I humbly call the angels of protection," Sarah murmured as each girl closed her eyes. She could see the white light circling her body and felt the slight crackling charge envelop her like a warm blanket. "Please allow only things that are good and from the Light to help us, to be around us, and to protect us. Keep us safe in all dimensions of time and space in which we exist. If anyone tries to do us harm, let only good come from it."

"Amen to that," Tami muttered, and got a swift kick from Hyacinth. "Ow."

Sarah cleared her throat, frowned, and pressed on. "We ask that the angels hear our prayer. We also pray for those students who weren't so lucky, who have gone missing or worse. We are all Light. *Ashe*."

Sarah opened her eyes, and her friends slowly opened theirs, waiting until the static charge around them withdrew before letting go. For the moment, Sarah felt empowered. They had done something proactive, but that certainly didn't mean the threat had passed. It was simply dormant, crouching and latent in the shadows.

"You think it'll work?" Allie asked quietly.

Sarah let out a weary sigh. "I guess only time will tell."

* * *

Thankfully, the rest of the school day was relatively peaceful. The girls' gym teacher, Ms. Akoben, hadn't even been there. An Upper Sphere student had taken roll and shown the girls the basic drills they'd do, but since no one had brought their sweat pants, sneakers or t-shirts to class, the Upper had only walked them around the equipment, telling them what to expect tomorrow. It was a wasted class period that the students had most likely spent gabbing.

The Upper Sphere girl had just shaken her head and fought a smile when Sarah explained about why they hadn't been in class. To Sarah's surprise, the older girl had a heart and simply placed four check marks on the clipboard next to their names and said sarcastically, "You owe me, kid."

Then Sarah braced herself as she saw her brother headed her way. Al was coming from the boys' gym class, and it would be impossible to avoid him. She was ready for an argument, but when his expression gentled and he touched her arm, she didn't know what to think.

"You guys okay?" he asked quietly, looking at Allie and Hyacinth. "I heard what happened. That was foul."

"We're okay," Allie said in a soft voice. "Just more humiliated than anything else."

Al shook his head and ran his fingers through his hair, seeming torn. "I heard 'Cinth got tripped a few times, too."

"I'll live," Hyacinth said, and cast her gaze down to the floor.

Al ignored Tami's crossed arms and hard glare, and looked at Sarah. "Sis, seriously…I know we don't always get along, but blood is thicker than water."

"Thanks," Sarah said, really needing to hear that from him. "It's nothing we can't handle, but watch your back Al, okay? Some people around here aren't what they're pretending to be."

She noticed that the other guys from the compound were hanging back, waiting for Al, but also giving him some space to talk to the girls alone.

"So did you already get what you wanted from that skank, Melissa? Is that why you're back here trying to act like you're with us? Or did you finally remember who your real friends are?" Tami said, clearly unconvinced that Al was being genuine.

"You're one to talk," he shot back, his tone hardening. "I'm not the one slobbering over that spooky kid—Stefan's a nice weirdo addition to your trophy case, Tamara."

Caught between her brother and her best friend, for a moment Sarah didn't know what to do. Truthfully, all she wanted was peace. "Al…"

"I'm out, Sarah," he said, glaring at Tami before turning back to her. "You be careful, too, okay?"

Sarah watched her brother walk off and merge with the other students milling in the hallway between classes. Part of her had wanted to say the same things Tami had, to get back at him for initially siding with Melissa over them, but another part of her totally understood where Al was coming from. How did one control a crush? Truthfully, they were all guilty of having one. In that moment, she wished that Tami could have kept her big mouth shut and just allowed Al's rare display of niceness to shine through.

"Good riddance," Tami muttered, and began to walk toward the Blends lecture.

"That's still her brother…our compound brother," Allie said, staring up at Tami.

"Yeah, and he did come back to us and really wasn't cool with what Melissa did to us. That counts for something," Hyacinth said, siding with Allie.

"C'mon, Tam…I know my brother can be a jerk sometimes, but ease up on him. We just did that prayer, and he came back to us acting nice. Like…just for once, let the grudge stuff go."

"Whatever." Tami hiked her backpack up higher on her shoulder, clearly ready to take on any challengers.

"I've got library orientation after Blends. I need to run over there and find out what I have to bring to that," Sarah said in a weary tone. She was glad to have an excuse to get away from all of them. "I'll catch you later."

For the first time since she'd arrived at school, she wanted—no, correction, needed—to get away from her closest friends. The bickering was wearing her out, and the constant obsessing about Melissa was getting old. She just hoped that with everybody so freaked out, Ayana's unity of strength ward would actually hold.

Plus, the more she thought about it, she really hated how Tami had embarrassed Al at lunch. If it had just been between the family, that would be one thing—but T had punked Al in front of some older guy, and a creep to boot. That was so not cool. But, of course, there was no way to say that to Tami without her blowing up. Right now Sarah just wanted a few hours where she could focus on anything but conflict.

Heading toward the sanctuary of the library, Sarah walked so quickly that she was almost running. When she rounded the corner, she skidded to a halt and her breath hitched. Wil was headed in her direction with a drop-dead gorgeous smile on his face.

"You got a minute?" he asked.

Sarah blinked and just stared at him for a second. Was he asking her if she had time to hang with him? "I've got Blends lecture—but not for fifteen minutes, so…I guess so. Why?"

"I was just wondering if we could talk. I heard what happened today…are you all right?"

"Yeah." A plume of butterflies took flight in her belly all at once, and she tried to keep her expression as neutral as possible.

"So can we just talk?"

"Sure."

"Cool," he said, opening the library door for her. "Let's go in here where it's quiet, and then we can run to talents. Afterward…maybe…"

"I, uhm…I have library orientation, but after that…"

"Cool. Well, I can come back after talents and track practice, and hang out at the library. I just wanna tell you something—it won't take long, if you've got a minute now, though?"

"Okay."

She wanted to kick herself. What was with the one word answers? But for the life of her, she couldn't think of anything witty or sophisticated to say to him. Keeping her responses aloof and simple seemed like the best option as she followed him to a table on the far side of the room, where nobody else was sitting.

She sat down, expecting him to take the seat across from her, only to be surprised when he actually sat down right next to her. Thoughts crashed inside her mind like a multi-car collision, and the first thing out of the pile-up and her mouth was everything she'd wanted to know about his relationship with Melissa.

"So what is the long story with you, Patty and Melissa?" She stared at him, waiting for some explanation that made sense.

Wil smiled, not seeming at all surprised that she'd gone there. "I knew you'd wanna know…especially after what happened earlier today. Listen, I heard all about it, and for the record, I'm not on their side. I really feel bad about the way Melissa is treating you and your friends. She can be a little over the top sometimes, if you know what I mean."

Sarah shrugged and looked away. "I don't know how you could even be involved with them. You seem so nice, and I don't know about Patty, but I sure know Melissa's not."

"Patty is different from her sister," he said with a long sigh, and then he dropped his gaze as though studying the fine grain of the gleaming walnut table. "It's all so complicated. We grew up in the same compound for a while…my dad had met my Mom in Italy when he was on a campaign there. My Mom got pregnant, had me, and I grew up in what was then Italy till I was three. It was a long time till he could come back and get me. He did when he heard she'd died. Took me to his compound back in old Boston and from age three until I was thirteen, I stayed there. Then he sent me to Italy for two years to get to know some of my mother's people and to train...Boston was under siege, and I think he wanted me out of harm's way. Last summer, they needed everybody's help. I came back—all the kids who were my age and older had to come back from wherever their parents had sent them to hide. But finally Boston fell, like a lot of the compounds on the East Coast. Things happened—Patty and I got together, even though she's a couple years older than me…wartime crisis can bring people together who normally might not even look at each other, but it didn't last. It was sort of a summer thing when I turned fifteen. She and I were, and still are, two very different people, but it's amazing what location, limited choices and hormones will do. So when my dad went back to Italy, I went with him."

"Oh…"

Wil looked up. "It's over, Sarah. We're just friends."

She didn't know what else to say. Part of her believed him, the part that was gazing into his magnificent sea-green eyes. But there was a part of her that felt cheated by not having known him first.

"Sarah…it was pretty rough back there in Boston," Wil said quietly. "Martial law, the whole area was flooded…food was scarce, and all up in the Salem region, Beantown, New Hampshire—the whole area—there are a bunch of really old covens that have made some serious pacts with the dark side." He let out a long breath and took one of her hands. "I'm not making excuses for Melissa's behavior, I'm just saying that her past might have something to do with it. There were months without fresh produce, people scavenged whatever meat they could from city wildlife."

"City wildlife?" Sarah leaned forward, thoroughly involved in what he was revealing to her.

"Strays," Wil said, looking down.

Sarah's stomach lurched, but she remained very, very still, listening and feeling his pain down into the marrow of her bones.

"Vermin," he pressed on, seeing that her eyes contained no judgment or laughter. He looked down again, speaking in a quiet confession. "Pigeons. Stealing canned goods from government checkpoint-controlled food outlets. Living wet, never being able to fully dry out. Mildew…I hate it to this day. Ragged clothes…man…and water was scarce, so you didn't waste it bathing." He looked up and sat straighter. "My Mom died keeping walkers away from our compound in Italy. The cities were overrun. Zaphon's agents of evil, his minions', goal was to starve out all resistance fighters, and he almost did. Trust me, he might have been driven back to the Dark Realms and injured during the Armageddon, but he's still got plenty who serve him and the Dark Lord. I was lucky…my dad called me back to Boston. That's why my dad is so into material things, because for a long time we didn't have them. It doesn't make it right, just explains why he is like he is. Patty and Melissa got sent here earlier, as little kids, for partial semesters when their parents needed to stash them somewhere safe. Finally when it all came apart, they got to come here when our compound completely fell and the team scattered. I don't even know what happened to their mom and dad."

Sarah gazed at him, trying to see past his irises and into his heart. Empathy washed over her. They'd never missed a meal in her compound, and neither she nor any of the kids she'd grown up with could fathom what losing a parent was like. All she could think of was the safe, warm beds they'd slept in and the luscious meals prepared by Aunt Inez's loving hands. She almost felt ashamed for hating Melissa.

"I'm sorry," she murmured, squeezing his warm hand.

"I was lucky. I got out," he replied with a slight smile. "But it wasn't all bad. I learned a lot. It made me stronger."

"It made you a Shadow," Sarah said, unable to hide her awe.

Wil looked away, seeming pleased by her compliment, and his bashful response only endeared him to her more. "You've gotta be on your toes in an environment like that. Anybody could have done it."

"No," she said in a gentle tone that brought his gaze back to hers. "A lot of other kids grew up there, but they didn't make Shadows. You should be really proud."

"If you met our Professor, you wouldn't think I'm lucky," Wil said, trying to lighten the mood.

"What's it like in Shadows?" she asked eagerly, scooting over closer to him.

"Aw, man…it's crazy. The Prof is a true hard ass. But I can tell you all that junk later. What about you? What was it like growing up in the Neteru Compound? Your Mom and Dad are like living legends. It must have been outrageous."

Shame singed her and she bit her lip as she watched the fire of excitement dance in Wil's eyes. Her life had been bland, boring and uneventful. Her parents were the ones who went out on patrols and saved the world, not her and Alejandro. Hearing just a tiny bit about Wil's life made her understand her brother a little more. Alejandro was looking for street cred, something he'd never get until he'd actually survived an adventure and had his own stories to tell.

Sarah looked down, not knowing where to start. How did she begin to explain to Wil that, comparatively speaking, she'd grown up in the lap of luxury, that her only true complaint was her dad's uneven treatment of her and her brother—and she really couldn't call that a hardship, since it was his over-protectiveness that kept all evil at bay and food on the table.

"Well?" Wil said, chuckling. "Don't let it all spill out at once."

She laughed with him, a soft, easy laugh. "It wasn't as eventful as you might imagine. They sequestered us up in the mountains and would come back from battles beat up, bloody and dirty. The Armageddon was supposedly over, but there were still demons popping up and border skirmishes happening, compounds being attacked…they never told us much—just that they had to go help fellow Guardians. We got told a lot of times not to bother them…sometimes they'd be gone for weeks, even months, at a time."

"Wow…" Wil murmured. "That had to suck."

Sarah nodded, realizing for the first time how much it did. "I was so scared all the time. I never knew if they were gone for a long time because they were dead, or just engaged in a long battle. Then there's the whole thing about my Dad…which is another long story."

"We won't talk about dads," Wil said with a sad smile. "You met mine, and I can't make excuses for him, either. He is what he is."

"Yeah, mine, too—he is what he is." Sarah let out a long, weary sigh, glad that Wil wasn't going to press for deeper information about her compound right now. Just sitting here with him in amiable silence holding hands was awesome. Too many words would ruin it.

After a moment of quiet contemplation, Wil drew her hand to his chest. "I know what that's like," he finally said. "Everybody here has scars…that's why I wish…" He let his words trail off and let her hand go, his open gaze becoming very sad. "I just wish people could realize that we're all the same, you know? Like, why do people have to fight and have factions? Nobody who came from a Guardian compound should be thought of as an enemy. Remember what happened in Everett's class?"

Sarah nodded. "Yeah…how could I forget? That battle…it felt so real. I forgot all about who I was angry at, and we all just pulled together."

"That's what I'm saying Sarah. That's how it should be…and that's sorta how me and Patty got together. But it was from wartime circumstances. It wasn't natural, like this."

Again, she was rendered speechless. Put in that context, in that framework, she could see how people living in fear and working as a unit could get together…how total opposites could attract. But he'd said, *It wasn't like this.* Meaning like being with her.

She didn't know what to do, what to say, and he seemed to sense that. Before she could respond, he leaned in and lightly brushed her lips with a soft kiss. When she opened her eyes, he was staring at her with a quiet smile.

"I've been waiting to do that since the first time I saw you," he murmured.

Stunned silent, all she could do was look at him as he stood. Being late for Blends lecture was in the distant background of her mind.

"I've got track practice after Shadows lecture…you've got library orientation, but I'll text you later, okay?"

Sarah nodded numbly. "Okay," she whispered, looking up at him as though in a daze.

Wow…She watched Wil gather up his books and head toward the door. Mrs. Hogan's voice echoed from somewhere in the distance, and that was enough to give her the will to stand. But she was fairly certain that she wouldn't retain anything the blue-haired lady was about to say.

"Sarah, Sarah," the high-pitched, pleasant voice called out. "Darling, I'm sorry I'm late. Bad faeries are such a pain—there's no place for Unseelies in the Seelie Court. But, wait a minute, you're early, dear…our orientation isn't for another hour. Oh, you new students do have to get used to the schedule. You're due to be in Blends lecture now, then you come here."

"Okay." Sarah smiled; she didn't have a clue what Mrs. Hogan was talking about, nor did she care what she needed to bring later for her orientation.

Wil Archer had kissed her.

Chapter 16

By the time they'd crawled out of Mr. Foggerty's Blends class, sleepiness had begun to wear on them all. Just as they'd noticed in his bio class, his boring stories of life in ancient Atlantis as an amphibian got interspersed between every problem he put on the board. Nobody in the room could stop yawning.

Sarah yawned again and wiped her eyes as her PIU vibrated in her skirt pocket. She pulled it out to look at it with another long yawn.

"Oh, great…just what I need," she said, closing her eyes and leaning against the wall. "A reminder that I've gotta go to library work-study orientation."

"And we have all this homework, too. Already. Like, these teachers are insane," Tami muttered, shaking her head. "They all act like their class is the only one we have, and they've dumped enough work on us that we'll never get out from under…and this isn't even exam time. How're you gonna do all your assignments *and* work in the library, Sarah? Why don't you just tell her that you committed too soon and can't help out, at least not 'til you get settled into your class schedule?"

What she didn't want to explain to Tami was that she needed a little space, somewhere to be that wasn't with the group…someplace where she could nurture what had just happened with Wil. She wasn't ready to share that with Tami right now for fear that Tami would say or do something to ruin it.

"I don't know how I'm gonna get it all done, but I'll figure it out," Sarah finally said, walking quickly. "I just want to be sure I've got access to any information we might need down the road."

She waved goodbye to Tami and kept hustling toward the library, dodging the other students crowding the hall. She wanted to get orientation over with as soon as possible…because then maybe she could see Wil again. Maybe he'd even sit with her at dinner. Then she tucked away that hopeful thought. He'd never single her out that way in public—would he?

But soon her footsteps slowed. She could feel Ayana somewhere deep in the belly of the school, somewhere secluded…like a stairwell, maybe an alcove, and something was very wrong. Rushing forward quickly and led only by the nervous energy that propelled each step, Sarah stopped by an exit and slipped through a door marked *Staff Only*.

The moment Sarah heard voices she froze, immediately recognizing Ayana's—and Brent's. She turned to leave, feeling the intimacy of the exchange before the words even made sense. But she couldn't go. She was rooted to the floor where she stood, not out of leering curiosity but from deep concern. Something within her told her that her big sister-cousin was in trouble, and Ayana would never tell her or allow her to help in a million years.

"You used to know how to have fun. Now that your little cousins are here, you want to play the straight-laced big sister? Give me a break."

"Brent, you're high. I can't talk to you when you're like this."

"Don't start with that again, Ayana. You know the pressure I'm under. You know I need to relax."

"But it's dangerous!"

Brent laughed. "Oh, please. I'm just taking the edge off." His voice turned petulant and nasty again. "All you ever say now is no."

"Brent, I just don't want our first time to be on the Shady Path!"

"Fine, I'll just find a girl who isn't afraid of a little thrill ride. Maybe I'll slip into town and find me a little something sweet to play with for a while."

"Brent, please, don't do this. You know how much I love you."

"Then prove it. Come with me into town. A few of us are going ZBing just outside of town. I need a seer to navigate for me. And you're the best, just like me, Yaya."

Sarah was stunned. They were still opening portals and going into town? Were they nuts?

Ayana's tone was soft and pleading. "I love being your navigator…but it's dangerous now. People we know have gone missing and—"

"Whatever. You in or not?"

There was a long pause, then Ayana said, "I can't, Brent! You know what's going on. What if something happens to you? I don't know what I would do."

There was a sound as if someone was getting up. Were they sitting on the steps? Sarah closed her eyes but saw nothing, but her cousin was an expert seer and would have had the whole secret meeting with Brent blocked. Undoubtedly the only reason she'd gotten this close was because one day Yaya would be her Neteru seer, so no matter what, they were linked.

She didn't have to see her cousin's face to know that she was crying. She could hear the soft muffled sounds of repressed sobs. Her heart broke for Ayana, but at the same time fury at Brent made her ball her hands into fists by her sides. The guy was a complete loser, and one day she'd tell Yaya what she really thought of him. But not now, not while Yaya was still nuts for the guy. She didn't want Ayana to freeze her out. If Yaya turned against her over a guy, she wouldn't know what to do.

"I don't know what I ever saw in you," Brent finally said.

A door below Sarah opened, then slammed, and then there was silence. Sarah pressed herself against the wall, trapped, listening to Ayana cry. After a while Ayana stopped sniffing and released a long, weary breath.

"You can come out now, Sarah."

Sarah timidly approached the stairwell and then hurried down the stairs to give Ayana a hug. She didn't immediately know what to say, so she allowed her embrace to speak volumes.

"I wasn't trying to be nosy…I just…"

"Sorry you had to hear that," Ayana said in a shaky voice.

"Yaya, why do you mess with that guy?"

Her cousin leaned her head against Sarah's shoulder and let out a shuddering sigh.

"Sarah, people aren't perfect…they're flawed. A lot of kids here have been through a lot, things you never went through. I was out there with my mom and stepdad, and I remember the Armageddon. I was there when I was like four or five. I've had a vampire actually grab me, but I got away. I've seen demons. A lot of kids have been through even worse."

Sarah stroked Ayana's back, for the first time really putting it all together. She'd *heard* about it; Ayana had *lived* it. But, still, that didn't justify losing herself to a complete jerk. People had problems, this was true—but they didn't all act like Brent. Wil came to mind. He wasn't anything like that.

"I know what it's like to be really scared," Ayana whispered thickly, as another large tear rolled down the bridge of her nose. "Brent and I kinda grew up the same way…we had that in common."

Sarah just closed her eyes and let Ayana get it all out, rocking her and holding her cousin close.

"And like me, he came from a pair of well-to-do parents who are amazing Guardians, and they put an incredible amount of pressure on him." Ayana lifted her head from Sarah's shoulder and stared at her with tears in her eyes. "Our parents are wealthy by comparison to most people, if you haven't already noticed. I understand that pressure to be a role model. I've lived with it all my life. 'Yaya, you're the oldest.' 'Yaya, you'll have a whole compound to lead as a seer.' Brent had to deal with that, too, and nobody else seemed to understand that maybe I just didn't want to do any of that!"

"Oh, Yaya," Sarah said, covering her mouth and trying hard not to cry. After a moment her hand fell away to touch Ayana's cheek. "I know how you feel," she said finally, taking her cousin's hand. "I don't want to be a Neteru or any of that. I'm the child of the Neterus, my dad was a Council Level Vamp—and I'm scared of the dark. We share that…You don't have to think he's the only one who'll understand."

The two girls stared at each other for a moment, and then Ayana released a sad chuckle. "We're a sad pair, aren't we?" she said, shaking her head.

"I don't care what he's been through, I still don't like how he treats you."

Ayana stared down at the floor. "He's not so bad…and like, who else is gonna really—"

"What?" Sarah said in a rush, grabbing Ayana by her arms. "You think just because he's good looking that—"

"Face it," her cousin said with a sad smile. "He could have any girl in here. There are more girls than boys in the school, and—"

"No, no, no, no, no, I'm not going to let you say these awful things about yourself, those poisonous things." Sarah dropped her backpack onto the stairs and dug into the front zipper pocket for her PIU. She yanked out her unit and held the shiny mirror-like back side up to Ayana's face. "I want you to look in that and tell me you aren't just as good-looking, just as worthy, just as…*everything* that makes you better than the way he's treating you."

When Ayana looked away, Sarah rounded on her. "I'm serious, Yaya. I'm not going away until you look."

Ayana took the unit, glanced into it and handed it back to Sarah.

"Say it," Sarah whispered, new tears of anguish rising in her eyes as she thought about her cousin's destroyed self-esteem.

"But—"

"No," Sarah insisted. "Say it! You are worthy of being treated better."

Ayana swallowed hard, and the tears began streaming again. "Okay."

Sarah shook her head no. "Say it with me. I…" She waited until Ayana repeated the word after her, then went on, the two of them speaking the words together. "Am worthy of being treated better than this."

Sarah went to Ayana and hugged her tightly. "You are. You really, really are. And for a seer, you are so blind. You are tall and beautiful, stylish, sexy, and you know everything, and you're popular and nice and wicked smart. You don't have to allow him to treat you like this. If I didn't know better, I'd swear a whole coven was working on you to make you blind to everything good about yourself."

"You're family," Ayana said, laughing sadly. "You're supposed to be on my side."

Sarah held Ayana away from her. "You have a body that would stop a firefight, Yaya. Pretty brown skin that's flawless. Gorgeous eyes, immaculate braids…I mean, why are you the only one who doesn't see the guys breaking their necks when you walk by?"

Her cousin shrugged and let out a long breath. "Force of habit."

"I think the jealous girls treated you so mean when you first came here that you finally believed them," Sarah said quietly. "I don't know how you did it, because I have the rest of the crew with me and it's still hard."

Ayana's eyes were sad as they met Sarah's, but a gentle smile graced her face. "Sometimes you need a second pair of eyes, I guess…Even the best navigators do."

"I'll be yours and you be mine, okay."

Ayana hugged Sarah. "I love you, girl. Thank you."

"I will always have your back till the day I die. Just promise me you won't go through any illegal portals."

"You don't have to worry about me," Ayana said, breaking their hug. "Listen, you be careful, too, all right? Don't let anybody talk you into doing something crazy. Only a few kids in Upper Spheres know how to open the portals—Casey was one of them. But please, please, *please* don't rat on Brent. He's not an opener, he just goes through them to get high in town. But he never hurt anybody."

"But, Yaya, how do you know that's all he's doing? He and Stefan are a lethal combination. Maybe he went through the portal the night Arthur and Casey disappeared."

Ayana shook her head. "No, he was with me that night."

"Whatever, you still don't need to be around somebody who's getting high like that. I mean, things can happen."

Ayana released another weary breath. "I know, but Brent is pretty safe. It's just weed."

Sarah raised an eyebrow but decided to let some of her argument drop. Brent, high, sounded anything but safe. Ayana's "just weed" comment didn't make her feel better, either.

"With all this stuff that's going on with missing students, tell me why these guys are still sneaking out and getting high and just doing crazy-ridiculous stuff, Yaya?" Sarah dragged her fingers through her hair and yanked out her ponytail scrunchie. "That's insane."

"Yeah. I know." Ayana let out a long, weary sigh. "Look…it's complicated."

"Complicated?" Sarah shook her head, annoyed. "And how are they keeping all this from all the teachers, Nana—all the seers in the administration?" Although she'd already pretty much figured it out, she wanted to hear it said out loud by her cousin for total confirmation.

"Blocker groups," Ayana admitted quietly. "That's what Brent wants me to do, too—help block against them getting caught. He's pissed because I don't want to be involved." She looked up at Sarah. "There are a lot of students around who want to do things that won't fly with the administration and are tired of being cooped up here, as nice as it is."

"Like?" Sarah folded her arms, and Ayana glanced away.

"Like…stuff. I'm not asking you to agree with it, I'm just asking you to be cool and not tell, okay, Sarah?" Ayana's eyes met Sarah's and held her gaze with a silent plea. "Don't put me in the middle of something just because you overheard what you weren't supposed to hear. That's not fair."

Sarah swallowed hard. She would never rat on her older cousin. "Anything you tell me stays with me. I promise."

"Thank you." Ayana smiled sadly. "Until you've mind-locked with a guy, you have no idea how unbelievable and…intimate it is. You've never felt closer to a person, and you feel like you never will again." She stared at Sarah, and silence stood uncomfortably between them for a moment. "He needs someone to believe in him, Sarah."

Sarah picked up her backpack and hoisted it onto one shoulder, feeling sad. Her cousin could do so much better. But apparently that was going to have to be something Yaya worked through on her own. Disappointment weighed more heavily on her shoulders than her backpack did.

"I want to be there for you, Yaya," Sarah finally said.

Ayana stepped forward and hugged her. "I want that, too."

"I'll see you later…go wash your face," Sarah said, kissing her cheek. "I'm late for library orientation."

"Thanks," Ayana said, grabbing her books off the steps. "Don't think badly of me, Sarah….I'm still working through all this crap."

Sarah nodded and headed up the dimly lit stairwell. Ayana had always looked out for her. Now it was her turn.

CHAPTER 17

Walking quickly toward the library, Sarah kept her head low and moved through the crowd as deftly as she could. But a touch on her arm jerked her out of her thoughts.

"You cool? No new developments on the all-girls war front?"

Sarah shook her head and gave Val a smile, glad that he cared. "No news is good news."

"Hold up," he said with a wide grin. "Where's the fire? You going to dinner?"

"Got library orientation for an hour first. I sorta volunteered."

"I'll be your bodyguard for a while, if you want—to make sure nobody from another compound tries you again, all right?" He moved into her and boxed her in near a locker.

She just stared at Val for a minute. "You don't have to."

He smiled. "I know I don't, but seeing as how you almost got slimed, I thought I'd get your back."

She smiled and gave him a little shove, then started walking again, glancing over her shoulder at him.

"Offer stands," he called out behind her.

"Okay," Sarah said in a distracted tone as she pulled out her PIU and looked at it. No text from Wil. She shoved it back into her backpack pocket and kept walking. Nothing in her life was going right. Nothing.

* * *

Bored out of her skull, Sarah listened to Mrs. Hogan and feigned interest even, though her stomach loudly growled.

"Are you clear on the check-out procedures?" Mrs. Hogan asked brightly.

"Yes, ma'am," Sarah said in her most studious voice.

"Good, good, good," Mrs. Hogan replied, clapping and making her blue marble wand spark. "Then let's have at it, shall we? I want to show you cataloguing, proper book and manuscript care, and shelving, not to mention how to help instructors when they need you to research for them or send up a bibliography to their classrooms."

Sarah felt her eyes glazing over.

Suddenly Mrs. Hogan yanked on Sarah's sweater, all the while glancing around to make sure that the coast was clear. Then the cherub-faced librarian spoke in a whisper behind her hand, chuckling.

"And glory be, child, I will show you how to discreetly help Miss Tillie. She's a wonderfully meticulous and lovely lady, but so painfully slow. Still, we cannot hurt her feelings."

Sarah nodded, her mind a million miles away. But when her stomach growled again—loudly—Mrs. Hogan simply sighed.

"Go have dinner, Sarah. Maybe this was a little ambitious for a first day. It's just so rare that I get a student who's interested in my library—most don't understand all the wondrous secrets and knowledge that it contains."

"Ma'am…next time, when I come back…"

Mrs. Hogan waved her hand with a pleasant smile. "Go eat. We have plenty of time to get together…but remember, destiny sends us on journeys and to places that may seem to be one thing when we begin, only to show themselves as a fantastic surprise later." She gave Sarah a wink. "This place is not as boring as it seems. Don't you give up on it, Sarah…or on yourself."

"Thanks," Sarah replied, gathering up her books. She had no idea what Mrs. Hogan was talking about. Adults had been speaking to her in riddles all her life; there was no reason to believe they'd stop now that she was in school.

Without actually bolting, since she didn't want to offend Mrs. Hogan, Sarah got out of the library as fast as she could and headed to the cafeteria, hoping Wil would be there though she hadn't heard from him.

The crush of the five o'clock dinner crowd was long gone, and only students who were coming from extra-curricular activities or who were just hanging out remained. Sarah fingered her green Blends pin as she surveyed who was seated where. Allie and Hyacinth had waited for her. Tami was nowhere to be found. Ayana wasn't around, neither was Brent—or Stefan. She kept walking, trying to act casual, trying to remain calm, but not seeing Stefan or Tami was sending off warning bells in her head.

To her complete disappointment, Wil was there but seated far off in a corner, alone with Patty. She tried not to stare, tried her best not to allow her gaze to linger, but it was next to impossible.

"You cool?" a familiar deep male voice said next to her ear.

"I swear, Val, I wish you wouldn't do that vamp-stealth thing," Sarah said, turning to glance at Val over her shoulder.

He shrugged, rolling a toothpick around in his mouth. "You know you love it, especially when I bring news from the front line."

Now he had her attention.

"Notice how Melissa and crew aren't here, but no authorities swooped down on you for that little altercation you guys had in the hall?"

"Yeah…" Sarah said in a non-committal tone, not sure which version of the story Val had heard.

"Word is, something spooked Amy Feingold—and Melissa's sister is over there trying to pump Wil for info to see if he knows anything."

"I hate how everybody in here is so sneaky and has an agenda," Sarah said, grabbing a tray. She almost wished Val hadn't come over to fill her in. She was exhausted and just wanted to eat. The politics of the Academy were maddening—and it had only been a day.

"Yeah, well, speaking of agendas…see if you can get your pal Tami to chill."

Val nodded when Sarah stopped adding vegetable stir fry to her plate and stared up at him.

"I'm just saying," he murmured, and then glanced at the table where Al, Miguel and Donnie were sitting. "She's gonna get your brother beat down, if she doesn't watch out."

"What're you talking about, Val?" Sarah hiked up her backpack with one hand, precariously balancing her tray with the other.

"You didn't hear this from me, but she left here with Stefan. Al ain't feelin' that at all…is all I'm saying, all right. That dude Stefan has more issues than you know—anger management kinda issues and a real violent history—so none of us are diggin' him rollin' solo with Tam."

"Neither am I," Sarah said, glancing back at the table where the boys were sitting.

Her brother's eyes had turned silver, he was so mad. But she knew that he wasn't ready to be embarrassed in public again by Tami, or get into a fistfight that he'd probably lose with Stefan. So he just sat there smoldering. None of the Upper Sphere girls that she knew were there. Jessica and company were probably off doing homework. Tina and Darlene were nowhere in sight, either.

"Cool…then talk to T soon as you can."

Sarah nodded as Val loped away. She got some juice, and then rushed over to where Allie and Hyacinth were seated. The moment she sat down, they began whispering feverishly.

"Tami has lost her mind," Allie hissed. "We tried to stop her, but you know how she is."

"He came over here and asked her if she wanted a tour, and we were like, Tami, are you crazy—and she just got up and told him sure." Hyacinth leaned in closer, whispering quickly. "A tour? Like she knows that guy well enough to be going off with him alone somewhere, Sarah—and going around this school at night without a hall pass, and—"

"I know, I know," Sarah said, taking out her PIU. "I'll let Yaya know, all right?"

Allie and Hyacinth sandwiched Sarah as she quickly typed in, *Need 2 tlk ASAP*, and then pushed send. She set her PIU in front of her as she ate quickly, all of them waiting impatiently for Ayana to text back.

"How come she's not answering?" Allie glanced at Hyacinth, who stared at Sarah, waiting for her to explain.

"Because she's probably with that jerk, Brent," Sarah said in disgust.

"Then what do we do?" Hyacinth looked from Allie to Sarah.

Sarah sat back and shoved her plate away in frustration. "The only thing we *can* do. We go back to our room and wait for her."

* * *

"Relax," Tami said with a wide smile. "I don't see why you all are making this into such a big deal."

"Relax?" Allie said, sparking. "We had no idea where you were and—"

"Yeah, you did. I was with Stefan."

"That guy is notorious, Tami!" Hyacinth fussed in a tense whisper.

"I know…" Tamara said, closing her eyes and hugging herself.

"Let it rest," Sarah said, now so disgusted she almost didn't care. "We were worried, Tami could give a hoot, so we're stupid for getting all bent out of shape."

Allie crossed her arms and stared at Tami. "You did it just to stick it to Melissa, didn't you?"

Tami shrugged and gave them all a devil-may-care look. Sarah closed her eyes. Tami was going to be the death of her.

"So where did you go?" Sarah asked, feeling resigned.

Tami plopped down on one of the desk chairs and stared at her roommates for a moment. "You promise not to freak out?" she finally whispered, glancing at the door.

Sarah crossed her arms over her chest. "No."

Tami rolled her eyes and let out an exasperated breath.

"Well?" Sarah said when Tami remained silent.

"Look, you're not my mother, okay—so let's start there." Tami gave Sarah a hard glare.

"Fine…fine," Sarah said, holding up one hand. "I'm going to bed."

Allie and Hyacinth just stared at Sarah's back for a moment before returning their attention to Tami.

Tami began picking at the wooden edge of the chair. Finally she looked up and whispered, "He took me into town."

Sarah turned around and stared at Tami as if she had heard wrong. A thousand warning gongs went off inside her head. "What?" The question came out in a furious whisper.

"Oh…my…God," Allie whispered, and covered her heart with her hand.

Hyacinth opened her mouth but no sound came out of it.

"I told you not to freak out."

"No, you tried to get me to promise not to freak out," Sarah said. "Are you crazy? Didn't you hear what they said during opening ceremonies? People are disappearing—dying! We're forbidden from going outside after curfew—not to mention from going to town! And how did you get there?" Her eyes got wider. "Did you take a portal into town?"

"How else would I have gotten there?" Tami offered her a casual shrug, but her eyes held a furious glare. "Don't judge me just because you're scared of the dark, Sarah."

Sarah sputtered. "Tami!"

"Sarah, look, I know what Baba said, but I was perfectly safe with Stefan."

"And how do you know that?"

"Stefan said that the administration always makes things sound worse than they are. Besides, he knows that town and these portals like the back of his hand and he said he wouldn't let anything happen to me." Tami smiled. "And it was *such* a rush!"

"Tami, if who- or whatever is taking people decides they want you, there is no way Stefan could protect you!" Sarah's voice was escalating.

"And how do you know that?" Tami said, getting truly angry now. Her voice was rising to match Sarah's. "Look, Sarah, I appreciate the concern, but believe me, I know what I'm doing." She smiled again. "And Melissa is going to know it, too." She got up, went to her dresser and pulled out her pajamas. "I'm going to take a shower," she announced and left the room.

Allie and Hyacinth grabbed their robes and dashed after Tami, no doubt seeking the juicy details of her excursion. But there was something in Tami's tone—something beyond the anger and know-it-all tone—that rubbed Sarah raw. She couldn't place her finger on it, but something was not quite right. Sarah's PIU sounded and she quickly looked at it, expecting Ayana's message. But it wasn't her older cousin. Wil had sent a text! He'd kept his word.

She stared at the simple message: *Hi ☺ srry I missed u @ dinner—drama—have a gr8 nite.*

Sarah's fingers flew across the keys, typing in *U2,* then she pushed send, pressed her PIU to her chest and closed her eyes.

CHAPTER 18

Tami having a twenty-four hour attitude was nothing new. It was something to be weathered, like the flu. But what really distressed Sarah was that Ayana never got back to her. Finally she saw Yaya at breakfast, and her cousin told her she'd been caught up with a project last night—which they both knew was a lie—and that she'd give them tips on the dance later. Ayana even took the news about Tami with a resigned shrug, which completely blew Sarah away.

And once again she was left all alone with things swirling in her head and no one to confide in. Her best friend had an attitude, Ayana was mentally AWOL—off in la la land with Brent—and somehow telling Allie and Hyacinth about Wil just didn't seem the same.

The three friends filed into Mrs. Gulliaume's chemistry class, minus one—Tami. She was already inside and seated at her desk, her mood aloof. Sarah let out a deep sigh of annoyance. Tami could be so stubborn, and moody didn't even begin to describe her. Later. They'd deal with it at lunch.

Sarah slid into her seat, noticing Val's sly smirk, which oddly made her feel better. Even Donnie's goofy grin and failed attempt to bump fists with her as she passed felt welcomingly familial. Miguel gave her an it's-all-good nod. It felt safe, having a lot of people around her who she knew, deep inside, she could count on. Al was still being relatively cool; his attention diverted fifteen different ways by the endless selection of pretty girls in the class. And then there was Wil's welcoming smile.

"Chemistry, ladies and gentlemen," Mrs. Guilliaume said, waving a large kettle and spoon around, "is art—not science."

The teacher smiled warmly at each student as she happily glided around the room while she lectured, her hefty frame hidden beneath a large floral print shift, accentuated by Earth Mother sandals, and an apple seed and handmade bead necklace. One long, thick, auburn braid hung down her back. She looked like an out-of-era hippie who was having a grand time running a classroom. Even though one could call her a little quirky, Mrs. Guilliaume was fast becoming Sarah's second favorite teacher after Mr. Everett.

A very studious-looking girl near the far wall raised her hand. "But, Mrs. Guilliaume, what about the periodic chart and all the stuff they showed us in the mini class yesterday and—"

"Yes!" the teacher said, running down the aisle to deposit her kettle on a burner. It immediately started to smoke, so Mrs. Guilliaume paused as Kimberly Wilkerson, one of the Olfactories, turned green from the smell, and bent over and hurled. Instantly the giant toad that was positioned by the side of the desk opened its wide mouth and caught the contents of her stomach. A loud "Eeeww" rose up in unison from all the students as three more *Ollies* followed suit.

"You may be excused," Mrs. Guilliaume said enthusiastically, and she waited as the four sick students dashed from her classroom. Those who remained made faces of disgust, but the teacher waved dismissively, staying determinedly cheerful. "As they should have explained on day one of class, this is why I've placed waste buckets by my *Olfactory* students. We must be good planetary stewards and recycle everything. A good nose is a must for developing the finest of blends and the richest of recipes.

"There is a science of molecular combination, certainly, but there's also the fact that no two compounds of the same element are ever of the same concentration. That is the art—getting the strengths of the mixtures right, based on the variables of the concentrations—and we shall learn to go beyond the basics to create chemical composition art."

Sarah just stared at the woman, her mind a million miles away and focused on finding Ayana as soon as she could. At least her little shadows hadn't come out of hiding since the Amy Feingold incident.

When the bell rang, Wil got up and stood by the door. He looked at her and smiled, but somehow Val body blocked her in the aisle, and it was next to impossible to see around him, given that he was more than a full head taller than her.

"What's the rush?" Val said, teasing her.

"No rush," Sarah said, laughing, trying to get past him.

"Did you talk to T?"

"I tried to catch her in the hall between classes, and you can see what good it did. Now she's totally not speaking."

"Hey," Val said, shrugging. "What can you do?" He glanced over his shoulder at Wil and then looked back at Sarah. "Remember, I've got your back, okay?"

"Yeah, Val, I know that," she said with a slight frown, not understanding why he seemed to take exception to Wil.

"Cool," Val said, and then loped past Wil, giving him a curt nod of recognition.

"Hi…" Wil said, when Sarah made it to the door at last.

Sarah could feel Allie and Hyacinth hanging back, wide-eyed.

"The big mixer is tomorrow…save me a dance, okay?"

Sarah smiled, her pulse racing. "Sure…okay."

"Catch you later, then—getting together with the guys from track right now."

The moment Wil jogged away, Allie and Hyacinth accosted her.

"OMG, Sarah," Allie whispered. "What is going on with you and Wil?"

Hyacinth squeezed Sarah's arm. "Is it my imagination, or…?"

Sarah just shrugged. "It's nothing." But she couldn't stop herself from beaming.

* * *

The balance of the day crawled by. Ayana was still preoccupied, but the teachers had handed out assignments as if they were handing out lunch. There was so much homework to get done, and all assignments had to be in the following day, on pain of being barred from the dance.

Everyone was on their best behavior all day Wednesday. Amy Feingold had come back to class with a newly repaired tooth but gave Sarah a wide berth. In fact, the only static Sarah and her friends got consisted of a few evil glances, which was just fine with her.

But by the end of Blends lecture, she was thrumming with anticipation. She was going to dance with Wil, and she could hardly wait.

However the real challenge would be what to wear tonight. It had come across on their PIUs—no uniforms required at the luau. A massive cheer had rung through the halls. Students could wear their own gear tonight. But for her and her friends, there was only dread. They'd never lived "off compound." They weren't sure what was considered the latest and hippest fashion. Sure, they'd gone on PirateNet to see what was what and asked around casually, so no one would know how out of touch they really were, but the feedback was vague. Just jeans, boots and a nice blouse.

Back at the dorm at last, Sarah studied her burnt orange midriff sweater with cap sleeves and chain belt. She'd seen the same style worn by an outlawed band star, although she wasn't bold enough to put a black lace bra under it and leave the front half opened—even she owned a black lace bra. Still, it gave what little figure she had a lift. The straight-legged jeans she wore seemed okay, and the metal hardware around her waist gave her a bit of edginess that she prayed looked cool. She just wished she could have done something new and dramatic with her hair, but at least allowing it to simply hang down on her shoulders was a departure from her perpetual ponytail.

Although nobody said it, she knew all her friends were thinking the same thing as they fretted and hunted through their clothing choices. They, like her, only owned whatever their parents had hot-zapped in from the outside world. Everybody depended on supplies coming into the compounds by way of her dad's white Light energy whirls, which had the upside of the cargo being safe and the down side of complete parental censorship.

Allie and Sarah stared at each other as Tami flung clothes out of drawers and closets like a mad woman while fussing at Hyacinth to make herself useful by reading somebody's mind. What had previously been a neat, orderly room was demolished by clothes all over every surface as the four friends tried desperately and in vain to reassure each other. Tami's previous attitude had been replaced by a new anxiety over not looking cool.

Ayana could have helped big time, but she was nowhere to be found.

"Try her again," Tami said, looking at Sarah. "Where the hell is Yaya?"

"Okay, okay, I'll text her again, but you have got to relax."

"Do you actually wanna go to the first mixer wearing something your Mom picked out for you?" Tami shrieked, holding up a floral print shirt with puffy sleeves from Hyacinth's dresser.

"I'm not going. I—"

"'Cinth, concentrate!" Tami begged. "Surely you can get a glimpse of somebody's brain, for the love of Pete. Where is Yaya—how could she leave us stranded like this? 'Cinth, you aren't concentrating!"

"Quit it, Tami," Allie said, hurling a tank top at her. "The poor girl is exhausted, and everybody around here with half a brain knows to lock it to all *Clav* invasions. We already asked people and even looked up stuff on the Net, okay?"

Hyacinth ran her fingers through her damp hair. "I would bust into somebody's mind if I could, but right now I can't, Tam! Wait, no I wouldn't—it's not ethical."

"What?" Tami turned away from her closet. "Ethical? Are you crazy? Desperate times call for desperate measures. What has—"

"Stop," Sarah said. "I'm going to try something else. Just find something to put on while I text Ayana's friends."

"Finally somebody with a plan," Tami said, settling down and beginning to drag on a pair of jeans.

Sarah picked up her PIU and frowned. She had texted Ayana an hour ago asking if she wanted to go to the party with them but hadn't heard back. She let out a frustrated sigh. She thought she and Yaya were past the my-boyfriend-thinks-we're-too-cool-for-you thing.

All right, don't jump to conclusions, she told herself, and shot off a two-way text to Darlene and Tina.

Have u seen Ayana?

A few seconds later Darlene wrote back, *Not w us. Prb w Brent somewhere.*

Doin somethin nasty! came Tina's reply.

Ignore her, Darlene wrote back.

"Thanks, I will," Sarah said, tucking her PIU into her fitted jeans. She didn't like thinking of Ayana with Brent, let alone doing something nasty with him. That guy would always be a jerk, no matter how much Ayana thought he could change.

Oh well, she would just see Ayana at the dance.

"Well?" Tami asked, waving her hands.

"They don't know where she is," Sarah said flatly.

"But did you at least ask them what to wear?"

Sarah just stared at Tami.

"Du-uh," Tami said, walking away and shaking her head.

Sarah pulled out her PIU again and sent Ayana's friends another message. *K about Ya. But what 2 wear?*

Cool jeans, boots, t-shirt, tank top, blouse, Darlene wrote back. *Easy.*

Yep, basic, Tina texted.

Thx, Sarah sent back and then sighed. She turned around and faced her roommates, and held up her PIU for them to read the messages. "We're panicking for nothing."

"Okay, I do feel better," Tami said, the edge gone from her tone. She held up a sexy, blood red lycra tank top that accentuated every curve and slipped it on, then began insertinb large silver hoop earrings. "And for the record, ladies, lose the pastel undies. Black, red, animal print, purple, go for something—anything—dangerous. Not all virgin white, lilac, baby blue and pink, puhlease. We're going to a *party*."

"Huh?" Allie said, glancing at Hyacinth. "Why? Like, who's gonna see those?"

Tami shot Sarah a meaningful glance. "One never knows…so a lady should always be prepared."

"Oh…my…God, Tamara," Hyacinth said, and closed her eyes.

"Do not listen to her," Allie said, slipping on a pink V-neck camisole. She turned away from Tami and began putting in her small silver hoops. "La la la la, Tami, we can't hear you."

"I am not listening to her," Hyacinth said, and then tied the pretty floral silk sashes of her halter top together. She slipped on a violet headband and shook her hair out over her shoulders.

Tami just laughed and shrugged as she slipped on her high heel biker boots, her jeans fitting her like second skin.

Sarah took a step back and surveyed herself one more time, wishing she had the nerve to wear thigh-high boots like Tami's, not that she even had them. Her basic knee-high ones would have to do.

"Ladies, we are going to knock their heads back," Tami said, smiling, as she stared at her own backside in the mirror.

Allie struck a pose, and they all laughed.

* * *

They arrived so late to the luau that they'd missed the meal blessing. Sarah could hear the music blaring down the hall well before they got to the cafeteria. The lights were dim, fireflies on the murals helping to light the way. But the moment they hit the entrance, she, Allie and Hyacinth had to body block Tami to keep her from turning around and leaving.

They'd obviously missed the memo that the current look was sexy warrior. Forget what they'd seen on PirateNet, the school apparently had its own unique style. They stared in horror, and Sarah wished she could find a dark hole to crawl into.

Everyone had on military green cargo pants or jeans, with rips and tears that made it seem like they'd been savaged by demon claws but had miraculously survived. The guys all wore black or white sleeveless t-shirts or fatigue vests that were threadbare and zigzag ripped, and the girls' tanks had major lacerations across the belly or down the back, as though they'd been vampire attacked...and their bras were dark colored, just like Tami had warned. Pastels were out. It was all about black, red, deep purple or animal prints that were hinted at through the rips. Jewelry consisted of heavy leather wristbands with thick buckles, and footgear was combat boots or graffiti-emblazoned hiking boots.

For earrings they wore sections of motorcycle chain or old tire bits, and everybody only wore *one*—not two—to give the effect that they'd battled so mightily they'd lost one earring somewhere along the way. Sarah discreetly brought her hand up to her right ear and slipped out one of her silver hoops, all too aware that in this crowd, burnt-orange seemed like a pastel color.

Allie and Hyacinth had to be dying, too. Pink and floral…There was no justice in the world. Only Tami was barely passable.

And the make-up all the girls wore consisted of red, red lip gloss glistening on their mouths, dark mascara and liner around their eyes…It gave them the surreal and dangerous look of a potentially turned vampire or a demon-infected warrior…which in some very bizarre way made them a risky and thus seductive choice for the guys in the room. The unspoken message was, really brave guys could handle a sexy vampire.

Sarah and her crew glanced at each other. Their faces were naked, save for pink lip gloss. The hairstyles around them were moussed to wildness, to mimic having been in an attack, not neatly combed like theirs.

Some of the other students had already spotted them, and were pointing and whispering. Some were outright laughing.

"Can we leave now?" Tami asked quietly, so bereft that she'd clearly gone past the point of panic to a place of abject defeat.

"No," Sarah said, squaring her shoulders. "I'm not going to have them laugh at us for running away."

"So it's better to have them laugh at us for totally not fitting in?" Resigned, Tami just shrugged. "Your call, fearless leader."

Allie and Hyacinth glanced at Sarah, waiting on her decision. Sarah didn't say another word; she didn't trust herself to verbalize anything. There was a fifty-fifty chance she'd talk herself out of being here if she did. But she wasn't leaving and letting Wil think she had stood him up for their dance. She just walked forward and kept her chin high, ignoring Melissa Gray's table and their rude snickers as she passed. Amy Feingold was back with them, teeth fixed and clearly ready for war.

"Losers," Amy muttered loudly.

Sarah ignored her and moved forward with greater resolve, her back straight as she headed toward the food. Then she spotted her brother and almost dropped fang. Alejandro was in dress code—of course. Someone—no doubt one of the girls fawning all over him—had obviously deigned to tell him.

Ayana was so gonna hear from her the moment she saw her!

Her brother wore a black sleeveless t-shirt, ripped so badly it was hanging off his buff body. Of course the guys from the compound had fatigues and army boots with them—hell, even Donnie was fashionably correct.

"Hey, I was looking for you," Val said, coming up behind her. "What's up?"

Her girlfriends grumbled a hello and hung back to find a desolate salad bar, as though trying to head off any additional teasing.

"Why were you looking for me?" Sarah asked, surprised.

He smiled. "I was looking for my dance, girl—what?" Val held out his hand to her. "You remember our moves from the Net-pound, right? Or did you get brand new on me?"

"Actually we're thinking about leaving," Sarah said uncomfortably.

"Why?"

"Because we look like idiots compared to everyone else!"

Val stepped back, and looked her up and down. His perusal was liquid slow and intense. Suddenly Sarah flushed, feeling as if he were almost stripping her bare. He had never looked at her like that before.

Finally he met her eyes and said, "You look awesome."

Sarah stared at him, dumbstruck.

Val held out his hand again. "So how about it?"

Sarah spotted Wil in her peripheral vision, making his way toward her, probably to claim his dance.

"I'm starting to feel like I'm being played here," Val said a bit sheepishly.

"Oh!" Sarah said, snapping her attention back to him. "Well, sure, but—"

"Cool," Val said. and swept her onto the dance floor.

Wil stared after them, and Sarah felt awful. But she didn't have long to dwell on that, because Val knew how to dance his butt off. She had forgotten how well he could bring it. Heavy bass thrummed through her body as Val mirrored every move she made, anticipating her like they were joined by one pulse. Then she saw Tami backing it up on Stefan, one leg raised and all.

"That girl," Sarah muttered, but then had to laugh. Tami was so outrageous that Sarah spun around to keep her back to her friend.

Val looked over at Stefan and Tami too. "Your girl likes to play with fire, huh?"

"And that's news how?"

Val just grinned.

Back-to-back songs kicked up the heat in the caf until the walls were sweating. Students whooped and called out, keeping time to the thundering beat. When the tempo switched over to a popular reggae cut to give everyone a chance to rest, Val surprised her by pulling her in close, still breathing hard, his movements becoming even more fluid. She wasn't plastered against him, but she could feel the strength of his body, could feel how light he was on his feet…could feel the heat rising off his damp skin.

The sensation made her heady, warmed her in a way that she'd never dared imagine when thinking of Val. She couldn't understand what had triggered it now. It had to be all the bodies moving to the beat, she reasoned. Had to be all the energy kicked up and the fever of the sweat. What was wrong with her? This was Val.

"I can hear your heart racing," he said.

She looked up and saw a hint of fang. He could hear the sound of her heart and the sound of her blood rushing through her veins? The vamp in him ignited something dormant within her. She couldn't help but respond. "You can hear that over the music?"

"Part vamp, baby," he whispered, leaning in. "But then so are you."

Sarah could feel his breath on her neck when he slowly drew his head back and stared at her. Then his attention suddenly snapped away from her. She looked up at him in surprise, wondering what in the world had happened.

Val was staring across the room. Sarah followed his line of vision and saw what had captured his attention.

Tami and Stefan were still at it. Difference was, Al was looking like he was about to have an apoplectic fit. Melissa looked violently unhappy, as well.

"Let me go get your brother before he does something stupid. I'll be right back," Val said, and then he was gone.

Sarah stood there, not quite sure what was happening. Then it hit her. She had almost kissed Val! And on the dance floor, in front of everyone. She glanced around, but no one seemed to be paying attention to her. But what about Wil? Had he seen what had almost happened? This was so not good and way too confusing.

She spotted Wil again, and thankfully he hadn't given up on her. He was making his way toward her once more. His gaze was locked on her, and his expression was unreadable. Oh, God, please don't let him have seen her and Val! Then again, would he be making his way over to her if he had? *Okay, don't panic.* She tried to put on her brightest smile and began walking toward Wil.

Suddenly a pair of hands seized her from behind.

"What the—"

She whirled around to see Jessica smiling at her. Allie and Hyacinth were behind her.

"Rescue mission!" Jessica said, locking one arm through Sarah's.

Sarah stared around the room. What on earth…?

Stefan's attention was on Al, who was glaring at him. Val looked like he was body-blocking Al as he stood in front of him, a hand placed on Al's chest while he said something in Al's ear. Using the male standoff to their advantage, Andrea and Bebitta—or Bebe, as she told them to call her—had no problem seizing Tami.

"To the ladies room!" Jessica declared, and dragged them away.

"Jess, wait—" Sarah started to say, but she couldn't stop her friend. She looked over her shoulder and cast a pleading look in Wil's direction just as she was dragged out through the doors of the cafeteria. Caught up in that female whirlwind, all Sarah could do was to leave Wil standing on the dance floor, watching her disappear. Her eyes had met his only for a few seconds, and she felt her stomach sink when he shook his head, then turned and walked away.

* * *

They all fell through the doors in a loud collision of female voices, and laughed hard as Jessica yanked off their scrunchies and headbands. Andrea whipped out mousse and began mussing up their hair, while Bebe flung a worn pocketbook so big it looked like a duffle bag on the sink and then began rummaging around in it.

"Since two of you are on our squad now, and just because we feel sorry for the other two of you, you've gotta get down with the latest styles," Bebe said.

Allie and Hyacinth gave Tami a look, and Sarah laughed. Tami had been so wrong about the older *Blends*. They *did* care.

"You guys really know how to do our make-up like we saw out there?" Tami asked, unsure as Jessica whipped her around to face her and accepted a jar from Bebe.

"Girl, please. We make it, distribute it and rule. Understand?" Jessica said with pride, and then high-fived Bebe and Andrea.

“Is it hard to make?” Hyacinth stood alongside Sarah and peered over Jessica’s shoulder as Jessica started transforming their friend’s eyes to a sultry demon-contagion look.

“It’s easy,” Jessica said without breaking the momentum of her chemistry lesson as Sarah gawked. “The basis of lip gloss is beeswax, and the color…our group makes the best stuff, because *Blends* have superior intellectual skills. We sell it to the other girls,” she added. “That is, when they grovel at our feet. We’ve got the compounds down for replicating Egyptian kohl and know how to coax a little honeycomb out of the Fae who tend the apiary. We’ve got the perfumes on lock. Ms. Guilliaume is soooo cool—she showed us how to infuse body butters and whatever. Our recipes are unbeatable.”

Bebe reached into the bag, came out with a small tube and squeezed a glob of hand cream onto Allie’s palms. “Mango butter, boo…the fellas can’t resist it. Plus has a little scent aphrodisiac in it—but if I tell ya, I’ve gotta kill ya,” she said, laughing.

“This smells divine,” Allie murmured, sharing some with Hyacinth.

“Look at your face, Tami,” Sarah gasped, thoroughly impressed.

“She’s gorgeous!” Hyacinth squealed. “Do me, do me!”

“Step right up,” Jessica said, laughing, and began to work on Hyacinth.

Andrea produced a razor and pulled off Tami’s shirt. “Good girl—black bra.” She glanced around. “If any of you have on white, I’m not cutting your shirt.”

“Tell em to go braless, then,” Bebe said with a shrug. “Live dangerously.”

When Allie and Hyacinth shared a gasp, the older girls doubled over laughing.

“You all are so precious,” Bebe said, wiping her eyes. Then she turned back to Tami. “There. How’s that?”

Tami stared in the mirror and looked at the deep gashes that showed off her tight midriff and then turned to examine the rents down the back of her shirt. “This is awesome.”

“Strip and gimme your jeans,” Bebe ordered. “I will have you so frickin’ hot in the next ten seconds, you won’t recognize yourself.”

“That girl is wicked with a razor,” Jessica said, turning Hyacinth to stare at herself in the mirror.

“Oh. My. God,” Hyacinth breathed.

The others gathered around behind her. The demure Hyacinth had been turned into a vixen with dark smudges around her pretty eyes, and dark lines along her cheekbones to give her cherub’s face a gaunt look. Dark sooty glitter covered her lids, and with red lipstick, the girl looked dangerous.

“Man!” Sarah exclaimed, completely impressed.

“I make it do what it do, babe,” Jessica said, yanking Allie into place. “Weinstein, your assets are the big gray eyes and curly hair. I say werewolf transition, don’t you, Bebe?”

“Definitely—give her wolf eyes,” Bebe said, nodding while Jessica began applying Allie’s make-up.

“The girls who buy from you…do they give you a trading number, Jess—like a fake bar code, so you can buy or sell in town?” Allie whispered, looking five ways before returning her gaze to Jessica. “But where could you spend it? Like, we can’t even get to town.”

“No,” Andrea said quietly. “Everything here is on the favor system.”

“You gonna tell them our biggest seller—the one item that keeps every smart female in here on her game?” Bebe dropped her voice in a way that made the others lean in to hear Jessica’s answer.

“We’re gonna make an exception for you, young *Clav* and young *Tactical*, and spill the secret in your presence,” Jessica said, smiling at Hyacinth and then glancing at Allie. She paused, then said, “Birth control.”

"Seriously?" Tami said, eyebrows raised. "You guys scored that up here?"

"You're joking, right?" Sarah said. "I can't imagine Nana stocking the school with birth control."

"She doesn't," Bebe said calmly. "This is why the *Clavs* might dislike us, but they don't mess with us. Not even Melissa and Patty—and Melissa and her crew just got cut off for messing with you guys. Trust me. We heard all about it."

Andrea nodded and leaned in with conspiratorial glee. "I can't wait till one of them has to come to us for a favor—boy, will they be surprised!"

"We hold more weight around here, literally and figuratively," Jessica said with a hearty chuckle, "than they do and they *can't stand it*. The *T-Rex's* worship us, *Specs* revere us, *Ollies* genuflect as we pass in the halls, and my dear *Audios* are at our beck and call for spy service night and day. They hate that we outrank them by creating strategic collaborations. We run the student government and most clubs, except athletics. We get everyone's vote. No matter what you may have heard, being a *Blend* means you have stepped into a sorority of entrepreneurs of the highest order. We've got a sure-fire barrier mix that's soaked into a little sea sponge plug that goes up you know where when you need it, and, voila! You're safe." Jessica met Andrea and Bebe's fists with her own.

"But, but…" Sarah stuttered. "What if it didn't work one time?"

The older girls laughed at her good naturedly, and slung an arm over her shoulders.

"You don't have to do it or use it, personal choice—abstinence is the only hundred-percent method…but you need to know options exist, kiddo. I know your parents told you the basic biology, but it wasn't like they were giving you access to a pharmacy, am I right?" Jessica said, and then gave Sarah a hug.

Bebe looked around the group with a wide grin. “Yo
you could try to wait till one of the Uppers comes back fr
condoms, which they always steal from the drug store, but that’s a long shot.”

Tami gave Jessica a sidelong glance, while Bebe added sooty smudges and fake bloodstains to her newly-ripped jeans. “So, uh…if I needed something, I could, like—”

“Come to Mama,” Jessica said laughing. She raised an eyebrow. “Stefan’s got you wide open, huh?”

“Well—”

“She’s not sleeping with him!” Sarah said, cutting Tami off.

“Gee, thanks, *Mom*,” Tami muttered, and shook her head.

“Okay, my bad,” Sarah replied in a sullen tone, trying to quickly pull herself together. But the very thought had sent a bolt of dread through her.

A look of pure satisfaction lit Jessica’s eyes as she finished Allie’s face and began working on Sarah’s. “But keep in mind that we’re the secret society of school pharmacists, you got that?”

“What Jessica is trying to say,” Andrea added with a dramatic sigh, “is that we’ll get in *big* trouble if Headmistress Stone finds out we’re making more than cosmetics.”

“Yep…just like Ernie and his best *Blends* buds make the best jewelry from hacked auto parts that get brought back from the outside. The guy is talented. Don’t let those beady little eyes and the weak chin fool you,” Bebe said with a wide smile.

“You guys don’t make...stronger stuff...do you?” Sarah asked cautiously.

“We don’t do black market drugs, if that’s what you’re asking,” Jessica said, cutting her off and looking at each new girl hard. “No mind-altering anything. Somebody else has that angle covered, and it’s a foul business. Stay away from that mess. Now be still.”

Jessica began to work on her make-up again.

Relief swept through Sarah. At least Jessica and her crew weren't hanging out with Stefan and Brent, or doing and selling anything really crazy.

"Ok, you're done," Jessica said, and then spun Sarah around with triumphant flair. "Looking undead on arrival. You like?"

"Wow…" It was all Sarah could say as she stared at her sooty eyes and wild hair.

Bebe laughed. "Now toss me your jeans and your shirt. We'll have you tricked out in a minute."

* * *

This time ,when they entered the caf, they had a different walk. Confidence was their new outfit, and attitude came with it. They passed Miss Tittle fussing at Headmistress Stone about the lyrics of some song or other, but Sarah worked hard not to catch her grandmother's eyes. The music thrummed through her body as a new wave of swagger thrummed through her spirit.

"These lyrics!" Miss Tittle argued in the shrill voice. "I know the outlawed bands supposedly have message music, but, Headmistress, really!"

"I don't listen to the lyrics, I just listen to the beat," Headmistress Stone said in a weary voice as Sarah and her crew passed by. "That's what keeps me from getting a migraine. We had our day, Miss Tittle, so let them have theirs."

Sarah and the others hurried to the beverage bar and grabbed cups of cold punch—it was a way of making a new entrance pass all the cute guys, a move that Bebe had highly recommended—and then they slowly promenaded to an open table that Jessica had scoped out. Melissa and her friends looked like they were about to die. Life was good.

Laughing to herself at their coup when male heads turned, Sarah took a sip from her cup and smiled. Val gave her a surprised look from across the room, and her brother, squinted, leaned forward and seemed torn, as though he was about to get up and come over, when Miguel put a hand on his shoulder.

"We look hot to death," Tami whispered to Sarah, and then squeezed her elbow.

"Yeah…" Sarah said, glancing around. She felt her heart sink when she didn't see Wil anywhere. Had he gotten angry and left?

The girls continued their conversation without missing a beat, giving each other the low-down on the newest music, who was dating who, but a male presence changed everything, so heads lifted and the girls parted as Stefan came up to their table.

Tami turned slowly with a big smile, but Sarah reached out in reflex to block the shadow that hung off him. It reached out as if it had claws, continuing to swath his entire body even as inky tendrils headed right for Tami's throat. Sarah frantically swiped at them, trying to arrest the progress of the darkness.

Stefan looked down and scowled. "What's your problem, newbie?"

"I—I thought I saw something," Sarah stammered, glancing up at him and then around the table.

"Like what?" he said in a low rumble. "Me coming over here to break your girl out of this hen fest?"

Sarah looked around for support, but apparently no one else saw anything. Stefan turned his attention to Tami. "You wanna get out of here?"

"Uhmmm...Well, like, sure," she said, and then stood. "Where do you wanna go?"

"Around," Stefan said coolly. "Maybe some places they didn't show you on the school tour."

"Cool…I'm game." Tami moved away from the table. "I'll be back later, guys."

"Tami, wait—" Sarah broke off, then watched, mute, as her girlfriend left.

Tami threw Melissa a triumphant look before she disappeared through the door with Stefan. Melissa and Al were matching storm clouds on the horizon.

The Upper Spheres at the table said nothing, just grinned.

"Tell me she'll be all right," Sarah said, mostly talking to herself.

"He won't make her do anything she doesn't wanna do, if that's what you're asking," Jessica said, laughing.

"No, I'm serious," Sarah said. "That guy has darkness around him...What if he…I don't know…forces her to do something with him?"

"If you haven't noticed, the last thing Stefan has to do is force anyone into doing anything," Andrea said with a patronizing smile. "Three quarters of the women in this caf would pay to be in Tami's shoes."

"Yeah," Jess said with a smirk. "The darkness you saw was probably horniness."

The older girls at the table laughed, but Allie and Hyacinth were silent, their eyes holding enough worry to make Sarah stand.

"Screw it, I don't trust him," she said as she got up from the table. She knew everyone was looking at her. She didn't care if she made a scene or did something stupid. Tami was in trouble; she could feel it in her bones.

Even if she just said what was on her mind in front of Stefan to let him know that, if her girlfriend came back with one hair out of place, one scratch on her that she didn't want, she'd be sure to make his life a living hell…that was her mission. To let that arrogant Upper Spheresman know that somebody was watching, somebody cared.

Sarah hurried out after Tami and then paused in the hallway, trying to gauge which direction Tami and Stefan had gone in.

"Finished dancing?" a voice said.

She whirled around to see Wil leaning against the wall, legs crossed at the ankles. He pushed off the wall and walked over to her.

Sarah put a hand over her heart. "I didn't see you there. You scared me."

"Yeah…it was obvious that I was invisible to you while you were dancing with your homeboy."

She so did not have time for this right now. "Val is like my brother. Gimme a break," she said, waving Wil off.

He caught her by her arm to keep her from leaving.

Still upset, she spun on him and yanked her arm away. "I have to find Tami. She went off with Stefan and—"

"Okay, okay, calm down." Wil put a hand on her face, and his expression changed from one of challenge to concern. "We'll find her together. Nobody is supposed to be wandering off alone anymore," he said, gazing into her eyes. "What do you think he's going to do to her?"

"I don't know! Maybe nothing, but I have to find her." Sarah could feel herself getting worked up again. They were wasting precious time.

"All right," Wil said, taking Sarah's hand. "Come on. I'll help you look."

CHAPTER 19

Wil took her through back hallways, hidden corridors and stairwells she'd never explored before. Beyond lost, all she could do was stay on his heels. But then she recognized the classroom level of the school and her pulse began to normalize. Okay, familiar ground, and nowhere too scary.

"Listen," Wil said to her in a quiet tone, stopping for a moment to catch his breath while holding her arm.

Sarah strained to hear, and after a few seconds she heard Tami's voice, heard her girlfriend giggling. Relief swept though Sarah and made her slump against the wall next to Wil.

"Thanks," she said in a near whisper, now feeling completely foolish for her panic. She closed her eyes and leaned her head back, wishing she could just slide into the mural on the wall and disappear.

"It's cool...I know she's your friend, and it's okay to be worried about a friend."

Sarah looked up at Wil, keeping her voice low like his. "I know it was stupid, but I just don't trust him."

Wil nodded and didn't tease her. "You're right to trust your instincts…something's not right with him, that's for sure."

"Glad it isn't just me," Sarah said, straightening. She looked up and down the corridor. "But how'd you know he'd come here and not the library…or the Great Hall, or somewhere else?"

Wil offered her a sheepish grin. "If I tell you, I swear, Sarah, you *cannot* tell anybody, especially none of the school officials."

She stepped closer to Wil and glanced around the vacant hallway, and then looked up into his honest eyes. “I promise,” she murmured, but it was more than words, it was a sacred oath.

He clasped her hand in one of his broad palms and then put a finger to his lips, leading her to a classroom door. Sarah peered in through the window at the top of the door but saw nothing except a large, dark swirling gray mass in the back of the room that obscured the second blackboard, chairs and part of the wall.

“Whoa…”

“Yeah,” Wil whispered. “They went in there.”

Sarah turned to him quickly, seeking answers in his expression, and then looked back through the closed classroom door.

“It’s a portal to town,” Wil said in a conspiratorial tone. “Right now, faculty is keeping a sharp eye on the Shady Path in the library, the Great Hall…most of the places everybody goes to so they can…you know—do whatever. So those are hot zones. But last month a couple of Uppers figured out how to pull the portal they found in town into Mr. Everett’s Inter-dimensional Shift classroom. Nobody monitors the classroom halls at night, especially tonight, during the luau.”

“Are you serious?” Sarah’s gaze went from the swirling mass to stare directly at Wil.

He looked at her and smiled, seeming pleased that he was able to offer her new information. “Yeah, pure truth,” he said stepping closer. “But it’s dangerous to go through unless you know how to fend off anything that could have been swept up in there.”

New worry creased Sarah’s brow, but Wil quickly allayed her fears.

“Word in the dorm is, Stefan practically grew up here—that’s why he’s more advanced than a lot of us. He’s not going to let your friend get hurt.”

“Yeah…but I wasn’t so much worried about the dark side, I was worried about *him*.”

Wil chuckled. "It's like an echo chamber—if she were in trouble or screaming, you'd hear it on this end…and last we heard, your friend was laughing."

"Yeah, she was."

"I'm in Shadows," Wil said in a casual tone. "And…I grew up in a pretty tough compound. If you really wanna see that she's okay, we could take a quick whirl and come back."

"Uhmmm…I don't know. We haven't even been in school a full week, and we'd be breaking a major rule."

Wil shrugged. "We'd only stay for, like, ten minutes, just to be sure your friend was all right. They'd never miss us. And if you're worried about an attack or anything, you'll have a Shadow with you."

The way he said it so calmly, without boasting, yet with no pressure for her to go along if she didn't want to, would have made going to the moon with him seem all right.

"Ten minutes? You promise?"

Wil beamed. "You have my word. Ten minutes."

"Okay…" Sarah said, nervously peering at the gray vortex. "What do we have to do?"

Wil clasped her hand. Again, there was that warm, firm, wonderful touch that was so awesome she felt lightheaded.

"Just walk forward with me and then hold on."

Sarah took a deep breath and squeezed his hand. This was the wildest thing she'd ever done in her life. The rational side of her brain told her there were at least a hundred reasons why this made no sense. Then there was the other side of her mind, which was completely occupied by Wil.

He took a few slow steps forward, all the while keeping his intense sea-green gaze on her. Then suddenly he gave her a little tug, she squealed, and his arms enfolded her. The next thing she knew they were speed-spiraling down a long energy tube so quickly that she couldn't catch her breath.

They came out with a soft thud, hitting a pile of hay in a barn. Wil threw his head back and laughed, hugging her. Sarah looked down, and then pried herself up and off his body.

"What a rush!" he said with a loud whoop, gazing up at her.

Truly, being pressed against him did feel divine, but embarrassment took over and made her get up and begin brushing dried hay off her jeans.

"Well?" he said, laughing.

Sarah had to smile and then all of a sudden laughter overtook her. "That was awesome! Crazy, but awesome."

"C'mon," Wil said, jumping up. "Let's get some wheels and go find your girl."

"Wheels?"

"Yeah. These border towns all have late model cars and trucks made just before the government started requiring GPS tracking chips, so the drivers can stay off the One World grid. We've gotta be a little careful when I zap it, though, because all the residents are armed to the teeth…but it should be cool if we borrow it and bring it right back."

Wil didn't even wait for her to answer or protest. He just jogged across the darkened barn, opened the door and peered out. Not wanting to be left in a dark, unfamiliar place, Sarah quickly caught up to him.

"Do you think that's such a good idea? *Borrowing* somebody's—"

"Sure, unless you wanna go the whole way through a dark town on foot?"

Since he'd put it that way…

Besides, Sarah said to herself, his tone was non-judgmental and calm. He didn't make her feel dumb or like a baby. Wil just gave her the facts and let her decide if what he'd said made sense or not. She liked that about him, and it was so different than the way she was treated at home by every guy in the compound. Well, every guy except Val.

Sudden conflict tore at Sarah as she watched Wil scan the streets for a vehicle they could use. Val had always occupied a special place as best-friend-and-slight-crush rolled into one. It was so odd—she and Val had started off as tight friends when they were little, and had almost a brother-sister relationship…but as they got older, the feelings started getting confusing, like on the dance floor tonight. Yet now Wil was quickly gaining ground in the best-male-friend-ever department, even though there was no doubt that he'd begun as a chemical-reaction crush. He was such a hunk—*and* nice. Whew.

Catching Sarah off guard, Wil turned back toward her quickly and gave her another dashing smile. "See that late model Ford pick-up over there? That's perfect."

Sarah strained to follow where he'd gestured. "You mean that rusted out tin can?"

"That's the one," he said, smiling broadly. "Those are the easiest to hot wire. C'mon. Follow me, but stay in the shadows."

If she'd been with anybody else, she would have told him that he'd lost his mind. Her? Sarah Rivera, staying in the shadows? But ducking down and running behind Wil seemed like the easiest thing to do.

He motioned for her to stay low as he pressed his palm against the door and a blue-white static charge crawled over the side of the rusted red metal door, making the locks pop up. He quietly opened the driver's side door a crack, and then helped her up and in. Staying down, she slid across the wide, worn leather seat and waited as Wil popped in next to her, shut the door and wrapped both palms around the steering column.

"I love these old vehicles," he said, staring at the blue static covering his hands. "No alarms, real basic wiring."

Then all of a sudden the engine turned over. Wil popped up, threw the vehicle into gear and slowly rolled it away from the curb.

"Oh, my God…when did you learn how to drive?" Sarah whispered as they went around the corner.

Wil laughed. "You can stop whispering now. Nobody but me can hear you. And I learned in the country with my Dad. Had to."

"Oh."

Sarah sat up and looked out the window. Then she watched Wil hand crank his window down, and she followed suit, enjoying the balmy September night breeze as it buffeted her face and lifted her hair.

People were out in groups dressed in fatigues, thick wool wraps, and thermal underwear and army boots, and everyone openly carried a weapon. She was actually among regular humans!

The town was built from logs and rocks and mud. It reminded her of old prairie shows and Westerns from bootleg DVDs her dad would bring back to the compound. The roads were dirt, muddy in some low-lying places. She couldn't stop gawking. This was the first time she'd been out in the world, and Wil had brought her. It was beyond mind-blowing.

"They probably only have a few stores. People don't risk stockpiling inventory anywhere anymore," Wil announced like a tour guide as they continued down the main strip. "If people have stuff to sell, they bring it out during the day and hawk it, and then they're gone by night. Same with people selling food and water. It's not like in the military-patrolled cities, where they have ridiculously high security. Things are on the honor system out here. Everybody knows pretty much everyone else, so if you steal something, they deal with you—frontier justice style."

Sarah glanced over at Wil, hanging on his every word. She hoped that borrowing a truck wouldn't be considered stealing it, if they got caught. The locals' idea of justice didn't sound good at all.

But the sights and sounds all around them stole her focus away from her fears. The adults in the compound had told her how there used to be clubs and movies and bowling alleys back in their day. These days, places like that were pretty-much gone, except in the government-run cities.

"Then what's the big deal about coming here?" Sarah said after a moment, growing concerned again because she still hadn't seen Tami.

"The bar," Wil said with a wide grin, and then nodded toward a long log cabin at the end of a row of one-story buildings and ramshackle homes. "At night, this place is pretty desolate, I'll grant you that. During the day you can buy stuff, eat, whatever. But at night, people are still scared of walkers, demons, vamps and werewolves…and with good cause. Not to mention any pirate drifters who might come through to raid for supplies. But the one thing that remains is the old watering hole. Guardians hang out there, because they aren't scared of jack. Usually the local town security hangs out in there…and so do the volunteer firefighters. It's sort of the local meeting place. People play pool, cards, gamble, watch illegal broadcasts…whatever. There's music. Probably the only place in town that serves food all night. Wanna go in?"

"Seriously?" Sarah looked from Wil to the building as he stepped on the gas and brought them closer to it. She'd never been around Regulars before, much less in a bar.

"Seriously," he said, and pulled the truck to a stop, then leaned over her in a dangerously sexy way, pressing his body against hers, popped the lock on her door, then scooted over to his side again and jumped out.

Flustered, she was still fidgeting with her door handle when he opened her door and gave her a hand down.

"C'mon. I doubt they'll serve us, 'cause we don't look old enough, even on a good night…but at least we can take a peek."

She just smiled at him, hurrying along, filled with excitement. She knew he'd said that for her benefit, and it was one of the nicest, most diplomatic comments he could have made. *He* could pass for old enough. She was the one who couldn't have passed on a good night. But he was taking her on a wild adventure, nonetheless, and wasn't even ashamed to hold her hand.

Two weary looking, gray-bearded, hooded men entered the bar ahead of them, and gave them a disapproving glare as they passed. They were carrying rifles and had on gray wool gloves with cut-off fingers.

"Watchmen," Wil murmured next to her ear. "Like town sheriffs…so we'll just stand in the doorway and make like we're looking for our parents or something, okay?"

Too nervous to do more than nod, Sarah could feel the heavy music thrumming through the planks of wood that led to the bar. The moment the door swung open, cigarette and cigar smoke, and the scent of roasting meats and alcohol, stung her nose. The thick fumes made her eyes water, but she stepped in behind Wil, clasping his hand, taking it all in, exhilarated.

Men and women sat on bar stools, and laughed and talked. The heavy clack of billiard balls echoed off a homemade pool table. Men playing cards joked and talked trash, which made her smile. That part of being there so reminded her of home. It was like the big rec room where her uncles and aunts got together, but with louder, unfamiliar music, smoke and a half dozen TVs blaring contraband channels all at the same time.

Several women draped themselves over men, and Sarah stared, wondering why such very public displays of affection were necessary. One glance at Wil and it was as though he'd read her mind. With a sly smile he whispered the answer in her ear.

"They're working."

Sarah's eyes got big, but she said nothing. Just standing in the doorway was a true education. But the best part of the place was the dance floor. People were out there having a good time, and seemed not to care if they were drunk, sober, had a partner or not. They were just out there moving and clearly having a blast.

The next thing she knew, Wil was pulling her by the hand until he had her out there on the floor dancing to a song she didn't even know. He spun her around, laughing.

"You owed me a dance," he said, then glanced over his shoulder at one of the watchmen, who'd gotten up and was headed their way. "But, it's time to go," Wil added, pulling her quickly to the door.

"You kids go home! You don't belong in here if you ain't looking for nobody!" the man yelled.

Sarah ran out the door with Wil, laughing, and then quickly jumped back into the truck. Wil turned it on with ease, backed up and then made a careening U-turn to head down the road the way they'd come. They laughed the entire way back, and kept getting a case of the giggles as he put his finger to his lips and quietly parked the borrowed vehicle back where it had been.

Very slowly and being quiet as mice, they rolled up the squeaking windows, softly pressed the doors closed, and then tip-toed away from the truck, finally making a flat-out dash back to the barn. They entered the dark space, shut the door behind them and gave in to the laughter.

"OMG," Sarah said, out of breath. "That was sooo crazy, but so much fun!"

"Yeah, it was, wasn't it?" Wil tugged her into an embrace for a second and then looked at the open end of the energy swirl over by the hay pallet. "C'mon…I'd better get you back. We didn't find Tami and Stefan, but I'm sure they're joy-riding somewhere around town like we just did."

Sarah nodded. "Okay," she murmured with a wide grin. He felt so warm and safe and good against her that her entire body ached when he let her go.

Wil jumped up on the hay and held out a hand. She eagerly accepted it with no fear this time, and then squealed as the vortex sucked them back up to land sprawled on the floor back in the classroom.

"Now do you see why a lot of kids do it?" Wil asked, helping her up.

Sarah nodded, laughing. "Yeah…I just wish Tami had gone with someone as nice as you."

Wil gave her a bashful smile and led her by the hand into an alcove. "We can wait for them here, if it'll make you feel better."

"Thanks," Sarah said quietly, sitting down beside him on a wide ventilation casing. "I really appreciate it."

"I'm not saying that Stefan is a knight in shining armor—far from it—but I don't think he'll force her or do something really stupid."

Sarah's eyes searched Wil's in the faux moonlight being cast from the murals all around them, worried. "I hope you're right...It's just that I saw something around him that scared me. Something stupid left over from old childhood fears, I guess."

"Like what?" Wil's expression was completely open, his eyes beckoning her to trust him…and she did.

"You're going to think I'm really crazy," she said, prefacing her revelation with a request. "So you can't tell anybody about this. They already wanna test me a gazillion more times, and I just want to fit in and be like everybody else."

He took both her hands, keeping them between his fabulously warm palms. "Sarah, you can trust me...I won't tell anybody anything you say."

"When I was like eleven or twelve…something happened to me," she said quietly, looking away.

Wil dropped one of her hands and put a finger beneath her chin, bringing her eyes back to his. "Show me," he murmured, coming closer, so close that she could see his pupils dilate.

She couldn't look away, couldn't move; her body felt like it was melting. She was sure that she was about to become a puddle right there in front of him as his hands slid up to gently cradle her face. Her palms slid over the backs of his to cover them.

"I've never shared a vision before," she whispered.

"It's okay," he said in a low murmur. "I'll go in with you, but we'll go easy."

"But if I say we have to get out…"

"We'll get out. You show me how far you want to go."

Her voice betrayed her; it wouldn't work at all. Her response was a slow nod as her lips parted and she sipped a shallow breath of air. Gentle pressure and heat filled her mind, and suddenly the terrifying childhood memory was back, but this time she felt safe, as though she were a dispassionate observer.

Al was chasing her, teasing her, and then he dodged outside the light barriers. She had her fist balled up, ready to slug him, when he sidestepped and she fell, her momentum carrying her forward until she was falling down the steep incline. The hillside was pitch-black at night, and terror almost broke through the memory, but Wil's soft voice prodded her on.

"Don't, it's all right…keep going."

Breathing heavily, she let the vision unfold. A light film of perspiration covered her body, and she watched Wil slowly lick his bottom lip. In the vision, she came to a thudding stop at the bottom of the hill, and then suddenly there were shadows all around her, reaching for her.

Her scream split the air, and she started to struggle, not realizing that she was pulling out of Wil's hold.

"Easy, easy, I've got you," he said.

"But they're coming for me," she croaked out.

"No, they can't get to you—you are light. Say it."

"I am light," she murmured, gasping.

Then she saw Val reach her and help her up.

"He didn't see them—no one else has ever seen them." Sarah dropped her head against Wil's chest, and a big tear rolled down her nose.

He crushed her to him hard, and she could feel his hands in her hair. "I believe you, Sarah. I saw them…but I don't think they were there to hurt you."

"You don't?" she said in a near whisper.

"No…it's weird," he said, nuzzling her hair. "But I have to ask you a question."

"All right," she murmured against his chest, loving the way his arms felt around her.

"Sarah..." he said, pulling back and looking down at her. "I really like you…a lot. You're not like some of the game-players around here, all fake. You're real, inside and out. I'd really like to get to know you better, but…"

"I like you, too." Sarah looked up, elated and confused. What had created the "but"? Maybe her stupid fears. Maybe Patty Gray?

"The tall guy, Val…the same guy who was in your vision just now. Should I know something about him? I don't want to run into a fist on my way to class tomorrow, even though it'd be worth it." Wil smiled.

Sarah quickly pulled away and wiped her cheeks, careful not to smudge her make-up. "Oh, Val?" A shy smile bloomed on her face. "We grew up together. He's like a brother to me. I already told you it's not like that." She took a deep breath, conflict tightening her stomach. Why was she suddenly so ambivalent about Val? Was it possible to like two guys romantically at the same time? Feeling unsure, but not wanting to give Wil a reason to stop this wonderful thing that was beginning between them, she pressed her point. "I believed what you told me about Patty."

Wil nodded, his smile gentle. "Yeah…and I'm acting like a jerk, aren't I?"

He was actually jealous? Sarah looked down. Staring at him now was too intense. Her belly was all tingly, and it was suddenly hard to breathe.

"You're not a jerk," she said quietly. "Far from it."

She felt so many things at that moment as he lifted her chin with his forefinger, forcing her to stare into those hypnotic sea green eyes of his...The first thing she could identify was hope—hope that what was happening between them wasn't just a case of proximity and hormones. Then total exhilaration that he was interested in her…and something else that warmed her inner thighs and completely terrified her.

But he never gave her a chance to pull all those scattered feelings together. He simply lowered his mouth to hers and gently brushed her lips with his. It was amazing. Warmth went racing from her stomach to each limb. She felt lightheaded and shaky all at the same time. He did it again, this time with a little more force, and she kissed him back, allowing herself to taste the tip of his tongue. He smelled so good, like fresh soap and something she'd never noticed before. Warm, warm hands covered her shoulders, but she didn't know what to do with her own as his tongue probed her mouth, finding all the delicate, sensitive spots within.

So she kept her hands clasped in her lap, even as she found herself leaning into the kiss, the sensation of it making her full to the point where she thought she might burst. She pressed her knees together tightly, wrongly thinking that might help. Her skin was on fire, every inch of her tingling, expectant, longing to feel the warmth that seemed to emanate from his hands.

She broke the kiss with a short gasp. "Uhmmm…I don't think we should be missing when they end the luau."

He nodded, breathing hard, and she glanced away from the bulge in his pants. "Yeah, that wouldn't be good."

It actually hurt to stop kissing him. She had to get out of there, but his eyes drew her back to stare at him…eyes now haunted in a way that made her both want to kiss him hard and flee.

"Just a little longer," he murmured and then pulled her to him slowly, opening her mind as he opened her mouth with a deep, soul-dredging kiss.

Her mind went in one direction, her body in the other. Her legs were entwined with his before she caught his hand at the edge of her shirt. He stared at her with both a plea and an apology in his eyes. She didn't have to say it—he knew without reading her mind. Things were happening too fast for her, this was all too new…and the mind-shadowing had opened them both up too intensely.

Laughter and voices coming down the hall created an instant solution. Sarah was on her feet in seconds, and quickly adjusted her clothes. Wil stood a little slower, then turned and faced the wall for a moment, seeming like he was about to die from embarrassment.

“Tami,” Sarah said, coming out of the alcove. “I was looking all over for you!”

Tami giggled and glanced at Stefan, who gave Sarah a sly half-smile.

“I have been on the adventure of a lifetime,” Tami said. She quickly kissed Stefan’s cheek, then ran up to Sarah and slung arm over her shoulder. “We’d better get back before they think we really went missing.” She glanced back at Stefan. “See you later.”

“Oh, most assuredly,” he said with a wolfish grin.

Sarah gave Wil a little wave as she passed the alcove. “Thanks.”

He just nodded.

“Dude!” Stefan yelled out, laughing, making Sarah walk faster and cringe.

“Don’t say a word, Tami,” Sarah whispered. “Not one.”

“’Kay,” Tami said, skipping along.

Sarah didn’t turn around. She was just glad when she heard Wil hurry off in the opposite direction.

Walking in a daze, she tried to listen to Tami’s happy chattering, but most of what her friend said was bouncing off her brain. Wil’s kiss and the mind-lock she’d shared with him had been awesome...She finally understood a little bit of what Ayana had been talking about, and maybe a little more about what had made Tami lose her mind. She had certainly lost hers—she had left the party and gone through a portal with Wil Archer and kissed him again!

Some things she wasn’t about to tell to a soul, especially not Tami—not right now, when her friend would be liable to blab the news to Allie and Hyacinth. No, this got tucked in her heart vault until things progressed a little more and it wasn't so intensely new. She'd tell her friends…soon. Just not this second, Sarah told herself, and forced her attention to the conversation.

To give their reappearance some casual flair, when they got back to the luau she and Tami swung by the beverage bar to stall for time, grabbed a couple of drinks and headed toward Jessica's table. It was agreed: what happened in the hallway stayed in the hallway.

The story they'd concocted was rock solid. Tami left with Stefan, Sarah got unnecessarily worried and went to find her, found her hanging with Stefan, and then the two of them decided to come back together. That was the story. Stefan was doing what he always did—roaming the halls somewhere without an authorized pass—and Tami didn't want to get in trouble, which was why she left him and hooked back up with Sarah. Nothing happened, everything was cool. Period. Sarah saw that Wil had already slipped back in and was chatting with some of the other Shadows.

The crowd was thinning out. The Hawaiian-dressed cafeteria staff was beginning to clean up food, and the chaperones were slowly standing and beginning to break up the event.

"Where were you guys?" Allie said, rushing up to them, out of breath.

"Yeah, geeze, guys…" Hyacinth said, shaking her head as she came up behind Allie. "We were—"

"Fine," Tami muttered, and shook her head. She looked at Sarah. "Now do you see why they make me crazy?"

Tami had a point, but Sarah couldn't get on board with it right now. Dread was roiling in the pit of her stomach, and she didn't know why.

Chapter 20

Before Allie and Hyacinth could launch into a full blown interrogation, everyone's PIU started vibrating. Sarah grabbed hers and gasped.

"Oh, my God," Allie said in a horrified rush, and before Sarah could say a word, the door to their room flew open and Headmistress Stone came rushing in. "Girls, I need you to come with me right now."

"Nana, what happened? What's going on?" Sarah said, running forward. She was so upset that all formality in the reference was gone. This wasn't 'Headmistress Stone' right now—this was her grandmother.

"Two more students have gone missing."

Sarah had never seen her grandmother like this before, so distressed. She felt a small knot of dread settle in her stomach.

Her Nana took a deep breath. "One of the missing students is Ayana."

They rushed down the hallway to her grandmother's office, barely able to keep stride with her.

"Your parents are all here," Nana Marlene told them.

"Where is everyone else?" Sarah asked, now running. "Where's Al and—"

"We already spoke to them before I came to your room," her grandmother replied. "The other members of the Guardian compound and the warrior-level faculty are searching the town and the forest for any sign of Ayana and Alexis."

Alexis Woodrow, an Upper Sphere, was the other missing student? Ayana wasn't with Brent? Now that really made no sense.

"The forest?" Sarah said, alarmed. They thought that Ayana might be in the blackened forest? Her heart began to pound even harder.

"Hurry," Nana Marlene said.

They arrived in her grandmother's offices, and saw her mother and Aunt Juanita there, along with a teary-eyed Aunt Inez. Aunt Jasmine and Aunt Heather looked like they'd been crying, too, and her Aunt Tara was wound so tightly that she couldn't retract her fangs. The girls ran to their mothers and barreled into their arms. Their mothers hugged them hard, and that was when Aunt Inez really began to cry.

Sarah's mother released her and went to her Aunt Inez.

"We'll find her, 'Nez...I promise you, I won't let anything happen to your baby girl." Sarah's mother's wings enfolded her Aunt as Inez's painful wails escalated.

"Dear God, Damali, after all we've been through with these kids, after all the death, hell and destruction we've kept them from—now this? My baby's gone!"

"We're gonna find her…me, you, Carlos, and Mike—three strong seers, two Neterus, and the best Audio on the planet...Marlene will help, too, so don't panic…just stay with me and stay clear in your head. Inez, you understand me?" Sarah's mother said, with tears streaming down her own cheeks.

Sarah wrapped her arms around herself as her grandmother came over and hugged her. The door burst open, and Mom Delores, Inez's mother and Ayana's blood grandmother, and her grandfather, Mr. Monty, aka Pop Pop, came in huffing and out of breath.

"My gran' baby…they got her," Mom Delores said, wringing her hands. "No, Lordy, no, jus' take me this time, not that young girl!"

"We're looking all over for both Ayana and Alexis," Mr. Monty said, his Caribbean accent thickened by his deep emotion. "School staff and warrior instructors are with that child's parents that have been energy whirled in."

When Mr. Monty tried to hold Mom Delores, she jerked away and hurried over to her daughter. The door opened again, and Hyacinth's and Allie's grandparents rushed in, everyone talking at once.

Bewildered, the girls gathered together in a tight little huddle and wept quietly as the adults tried to comfort the wailing woman in the middle of the room. The loss of one child from the compound was a loss to everyone, and a pain so deep and visceral gripped Sarah that she literally couldn't breathe. General pandemonium reigned until the steady demeanor of Nana Marlene, the family matriarch, drew everyone's attention.

"We have to summon calm," Nana Marlene said, and the room gradually went quiet in the wake of her words. "That's the only way we're going to find Ayana and all the others who are missing—and we will find our students, even if we have to go to Hell and back. We've done that before with much less at stake, and I have no problem going back down there again for any of these kids."

Angry nods of agreement went around the room. Nana Marlene looked at Sarah's mother, who stepped forward to explain where they stood so far.

"We've got people checking both kids' rooms and searching the school grounds," her mother said, then went on to explain what the armed and motivated searchers were doing.

At a natural pause in the narration, Nana Marlene turned to Aunt Juanita and asked, "Would you go to the teachers' lounge, and get Inez and Delores some tea?" She gently touched the distraught women on the shoulder, guiding them to sit down as Aunt Juanita hurried out.

"Girls," Nana Marlene said, "we need to know if you saw or heard anything. We're also asking any student or faculty member to come and talk to us if they saw or heard anything. The hard part of all this is that every student who has gone missing left their PIU in the dorm, so we can't even track them that way." Nana Marlene let out a long breath in frustration. "When was the last time you saw Ayana?"

"We couldn't get her before the party," Sarah said, glancing around the room with tear-filled eyes. "We kept texting her, but she never answered." Her bottom lip trembled with grief as she realized why Ayana had never responded, and every mean thing she'd ever thought crashed in on her with one big sob. "We thought she was ignoring us...had stood us up for her boyfriend! I just figured that was why she wasn't at the luau." Sarah covered her face with her hands. "But she was missing, not avoiding us."

Nana Marlene frowned. "Do you know who this boy is?"

All eyes were on Sarah, and it was so quiet that the only thing she could hear was Aunt Inez's labored breathing.

"His name is Brent Wilson," Sarah said, glancing around the room. "And for the record, he's a world class jerk. We didn't see him at the party last night, either. So we just figured they were off together somewhere."

Her mother and Nana Marlene exchanged a glance as Aunt Juanita returned to the room with herbal tea, which both Aunt Inez and Mom Delores refused.

"Anything else?" Nana Marlene stared at Sarah.

Sarah glanced at Tami and then bit her lip. It was Wil's secret, just like it was Tami's, but this was so much more important than that...yet the thought of telling where they'd been...here...in front of everyone in the family...tied Sarah's stomach in knots.

"Well?" Sarah's mother said, walking over and grabbing her by both arms. "This is serious, Sarah! And I know you know the answer. It's written all over your face. Tell me."

"I—I went through a portal to town with a boy from school…when I was supposed to be at the luau," Tami said, quietly. "Maybe that's where they went, too. I don't know for sure…but Sarah didn't want to tell on me."

"But I—"

"What!" Tami's mother shrieked, cutting off Sarah's attempt at a confession, then crossed the room so quickly that she was practically a blur. She got in Tami's face, glowering at her, breathing hard, full fangs presented, and impatiently waited on a full explanation.

"It's not her fault," Sarah said, coming to her friend's defense and trying to confess herself. "I—"

"Some Uppers opened a portal—like Baba Shabazz said during opening ceremonies," Tami said, meeting her mother's furious gaze and then turning to Nana Marlene. "Stefan…he didn't open it and doesn't know how, but he did take me to town on a joy ride. Sarah was in the hall with Wil looking for me when I got back, because she was worried…"

"But…" Sarah stammered. "I also—"

"Where's this new portal?" Uncle Richard said, interrupting Sarah and checking the clip on his nine millimeter.

"In the back of Mr. Everett's classroom." Tami began twisting the hem of her shirt as her eyes filled with new tears. "But we came back, and…and everything was fine. He said someone would shut it down before anyone found it, so I forgot about it once we got back. Maybe Ayana and Alexis went down that portal with Brent, or maybe looking for Brent, and something happened to them. Oh God, I'm so sorry...I didn't think anyone would get hurt." Tami's words trailed off and then became wracking sobs, as her mother grabbed her and clutched her to her chest.

"I didn't think anything would happen, either," Sarah said, tearing up, and then squeezed Tami's hand.

"Get Titan Troy, Jose and Mike on detail with you, Richard," Nana Marlene said as he headed for the door. "Professor Raziel is out in the forest flying reconnaissance with Valkyrie, and Shabazz is working at ground level. I'll mind-lock with Shabazz and give him a remote update. Shut that portal down hard, gentlemen."

"This Brent," Nana Marlene said, turning back to the girls and staring at Sarah. "Is he definitely Ayana's boyfriend?"

Sarah nodded, feeling uncomfortable. "And...I overheard them arguing a day before the luau. He wanted her to go down the Shady Path and into town with him to get wasted, and she didn't want to go. But maybe she decided to go find him?"

Her grandmother closed her eyes as Aunt Inez stood and paced toward the window. "Give me strength," Nana Marlene said, and then looked at Aunt Juanita and Aunt Tara. "Please alert security—I want Brent Wilson's butt in a chair in front of me, pronto."

"Done," Aunt Tara said, glaring at her daughter. "You and I will talk later."

Aunt Juanita nodded, and both warriors slipped out of the room.

"We will find them. We will!" Nana Marlene said, grabbing Delores and Inez by the hand.

"Nana," Sarah said, "how did this happen?" New tears filled her eyes. "And why does this keep happening? Where is she?" She couldn't help it. She burst into tears.

Damali rushed forward and hugged Sarah again. "We don't know, baby, but we're going to find them. I promise you that."

"But why Yaya?" Sarah sputtered through her tears.

"I keep asking the same question," Aunt Inez said, twisting a tissue in her fingers until she'd shredded it. "Why my baby?"

"None of it makes sense," Sarah's mother said, stroking Sarah's hair as she spoke. "She doesn't fit the pattern we thought we'd figured out," she added, looking at Aunt Inez. "All the other children who were abducted were orphans, kids who would be missed by their friends but who didn't have an entire compound or an extended family to get up in arms about them." She squeezed Sarah to her closer. "And the missing adults…The Rogue Guardians, by definition, travel alone…and the staff members from Nod, like the Fae, were refugees—and many of them were already alone in the world even before they came here. The witches who were taken were soloists, not part of a working coven."

"Then they really screwed up when they took my chile," Inez said bitterly, and then wiped her face with the backs of her hands. "'Cause they oughta know I'ma hunt 'em down till I draw my last breath."

For a moment no one spoke; in fact, they barely breathed. The hurt and rage roiling within Aunt Inez were so intense that they filled Sarah's lungs, threatening to suffocate her.

"Girls, there is something that you should know," Nana Marlene finally said. "I'm strongly considering shutting the school down until this matter is resolved."

"Damn right we're shutting the school down," an angry male voice said behind Sarah.

They all turned to see her father standing in the doorway. Uncle Jose, a distressed Uncle Mike and Uncle Dan were behind him. Uncle Mike immediately went to Aunt Inez, who collapsed against his tree-trunk frame.

Her father walked into the room carrying a grenade launcher on his shoulder.

"Did you find anything?" Sarah's mother asked.

"Same whole lot of nothing we found at every other scene," her father said, disgusted. "No one else found a thing, either. We haven't got jack." He made a slashing motion with his hand.

"Mike, Inez," Nana Marlene said, worry and concern shining in her eyes, "how are you holding up?"

"Not well," Uncle Mike said, his voice tight. "And I won't be until I have my baby girl back."

Marlene nodded and looked away.

"I think we need to get these kids out of here, starting today. Get the parents on the PirateNet and let them know what's going on. I can start transporting students out as soon as they're ready," Carlos said.

Nana Marlene rubbed a finger between her eyebrows. "I'll get my staff started on contacting the parents. In the meantime, we'll begin informing the students." She went behind her desk. "You girls try to get some rest. If you think of anything else, let us know immediately." She looked up at Dan. "Can you get our girls back to their dorm?"

"Sure," he said, hugging his daughter Allie tightly. "Come on, pumpkin. We'll find Yaya, don't worry."

Sarah stood watching as everyone prepared to go off in different directions. No! The thought screamed out to her so loudly that she thought for a moment one of her Aunts had yelled it. This wasn't right. They couldn't leave. The school had to stay open. Something deep inside her knew they couldn't go. They had to stay if there was any hope of finding Ayana and the other students alive. She felt it like a vibration deep within her.

"No. We can't leave," she said in a quiet, far-away tone. She didn't move, didn't turn away from her father's look of impatience as she slowly began shaking her head.

Everyone turned to face her.

"What?" her father said with a frown.

Sarah stared at them, wiped her cheeks and repeated herself, "We can't leave. Ayana's still out there, and if we leave, we'll never find her. I know it." Then she stared off into space and said, almost as an afterthought, "Ayana wasn't supposed to be taken. It was a mistake."

Aunt Inez put her hand over her mouth, and Uncle Mike hugged her even closer. For a moment, everyone in the room paused and stared at Sarah as her mother and grandmother became eerily still.

"Baby…how do you know?" her mother asked in a quiet, intense voice.

Sarah swallowed hard. “I don’t know, Mom…I just do.”

Her grandmother shot a glance toward her mother, but her dad hesitated for a second and then crossed the room, seeming to dismiss her statement with a tense shrug.

“Baby girl, I know how you feel,” he said, trying to convince her to leave. “This is eating me up, too, believe me. But you can’t stay. It’s not safe. I wish that everyone had listened to me earlier and that none of you were here—but it is what it is. Now me, your Mom and the rest of the family have to fix this and make it right. Okay, baby? You understand me?”

Sarah shook her head stubbornly, becoming frantic. “We can’t leave. We have to stay and find them, Papi.”

Her father put his hands on her shoulders, leaned down and looked her in the eyes. “We will find her,” he said, and his voice was full of strength and conviction. “No matter what, we will bring Yaya home. We’ll bring all those kids home. There ain’t no doubt about that, ok? Just leave it to us. But we need you at home, safe, so we can do what we need to do.”

Pure terror entered her, and she held her father’s t-shirt in her fists as full-blown hysteria suddenly overtook her. “No, Daddy, you don’t understand. She’s my mother-seer! We’re linked! I feel her, I know…I can’t explain it, but I know—if you shut down the school, you’re sentencing her to death. Don’t do it!”

“Carlos, listen to the child,” Aunt Inez said, going to Sarah and hugging her, pulling her away from her father and staring into her eyes. “Tell us what you see, baby,” her aunt implored. “I’m a seer, your mother is a seer, your nana is a seer—and so’s our Yaya. Tell me, honey…can you feel her? Is she all right?”

Sarah nodded, crying harder in her aunt’s embrace. “They’re alive. It’s dark. I can’t see where they are…but I know inside my soul that if you shut the school down now, we’ll never find them.”

"I think the people who have the final say are those who have the most already at risk," Nana Marlene said calmly but firmly, looking at Sarah's father. "That would be Inez and Mike."

Aunt Inez snapped her head up to look at Sarah's father. "Carlos…it's my baby girl who's missing. Sarah is the only one who's linked to Ayana this strongly. The mother seer bond between them has been growing steadily. It's even tighter than the mother-daughter connection."

Even Sarah's mother nodded. "I don't need to remind you that there is a strong link between a future mother seer and her charge, Carlos," she said.

Nodding in agreement, Nana Marlene walked over to Carlos and put a hand on his shoulder. "It has begun, and neither you, nor anybody else, can stop it. This is the order of things. The babies leave their parents and form the link with the mother seer, and you have got to let Sarah's instincts about this prevail."

"If Sarah says we keep the school open, we keep it open," Uncle Mike said, looking hard at Sarah's Dad.

Clearly outnumbered, her father finally nodded.

"I'll work with Nana Marlene to contact the parents, so they can make their individual choices," Sarah's mother said. "Some may pull their children, but we will honor Sarah's instincts, Carlos." Her mother went to Inez and brushed back her hair. "We're gonna get those kids back safely. All of them."

PART THREE
DISCERNMENT

"...Do not be hostile to me in the presence of the Keeper of the Balance..."

—The Book of Going Forth by Day

CHAPTER 22

Sarah looked up at her uncle Dan as he guided them all back to the dorm. Strain was apparent in his deep blue eyes, his normally neat blond hair was mussed, and fatigue had cast a gray pallor over his normally robust complexion. She hated to wrest him from his deep thoughts as they trudged along like a defeated huddle of humanity, but she had to make a stop along the way. She had to *feel* Ayana's room.

"Uncle Dan…I've got to go into Ayana's room."

The group stopped walking and simply stared at her.

"I have to," Sarah insisted, beginning to twist her shirt into a knot. "I have to feel what the room can tell me."

"All right," he said hesitantly. "I'm no seer—I'm just a Tactical—but I've witnessed how sensing is done. I don't suppose there'd be any harm in it, especially since your grandmother and mother, as well as your aunt Inez, have all been in there already to try to pick up impressions."

"Thanks," Sarah whispered.

"Dad, if anybody is connected to Yaya, it's Sarah," Allie said with a trembling voice as she put an arm over her friend's shoulder.

"Okay, let me get you three into your room—and I'm waiting 'til I hear you lock the door, got that? And then I'll take you, Sarah."

Just having a plan, having something to do, made her walk more quickly and added intensity of purpose to her stride. She waited impatiently for her uncle to herd everyone else into their dorm room and for him to say goodbye to Allie, knowing how parting with his daughter was tearing him up now more than ever. It had been on every parent's face in Nana Marlene's office, that sense of relief amid doom. It was telegraphed in the extra tight hugs, in teary eyes and wavering voices. All of it said, there but for the grace of God go I—that could have been my baby who's gone missing.

But soon her uncle's warm arm covered her shoulders as he steered her to Ayana's room. He opened the door and stood back, allowing Sarah to enter under his watchful gaze.

She stood in the middle of the floor and closed her eyes. Nothing seemed to be out of the ordinary. Ayana's bed was made. Her books were stacked in the corner of her desk. Her roommates' tension still thickened the air like a heavy residue…crying. Tina and Darlene were terrified and had been crying just like she, Tami, Allie and 'Cinth had been. They had been moved to a new room for safety's sake and clearly hadn't wanted to leave. Sarah opened her eyes and hugged herself for a moment, then caught a glimpse of the shadows in the corner.

They were back, and tonight they seemed particularly agitated. They kept running back and forth along the baseboards, then jumped up and down on Ayana's desk near the small shelf that held her toiletries. Not a thing appeared to be out of place—until Sarah realized that the toothpaste was there, but the toothbrush and cup weren't. But with the shadows stretching and popping wildly, she couldn't really think about that. Knowing Yaya, she had those items stashed in a plastic baggie in a drawer or something.

Just stop. Would you please stop! Sarah thought, then she looked at her uncle. "I'm sorry. I couldn't pick up anything other than how upset her roommates were."

"It's all right, honey. We're all working on it. We'll find her, I promise. Why don't I walk you back to your room?"

There was nothing left to do but comply. She walked with him down the corridor, and he waited until she knocked on the door, then slipped inside, but not before leaving him with a kiss on his cheek.

"Well?" Allie asked, wiping her nose with a tissue. "Any luck?"

Sarah shook her head no as Allie, Tami and Hyacinth crowded close, eager to hear whatever she had to say.

"I feel sick," Tami said quietly, then sat down slowly on the bed. "This is Yaya. We should go back to the library tomorrow and sneak into the Shady Path to see if we can feel anything there. We can't just wait for everyone else to figure it out."

"That sounds like a plan to me, but right now I can't even think straight," Sarah said, resting her forehead against the door. "I know there's something they're overlooking, something all of us aren't seeing." She looked at her friends and wiped her nose with the back of her hand. Her eyes felt grainy, like someone had shoved sandpaper under her lids. "I wish we'd all stayed home, like Dad wanted, especially Yaya. Then none of this would have happened in the first place. I have to wash my face."

"I'll walk you," Tami said, starting to get up from her bed, but Sarah shook her head.

"It's just down the hall. Nobody is going to come back in here with all this heat in the system right now, and I really just need to be by myself for a minute. She's my seer…my sister…my…" Sarah covered her face with her hands and broke down, which made Allie, Tami and Hyacinth wrap her in loving arms. "How could they have taken Yaya?"

Slowly but surely the tears abated, and her compound sisters released her, wiping at their own tears.

"You go wash your face and then get your butt right back here," Tami said and gave Sarah a quick squeeze.

Looking both ways, Sarah crept down the hall to the girls' bathroom. How did things like this happen? None of the missing students, except

Ayana, even had the benefit of parents, which was horrible enough in itself. All of it was a nightmare, all of it was tragic, but until Ayana had disappeared, the other students who had gone missing were just names to her. Plus two Upper Sphere students had actually died. Now with Ayana and Alexis, that made four missing and two dead. All of it made her shiver.

Sarah's conscience weighed heavily on her as she stood there in the bathroom. Yes, she cared, but in a removed kind of way. Now tragedy had a face, and that made everything deeply, painfully personal.

She went to the sink, then bent to splash cold water on her face. Was it a sin that she cared more now that Ayana had been abducted? she wondered, then looked up and grabbed a paper towel, staring at her red eyes and nose as she blotted her face dry. There had to be something they could do. Tami was right—they couldn't just sit and wait for their parents to fix this.

Frustration claimed her as she tossed away the used paper towel and headed back to her room. But the hair stood up on her neck as the shadows that she'd almost forgotten about began moving along the hall in what looked like an agitated little dance, stopping near an exit.

Sarah froze for a moment, then, lured by the shadows, she chased after them. What if they knew where Yaya was or could point her in the right direction? Was that why they'd been in such a frenzy when she walked into Yaya's room? If they could lead her to a clue, she would risk going after them.

Running down the hall as quietly as possible, she stopped by the door marked EXIT, slipped behind it and then listened hard. There were voices. Something was going on. She was instant motion, hurrying down the steps as softly as she could, then listening momentarily at the next door down before exiting there, and rushing down the hall to find a service corridor extension. That was when she heard the voices more clearly, both of them familiar.

Sarah stopped, pressed her body into the shadows of an alcove and listened.

"If you ever take anything from me again, I swear you'll regret it, Melissa!"

It was Stefan, and he sounded pissed.

"I swear I didn't."

"And if you mess this up for me, I swear, I'll—"

"I would never do that!" Melissa said, her voice fracturing as she spoke.

"You'd better make sure you don't!" The threat in Stefan's tone was unmistakable. "Do you know what's going on? Everything around here is about to get hot, and they're looking for me. They've already got Brent in there, grilling him about Ayana, and now you pull some stupid shit like this? He'll get a pass, on account of who his parents are—you know that. Me, they'll expel, and where am I gonna go, you spoiled flake? I don't have parents and a home compound waiting for me, Mel! What'd you tell them, huh?"

"I didn't tell them anything. I wouldn't do anything to get you in trouble, I swear," she said, beginning to cry.

"Don't play me," he said. "You've got your new dude, Alejandro—so leave me alone. It's over!"

"I was only messing with him to make you jealous," she said, her voice a desperate plea.

Sarah could see them as Stefan stormed out of the alcove they'd been in, Melissa grabbing his arm. As much as she hated the girl, it was still heart-rending to watch her cling to his arm even as he shrugged her off.

"You don't do werewolf. Remember?" he said, sneering.

Sarah flattened herself against the wall again, but this time with her hand over her heart and listening intently as Stefan walked off. Werewolf? Did the guy say he was a werewolf? That explained the darkness she saw around him. Werewolf blood was so different from Baba's shape-shifter powers. There was a lunacy that took over, a loss of the human self inside the primal bloodlust of the flesh-eating wolf. That was what Stefan was? Not a shape-shifter but part frickin' crazy wolf? And Nana had let him into the school? Holy…

Sarah inhaled deeply to calm herself. She had to remember that her nana was a veteran seer. She had to know that Stefan was a werewolf. But then again, sometimes it seemed as though there were things she could see that others couldn't, even her nana. Like the shadows. What if he was turning and able to hide it from people? What if he really was dangerous? What if he was abducting students and feeding on them!

The sound of adult voices patrolling the halls shot another wave of panic through Sarah. They were in the same stairwell she had just left. She made a mad dash, following the direction Melissa and Stefan had gone, found another stairway and ran down two flights, then found the service corridor. She ran as though a demon were chasing her and didn't slow down until she got back to her room.

"Where have you been?" Allie said, racing over to hug her. "We were worried sick and almost called Nana Mar!"

"Yeah, you promised to come right back, and when you didn't, we got scared," Tami said, hiding her fear behind anger. She pointed at Hyacinth, lying on her bed. "'Cinth is so upset she's ready to hurl."

Hyacinth just looked up at Sarah with bloodshot eyes. "I can't take any more, okay?" She turned over and drew herself up into fetal position.

"You can't go out with Stefan, Tami," Sarah blurted out, ignoring all the charges her friends had lobbed against her. "Something's not right about him."

"What are you talking about?" Tami grabbed Sarah by both arms as Allie stood in the middle of the floor, gaping. "Yaya is missing, and all you can think about is why I shouldn't be with Stefan? Get over yourself, Sarah!"

"I saw him. Melissa was trying to get him to get back together with her, and he blew her off. It was a disaster."

"Good," Tami said flatly.

"Not good. She's playing Al to make Stefan jealous."

Tami let go of Sarah. "And…?"

For a moment Sarah didn't answer. Guilt lacerated her. She hadn't stepped forward and admitted that she'd also gone into town—she hadn't, and that fact was damning. She had to do better now. Stefan was clearly into some dangerous underground scene, and his confession that he was a werewolf had freaked her out. Sarah released a breath of frustration.

"Look, Melissa took something from him. I don't know what, but…Look, all I'm saying is he could be dealing drugs right here in the school, or maybe he's into something worse. In any event, he told her he was a werewolf—that much I'm sure of. And whatever other stuff he's into, it didn't sound good."

"First of all, you don't know that for a fact. Melissa is pathetic. She could be lying. She'd do anything to get him back, I bet." Tami frowned, then her expression slowly changed to one of awe. "I thought Baba Shabazz was the last of the shape-shifters. If you're right about Stefan, then…cool."

"Cool. *Cool*? Do you hear yourself? A shape-shifter is one thing, but somebody who gets crazy and eats people when the moon goes full is something way different." Sarah began to pace. "Like, I think you need to know a lot more about Stefan before you get all caught up, *especially* before you ask Jessica for anything—you know what I mean? And especially since we don't know if he was involved in opening portals and—"

"Hold it. Now you've crossed the line, Sarah," Tami said, kicking off her slippers and climbing up onto her bunk. "I didn't say anything to you about Wil and the fact that something's obviously going on with him and Patty, so don't you judge me! Not to mention, I already admitted where I was. I might have gotten the poor guy expelled for doing nothing more than a lot of kids are doing. He's certainly not a kidnapper or a…a…I don't know what."

"I'm not judging you, Tami. I'm just—"

"Back off. It's my choice! I like the bad-boy types, so sue me. This hasn't got anything to do with Ayana being gone. This is about you not liking my choice and not respecting it! I have always had your back, Sarah—when are you going to start having mine, huh? It's always crazy Tami's fault, isn't it?"

"Well, at least cut Al a break in public, then, all right," Sarah said, feeling her face getting hot. "You almost got my brother beat down by a real live half-were at the luau."

"First of all, you're one to talk!" Tami shouted. "What was that thing with you and Wil after dancing up close and personal with Val? I guess it's okay for you to let Val be ready to punch out some guy's lights over you, but when—"

"What the hell has any of this got to do with you staying safe, Tami? You always try to change the subject when you're dead wrong! Tonight I'm not in the mood for it!"

"I am so sick of your holier-than-thou crap, Sarah!" Tami shouted back, veins standing out in her neck. "Everything is always about what you're worried about, what you think, what you're scared of, you and all your little problems! Everything always revolves around you, Sarah! Well, who made you the center of the frickin' universe? Who made you the leader of our group? I bet your parents had a nervous breakdown when they found out you were a Blend like me and Donnie. Don't even try to deny it—they were sitting on the edge of their seats at the ceremony praying for a last-minute change, just like you were. Admit it! But the sick joke is that you got stuck in Blends with me, so now you're trying to suck up to Mrs. Hogan in the library and do extra work, hoping somebody will finally rank you higher. Don't speak to me or try to tell me how to live! For once I have somebody who likes me waaay more then they like you, and I don't have to stand in your stupid shadow!"

Pure hurt made Sarah's words explode past her dropping fangs. "You really feel that way about me, Tami? And you call yourself my best friend?"

"Why are you two arguing?" Allie shouted, coming between them as Hyacinth placed her pillow over her head. "Just stop it!"

But Sarah couldn't disengage from the emotions imploding within her, and she leaned past Allie's small frame to get in Tami's face. "Net compound sticks together, like we should be sticking together over this horrible thing that's happened to Ayana. I'm telling you about Stefan because I care! I don't want anything to happen to you! If Al had swung on Stefan trying to protect you, he might've gotten hurt. So give him a break—"

"What?" Tami pushed Allie out of the way and squared off with Sarah. "Since when do you give a crap about your brother? I thought I was your BFF, through thick and thin. When those two are too chicken shit to go on an adventure," she said, pointing at Allie and then Hyacinth, "who's got your back? Me, that's who. Who always stood up to Al when he was in your face? Me. And now, just because I'm interested in a guy you've decided not to like…now I'm wrong? Puh-lease! Plus, I don't like your brother like that—never have and never will!"

Sarah held her hands up in front of her. "You said you're my BFF, then run me down like you just did, actually sounding like a hater? And however you feel about my brother, just on general principle, not to care if he's totally humiliated…okay, now that's deep." She shook her head as tears rose in her eyes. She let her arms drop to her sides and walked to her bed, then spoke to Tami with her back turned. "I shouldn't have to take that from anybody, but from one of my compound sisters, especially from you…Wow."

"Whatever." Tami stalked away to climb back up into her bunk on the other side of the room.

Yeah, whatever, Sarah thought as she climbed into bed and tried to make her mind stop whirling. Sleep would be impossible. She could barely force her eyes to stay shut, so instead she stared at the wall. Ayana was missing, but somehow she also could feel that her beloved Yaya was still alive. None of this bull with Tami meant anything compared to the need to find their compound sister. Tami was so self-absorbed that Sarah could almost scream. In this moment, hurt quietly collided inside of her with fear and anger. Why, of all times, would Tami be worried about some stupid maniac dude and not focused on the serious fact that Ayana was missing! And then to pick some ridiculous fight?

It took everything within Sarah not to get out of bed and kick Tami's stubborn ass.

CHAPTER 22

Morning came with a vengeance. Sarah rubbed her temples and climbed out of bed as her PIU gently chimed. She squinted and read the message being blasted out simultaneously to all students from Headmistress Stone. An emergency assembly would be held right after homeroom, so each student could be counted present before their parents came to collect those who were leaving. Sarah sighed. Things were so bad now that the administration had to do a headcount. Just great.

Gathering up her toiletries and robe, she moved like the walking dead. Bizarre dreams of everything in her life running in reverse had haunted her all night long. There was still a trace of a nagging headache that she was sure was the result of too much crying and the final blowup with Tami. Each girl in the room had awakened slowly and unhappily, then navigated her way to her closet without a word. Tension was wound so tightly that Sarah finally bolted toward the showers just to get away from them all.

As she stood in the spray and closed her eyes, the comfort of darkness lessened the headache and almost managed to mute the pain in her spirit. If she could just stay here for a little while, just to avoid going out and facing the harsh realities waiting for her. Ayana was gone. She couldn't take another argument with Tami and didn't want her mind cluttered with bickering, anyway. Didn't Tami understand that the only reason she was making such a stink about Stefan was because she loved her? If something bad happened to Tami, she would die.

But obviously Tami was too pigheaded to recognize true friendship and sisterly love when it smacked her in the face. All over some dude. That was what pissed her off the most. Her compound sister was yelling at her for worrying—all because she was so caught up with some guy that she didn't care if he ate people or not! And *she* was the crazy one?

It was more than that, though. Remembering all the hurtful things Tami had said stung so deeply that new tears rose in Sarah's eyes. She angrily wiped them away, trying to collect herself before she went to class. There was always an edge to Tami, and her tongue was always as sharp as a razor, but this time Tami truly resented her. Now that it was fully out in the open, there was no denying it, and it hurt.

She was so upset that she couldn't even shore up Allie or Hyacinth; it was hard enough trying to keep herself together. Right now the warm water felt good, like a clean, hard rain washing through her system, and she closed her eyes against the spray. But she had to get out of the shower and get to homeroom. Finally she opened her eyes to shut off the water, then stood very, very still. For a moment there was nothing but darkness enveloping her, then it lifted and dissipated like a dark mist.

The urge to scream bubbled up inside her, but the very second it did, an eerie calm befell her. What was going on? The sensation was both fascinating and frightening, and she privately pondered it as she dried off, pulled on her robe and finished her morning routine in the now-quiet bathroom. Then sudden panic hit her as she realized what that silence meant.

She was late!

Running into her room, there was no way to erase the knifing disappointment when she saw no one there. Her friends had all left her.

Glancing at the clock, she hurriedly pulled on her uniform, then dragged a comb through her damp hair before giving up and simply yanking it up into a ponytail before dashing out the door. It felt like she was walking through molasses as she hurried along the hallway, then everything began to go wrong.

Just like in her dreams, everything seemed reversed. The atmosphere around her was suddenly too dense. She kept finding herself walking in the opposite direction from what she intended and realizing it only after she'd gotten to the wrong end of a corridor. Though she was running now, with only seconds to spare, Miss Tittle's classroom might as well have been on the moon. The bell sounded just as her PIU shrieked an agonizing truth—she was late.

As if an invisible haze had been lifted, she suddenly saw where she was—only a few classrooms away from where she needed to be.

Sarah cringed as she opened the door to Miss Tittle's room. Hyacinth and Allie stared at her with compassion in their eyes. Hyacinth shot her a mental message. *We left because you two were fighting and we didn't want to be late. We figured you knew where class was. If we had known you didn't, we wouldn't have left you.* Hyacinth lowered her gaze just as Tami glared at her, then looked away.

"I cannot believe you are three minutes late, Miss Rivera," Miss Tittle chastised. "And on a morning like this, where there is so much going on. What have you to say for yourself?"

Miss Tittle's shrill voice sliced into Sarah's head and sent a shiver through her like fingernails raking down a blackboard. At a momentary loss and with twenty-nine pairs of student eyes on her, she tried to muster her voice to speak. Then a snicker from Melissa Gray broke the deadly silence.

Full comprehension hit Sarah as the brittle seconds passed and Melissa whispered to Amy, "Her white light needs batteries."

Amy giggled behind her hand.

Any barriers Sarah had up had dissolved by that morning. She and her crew hadn't been able to reinforce their protections after her fight with Tami, hadn't been able to come together and renew the ward Ayana had suggested, and she herself had been further weakened by the ordeal of getting to class. Sarah gave her friends an accusing glance. They'd left her alone and at risk. Had Melissa sensed her vulnerability and targeted her? Had the strong Clavs gone after her and shifted the hallways on her, or was something scarier, something more dangerous, going on?

She stared past Miss Tittle to Melissa. Had they actually attacked her when Ayana was missing? That was so cold…so unforgiveable. Fury imploded within Sarah as Miss Tittle tapped an impatient foot, waiting on her answer. Sarah would have ratted Melissa out if she'd been sure the other girl had been jacking with her.

Staring at Melissa's too smug expression, Sarah suddenly realized her guess was right. She wasn't sure how, but the truth hit her in the gut like a punch. Now, on top of everything else, she was about to get a detention because of Melissa Gray? She should have hung her out to dry last night, should have gone back to Nana Marlene and told her everything that she'd heard in the hallway. But somehow there just wasn't enough satisfaction in that. She wanted to take care of things herself—maybe wrap her hands around Melissa's throat.

"Well, young lady, what have you to say in your defense? Why are you late?" Miss Tittle continued to tap her long, narrow, birdlike foot, then crossed her arms over her flat chest. Her beaklike face was contorted into a scowl, and her red hair piled up into a beehive was smoking on top.

Sarah looked away from Melissa to Miss Tittle, ready to tell all.

The class issued a collective gasp, and Sarah realized her fangs had dropped.

Miss Tittle jumped back and began to screech as her hair actually caught fire. "You dare to threaten me to my face in my own class, young lady?" The distraught phoenix dashed back and forth in front of the class, flames sparking in her eyes as she waved both her hands and a pointer. "I feel a transition coming on—I am about to flame over this outrage! Do you think your parents' station gives you the right to disobey the rules of this institution and threaten a teacher in an outright display of hostility?"

"No, ma'am," Sarah said, trying desperately to retract her fangs. But she couldn't. Not while Tami shook her head knowingly, and Melissa and her crew laughed behind their palms.

"Get out of my classroom! Report to Headmistress Stone immediately," Miss Tittle shrieked, picking up a PIU and quickly transmitting her complaint to the school administration.

A low, ominous "Ooooh" buzzed through the classroom as the edges of Miss Tittle's dress began to smolder.

"The one thing I detest more than tardiness is impudence—I *will* be respected in my classroom! I would have given you one evening kitchen detention demerit, but, but, but…!" Miss Tittle exclaimed, sounding like a giant, squawking chicken. "Off to the Pegasus stables with you, Miss Fangster! Let's see how much good those puny little incisors will do you there. You can report to Mr. Milton, our stable keeper, at four A.M. sharp for the rest of the week—and for every day that you show up late, I will add a week! And I *will* be watching!"

This was *so* not how this day was supposed to go. Didn't that old battle-ax understand that her compound sister was missing? Didn't that dumb Clav understand that this was like having a death in the family, or at least the closest thing to it that she'd ever experienced? Didn't anyone know anything about compassion? What bitches—both of them!

Guess with your big sister falling down a demon hole you'll be doing detention all the time, Melissa mentally shot into Sarah's unprotected mind. *You're wide open, newbie, and even your friends aren't loyal anymore.*

Sarah glanced briefly at Melissa Gray and something very dark slithered through her system. The shadow cast by the adjacent desk near Melissa seemed to grow. Melissa had hurt her. She'd gone after her crew—and now she was taunting her about the loss of Yaya?

Every offense built inside Sarah as Melissa tossed her glossy hair over her shoulder. The shadow beside the globe scampered to the back of the class, seeming to find its partner there. Then Sarah blinked.

It was a slow closing of her eyes as something dark raced down the aisle from the back of the room. She reached out her hand toward Melissa in fury, and an invisible power pulse flipped the books off her desk and blew the girl out of her chair. Students shrieked, but Melissa never hit the ground. Two squabbling shadows that emitted a low, gibberish-filled hum yanked her by the hair, tore at her clothes and began dragging her down the center aisle of the classroom.

Chaos broke out as students rushed out of the way. Miss Tittle began screaming and running back and forth in front of the room again. Another teacher burst in, shouting. But Sarah heard none of it as static blue energy lifted her hair up off her shoulders.

"Sarah!" Al shouted, leaping over his desk and shaking her. "Make them stop!"

She snapped out of her daze and stared into her brother's eyes.

"Are you crazy?" he said, then went over to Melissa, who was bleeding and crying on the floor. He turned accusing eyes back to Sarah. "What the hell was that? What did you do?"

Sarah just stared at her brother as he helped the sobbing Melissa. Someone else had finally seen her shadows. She wasn't insane. They really did exist.

"The girl's a freak, man," someone mumbled from nearby.

Tami, Allie and Hyacinth just stared at her, petrified. Val looked like he was in shock, and Wil was paralyzed at his desk. Only Al seemed brave enough to move, as he helped Melissa up. Sarah's vision blurred as tears stung her eyes.

Dear God, what had she done?

Blood dribbled down Melissa's chin and her crying grew louder. It would take a full cosmetic healing to repair the damage to her face.

"Someone help this young lady to the infirmary," Miss Tittle shrieked, rushing around in a smoldering circle.

Three guys in the front of the room jumped out of their seats. Wil just stared at Sarah, his eyes holding both pity and worry. Val's eyes seemed to be trying to tell her that it would be all right, but her brother glared at her and was the one who picked Melissa up when she fainted.

The moment Melissa passed out, Miss Tittle whipped out her PIU and sent another complaint to Headmistress Stone. "Get out and report to administration!" she yelled at Sarah, stamping her foot.

Sarah quietly backed out of the classroom. She closed the door softly behind her and this time navigated the corridors with ease. If she and her friends hadn't been distracted, hadn't been fighting, she would have known to reinforce their barriers, but they'd gotten caught up and distracted. The pandemonium after losing Ayana had made everybody turn on one another and argue about nonsense.

But the real question was, what had just happened?

She felt so stupid as she trudged up to the pristine, snow-capped hallway of the administrative area. This was the last thing her grandmother needed this morning.

Sarah reached out and placed her hand on the silver-etched doorknob. Cold sent a shock of added dread up her arm as she opened the door and entered the outer office area. Beautiful landscapes of snow thawing in the spring frost surrounded her, pink buds and green shoots trying to push through, along with imposing mahogany furniture and huge file cabinets. A stern-looking older woman stopped zapping the teachers' mailboxes with white light and gave her an admonishing glare. This was so different from her frantic visit the night before, when she hadn't noticed anything through her upset and tears.

"Are you Sarah Rivera?"

Sarah nodded. "Yes, ma'am."

The woman shook her head and clicked her tongue, then adjusted her half-glasses. "Headmistress Stone will see you—she's been expecting you. Don't keep her waiting."

Apparently news traveled fast around here. Sarah just wondered why it was the trivial news of students fighting in class and not the real issues, like drugs, sex and student-on-student sexual harassment. Steadying herself, she walked around the large gleaming wood counter and past the mean-looking secretary's desk to knock on her grandmother's door.

"Come in," Nana Marlene called out, then looked up from a pile of papers on her huge credenza.

Sarah stood in the doorway, paralyzed as she waited, barely breathing. All Nana Marlene did was motion with her chin for her to sit down, then rounded her desk to sit behind it. Damn…no kiss hello, no glad to see you. On top of everything else, this was bad.

Nana Marlene was in full Headmistress Stone mode this morning. Gone was the warm nana who was upset and worried about the loss of one of her children. Sarah sank down into the overstuffed velvet-covered Queen Anne chair that faced the huge mahogany desk that seemed to put too much distance between her and the family matriarch. Sweat moistened Sarah's palms, and her heart was beating so fast that she began to feel dizzy.

Today her nana was wearing mauve, and she pushed up her exquisite Kemetian robe sleeves and leaned forward on her elbows while seated in her high-back, burgundy leather chair, making a tent in front of her mouth with her fingers, momentarily lost as to where to begin.

"Before I share my perception, I want to hear your side of this, Sarah," her grandmother finally said. "With everything else that's happening, *why*?"

"Nana," Sarah mumbled, but then quickly revised the title. "I mean, Headmistress Stone."

Her grandmother held up her pointer finger to stop Sarah's stilted flow of words. "I will *always* be your nana. Headmistress Stone is only a public formality for your benefit, not mine. You know I will not play favorites, and if anything," she said with a deep, disappointed sigh, "I'll be harder on you and the other compound kids because I know you know better. Attacking a student in class?"

"I *do* know better," Sarah said quietly. Tears welled in her eyes, not from fear of punishment, but for having so disappointed one of the people whose opinions mattered most. "I wasn't bearing fangs at Miss Tittle. I was just so angry at this jealous Clair-V girl who'd set me and my crew up that when she laughed at me for being late—after she'd reversed my corridor memory mapping—I lost it."

"Good," Nana Marlene said, sitting back in her chair. "So what have we learned from this incident?"

Good? Had her grandmother said *good*?

"Stretch your mind past the emotion and search for the lesson."

Sarah let out a sigh of frustration. "Don't fight in-house…save it for the demons outside." It was one of the canons of the compound that she knew by heart, and she felt really dumb for forgetting that.

Her grandmother smiled and considered her with a slight tilt of her regal head. "Yes, and I wouldn't go so far as to call the unnamed young lady who pranked you a demon, although the green-eyed monster can feel just as treacherous and is truly just as ugly."

"You're telling me," Sarah grumbled. In that moment she wished her grandmother would use all her superior psychic powers to look into her mind and see what she saw. That was the part that just boggled her mind—why wouldn't Nana Marlene just go through every student's brain and simply weed out all the bad apples? Why did they even allow people like Stefan, Brent and the Gray sisters in this school?

"You know, Sarah..." her grandmother said thoughtfully, pausing as she stood and then began to leisurely walk around the room. "There's an old saying that goes way back before your time and mine, one that we had in South Carolina, where my mother was from. It goes like this: *Every shut eye ain't asleep.* I don't miss much, but if you elect to allow some things to slide, a greater good will come from it."

The revelation was startling, and Sarah's gaze locked with her grandmother's. Did Nana have a clue about some of the stuff happening behind closed doors after all? If so, then why was it still happening?

"I'm not going into your mind...that destroys the fabric of the lessons about leadership that you all must learn. But even without a mental probe, I can pretty much figure out what happened—age gives me that advantage. I've seen this a hundred times if I've seen it once. But what I want to know is how did one young lady get her front teeth chipped and another get her face cut...and no one ever saw you move?"

Cold sweat dampened Sarah's entire body. "I don't know," she breathed.

"Miss Tittle said the shadows just reached out and clawed Melissa Gray. Just leaped out and attacked her right there in class—after you hit her with a power strobe, blowing her out of her desk. And I suspect a shadow might have tripped Amy Feingold, too." Nana Marlene folded her arms over her chest.

Sarah closed her eyes. "I never meant...I never told anything to attack them—I swear, Nana."

"I want to go back to when you had those dreams when you were little," her grandmother said quietly.

Sarah leaned forward and hugged herself. "I hate thinking about that."

"I know, sweetie, but it's vitally important that we do. Especially now."

Sarah looked up slowly. "You think I'm doing this, don't you? That I'll hurt someone." Her voice wavered. "Am I evil?"

Nana Marlene got up and walked over to Sarah and took her hands. “No, baby, but tell me. Have you been seeing the shadows again?”

Sarah nodded, her grandmother’s face blurring as tears formed in her eyes.

“When?”

“Recently,” Sarah finally hedged, but her grandmother leaned down in her face.

“Don’t make me go in hard, Sarah—tell me. This is important!”

“We heard Mom and Dad arguing,” Sarah stammered, staring into her grandmother’s eyes. “We were upset, so the night before school, we went beyond the barriers, and the shadows started chasing me. And then I fell, just like before. There was a lady who said a funny word to me…uh…*Nexse,* then I was back and a demon was burning beside me.”

Her grandmother pulled her into a hug, her arms holding her tight and safe. Then she held Sarah away from her so that she could stare deeply into her eyes. “Sarah, there’s no dispute about it now. I finally know what you are. You’re a Shadow Walker.”

Chapter 23

"A what?" Sarah said, fear making her palms sweaty.

"You weren't falling, you were shadow traveling—slipping between dimensions in the dark to get away from what was chasing you, the same way a vampire would, but instead of hell tunnels, you were using the shadow paths. Then you shadow-boxed what was chasing you, caged it in darkness so it couldn't follow you. All of that was survival instinct. And those shadows weren't chasing you, baby. They were guarding you. Their job is to snuff out anything that tries to attack you—to go after anything that means you harm. They killed that demon."

"But a Shadow Walker? What kind of freak is that?" Sarah pulled away and stood, walking to the far side of the room. She hugged herself suddenly as if cold.

"A Shadow Walker is not a freak," her grandmother said quietly. "It's a type of angel hybrid, a member of an elite fighting force." Her grandmother closed her eyes with a smile. "It makes so much sense now why Counselor Z couldn't figure out how to place you. You're so much like your father. We were all looking to Al to mirror him, when it was you all the time."

"No, no, no, no, no, no, no! I am not adventurous; I am not the one who likes playing in the dark and taking dares—uh-uh…no."

"You've been suppressing your talents because you fear them, so—"

"Yes, I fear them, Nana! I'm so scared all the time you have no idea," Sarah said in a rush, then began crying. "I see things in my head that frighten me!" Her voice broke as words gave way to sobs, and walked over to hold her again.

"Let it out, baby," Nana Marlene said, rubbing her back. "You've been carrying that weight since you've been born."

"I've had nightmares since I can remember," Sarah sobbed, "and I just wanna be like all the other kids. And I want Ayana back!"

A warm, moist cheek rested against hers as strong arms rocked her until the hiccupping sobs subsided.

"They sent you my daughter as a guide," Nana Marlene said quietly. "She came to me the night you kids went outside the light barrier back home at our compound, just before you were to go to school." Nana kissed Sarah's hair gently. "I'm an old seer, baby—not too much gets pass me. I don't speak on all that I see or know because some of this you kids have to learn on your own."

Sarah looked up, teary-eyed. Her grandmother was simply amazing. It always blew her mind that the woman was so wise.

Her nana nodded. "Christine was lost to me when she was about your age. Vampires took her and turned her. I went after her, but your mother did the job." A pair of wise eyes filled with tears that burned away as they stared at Sarah. "*Nexse* means awaken. She's telling you to awaken to your path, and she's there for you now as a beacon of light. She was taken by the Light because she was too young for the dark side to lay claim to. But she walked that path—the shadow path—for years, which is why they sent her to help you learn how to navigate it. Call her by name when you need her, and she will guide you."

"How do you know all this, Nana?" Sarah buried her face in the crook of her grandmother's neck, wishing she could climb into her lap like she had as a toddler.

"When I lost the first two students, Christine came to me and said she would watch over you, and she told me how you came to be, but she didn't reveal your talent."

"How I came to be?" Sarah looked up, spent, but if her grandmother had any more terrible revelations, she wanted to look her in the eye to hear it.

"Your mother lost a baby, years before you and Al were conceived. The dark side clawed that small life right out of her womb, and…that life was you."

Sarah didn't blink or move.

"Angels came and got you, but your mother and father wept as though their souls had been shattered. This all happened before your father crossed over."

"Wait a minute," Sarah said, pulling back. "Before he crossed over…You mean when he was still a vampire?"

Her grandmother nodded.

"But vampires can't have children, grandma!" Sarah tried to pull away, but two hands held her body still, and ancient eyes held her gaze steady.

"Normally they can't. Their seed is dead. That had never before happened in the history of the vampire lines, and it's never happened again since. Do you hear me, child? Are you listening with both ears? Your father loved your mother across the lines of life and death, and trust me, what he suffered was something that no one else on this planet could have endured." Her grandmother released her and paced away, talking with her hands, then suddenly zapped a hard snap at her that sent static electricity across the room. Papers flew off the desk, and a blue charge ran over the surface of the furniture.

"The angels said they would replace that which had been wrongfully stolen from your mother's womb, and your biological grandmother—angel Sarah, your mother's mother—held your soul in her palm until the time was right. When your mother got pregnant with Alejandro, you were placed in your mother's womb right alongside your brother. This is partly why Alejandro resents you—you are the true firstborn. His spirit feels it, and your mother and father down in their souls know it but cannot articulate it, and until now, it was not for me to tell them, but the time has come."

Sarah fell down into the chair she'd been standing in front of and took several deep breaths. "So Al and I aren't really twins?"

"No, baby."

Sarah looked at her grandmother. "I don't know what to do. I didn't mean to hurt Melissa like that, even though I was angry at her. How do I control this…thing?" She bit her lip for a moment and clasped her hands in her lap. "I don't want to see scary things anymore, Nana. I don't want to live the rest of my life scared to death of everything."

"You have to trust the Light. The angel legions aren't going to let you see anything that will damage your mind, but they *will* let you be a lethal weapon for us against the dark side. Our job here at this school is to teach you how to control this powerful force within you. Right now, of course it seems frightening. But, Sarah, what you have is a magnificent gift. Your mother is a descendant of Powers angels. Your father…well, he used to be one of the highest ranking Vampires of all time until he got saved. So there you have it, a blend of talents. Shadow Walkers are as rare as Neteru, so it stands to reason that the Light would send one to the planet during the end of days."

"I'm not brave enough to do this, Nana," Sarah whispered.

"Bravery comes with confidence in one's own abilities." Her grandmother smiled softly. "Baby, being brave doesn't mean being fearless. It means doing what you have to do even when you are most afraid."

Sarah let out a long breath of frustration. She'd do the detention, take a suspension, even accept it if they expelled her from school. But she *did not* want to be some shadow controlling freak!

Reading Sarah's mind gently, her grandmother kept her voice soft yet firm. "Honey, you have to train for this or you can hurt people. You have an inner rage that must be directed against the right sources, not fellow students who simply get on your nerves."

"Am I the only one like this?"

The question hung in the air for a moment, then her grandmother pursed her lips. "No," she said, standing. "Follow me."

* * *

Sarah found herself almost jogging to keep up with her grandmother. The halls were empty, and Headmistress Stone swept through them with sudden purpose. Her long Kemetian robes billowed out behind her as she marched forward with her age-old ebony walking staff held tightly in her grip. Descending flight after flight of seemingly endless stairs, they arrived at a desolate place so barren that the long corridors contained no murals. A small sign made Sarah's breath hitch. It read *Crematorium.*

Using her staff, Headmistress Stone knocked twice on the large metal door, then swung it open. And there, standing in front of what looked like a long metal hospital gurney, Sarah saw her parents and a man emanating such power that she could only stop and stare.

Simply gazing into his eyes, she immediately knew he wasn't a normal human. His large irises were midnight blue and almost eclipsed the white in the rest of his eyes. His thick hair was disheveled and as dark as a raven's, with silvery gray at the temples. Dark stubble covered his jaw, and his face had a long, ancient, vertical scar that began at his hairline, crossed through the plane of his left eye and stopped just above the edge of his jaw. He looked up and fixed those amazing, frightening eyes on her. He had her father's height and build, but his weathered face showed him to be much older than Uncle Jack. He wore an old sleeveless white t-shirt and a pair of olive fatigue pants. A cigarette smoldered in an ashtray before him, then he tilted his head, studying her with a frown.

Sarah glanced around the room, growing more frightened by the moment. The lights were dim, but the furnace was burning red hot, and suddenly she was so panicked and perspiring so badly that her shirt clung to her like a second skin. There was no air-conditioning, and all around her were implements of death. Battleaxes, scythes, chains, sharp knives, bone saws…Dear God, the school had a torture chamber?

"What's my daughter doing down here, Marlene?" Sarah's father finally said, stepping away from the table. "She should be in assembly with the other students, listening to Shabazz's security update."

"She's here to meet Professor Zachariah Raziel," her grandmother said in a calm but firm tone.

"Professor Razor fits better," the ominous being said in a disinterested tone, walking slowly toward Sarah.

"Why?" her mother said in a horrified whisper, hurrying toward Sarah and getting between her and the professor.

"Because it's time," Headmistress Stone said firmly, then gentled her voice. "Although it was an accident, she activated the shadows and severely injured a student today, Damali. She has to learn how to control her power. It's time, even though she'd initially been placed in the Blends division. I don't know how Counselor Z could have made such a mis—"

"No!" Carlos shouted. "I forbid it! Especially with everything else that's going on."

"It is her destiny," Headmistress Stone said calmly.

"I didn't mean to, Dad," Sarah said, beginning to tear up. Her panic-stricken gaze went from her parents to her grandmother, then to the furnace silhouetting Professor Razor in its orange light. "I didn't know about the shadows. I didn't know I could—"

"Are you mad?" Professor Razor said, changing course and walking up to Carlos to get in his face. He spoke in a quiet, lethal tone as he stared at her father eye-to-eye. "You've allowed this child to be afraid of a talent like this, as well as remain unaware of how to properly use it? That's like throwing a loaded gun into the middle of a schoolyard filled with toddlers. Guaranteed, one of them is going to pick it up and pull the trigger!"

"She's my daughter!" Carlos said. "Don't lecture me, Reaper, when you've never had a child of your own!"

"In this school I have three hundred children, Vampire!" Professor Razor said through clenched teeth. And as fast as light he called a scythe off the wall to come whirling into his hand, then caught it in his grip and brought it with a clang against Carlos's quickly drawn sword.

"You were the only one that got away, Rivera. The only Vampire I chased into the depths of Hell all the way to Level Six and missed. But a Reaper always reaps what is sown. Do not make me forget that you are now a being of the Light."

"Any day or night, mother—"

"Carlos!" Damali shouted.

"Gentlemen!" Headmistress Stone said loudly, and banged her stick on the ground.

"Mom, Dad, I'm so sorry," Sarah said, wiping at tears that wouldn't seem to stop flowing. "I know with Ayana missing this is the last thing you need, but—"

"No, Sarah," Professor Razor said, stalking away from her father, still swinging his scythe. "Your father owes *you* an apology."

"I don't have to explain myself to a fifteen-year-old! I did what I did for her own protection!"

Sarah's mother left her side as her grandmother closed her eyes. "Carlos…what did you do?" She grabbed Carlos's arm, then looked at Professor Razor.

"He made a deal with Counselor Z to hide Sarah in Blends," the professor said. "You can't lie to a Reaper—and now that I have you both in the same room, I know my gut hunch was right! He thought that if she was with the less developed students she wouldn't be so competitive and her ability would lie dormant for years." Professor Razor looked at Carlos hard. "Tell her! Tell them! You have the strength as a Neteru and an ex-Vamp to block seers, but not a Reaper angel!"

"Carlos…" her mother whispered, hurt singeing her tone.

Sarah's grandmother simply closed her eyes.

"Dad?" Sarah ran forward. "You put me in Blends—made me test three times to be where I wasn't supposed to be?"

"Z wouldn't have done that unless coerced," Sarah's grandmother said quietly, her gaze now fixed on Sarah's father, and the weighted accusation went off like a siren in Sarah's head.

"You put our daughter through that?" Sarah's mother said, her voice a near whisper.

"Tell the truth, Carlos," Sarah's grandmother said in a calm voice. She gazed off into the distance as if seeing something the rest of them could not. "I should have seen this before, but I had no reason to vision-check family. Counselor Z tested the girl three separate times just to try to give you a chance to accept the truth…a chance not to ask her to do something that went against her core values as both an oracle and a guidance counselor. But you knew Z would do anything for you."

"You had no right to do that to her," Sarah's mother said, tears shimmering in her eyes.

"I had every right!" Sarah's father shouted, exploding. He used his sword to point at Sarah, his haunted gaze going to each face as he spoke, but landing on Sarah's last and longest. "You don't know, but I did. From the day she was born, I knew. It was in her blood, in her skin. I could smell her. I knew she was the one we'd lost, Damali! She's not a twin. She's our firstborn, my baby girl that Hell snatched from me once. I will not, do you hear me, *I will not*, send her into the darkness to hunt anything! I don't care about destiny. Damn destiny! And she's definitely not going to learn how to smoke demons in Hell from a Reaper! Never!"

"Destiny is the province of God, and the last time I checked, you ain't the One, son!" Professor Razor shouted, lowering the scythe at Carlos. "Don't forget your place in the food chain, Neteru. Switch sides like Lucifer did in a fit of hubris, and it's your ass."

"I don't want her in the Shadow class," Carlos said in a low, warning rumble. "I ain't having it."

They were arguing about her as if she wasn't even in the room! Didn't she have a say about anything happening in her life?

"It's my choice," Sarah said firmly. She looked her father in the eye. "Who I am, who I will be, what I do with my powers and which battles I choose to fight—they're all my choices. You had no right to take that away from me. Do you know what you've done to me? Do you know how scared I've been? And all because I didn't know?"

Her father walked back toward her with his sword in his hand and punched the metal table, causing her to jump. "As long as I'm your father, *I* will decide on matters like this! You have no idea what the Dark Realms can do to you if they get their hands on you. I've kept you safe!"

But her mother's stricken gaze left Carlos and went to Marlene. "Is it true what he says? When did you know she was the one I'd lost, Mar?"

"If you had known too soon," Marlene said with her eyes closed, not fully answering the question, "you would have mothered her differently—and it is her destiny to be a Shadow Walker."

Her whole family had kept secrets and told lies? The closest people in the world to her? Her father turned to her mother and held her with his troubled gaze. "Don't fight me on this, Damali." Then he turned and walked out of the Crematorium. Her mother ran after him.

Sarah couldn't believe that her father had just left like that. He had lied. He had tried to keep her back because he didn't want her to even try. Did he think so little of her?

Fury rose inside her, and Sarah took off after her parents. As soon as she stepped through the door, she held up her arms in front of her face. The hallway was filled with gale force winds as her father began to open an energy fold-away.

"It's my life!" Sarah shouted behind him. "I'll do whatever I want to with it!"

She hugged herself, crying tears of outrage and betrayal, then slumped against the wall when he didn't even look back at her. He simply walked away into nothingness. Then the winds died down and he was gone. "I hate him!"

Her mother walked over to her and drew her into a hug. "Don't hate him, even when he messes up, even when it's this badly. Sarah, your father loves you. He just has a strange way of showing it sometimes."

Her mother's arms and wings surrounded her, and though she tried to stiffen against the embrace, the heartbreak of the one person she looked up to the most failing her the most was too much to bear.

"He lied," Sarah said angrily against her mother's shoulder, breathing hard.

"I know," her mother said softly.

"I will never forgive him for this!"

Her mother stroked her back. "Never is a long time, baby, and forgiveness is divine. He was wrong. He was pigheaded. He was a lot of things, Sarah," her mother said, finally holding her away from her to look into her eyes. "But your daddy loves you. That doesn't make him right; it just makes him more human than most people realize."

Tears streamed down her mother's face, and she didn't try to hide them. The sight of her mother so upset by something her father had done was as upsetting as anything else that had happened that morning.

"One day, maybe you'll understand just how scared your father had to be to do something this outrageous. I'm not going to apologize for him anymore. It is what it is. He owns this all by himself." She wiped Sarah's face and then her own. "But I want you to put this anger to good use. Go in there and soak up everything you can from Razor, you understand me? He's got a lot of experience. Remember how your Nana Marlene used to say, 'You can show 'em better than you can tell 'em'? Show him, Sarah. You become the best with whatever gift you were given. Nobody, not even your father, can take your destiny away from you."

Sarah sniffed hard and nodded. Yes, she'd show him. And she'd use every skill she had to help find Ayana.

CHAPTER 24

Professor Razor opened the door and came out into the hallway with her grandmother. "Let's me and you take a walk, kid. Go get some fresh air. It's the only thing that clears the head after a good hell fight."

They walked along the corridors in companionable silence, and Sarah was surprised to find Professor Razor wending his way up toward the Great Hall. The moment they passed the barriers, he looked up at Mojo and snapped his fingers, waking the surly dragon.

"G'morning, Mojo. Normally, I'd light you some incense and leave an offering, but this morning I just want you to meet a jumper." Professor Razor turned to Sarah as he walked her toward the huge doors. "If you decide to break the rules and go for a stroll out here one starry night, bring him something and say a prayer, otherwise you and your date will be dragon treats."

The old dragon grumbled and resettled himself as they strolled out of the building into the small courtyard.

Professor Razor held Sarah's arm. "We're going up to the top. But on the way up, I want you to think about three things."

She simply looked at him, frighteningly aware that if her grandmother and parents hadn't introduced him to her, she would have run headlong screaming to get away from him.

"One," he said, ticking off his points on his wide, calloused fingers. "People screw up, so what are you gonna do? Spend your whole life whining about your mom or dad and what they did to you, or are you gonna suck it up and move forward with your own life? Two, like Headmaster Shabazz told you guys at the opening ceremonies, we aren't stupid. We know students have been opening illegal vortices around the school to sneak out and do what young people do. We also know that too often they're also getting high while doing something dangerous. Foolish. No newsflash, but we *will* find the culprits," he added when Sarah's eyes got wide. "What, you think with all the advanced seers in this joint we wouldn't know?"

He shook his head. "Yeah. We know. The problem is, these kids've gotten really good at masking who's doing it and when. More about that later, during my class, but I'm going to show you a known danger area right now. Seeing it is better than reading it on your PIU—since I've heard you're the adventurous type, prowling the halls unescorted. Need I say more?" He gave her a meaningful look, then began walking toward the steps that would take them to the top of the Great Hall.

"You said there were three points?" Sarah said, catching up to his long strides.

"Oh, yeah," he said, not bothering to look at her. "Don't fall. It's a long way down."

She peered over the edge, stepped back and shut her eyes for a moment.

"You coming or what?"

Summoning her courage, she took a deep breath, said a quiet prayer, then began the steep climb up to the last platform that separated the school from the floating capstone. Moving very carefully, she placed each foot with precision, going up sideways so her entire sneaker would fit on the narrow steps. But Professor Razor took the steps two at a time, without holding onto anything, and only hit each step quickly on his toes, since his large combat boot wouldn't fit no matter what.

"Don't look down," he said with impatience, waiting for her on the platform, half of his boot hanging over the edge. He popped a cigarette in his mouth and lit it with a snap of his fingers.

Sarah stopped for a moment and squeezed her eyes shut to stop the feeling of vertigo.

"A demon is on your ass, kid! Move it and get up here pronto!"

She began climbing again with a little more gusto, and when she finally reached the top, he held out a hand and pulled her to stand beside him with amazing strength.

He looked at her, then looked up at the sky, blowing out a stream of white smoke. "You almost feel like you're up in the clouds from here." He let out a wistful sigh, took another long drag on his cigarette, then sent his gaze out toward the horizon.

Sarah stood beside him, captivated. "It's beautiful," she said quietly, taking it all in slowly.

Gorgeous snowcapped mountains rolled out in a blue-mist range before her, and as she glanced down she saw a black ring of burned-out forest. Beyond that, the leaves of the dense tree line in the valley below made everything seem to be nestled in a sea of fire-orange, red and yellow confetti.

Above her, the huge floating capstone cast a shadow on the platform, but there was enough light that she could see into the base of it. The way the stairs spiraled up and the way the shelves were built into the walls reminded her of looking into a seashell. Her mother had brought her one from one of her many journeys when she was just a little girl. For hours the queen conch shell had fascinated her as she tried to spy into the pretty pinkness by holding it up to the light, wondering how the thing that had once lived inside it might have made such a winding place of beauty its home. Now she wondered how students got up into the ultimate library in the world, and once in, how in the heck did they select an Akashic Record or sacred text, much less find a place to sit and study?

She craned her neck to stare up and almost lost her balance.

"Counselor Zehiradangra has her living quarters up there." Professor Razor cupped a hand to the side of his mouth, holding his cigarette in the other hand and called out, "Hey, Z, I've got Sarah up here. Yeah, yeah, she's in my class now." Then he turned to Sarah. "Counselor Z says she's sorry and really feels bad about what happened." He let out an impatient breath. "That's the one thing I can promise you. I *will* give it to you straight. If you screw up, I'll tell you. If you do good, I'll tell you that, too. Angels cannot lie—well, one did, and we know how that turned out."

"You're an angel?" she said, looking at the cigarette he held.

"Gimme a break, kid. None of us is perfect—except the One. This is my one vice since they took me off Hell patrol." Professor Razor took a deep drag of his cigarette, let the smoke come out his nose and briefly closed his eyes. "Headmistress Stone and about a hundred thousand white wingers tell me it'll be the death of me one day, but, hey, I'm immortal, remember? Besides, it reminds me of the good times me and my buddies had down in the black sulfur smoke of hellfire and brimstone, kicking demon butt." He took another puff, then crushed out the smoldering butt between two tobacco-yellowed fingers, and finally made it disappear. "Just because I do it doesn't mean you should, though. You're not immortal, and your lungs are still pink and alive. Mine are tar pools after working in the mines demon hunting for so long."

She had no comeback to that. The professor was so not what she'd imagined a hell-fighting angel to be. Looking for a graceful way to change the subject, she stared out at the horizon.

"Thanks for bringing me up here," Sarah said, casting her gaze around as she turned in a slow circle. "I think I needed this."

"All right, but I'm going to make this lesson quick, so you don't miss the rest of your classes today. Assembly is going to inform everybody about the things you already know. Then your dad is gonna whirl out those kids whose parents are nervous and want them home. But what you need to know is this: No matter how upset you were or whatever they might have done to you as a prank, going after a fellow student is something that has to be addressed—especially when you've got powers like you do. Next time, you could kill somebody. So this isn't a hooky session or a reward for screwing up in Miss Tittle's homeroom. I'm just giving you a little time to get your head on straight so you can go back to class without doing more damage. We clear?" Professor Razor said, breaking her quiet communion with nature.

"Yes, sir," she said, feeling the sting of his reference to what she'd done to Melissa. Up here in the fresh air and cloaked by peace, she'd almost forgotten about it.

"See that black ring in front of the tree line?" he said, stretching out a long arm and pointing for her gaze to follow. "That's the no-fly zone. You don't have to worry because none of you guys in my advanced class have that gift. But every year there's at least one winger who thinks he or she knows enough about aerodynamics to fly over the ring of darkness down there and make it to town. Tell your brother not to be stupid."

"Is Al about to move up from Specials into the advanced Shadows class as a flier?" she said, suddenly feeling dejected.

"In his dreams," Professor Razor said, and then kicked a small pebble over the edge of the platform.

Mixed emotions coursed through her. This was a first. She was in a talent division class that was more advanced than Al's? All her life she'd thought it would be great to one-up him, but now it felt really strange…and she felt oddly sorry for her brother. This kind of recognition meant more to him than it did to her.

"He's not so bad," she offered quietly.

"Reminds me of your father—needs a lot of discipline before he's ready for my class."

"So…am I really in your division now?"

"*Hmmm*...let me think about that some more while we're up here. To be a Shadow, you've gotta really want it. If—and I do mean if—I agree to take you on, you'll meet everybody tomorrow, last period, at which point I'll become your living nightmare." Professor Razor gave her a sidelong glance. "Today, spend your time getting your head together and following your normal roster." He hesitated, then looked away from her. "Everybody is a little thrown off by what's been happening lately. It's tough losing a compound sister. I'm sorry about what happened to Ayana. But tomorrow, I will have no mercy. You can't be a loose cannon or do anything that could hurt a fellow student, regardless of what's going on."

She noted that, unlike her grandmother and parents, Professor Razor didn't tell her everything would be all right and that they'd find Yaya. He just said he was sorry about whatever had happened to her. His statement was true but not comforting.

"I already have detention from Miss Tittle," Sarah finally said, hoping that would help mollify him. It didn't.

"Tough break. But if I were you, I'd honor it as a matter of principle—just so it doesn't look like your grandmother gave you a pass on a serious school infraction. Sure, you could argue that Miss Gray provoked you with an earlier prank, *blah, blah, blah*, but in the end, the Academy has a zero-tolerance policy on student-against-student violence, for obvious reasons. Kids can die. If the other students see you walk and not get punished just because you were extra upset about Ayana, you'll never live it down. Plain and simple. So suck it up. Other kids around here have gone missing, too. The only difference is, they were all orphans and didn't have an entire posse of family to come barging into the school to turn everything upside down. Yeah, there was an exhaustive search for them—an ongoing search, just like this one—but there were no parents, aunts, uncles and cousins coming to school in full-metal-jacket mode, ready for war."

He shrugged and looked off toward the horizon again. "Sure, you could cop a plea and probably get your grandmother to tell Miss Tittle to back off and not make you do detention. Suit yourself, but do you truly want to do seven years here as 'that privileged Neteru bitch' and be hated by everyone because of that?" he asked, making little quotes in the air with his fingers as he glanced at her over his shoulder. "Or would you rather fit in as best you can? Your choice, but if it were me…"

Sarah just stared up at her newest instructor, hanging on his every word.

"I thought so," he said. "Good choice. Now, back to why you don't base jump from here, and I'm telling you this because you came in here with a couple of fliers. Earlier this year we lost two seventh-year Uppers because they were showing off for a couple of girls. Sure, they claimed it was all about trying to locate the missing students—but if you ask me, it had more to do with trying to impress the two Clavs they came up here with." He let out a hard breath and looked off toward the horizon again. "Damned shame, too. So much life yet to live, so much promise, and gone—for what? Just because they couldn't follow some basic rules."

He turned his attention back to Sarah, and his gaze was penetrating. "So I guess you wonder why am I telling you this. Because after the shadow attack, you might suddenly find yourself being very popular with a few bad asses. Why am I concerned? Because those bad asses are dumb asses at your age."

He walked to the edge of the platform and slapped his chest. "I'm a supernatural. Was never a kid. Was always this age since the beginning of ages. I can fly in where normal angels fear to tread, you read me? Problem with an inexperienced flier base jumping from here is that this entire structure is being shielded by a Neteru energy distortion, courtesy of your dad. Once they come out of that at the base of the pyramid, things are a lot closer than they appeared." Professor Razor shook his head. "Ground just comes right up on you—*whack*."

She cringed and thought about Al and Val flying out past the light barriers at the Neteru compound. If they had managed to land out there, God help them. Maybe the only reason they'd made it back safely that night was because they'd had to turn back when they heard her screams.

Her voice moved up her throat and past her lips without consulting her brain. She thought of Val's expression when he took flight, just as he took a running leap. "Or maybe," she said, closing her eyes and opening her arms wide, feeling the breeze caress her soul, "maybe if you had wings you feel like you *have* to do this. Maybe not giving in to the wind and hurling yourself off the edge of the world would feel like you were in a cage, maybe you have to just let the nothingness catch you until you became lighter than air."

"That must suck," he said quietly. "You've got the soul of a flier but no wings."

Sarah opened her eyes.

"Tough break. But everybody's got issues."

For a moment she just stared at him. "Yeah, I wanted the wings but got crazy demon shadows that hurt people. Go figure."

"They aren't demons, and for the record, I wanted white wings and a frickin' harp but got raven wings and a scythe, then a class of newbies with problem parents. You learn to play the hand you're dealt. Not much work after the Armageddon for us Reapers. Just a little border patrol duty, the occasional riffraff to drag back to Hell, nothing major. Gotta wait until the next big one, I suppose. Like I said, kid, we've all got issues."

"What's a Reaper, exactly?"

Professor Razor let out a long, weary sigh and rolled his shoulders. "Didn't they teach you *anything*?" One moment he was standing beside her like a normal old dude with weird eyes. In the next moment, darkness fell over her. His twenty-foot, muscular wingspan eclipsed the sun. Blue-black feathers glistened as his eyes turned midnight blue and a silver scythe materialized in his hand.

"This is a Reaper," he said in a low, ominous rumble. "If one of us is on your ass, you've obviously made some very unfortunate choices in life."

Sarah stepped away from the edge of the platform on wobbly legs. "You were after my dad?"

Her shadows leap-frogged over each other and let out tiny squeals before jumping into his larger shadow to disappear entirely.

"Yeah," Professor Razor said, then folded away his wings and flung his scythe away from him into the clouds. "But he got a last-minute pardon. Luck of the draw that never sat right with me, but I don't make those decisions. Then again, you're here as a result, so somebody must have had a reason for sparing him."

"Oh." What was she supposed to say to that?

"And those little shadow guys who scare you? Those are Collectors. And they don't like being confused with gremlins, hobgoblins or demons. It's an insult."

He tapped his foot and waited as they came sliding over the edge of the platform, then began bouncing up and down like tiny balls.

"Collectors?" Sarah hugged herself, making sure she kept her distance from the Reaper.

"We Reapers are like bounty hunters," he said matter-of-factly. "We drag things down to the Pit, and those little guys are like our bloodhounds. They help—and they love to play go fetch. Yours are still young. Your Collectors are like big puppies, really, when not on the hunt. You just have to give them plenty of love and discipline, let them know who the alpha dog is and tell them no when they grab the wrong creature occasionally. But I like 'em." He motioned toward the small moving orbs with his chin. "You oughta name them."

"Name them?" Sarah couldn't believe what she was hearing.

"Yeah, like give…them…a name," he said slowly and deliberately, without a smile.

Sarah shook her head and walked away from him and the little nuisances that had bothered her all her life. They looked like ink spots, just strange splats against the stones, when dormant and not three dimensional. The really weird part was when nothing was going on, there'd always just be two of them—but when things got crazy, it was as if they'd multiply and divide into a bunch of smaller dark orbs. Yet after things calmed down, they always came back into the main two blobs they'd originated from. And now she was supposed to *name* them? Was he nuts?

She hadn't a clue as to how to name a shadow, especially when they began stretching like an old Slinky toy when they tried to follow her down the stairs. "Inky…Slinky? Professor, help me out here," she said, opening her arms wide. "I don't know! Who names scary shadows?"

Shrill noises that degenerated into grumbles emanated from the shadows.

"It might be me," Professor Razor said, trying hard not to smile, "but I don't think they'd like that. The whole Inky and Slinky thing? Rhyming…uh…not so great."

"Well then…what?" Sarah dragged her fingers through her hair, grabbed her scrunchie and slipped it around her wrist before placing both hands on her hips. "How's Beep and Bop, since that's what they sound like when they're playing around and not fussing at me?"

Squeals of delight ricocheted off the stones, and her instructor cracked a smile.

"Wouldn't have been my choice, but I guess it works for them," he said, trying to remain stern.

"Okay," Sarah said, blowing out a breath of annoyance. "Beep and Bop—but how the heck do I tell you guys apart?"

"I wouldn't worry about it, since they work in tandem…sorta like twins are supposed to," Razor pointed out. "Anyway, now that they've been named, your Collectors should behave a little better just knowing you've finally claimed them, which should also stop any unauthorized attacks.

Rather than acting on your behalf, they'll wait for your command. But you've really got to practice some anger management, kiddo."

"They grabbed Melissa," Sarah said, and hung her head. "They bit her, yanked out her hair and cut her up."

"Yep. But they'll fix her up in the infirmary and her face will be as good as new—courtesy of our expert healers," he said with a shrug. "Unfortunately for Melissa, the green-eyed monster is hard to tell from other demons, then add in a jigger of malcontent, lies, whatever else she had stewing in her, and then an attack that sent you to a very dark place inside your mind, and your Collectors flipped out. It was the perfect storm."

"Were they really gonna drag her to Hell?"

"Yep," he said in a casual tone, going to the edge of the stones to peer over them. "Like I said, they hunt and fetch what a Reaper or Shadow Walker tells them to go collect. They would have belched her out of there eventually. It's not her time. Once she got down there, the Reapers on patrol would have checked with their commander, The Grim Reaper, and she would have gotten a pass—although she'd have been traumatized for life, but hey."

Sarah squeezed her eyes shut. "I never, ever, *ever* want to be responsible for anything like that. What if she'd burned like that demon did or something?"

A pair of rough hands suddenly held Sarah's arms tightly, forcing her to peer into Professor Razor's hard glare.

"What demon, Sarah?" he asked in a no-nonsense tone, almost shaking her.

"Not here at school," she said quickly. "The one at home. We were out at night—weren't supposed to be, but that's a long story."

"Aren't they all?" he said, letting her go and seeming somewhat relieved. "But what happened?"

"I got separated from…one of my compound sisters," Sarah hedged, not wanting to implicate any of her friends in her confession. "Then, out of nowhere, a demon jumped at me. Then everything went black. I started falling, and I went into this…I don't know. This dark place—a demon hole, I guess. Except it wasn't like demons were there. In fact, there was this being of light instead. Nana said it was Christine—the daughter she lost a long time ago, who is now my guide. And when she sent me back, the demon was burning." Sarah looked at her teacher, searching his expression for answers. "Is that where Melissa would have gone?"

A slow smile spread across Professor Razor's face, then he raked his hair with his fingers, beginning to pace. "I'll just be damned!" he exclaimed with a wide grin, then he threw his head back and laughed. Staring up at the sky, he said in a loud, booming voice, "First she shadow pulsed a student out of her chair, and now she says she can torch demons? Do you hear that! *Do you hear that?* The girl can already throw shadow fire, and she can even create a shadowbox!"

Not sure if what he was saying about her was a good thing or a bad one, Sarah just hugged herself and stared at him. Her grandmother had just used some of those terms the professor mentioned when they'd spoken in her office: shadowbox, like a cage. And what was shadow fire? She had to learn more.

"Sarah," he said with a big smile, then went to her and placed his hands on her shoulders, "you are so gifted." His expression and voice took on a gentler quality that she hadn't known he was capable of, and he bent down so they were eye-to-eye. "When you went into the darkness, your guide didn't save you. You saved yourself. It's called shadowboxing—you put yourself in a black box to hide yourself from what was chasing you. Then you blew the sucker up with shadow fire. Dark energy, not to be confused with evil or dark consciousness…It's like the spectrum of ultraviolet light that actually becomes a black light—but concentrated. We call it shadow fire. The demons can't see it, especially inside a shadow box, but when they trip over it…kaboom."

He stepped away from her and laughed out loud. “Only fifteen years old and already blowing demons to smithereens. I love it!”

“I did?” she said in a very small voice, but down deep inside his pleased assessment made her stand taller.

“Yes, Sarah, you did,” he said, then folded his arms, still smiling. “Have you ever been so upset or afraid that everything around you just went dark, but somehow you didn’t feel terrified, just safe, like you’d thrown a blanket over your head or something?”

She looked off toward the horizon and thought about his question hard, and after a moment she turned back to him and began sputtering excitedly. “Yes, yes, just this morning! In the shower—I was so upset, I just wanted all this stuff to go away, and my roommates…” She hugged herself again and looked down. “I lost track of time. Everything went dark. It was so quiet and peaceful, then I realized I was late for homeroom.”

“It’s all right, Sarah,” Razor said in a quiet tone filled with pride. “One day, you might grow into shadow sight or even learn to shadow speak or hear what the shadows say. You already hear the little noises your Collectors make, right? If you’re really adept, you might even learn to strengthen your skills enough to regularly shadow travel.”

Sarah peered up at the man who had finally given names and clearer definition to the weirdness in her life. Overcome with emotion, she closed the gap between them and simply hugged him. He awkwardly patted her back and returned her hug. Somehow words weren’t necessary for him to understand what it had been like living with this thing and not having a name for it.

“I don’t want to hurt anybody,” she said, keeping her eyes tightly shut as she held onto him. “I’m so, so sorry for what I did to Melissa.”

“I’m not going to let you hurt anybody, honey,” he said softly, then held her away. “But that was why I was so angry when I found out that no one had told you.” He released a long breath and shook his head. “You needed to know. Ignorance is a sure recipe for fear. And had you known your power, you could have been trained like a black belt not to get into petty street fights with amateurs, knowing full well you could kill them. But without knowledge, you were just spontaneously ejecting all over the place—not good."

"My father always said knowledge was power," Sarah said in a bitter tone, feeling outrage beginning to rekindle within her.

"Yeah, I bet he did, and I'm pretty sure where he got the quote. Be that as it may, let's not focus on what people did wrong. Let's focus on your learning, your improvement, your talents, all right?"

"Okay," she said, finding a smile. It was hard not to be angry, but it was also hard not to feel empowered—and that felt so good. "Can I like…maybe…just come to you sometimes after class just to ask you questions, sir? Like…there's nobody who really understands this stuff, not even Nana—I mean, Headmistress Stone." Sarah bit her lip, waiting, hoping, praying that Professor Razor, who only took the super-advanced kids, might share just a little of his time and expertise with her. If she could learn how to use her talents with him, maybe she could learn fast enough to help Ayana. What good were special powers if it didn't help the people you loved?

He shrugged and stepped back, looking down at her. "I don't know, Sarah. Are you willing to work hard?"

"I am. I really am," she said, almost breathless at just the chance to study under him.

"Then I'll do you one better than just some casual tutoring after class." Professor Razor stared at Sarah, then he reached into his pants pocket, extracted a little onyx-and-sterling pin in the shape of an Egyptian Ankh and attached it to the collar of her sweater. "There. You're now officially in the Shadows division. You are not in the Blends talent division anymore. Normally I give these out during the first day of class, but why stand on ceremony? You sure don't, Miss Rivera."

"Oh, my God!" she said excitedly, and after a moment she touched the small black pin and looked up. "I don't ever want anything like hurting another student on my conscience. I promise you won't be disappointed in me. I'll study hard. I know this is a big responsibility, and I swear to you that I'll only use what I learn for the good. I don't want to be responsible for dragging another kid to you-know-where."

"I didn't think so," he said firmly. "So learn to control your gift and make your Collectors behave."

"I don't know how to," she said.

"That's why I got the job of working with you. Oh joy," he said with a lopsided smile and a wink.

* * *

By the time she'd gotten back to the purple corridors, homeroom was over and so was first period. Sarah dashed down the hall to make it to Miss Tittle's English class a full minute early, then put on her most contrite expression, walked up to the high-strung woman and apologized in front of all the other students.

"Thank you for allowing me back into your classroom, Miss Tittle," Sarah said in a solemn tone. "I am very sorry that I was disrespectful earlier and retaliated against another student. It won't happen again. And I'll be at the stables on time—I promise."

"Well, that is more like it—and I do hope Headmistress Stone reinforced with you how unacceptable disrespectful behavior is." Suddenly Miss Tittle came to a halt. She stared at Sarah's collar. "Oh, my," she said. "Your powers…that explains it…you're in Shadows now."

Murmurs broke out in the class as Sarah went to take her seat in the back row next to her brother.

"What'd you do?" Amy Feingold muttered. "Go get a free pass from your grandmother? I guess everybody in the Netpound sticks together, huh?"

"You know they do," Angelica Roberts griped under her breath.

"Back off," Al said, giving Melissa's girlfriends a warning glare. "If Sarah's a Shadow, it's because she earned it. And after what Mel's been doing to Sarah and her friends, then what she said about my cousin Ayana…well, Melissa is just lucky my pop doesn't go in for hitting girls. But as you can see, my sister can take care of herself."

Dumbstruck, Sarah slid into her seat. "Thanks," she whispered, staring at him. She'd thought he was on Melissa's side from the way he'd gone to her rescue earlier, but it was clear now that he'd simply been upset like everyone else and had just reacted without thinking, trying to save her.

"That's awesome," Val said, leaning over to her to bump Sarah's fist with his own.

Allie passed a note to her quickly, and Sarah read it, then hugged herself with a big smile. The paper had little smiley faces and hearts all over it, and said: *We are so sorry. Sit with us at lunch. Still BFFs, right?* Hyacinth mentally shouted *OMG! I'm so proud of you*! so loudly that Sarah squinted. Donnie shook his head and looked completely amazed. But Tami's eyes held something Sarah didn't want to quite name. It seemed to be a strange combination of hurt and deep sadness—along with resentment. That stabbed Sarah in the heart, numbing her good news, muffling the voices around her.

"You go, sis," Miguel said with a wide grin, drawing her attention away from Tami.

"Sweet," Wil said with an affirming nod. "I'll see you in lecture. Razor is…what can I say?"

"Okay now, class, let's settle down," Miss Tittle said, tapping the edge of her desk with a ruler. "This is all very exciting and positive, given some of the more unfortunate incidents we've been experiencing, but Sarah will still do detention. Disrespect is not allowed under any circumstances. Of course, there is also the matter of Melissa's injuries, however, I was made privy to some of the details surrounding that situation, and she is in trouble herself for pranking several of you earlier. Even while this nasty business of the missing students is being addressed by the administration, we must adhere to rules—must keep a sense of normalcy. Understood?"

Both Amy Feingold and Angelica Roberts gasped.

"You little rat," Angelica muttered under her breath, glaring at Sarah.

"No, more like a big rat," Al said, defending his sister in a low, warning tone. "*I* told when I took Melissa to the infirmary, so if you've got a problem, tell Mel to see me. And for the record, my grandmother doesn't play favorites. Like I said before, if Sarah's in Shadows now, you can be sure she earned her place there."

"Yes, well," Miss Tittle said, walking over to the board. "As I said, all of this nonsense must stop from here on. Melissa is in trouble, believe me—even though we must verify the voracity of Al's claim," she added, her tone skeptical, "given that he might be motivated as a sibling to, umm…shall we say, *embellish* circumstances on his sister's behalf."

Amy cut Al a mean-spirited smile as Angelica rolled her eyes at him in triumph.

"But Melissa must heal first, and what becomes of her for conspiring to harm a fellow student is a matter for the administration, not the speculation of this classroom. As to you, Miss Rivera, while your reaction to Melissa may be viewed as self-defense with cause—if we find out these allegations are true, and if you thought you were under attack again—regardless of your latent shadow talent, you must learn how to control said gift, and you most assuredly cannot disrespect an instructor, least of all, me. There will be order in this Academy!"

"Yes, ma'am," Sarah said, just happy to not be expelled. She glanced at her brother and gave him a rare smile of gratitude. Miss Tittle was such a sore winner. But that didn't matter. She now had something and someone to work with. For the first time in her life she didn't feel like a complete weirdo. There was a name for what she had and for what she was.

Sarah briefly closed her eyes and tried to send some light to Ayana with her mind.

CHAPTER 25

Sarah wasn't sure how she'd made it to lunchtime. She went through the motions for the balance of the morning feeling emotionally wrung out and numb. Ayana was missing, plain and simple. Wil alone seemed to know that, above all things, Ayana's disappearance had injured her soul, and his sad eyes told Sarah he understood that in every class.

"Hey, Sarah," he said quietly, waiting for her at the door as class broke up. "I just want you to know how sorry I am about everything you're going through. I'm here if you need me."

"Thanks," she said in a barely audible tone. "Means a lot."

Then she watched as Val, Al and the others from her compound walked toward her. Sarah noticed how Tami hung back and seemed to separate herself from everyone. Resentment flared, but she dragged her attention back to Wil.

"I understand," he said, nodding toward the family coalition heading her way.

He didn't have to say more; she knew what he meant. This was a time for her to be surrounded by the people who would be grieving with her. There would be time later for those who supported her individually, but right now everything was still too raw.

Val reached her first, followed by Allie and Hyacinth, then Donnie and Miguel. Sarah watched her brother stand back with Tami.

"Everything is gonna be cool," Val said gently, touching Sarah's arm. "Al's gonna talk to Tami—hip her to a few things. But you need to eat."

"I'm really not hungry," she said, looking up at him. Allie and Hyacinth squeezed her hand.

"One team," Miguel said in a somber voice.

"Net-pound sticks together," Donnie added. "It's time for everybody around here to know that."

Val slung a protective arm over Sarah's shoulder and gently urged her forward. She didn't fight him. It felt good to have someone else take the lead, just for a little while.

They all entered the cafeteria and headed straight to the table where her brother and Val normally staked a claim. It was then that she realized just how fractured their team had been. The first few days of school, the boys and the girls had split. Now it seemed that the girls themselves were falling apart. Sarah set down her books, and Wil gave her a nod from across the room. He had found a seat with a bunch of his track buddies. Melissa's crew was with Patty now. Al wasn't there yet, and neither were Tami and Stefan. Brent was nowhere to be found. In fact, just like in her classes, almost half the students were missing, no doubt called home by nervous parents.

Just then Jessica and her girls rushed over with Ayana's friends, Tina and Darlene.

"Guys, we are so sorry about what happened to Ayana," Jessica said in a shaky voice.

Tina and Darlene just nodded, shredding the tissues they held in their hands. Val, Donnie and Miguel nodded back, then stepped away to head for the food stations.

"Tonight, in the library, right after dinner, we want to hold a secret meeting with a few of us students," Jessica said as Bebitta and Andrea joined them. "The inner circle, if you get my drift."

Tina nodded. "We can't just sit around. We have to do something. Maybe we can all work as a group to…you know, like, try to mentally track her."

“I know the Shady Path is off limits,” Darlene said with a hard sniff, “but it’s the only portal we know of that they can’t close. Last night they shut down the one in Everett’s room.”

“Plus that rat-bastard Brent went home today. Just left, as polite as you please, with his parents.” Tina shook her head. “That’s what made me and Dar rally the troops.”

“Are you serious?” Sarah said, both angry and incredulous. “He left her?” She looked at Allie and Hyacinth in amazement, and they stared back at her with tearful, angry eyes.

“Yeah, and I doubt his buddy Stefan is giving up any real info to Headmistress Stone. They’ve had him in there for over an hour,” Darlene added, clearly furious.

“We need you there in the library tonight when all of us Upper Spheres who lost a friend come together, Sarah,” Jessica said, earning nods from Bebitta and Andrea. “We heard you’re in Shadows now, so you must be super strong. And Ayana was supposed to be your mother seer, so if anyone can jumpstart a serious telepathic search, it’s you. And if we can find Ayana, we’re hoping we can find the others.”

“Yeah,” Bebitta said. “We’ve just gotta distract Mrs. Hogan and any of the library staff.”

“We want you guys to know we’re with you,” Andrea said, her voice thick with tears. “We’re not going to stand around and just watch our friends disappear without a fight.” She wiped her nose and then hid her face against Jessica’s shoulder.

Andrea’s crying jag set off the rest of the girls. Sarah watched as Val walked up with his tray, hesitated, then found a faraway table. She knew the guys from the compound would never come back to their table now, afraid they’d start crying in public, too. She couldn’t blame them. It was all so heartbreaking, and she found herself swept away by the emotional flood, with the only thing to hold onto being the other girls around her.

Allie and Hyacinth put their arms around Sarah in a group hug as everyone collectively wept. Sarah cried even harder because of all the times when her best friend should have been right there by her side, Tami was off in her own little world nursing her jealousy. It was just another deep gash in Sarah's heart.

"Some of us can't even go back home," Jessica said, her words punctuated by sobs. "We don't have a home. This is it."

* * *

Somehow Sarah had managed to stay awake in Mr. Everett's history class, even though he'd spent the whole period on the boring American history dateline. And not wanting to further traumatize his students, he hadn't even used his more flamboyant methods of maintaining student attention. The quiet, calm pace of his lecture was both a blessing and a curse. While it relaxed her frayed nervous system, it also made her fall out of her chair in a coma.

By the time the bell rang, her eyes were crossing. Her last Blends lecture was going to be torture, though. Tomorrow, according to Razor, she'd start anew in his class and wouldn't be reporting to her old division. It was as though Professor Razor really did have a heart beneath his crusty exterior. He had to have known that, as anxious as she was to get started with his elite skills training, her mind was fried and her emotions were beyond wrung out. One day to pull herself together was what she needed, but not necessarily what she wanted. If she could have snapped her fingers and made everything work out, she'd sic her shadows on whoever had Ayana and the others. She'd send them to track her compound sister and find her alive. Unfortunately, she didn't have that kind of juice yet.

Just seeing Tami sitting off by herself, head turned, ignoring her, would knife at Sarah's soul. She wouldn't be officially moved into Razor's class until tomorrow, and all the waiting for closure on things felt like her fingernails were scraping against Styrofoam, with her nervous system playing the role of Styrofoam.

* * *

Dinner was a repeat of lunch, an emotional free fall. But at least she had a chance to tell Val the plan. Her stomach was in knots, and food was the last thing she wanted to think of right now. Tami was still not speaking to her, and she was not going to kiss Tamara's butt to get her to stop acting like a complete jerk.

Sarah shoved a couple of apples into her backpack for later then headed to the library with the rest of the girls. Val and the guys hung back, claiming they'd be right behind them.

But as she passed Wil standing by the door and glimpsed his sad eyes, Sarah stopped. "Hey, I'm sorry it's been…"

Wil reached out and touched her arm, stopping her words. "I know it's been rough. No apologies, okay?"

Sarah nodded and hugged herself. "We're all going to the library to see if, you know, maybe…"

Wil nodded. "Word travels fast around here. You guys do what you've gotta do. Me and some of the guys," he added, his eyes getting hard, "we're gonna do what *we* need to do."

Nervous, Sarah looked up, searching Wil's normally easygoing face. "What's that supposed to mean?"

"We wanna ask Stefan some questions about his boy—where he goes when he's in town—and ask him in a way that maybe Headmistress Stone didn't."

"Please don't do anything that's gonna get somebody hurt or kicked out of school, all right? Promise me. I would die if that happened."

Wil kissed her softly on the forehead. "It'll be okay, Sarah. You just do what you can, okay?"

She left Wil standing by the cafeteria exit, now more worried than before. Val, Miguel, Donnie and her brother were nowhere to be seen. Tami was who knew where. All of this was so not good.

* * *

"Time to get started, I guess," Sarah said to the group, once Mrs. Hogan was done with her teary pep talk. "Somebody has got to get her and her staff away from the front desk so we can start the vision quest."

Hyacinth and Allie nodded in agreement. Jessica let out a frustrated breath and nodded. She glanced at Bebitta and Andrea.

"Okay, Bebe, you and Andrea have to be on distraction patrol because we've gotta get me, Tina and Darlene in there with Sarah and maybe even Hyacinth since she's from the same compound. Allie can use whatever tactical strength she has to help jumpstart the session with white light. Okay?"

All heads nodded as the girls glanced in four directions to be sure no teachers or adult staff were watching. Sarah looked at the front desk, surprised to see Tami suddenly standing there with Al. She wasn't sure what was going on between them, but at least they were talking and Tami wasn't trying to make Al look bad in front of anyone.

But it was really strange to see Stefan enter the library with Brent's crew, without Brent. What the heck?

Sarah could feel it. She was sure Stefan had to know the guys were coming for him. Wil was off in a corner talking to Patty, of all people. Why that bothered her so much at a time like this, Sarah couldn't say. But it did. Just like the guys' plan to somehow get information out of Stefan felt much riskier than what Jess and Tina had cooked up.

"Why's Wil over there talking to Patty?" Allie asked, whispering to Sarah as the older girls got up to go distract Mrs. Hogan.

"I don't know, but I don't like it," Sarah muttered. Try as she might, she couldn't shake the irrational jealousy that came over her when Patty was near Wil. Yet that made no sense, because she also had a strange combination of feelings for Val.

"I know she's Melissa's sister," Hyacinth said, hedging, "but maybe she's just upset like the rest of us. You know, if she were on our side, a Clav as strong as Patty could help. Maybe that's why Wil is over there to ask her to put the other stuff aside and help find Yaya."

Sarah nodded, suddenly feeling small. "Yeah, you're probably right, 'Cinth."

Jessica placed her hands over Sarah's. "Okay, we've gotta start slipping in there one by one, so we've gotta focus. We need your head in the game, 'kay."

"Okay, but…" Sarah looked around as a dark worry swept through her. "Where'd Tami and Al go?"

Allie's gaze raked the library. "A scarier question is, where's Stefan?"

"Oh…nooo…what do we do?" Hyacinth grabbed Sarah's arms.

"Okay, let's not blow this whole thing because we panicked," Tina said as calmly as possible. "Stick to the plan."

"Can't you feel it?" Sarah said. "Something is really wrong."

Darlene nodded, beginning to rub her temples. "I think Sarah's right. I know everybody around here is blocking, but there's something else I can't put my finger on."

Sarah stood. "I've gotta go find Tam—"

"You two aren't even speaking!" Hyacinth whispered harshly. "So…no. Not by yourself."

"You've really lost your mind, Sarah. You know that, right?" Allie said calmly. "Like, you know there's no way we're gonna let you go trawling the halls alone to find Tami and Al, with Stefan who knows where…you're clear about that part, I'm sure."

"But if we all peel out together searching the halls and we bump into any teachers, it's gonna look so fishy. They'll get suspicious, and our whole plan falls apart." Sarah leaned forward and rubbed her temples.

A shadow over the table made them all look up.

"What if I walk you?" Val said quietly.

"How much of what we were talking about did you hear?" Hyacinth sat back and placed her hands on her hips.

"You're a Clav, li'l sis." Val shrugged and chewed on a toothpick he'd gotten in the lunchroom. "But it doesn't take a rocket scientist to put together the fact that my boy Al is AWOL. Sarah is clearly stressing over here, because her BFF is gone, which wouldn't be a problem, except that there's a sick bastard on the loose."

Sarah glanced over her shoulder and saw Wil, alone now, trying to look nonchalant. Then he simply closed the book he'd been pretending to read and came over.

"Everything cool?"

"No," Sarah said quietly. "My brother left with Tami, and Stefan is gone, too. That's not good."

"I'll go with you. We'll search the halls together—"

"This is family business," Val said roughly, glancing at Sarah and then Wil. "My boy, her girl, her brother."

"And you do not want to run up on Stefan solo, man," Wil said quietly, but his tone was firm. "Anything else we need to sort out can be handled later."

"That makes sense," Allie said slowly, looking at both guys.

"It's the most reasonable thing I've heard so far," Jessica said, then glanced over to see how the Upper Spheres were doing. "We're gonna need a few minutes to make sure the coast is clear, anyway."

Sarah looked from Val to Wil. "The main thing is, we find them, okay?"

"Right," Val said, eyeing Wil. "Maybe you wanna roll with Miguel and take one half of the school while me and Sarah take the other half."

"Guys, it doesn't matter—"

"How's your head?" Val cut off Hyacinth's protest and looked at their friend hard. "Why don't you try to get a mind-lock on Tami and leave the details to me and Sarah?"

"That was uncalled for," Hyacinth snapped.

Sarah closed her eyes.

"I didn't say that to be mean." Val folded his arms over his chest. "I said that because Miguel's got a mental safety line on me, and I thought, if you were cool, you might want to put one on Tami, then me and Sarah could go make it do what it do. All of us want the same things: to be sure Al's not getting jumped by Stefan and to find Yaya."

"Enough talking. Do it," Sarah said firmly.

Wil seemed a little hurt, but apparently he was okay with her choice to hunt for family with family for now, because he didn't object. Good thing, Sarah thought, because she just didn't have time to worry about him at the moment. Ayana was missing, and now her brother and Tami were gone, too. This was a search-and-rescue mission for her and Val. Their two best friends—one of them her twin—were in serious jeopardy.

* * *

The first place she took Val to was Mr. Everett's classroom, explaining as much as she knew as they went. She told him about the shadowy scratches she'd seen on the floor and filled in the blanks, really valuing the connection that only years of friendship and knowing someone could create. Val walked, listened, just took it in quietly, his senses keen as she jogged beside him, murmuring critical information and telling him everything she'd learned from overhearing Brent and Ayana, as well as Melissa and Stefan.

But when they got to the classroom, nothing was swirling. No portal was opening, and there was no sign of any kind of disturbance tonight. They searched high and low, through dim classroom corridors, through the auditorium, labs, broadcast studios and restrooms, and still no sign. Mental beacons came back with dead air, zero vibrations. Just like Jessica had told them, that portal had definitely been shut down, and they couldn't find a sign of anything else—including their friends. And they were running out of time—dorm lockdown had been moved up by two hours due to the missing students and faculty, which had the administration spooked.

"Maybe they've left the building?" Sarah said, growing genuinely frightened.

"I don't think Al would risk going up against Mojo alone at night or put Tami in harm's way like that…not even to be by himself with her. To mind-stun that old dragon you'd need two or three Specs or Upper Sphere Clavs with laser focus to keep him dazed while the others escape. That's how those other fliers did it." Val leaned against the wall with a thud, frustrated. "Damn!"

"Wait. You mean my brother isn't just trying to talk her out of hooking up with Stefan or filling her in about all the stuff going on? He's…" Sarah stopped walking for a second.

"Yeah, girl, where've you been?" Val shook his head and kept walking. "He's liked Tami ever since we were little."

"But they always fought and…"

"And what?" Val stopped walking to look at her. "She's the only one that ever gave him as good as she got and wasn't impressed with him. That's probably what blew his mind."

Sarah jogged to catch up with Val. "But…but…what about Melissa?"

"You know Al…his ego got crushed when Tami kept blowing him off. Hey, what's a brother to do? At home, there weren't many options, here it's like—dayum. So when this tall, pretty girl got in his face, he was on it, especially since Tami was acting funny. But he never liked Melissa the way he likes Tam." Val shook his head and stopped briefly to stare into Sarah's eyes. "You have no idea how deep somebody can feel about a person they've grown up with. All the other options around here are just a distraction."

Val turned and began walking quickly. "That's why I've gotta find our boy. If Stefan finds him first and Tami is between them, there's gonna be blood."

"So if they're not outside, and if they wanted to be alone to talk, where would Al take her?" Sarah pulled off her scrunchie, ruffled her hair up off her neck and then redid her ponytail as she kept pace with his long strides.

Val looked at her. "The gym."

Sarah looked at him for a second, and then they both started running.

There would be private blue corridors, romantic aquatic alcoves—like the locker rooms—full of darkly shaded marine life, bleachers to sit on, a place to talk and kiss in the dark. The pool was down one level and enclosed by tempered glass, but the serene water was beautifully lit at night. Poolside benches and lounge chairs offered a quiet sanctuary for lovers. By now Mrs. Gillison, keeper of the pool, was back in her deep sea mural, at home with her merman. In other words, there were plenty of places and a lot of time for things between two guys with a beef over a girl to go very, very wrong.

Val had outstripped Sarah, his long strides driven as he raced down the stairs toward the pool. She skidded into the blue corridor at the bottom behind him, and they both began yelling for Al and Tami in a sudden panic.

"Tami! It's me, Sarah. Look, I'm not trying to be in your business, but we're worried!"

"Yo, Al, man, this ain't a good time to be caught out on a limb. I got your back. Just holla and lemme know you're okay!" Val shouted.

"Everything's cool," Al yelled from the opposite end of the hall. He stepped out of the shadows, and Tami giggled.

"We were just talking, catching up on all this craziness that's been going down," Tami said, but she still didn't show herself.

"Okay, man," Val said and slumped against the wall. "My bad, carry on, I see no evil, hear no evil."

"I feel so stupid," Sarah whispered, shocked but relieved that Stefan was nowhere in sight. "We should probably go."

"Yeah, we should, but the hair is standing up on my neck."

She looked up into Val's serious eyes. "I know." Glancing back toward Alejandro, Sarah walked forward. "Al…Tam…listen, I know this is probably the last thing you wanna hear right now, but we've got a really, *really* bad feeling. Nobody can find Stefan, and if you guys are making out, you won't—"

The scream left Sarah's throat before anything intelligible could enter her brain. A blurred figure had body-slammed into her brother. His head had hit the cement pool deck hard—too hard. He was on his back, and the figure crouched above him released a horrible roar. Tami had tackled it, landing on its back, but it flung her off like she was a rag doll, and she hit her head on the wall and went down hard. Val was like a breeze, long strides pumping, carrying him forward. Her shadows rushed from beneath the pipes, scampering toward her brother and Tami.

All Sarah could make out was the glint of fangs in the emergency lights—massive upper and lower canines in an elongated snout headed toward her brother's exposed throat while that blood-curdling, moon-wailing howl still echoed.

Her twin was going to die. Her shadows leaped forward, making the beast hesitate for a second. She saw death in that murderous pair of crystal gray eyes, and her hand hit the wall, adrenaline spiking in her system as her scream hit a glass-shattering pitch. Shadows—hers and a dozen more like them—leaped from behind the pipes, out of the murals and from somewhere behind her, and then there was nothing but water.

Everyone and everything in the hall was swept away by the displacement current as the murals literally surged and water filled the hallway. Dolphins leapt from the murals, searching for survivors; schools of fish bumped her and sent her careening into the walls as the hallway filled. Dark shadows swam and swirled, clawing the water. Seaweed stuck to her hair, and she found herself unable to hold onto anything as the water carried her, as if she were riding white water rapids.

A hand yanked her up until she could grab the ceiling pipes. Sputtering and coughing, she clung to them, dangling there with Val, who was shimmying in the opposite direction, trying to get to Al, who was bobbing up and down in the maelstrom. Suddenly Al came up coughing. The werewolf was farther away and had hoisted himself up. He took one look back, snarled at Al, then scrambled away using the ceiling duct work for purchase.

"I can't find Tam!" Al shouted over the din of the rushing water. "Stay with my sister, man! Don't you dare leave Sarah!" And then he dove back down.

Fins—dangerous, ominous fins—sliced through the water as the mural continued to empty itself out.

Sarah's voice became a hysterical refrain. "Sharks! Mrs. Gillison, help! *Sharks!*"

A swift-moving fin headed right toward Val as he hung from the pipes, and he swung himself as far up as he could, squeezing his eyes tight. The water was so high now that his sweater was skimming the surface. Then suddenly a huge pink and green tail flipped up, a golden Trident slammed against the wall, and all the water was gone, leaving only a few flapping fish that hadn't made it back—along with Mrs. Gillison, the mermaid who'd driven back the flood.

Val dropped down to the floor and stood under Sarah. "Just let go, I've got you," he called up to her.

She did as he instructed, too freaked out not to trust him. He caught her easily, didn't even let her feet hit the wet, slippery floor. At one end of the hall was a sputtering mermaid, her green hair covering her face as she tried to right herself. But Val and Sarah dashed into the gym, where they'd seen Al and Tami carried by the flood.

Al was hunched over Tami's body, his magnificent white wings spread, working feverishly at administering CPR. "C'mon, baby, breathe," he said, sounding like he was about to cry.

Sarah went to Tami's side and put her hand on her brother's arm. "Clear!" she said, helping Al to send a white-light jolt into their friend.

Tami rolled over onto her side with a groan and coughed up water. Sarah and Al fell back on the floor, breathing hard, saying nothing as they released a simultaneous sigh of relief.

Star fish, sea anemones, broken bits of coral, tiny clown fish and huge blow fish, along with a few scattered angel fish, littered the floor.

"We are *so* in trouble," Sarah said, closing her eyes.

"If we don't get kicked out," Al said quietly. "This looks like a month of gym cleanup." Then he looked at Tami. "But, shit, who cares…none of that matters if she can breathe, right?"

"Listen, we found out Stefan goes wolf when the moon is full. I think somebody oughta know about that," Val spoke up.

Tami started to push herself up into a sitting position, and Al helped her. "But we need to find Ayana," she said, coughing. "I'm so sorry, Sarah. I don't want us to be mad at each other anymore."

"Me neither. But I think we need to scratch whatever plans we had and just tell Nana about everything we've learned," Sarah said, quickly glancing around.

"That's assuming we don't all get kicked out tomorrow," Val said, slowly standing and helping Sarah up. "And I agree with Sarah. It's getting too dangerous around here, man."

"Big assumption about us not getting sent home," Sarah muttered. "But what if I take the weight on this one, since I'm already in trouble for what happened with Melissa? No need in all of us going down."

"No way," Al and Valencio said in unison.

"Hear me out," Sarah said quickly, as the mermaid's fussing in the hallway intensified. "It was my energy signature that called the mural down, not yours. I can say I was trying to find my way to the gym in the dark, since I have a six A.M. detention right after my four A.M. detention…the first one for pissing off Ms. Tittle, the second one for what happened with Melissa, remember? And they know my powers are wonking in and out. Nobody else needs to get in trouble, and I can let Nana know what's up alone."

"But what if they kick you out, Sarah?" Tami whispered hoarsely.

"Just get out of here, you guys, and pray for me."

"I demand that somebody come right this instance and put me back in the pool so I can go home! Look at this mess!" Mrs. Gillison shrieked.

"You guys go hide in the locker room until I can drag her back to the pool. Run—before she sees you."

Sarah waited as the others finally gave in and quickly escaped to the locker room.

"Do you hear me, young lady? Look at this mess!" Mrs. Gillison complained as Sarah approached.

"Sorry, Mrs. Gillison," Sarah said with a fake cough. "I almost drowned."

"Drowning should be the least of your worries! That I can correct, albeit you'd have to live in the sea for the rest of your life—but the sharks, the orcas!"

"Yes, ma'am," Sarah said, stooping to lift the thick-bodied mermaid.

Mrs. Gillison's green eyes flashed with rage as her equally green hair practically stood straight out from her head. She slapped her broad tail on the wet floor for emphasis, the same way a person would stomp a foot when furious.

"Do you know how delicate a balanced sea life is? How damaged the environment already is after so many wars, not to mention pollution and acid rain? For you students to hit the alarm out of pure folly is simply unforgivable!" She swept her trident around, intermittently zapping expiring fish and sea vegetation back into the mural. "Look at my anemone beds! And my coral reefs! Oh, my poor sea horses and star fish have been traumatized!"

"I didn't do it on purpose," Sarah said in her most sincere tone. "I'll help clean this all up."

"There were more of you," Mrs. Gillison shrieked. "Where are the others?"

"They didn't do it, I did." Sarah let out a long, dramatic breath, sat down hard on the floor and stared at the mermaid. "We had all gone to the library, and we were walking back to our rooms, but then we decided it was still early…and since this is the most beautiful section of the school, we wanted to walk through to appreciate it at night."

"At least you remembered the buddy system." Mrs. Gillison flapped her tail, but clearly the compliments had helped considerably. "But do go on," she said, folding her arms over her askew seashell bra.

"Then something snarling and fast-moving came out of nowhere." Sarah shuddered. "We all scattered. But I was trapped at the other end of the hall, and I simply panicked. I just had a spontaneous powers explosion. I was a Blend and now I'm a Shadow, and that happens to me from time to time. I'm not sure what my true talent will be."

"So you'll be studying under Zachariah Raziel?" Mrs. Gillison asked, sounding impressed, and then she leaned forward to peer at Sarah's pin. "Well, that does make a difference, doesn't it? If you say you saw something ominous in this corridor, given the horrible disappearances we've experienced at this institution, then…I suppose we should investigate, rather than seek redress."

"Ma'am, I swear," Sarah said, using every negotiating skill she owned, "the water just came out of the walls and scared me to death. That's why I screamed your name—if I was pranking, why would I call a teacher, knowing I'd get in trouble?"

Mrs. Gillison stared at Sarah for a moment and then frowned. "You poor child. Were the others hurt?"

"No," Sarah said quietly. "Thank God."

"Yes indeed," Mrs. Gillison said. She looked around and let out a deep sigh. "There's a great deal that will need to be repaired, and the Fae staff and Mr. Monte will not like that one whit, but the fact that we didn't lose a student is of far more importance." Her troubled gaze sought Sarah's face. "I will have to report this to Headmistress Stone and Headmaster Shabazz, of course. If there's an entity in the building, we must all take precautions." Then she squinted and reached out to touch Sarah's pin. "You're definitely a Shadow, child. Professor Raziel doesn't give these to students unless he feels they belong in his very advanced division." She met Sarah's eyes, her own serious. "And we so need you in this school right now."

* * *

Sarah had barely turned the corner when a seven-foot-tall sentry blocked her path. Titan Troy lowered his blade and shield when he recognized her.

"Are you well, Miss Rivera?" he boomed. "Have you sustained an injury?"

Before she could answer, a black jaguar came slinking into the other end of the corridor, its magnificent golden eyes gleaming in the shadows.

Paralyzed by fear, she watched the huge beast move into a pool of light, then back into the darkness. The animal stood three feet tall at the shoulder, and she couldn't even speculate as to its length. Massive fangs filled its mouth, and its long, thick, velvety tail twitched back and forth in agitation. She couldn't take her eyes off of it, and it seemed as though Titan Troy had been transfixed by its hypnotic eyes, because he was just standing there as if waiting for the creature to lunge.

Then, barely visible in the shadows, the jaguar form morphed into a man who straightened from the beast's crouch to stand in front of the light. She couldn't see any detail, only his silhouette, but something familiar arrested her. Long dreadlocks swept his shoulders, and her fear became relief.

"What are you doing out alone like this, Sarah?"

"I—"

"Your grandmother is worried sick. Go to her quarters—immediately. Titan Troy will escort you while I try to find the intruder of whom you spoke to Mrs. Gillison. This academy is on complete lock-down until further notice."

Then her grandfather was once again a hunter of the night who took two graceful bounds and was gone.

"Stay at my flank, Miss Rivera," Titan Troy ordered.

She did. His massive size was a great comfort as they passed shadowy corridors and disorienting blue streaks of energy began to blur her vision. She kept up with his impossibly long strides only by taking two steps to his one, not wanting to be even a few feet away from his thickly muscled arm and gleaming blade.

She was soon panting, and disoriented with it. Her head was spinning from the bisecting and intersecting blue lines that crisscrossed the opening of every corridor they'd passed. Occasionally she'd see the transparent image of a person at the end of a line—or maybe it was the beginning of it. She couldn't tell. These weren't ghosts; that much she was sure of, because the people she saw were very much alive, despite their transparency.

It was as though she could see where everyone in the entire school had walked that day. Close to nausea she trailed her hand along the wall to ground herself, but that only seemed to annoy Titan Troy. He frowned and halted abruptly to issue her a sidelong glance of disapproval, which was enough to make her hug her sopping wet sweater and quickly start walking again.

Maybe she'd hit her head when she was caught in the rapids? It didn't really matter. All she knew was that being ill was not going to help her cause with her grandmother.

Titan Troy raised his huge fist to pound on the door of her nana's private suite, but Nana swung open the door before he could make contact.

"I present to you Miss Rivera," he announced, seeming a bit startled. "I shall wait outside your chambers to return this errant student to her dormitory once you are finished."

"Thank you, thank you," Sarah's grandmother said, brandishing a bath towel and yanking Sarah forward. Then she slammed the door, wrapped Sarah up in the towel and hugged her so hard she could barely breathe.

Kisses pelted Sarah's wet hair. Headmistress Stone had transformed into Nana Marlene. Sarah clung to the familiar warmth for a moment, soundless tears soaking into her nana's thick, white embroidered robe.

"Don't you ever, ever, *ever* frighten me like that again, Sarah Rivera, or I will zap you into tomorrow with my walking stick. Do you hear me, child?"

Her grandmother held Sarah away from her, tears in her wise old eyes and emotion in her voice, as a small purple disc began to glow in the center of her forehead as it scanned Sarah's entire body.

"In your own words," her grandmother said, hands still trembling, "what happened?" She took the towel, not waiting for an answer, and began helping Sarah out of her wet sweater.

Nana Marlene tossed the sopping garment in a waiting laundry basket, then walked past the gold brocade sofa to fetch a white robe from where it was warming on the radiator, along with a pair of fuzzy slippers. She thrust the offering toward Sarah, who gladly accepted it, then turned around to give her granddaughter privacy.

"Strip," Nana Marlene ordered. "Quickly."

Sarah followed her directions and dropped the rest of her wet clothes in the basket. The warm robe and slippers felt so good that all she wanted to do was curl up on the couch like a lazy cat.

But Nana Marlene spun on her and, with an outstretched arm and a pointing finger, issued a one-word command. "Sit."

Sarah did, quickly and quietly, the sensation of being in a safe haven immediately evaporating.

"Talk," Nana Marlene said, her gaze hardening by the second, now that the shock of potential peril had worn off.

Sarah twisted the sash of her robe, trying to decide where to begin. She'd heard that no-nonsense tone from Nana before, but never quite like this—well, at least not directed toward her. Sarah blinked several times; the blue streaks were still there, even in Nana's room. They fractured her attention, made her temporarily lose focus as she foolishly allowed her gaze to wander around the room.

The effect was disorienting but also eerily cool. Ferns were everywhere, and blue streaks went from each plant to a back room and returned, as though marking the trail of whoever tended the plants.

Nana had two sofas facing each other, with a small oval mahogany coffee table in between, littered with white candles and yellow flowers in silver vases. Two golden velvet Queen Anne chairs completed the grouping, and Sarah could see through open doors to the bedroom with its large four-poster bed covered in pristine white and private bathroom, and into the kitchen, with more blue lines weaving everywhere.

"Do *not* test my patience, child," Nana Marlene said in a low, warning tone.

That was all it took to make the blue streaks go away and snap Sarah's attention back to the real problem.

Chapter 26

Sarah kept her gaze focused on the end of the sash she was turning as she spoke. It was easier than keeping the intermittently reappearing blue streaks out of her line of vision, and way easier than meeting Nana Marlene's expression.

For some strange reason, everything that she'd wanted to tell her grandmother seemed to be slowly glazing over in the back of her mind, as though someone or something was sucking out her memory through a dark straw shoved into her brain.

Forcing herself to concentrate, Sarah kept to the highlights: walking down the hall, getting scared by a beast she couldn't fully see and hitting the wall—to release what had seemed like Noah's flood.

Her grandmother let out a long sigh and wiped her hands down her face as though trying to find something to do with them—other than strangle Sarah.

"I want the *full* story," Nana Marlene shouted, beginning to pace. "The entire spectrum of nuance and detail—your compound sisters' lives depend on it!"

Sarah sat back, eyes wide, breath caught inside her chest. Nana had screamed at her! And had she said *lives*, as in *plural*?

"That's right!" Nana Marlene shouted, her magical hands slicing the air and making blue sparks fly. She stopped pacing and placed her hands on her hips. "Sarah, I swore to the Creator that I would never break into your mind and violate you by taking you to the rock—prying your mind open by sheer psychic force and making your poor little soul hit the rock bottom of truth, girl, but so help me, if you don't tell me the information I need, I will. Hyacinth is lying in intensive care right now, her body gray. Shall I take you to see her?"

Sarah shot up off the sofa. "Hyacinth? Oh, no! She must have gone into the Shady Path alone!"

"Tina, Darlene, Andrea and Bebbita are sick, too—shall I go on? And they're in worse shape than Hyacinth, because from what I could sense, Hyacinth had a dwennimmen protective white light ward around her. Now you speak to me like you've got some danged sense!"

Nana Marlene reached out her hand and her walking stick filled it. In one deft move she slammed it against the wall over the mantle, and the wall lit like a big-screen HDTV. Horror filled Sarah as she took in her friend's dire condition. Hyacinth was barely breathing. An oxygen mask covered her face. Mrs. Guilliaume, the chemistry teacher, was by her side, taking the blood samples the doctor handed off to her. Uncle Richard was assisting the school doctor as he tried to give Hyacinth a transfusion, but her skin was still gray. Black cracks marbled their way through it in terrible, inky veins. Dark circles stained the skin beneath Hyacinth's once-pretty eyes.

Tears formed and fell, but Sarah only stared past Nana Marlene at the images on the wall. Slowly darkness began to surround her, but she breathed through it, pushing it away, until all of a sudden there was clarity, like a fog had lifted from her brain.

"It wasn't supposed to happen like this."

"It never is," her grandmother said, now leaning on her walking stick. "Mrs. Hogan told me that you and Hyacinth stumbled your way onto the Shady Path the other day—a path that was off limits due to the abductions, and is particularly off limits to students. Whatever got released through those illegal vortices is now spreading a deadly virus to whoever enters."

"But I went in and I'm not sick." Sarah's statement hung in the air like a giant question mark between them.

Nana Marlene pointed at her. "How many times do I have to tell you? You're special. You have to be mindful of the dangers that can harm others. If your parents weren't off looking for Ayana and the other missing students, I would be moved to send you home! Do you know how lucky you are that you've got Neteru DNA that makes you immune to most dark spiritual attachments and even a vampire or werewolf bite? If not for that, you would be lying in the infirmary with Hyacinth and the other girls right now!"

She walked back and forth, and then sent her stick away by simply tossing it into the air to disappear. "Earlier tonight someone distracted Mrs. Hogan's library aides, Mr. Anansi and Miss Tillie, with a mysterious gift of fruit and fireflies. When Mrs. Hogan got a call—a call that turned out to be a ruse, I might add—that her presence was needed at the unicorn stables, she thought the area was being monitored, but it wasn't. When she got back, there was a true medical emergency—Hyacinth and the other girls were lying on the library floor. I can't lose another student. I *won't*!"

Nana Marlene shook her head, her long, silver dreadlocks swishing, and then her voice fractured. "Those two fine young men who died…they were Valkyries rescued from Nod. They had no parents. We couldn't even give them a decent burial, just a memorial after cremation, because your grandfather, your father, Professor Raziel and Mr. Hubert could only find parts of them. That's what they didn't tell you kids in your big orientation. Everybody thought that was TMI, but maybe we should have told you."

Nana Marlene closed her eyes and drew a steadying breath, and it was only then that Sarah realized how stricken her grandmother was at the losses.

"We've tested all the sick girls'—all of them Clavs—blood. Tina and Darlene are at the curtain of death. Bebitta and Andrea aren't far behind. Whatever this plague is, it seems to slam Clairvoyants especially hard," Nana Marlene said in a strained voice. "We're running out of time, Sarah. These girls went immediately into the advanced stages of dark energy sickness. So, baby, if you know anything that will help, now is the time to be a leader and let me know."

"They were going into the Shady Path to try to put a tracer on Ayana," Sarah said. "I was going to go, too, but something came up. I had to leave, so I didn't think they would go in without me. Jessica was going to stay outside the door with Allie as our ground wires. They were going to try to bounce a signal off my deep connection to Yaya. Without me, I guess…I don't know what happened, but it must have been awful." Sarah rubbed her temples. "It sounds lame now, but I was going to tell you this Nana, but it was like a dark cloud came over my thoughts. Like someone or something was trying to block me from telling you what I needed to."

"What?" Nana Marlene's whisper was threatening and incredulous. "Can you still feel someone trying to block you?"

Sarah looked Nana Marlene directly in the eyes. This was too serious for her to be afraid. She pushed through the pain as the darkness suddenly returned, beginning to breathe heavily. "Yes, and do you also know students have been going into town to get high? You must. That's why you tested their blood. Those girls weren't—*aren't*—into any of that. But I overhead a conversation between Melissa and Stefan…he said something crazy about being a werewolf and was really mad at her because she supposedly took something from him, and it sounded to me like he was talking about drugs. I can say for sure that every time I saw him and Brent together, Brent was high. Maybe none of this has anything to do with the abductions or the girls getting sick, Nana. All I know is, we were just trying to help in any way we could to get Yaya and the other missing kids back."

Her grandmother nodded. "You're right, it is related…although Stefan's past is just that—his past. He was indeed infected years ago as a baby, but I cannot believe…No." Her grandmother briefly closed her eyes and sighed before she began speaking again. "He's been at the center of speculation before because people got nervous. I will only act on what we do know for sure and we are watching him closely, trust me. However, we do know that there's been a lot of underground activity going on at this school. We found illegal substances in the remains of the fliers, but the two Clavs who were their ground navigators didn't have a trace of anything in their systems. Somehow all of this is related. I just can't see the pattern—and that's what's making me crazy, baby." Her grandmother let out a hard breath. "That's why I don't need you kids meddling in things you don't understand. There are Upper Spheres blocking us from seeing what's going on, so unwilling to tell or snitch, as they call it, that lives are at risk. Those two girls who were out there on the platform above the Great Hall hadn't taken anything, but they wouldn't tell us where their boyfriends got it, even after those poor boys were dead. Insane!"

Sarah shut her eyes for a moment, thinking of Val's comments, locking in on them, and knowing that her father would have told Val and her brother about the dangers the two strong Upper Sphere fliers had faced.

"The guys who died were trying to find Art and Casey. Their girlfriends had to stay clean so they could mind-stun Mojo while the guys got away." Sarah felt her stomach roil. "Nana, what if the girls didn't tell you where their boyfriends got the drugs because they *couldn't* tell you? What if something blocked them like something just tried to block me?"

But before her grandmother could speak, Sarah shut her eyes against the pain and held her forehead and calmed her breathing. And then, in her mind's eye, she saw Beep and Bop frantically trying to get Hyacinth's attention before she entered the Shady Path. But Hyacinth couldn't see them, and she and the other girls just kept going.

"The Shady Path is booby-trapped, Nana," Sarah said, opening her eyes. "If a teacher went through there, he'd get sick, too."

Nana Marlene stared at her and nodded; it was a silent confirmation that what Sarah had shared was also what she'd heard. Nana Marlene snapped her fingers and made the images on the wall fade back to the original pristine white paint.

"That's why only your father, your mother and Professor Raziel can go through there now. They have genetic barriers to all dark consciousness contagion, just like you and your brother. You were meant to be hell warriors, Sarah, so I'm all the more disappointed in your behavior. I thought you would rise above peer pressure, that you'd be a voice of reason instead of going along with the crowd to make yourselves look cool."

"I *did* rise above peer pressure!" Sarah suddenly shouted. She pointed at the wall where the images had been. "This wasn't about looking cool, it was about finding Ayana! You said we're supposed to be Hell warriors, supposed to hunt the darkness. Well, as far as I'm concerned, the darkness has my sister, and I can't just sit around and do nothing! But I can feel it, Nana. Something evil is trying to pry open my mind."

Her grandmother rushed over and placed her hands on either side of Sarah's head, then began to loudly chant a prayer of protection. "A thousand may fall at your side, ten thousand at your right hand, but it shall not come near you."

Immediately recognizing Psalm 91, Sarah said it in her mind until she could get the words to coordinate with her mouth. Soon she was speaking the words out loud, and the fog that battled her mind, along with the pain, rolled away.

She slumped against her grandmother's body, and after a moment she felt a gentle kiss brush the crown of her head.

"Better?" her nana murmured.

Sarah nodded and looked up into ancient eyes holding wisdom. "We had no idea there was a booby trap in there. We wouldn't have sent people in there to get sick, no matter how upset we were or how badly we wanted to help."

Nana Marlene closed her eyes. "Oh…child…you girls shouldn't have been playing cops and robbers when you were so upset and angry. It takes a lot of maturity and self-discipline to deal effectively with one's attackers." After a moment she opened her eyes and sat down beside Sarah. "Sit back and hear me well," she commanded and then rubbed her temples. "I want to explain to you, here and now, how dark consciousness works, all right?"

Sarah sat back slowly and simply nodded.

"Malevolent intent is a dangerous thing. If anyone goes in there wishing for payback or vengeance, then the dark consciousness already swirling in there simply magnifies itself, feeding on those emotions. This is why our medical team is working overtime to keep the infected girls from flat-lining. When you're walking between the realms, until you're strong enough to stay focused, you can get hurt."

"Nana, I swear," Sarah said quietly, "none of us knew that was in there."

Nana Marlene leaned forward to grasp Sarah's hands between her own palms. "Negativity has its own dark tendrils, its own black grid. Demons and nasty little creatures run along its axis of evil. That's why we send out love, not hate. Love will burn away anything that's not right."

Pain and worry and disappointment filled Nana Marlene's gaze as she stared deeply into Sarah's eyes. "But we must never, ever, *ever* get caught skating the razor's edge between the light and the dark while using our white-light gift to exact a dark consciousness energy, like vengeance. *That* is an oxymoron…Light and revenge. Bad juju. The light doesn't do vengeance. Can't coexist in the same time-space, and the attempt will lower the vibration and leave you vulnerable. Some of those girls who went in there after Yaya took that dangerous vibration through the door to the Shady Path with them."

Nana Marlene released a long breath. "Who- or whatever is abducting students got to them through the illegal portals. Apparently they got wise enough to booby trap their travel route after they took Ayana, trying to make sure we couldn't send in seers or actual hunters behind her. We're pretty sure that Ayana's abduction was a blunder. Every child taken before, even the faculty members and Rogues, were loners or without families. What they didn't bank on was our love of those people, too—that this institution is one big compound where everyone is connected to everyone else. Even those poor boys we lost. The thing that got them up on that platform was that they wanted to look for the students who were already missing. It was in the very fabric of their spirits to help. Everyone here matters." Her grandmother wiped her eyes, which were beginning to tear up. "Everyone, Sarah. Even the kids with problems."

"How can I help 'Cinth and everybody get better?"

"Pray," Nana Marlene said, standing. "Now, what happened in the hall by the gym? I want details this time."

"A few of us left the library early," Sarah admitted, eyes downcast, each word weighed by despair. But she still wanted to protect her friends and brother; there was no reason to drag anyone else into this. "We decided to take a walk by the pool."

"Ummm-hmmm. Our indoor Lovers' Lane," Nana Marlene said, sounding weary.

Sarah glanced up and then went back to studying the floor. That wasn't why she and Val had been there, and she wouldn't bust Tami and Al. If nothing else, it wasn't relevant to everything else that was going on.

"We were walking, and something came out of nowhere. It was huge, a creature with a long snout and long teeth, but it stood upright like a man. I freaked out and a spontaneous discharge from me hit the wall—the next thing I knew I was screaming for Mrs. Gillison and half drowning."

Nana Marlene leaned forward. "You said the creature had gray eyes?"

"Yeah."

The older woman sat back and looked off at nothing. "And a snout?"

"Yes, Nana. It was like half-person, half-wolf."

Her grandmother closed her eyes. "I have suspected for a long time that students taking contraband into the Shady Path were weakening the integrity of the barriers. We've expelled some students from this academy, have purged the portals, and created strict rules about who could enter, and then only with an instructor involved. Apparently more have been sneaking in than we've known, and with the addition of drug use, it may have had especially deleterious effects on one student in particular."

"Nana, that other portal that was opened in Mr. Everett's room—the one that's gone now because the uncles shut it down—I could see shadow scratches on the floor where the opening had been."

"What!"

Sarah shook her head, feeling completely foolish for not thinking to disclose the information earlier. "I thought I was seeing things because nobody else could see it. That's the way my life has always been—I see stuff other people can't see and then they tell me I'm crazy. So I kept my mouth shut. Then, when Yaya went missing, we were all hysterical. That was the last thing on my mind."

"Oh, baby…I know, I know," her nana crooned softly, grasping her hand. "But if you see anything, anything at all, you have to tell me. It's vital."

"When I went to class and Mr. Everett opened up a dimensional moment, I saw shadow scratches on the floor then, too."

"Dear Lord…" Nana Marlene held out her hand. "Please give me your PIU so I can dry it. Kids are playing with fire, moving vortices around the school and letting in God only knows what."

The tone of Nana Marlene's voice was so resigned as Sarah got up and riffled through her wet clothes that there was simply nothing left to say to her. Sarah took the pin off her sweater and tucked it into her robe pocket, not wanting to lose it in the laundry. Being a Shadow meant something. Right now it was the only thing she had left to be proud of. But as she stared at the water-logged unit before handing it over to her grandmother, she noticed that the alphabet was backward.

"Nana, are you sure I can't get sick?"

Nana Marlene accepted the PIU from Sarah and held it between her palms, causing a warm purple light to surround it as she closed her eyes. "No, child. I told you. Your system doesn't allow for that."

"Then how come the letters on my PIU are backward, and I'm seeing blue streaks all over your pretty Oriental rugs, and I feel nauseous. Even that spontaneous zap that hit the mural…I—"

Sarah took two steps, then stumbled and collapsed on the floor.

Nana Marlene opened her eyes at the sound. "You're seeing shadow echoes?" she whispered, getting up to help Sarah off the floor.

"Huh?"

"Come, child—into my kitchen with you. Tea is in order." Nana pushed a button on Sarah's PIU. "You need to read the help notes," she said. "Each unit now contains a guardian within the crystals. That's our spiritual version of a GPS. We added that feature after we lost those two Valkyrie students, Peter Matthews and Gregory Duncan, in the woods. Your unit protector is Sarina—Mr. Hubert's wife."

Sarina spilled out of Sarah's PIU in a colorful, coughing haze. "Oh, my goodness—sakes alive, headmistress! I thought those children were going to drown!"

Sarah just stared at the tiny being in the middle of the floor. Her PIU had a genielike little entity embedded in its crystals?

"Are you all right, Sarina?" Headmistress Stone said, her tone worn and somber.

"I believe so, but that was just an awful experience."

"She did it without you, Sarina," Nana Marlene said with no small measure of pride in her voice. "Sarah had enough electromagnetic charge on her own under battle conditions to bring the murals to full life. Most of the time not even my most advanced Upper Sphere students can do that. It requires pure white light, laser intent and selfless sacrifice—a willingness to give every ounce of your own life force to save another. Not bad for a Blend…or a Shadow."

The small multi-hued nymph did the happy dance in the middle of the rug, stamping her teeny-tiny feet.

"She's also seeing shadow echoes, plus she's beginning to read backward." Nana Marlene went to Sarah and hugged her.

"Oooooh…" Sarina gushed, then covered her mouth. "Like the old texts were written in relation to current-day English?"

"Yes, this child is beginning to read in ancient text—from right to left, instead of left to right, as well as horizontally from top to bottom and bottom to top like many of the old hieroglyphics were presented, so please help her in her normal classes when it's time for her to read assignment or copy notes from the board. This may be a permanent development or it could self-correct, I'm not sure. But Sarah will need your help to navigate through this."

"She'll be reading in the Tehuti Library in the capstone in no time! Oh, Sarah, I am so proud."

"We *are* proud, Sarah," her grandmother said, releasing her. "But, Sarina, since she is determined not to divulge who her partners in crime in the hallway were, would you visit those PIUs and help dry them? They're expensive equipment, as you well know, and the students need them for class."

"Yes, headmistress," Sarina said with a squeal, and then disappeared in a rainbow-hued, opalescent streak under the door.

Nana Marlene placed an arm over Sarah's shoulder and began walking her toward the kitchen. "We will have a cup of tea, over which we will discuss what these new talents that are beginning to bloom truly mean—and the responsibilities that go with them. And you will dwell on what I have said, as well as this very unfortunate incident that you had a hand in exacerbating. I have not even begun to assess the punishment that something so serious requires, but perhaps seeing how quickly things can get out of hand is enough laceration for one soul. I honestly don't know, Sarah. But I do know that tomorrow at 3:30 A.M., Titan Troy will escort you to your detention—if you are still going to take Professor Raziel's advice and go. With everything going on, no one would blame you if you didn't."

Sarah's and her grandmother's eyes met. Sarah knew her nana was so bone weary and so upset that she didn't have it in her to enforce a punishment that now seemed moot, given all that was going on.

"Maybe not right now they wouldn't," Sarah finally said after a moment of reflection, "but in the long run they would. I don't want them thinking you play favorites. I could care less about what they think about me at this point, but I don't want them thinking badly of you. I'll go."

"If that's what you want, I will respect your wishes."

Sarah stopped walking and stared at her grandmother. "I don't mind doing the detentions. I just want to know how we can make 'Cinth and the others get better."

"*You* can't do anything, Sarah—and I want you to promise me that you won't. But the staff here, while holding each student's life-force in the light, will send a dispatch to find the source of the contagion. And we will be scouring the school to shut down all additional unauthorized portals. We never found the PIUs from the two students who died in the forest, and having those crystal-lit units out there in a den of negativity is of deep concern. They didn't have a crystal keeper in them like yours does, and we must find them, which will take time—something I fear we don't have. And all of this while we try to save your friends' lives and find the missing students."

* * *

Sarah's room had become the impromptu command center. She said good night to Titan Troy, opened her door and was greeted by an entire cadre of overwrought friends. Tami quickly shut the door behind her and locked it, while Allie and Jessica shushed loudly to bring order.

"What happened?" Tami asked, thrusting a chair forward so Jessica and Allie could make Sarah sit down hard in it.

"It was all so messed up," Jess said, not allowing Sarah to answer Tami's question. "The moment you guys left, we got old Hogan away from the front desk on a phony stables call, then the Upper Sphere crew went in without you."

"Right. That's when it got crazy," Allie said, sounding out of breath. "Hyacinth wanted to help. She could feel something just behind the locked door. I begged her to stay with me and Jess, but she wanted to be a part of the mission."

Sarah held her head and groaned.

"Now they're all sick," Allie said thickly, then swallowed hard, as if holding back a sob.

Jessica cast her gaze around the group. "Who knew everybody would get sick?" she asked in a tense whisper.

"The vortex is booby trapped," Sarah said, looking up at her friends. "Whoever took Ayana wanted to make sure no one could come through the portal after them. It's unsafe to go through them unless you've got DNA like Razor or my parents."

"Shit!" Jessica exclaimed, then covered her mouth.

The room fell silent for a moment, everyone wide-eyed, looking at Sarah.

"We know all about Stefan's attack and the pool murals," Allie finally said, glancing around. "Tam filled us in. Uncle Richard is at the ER. Pop Shabazz is patrolling the halls in a full shape-freakin'-shift! Teachers are running everywhere."

Jessica thrust out her PIU. "Look at the broadcast. Stefan Oahspe is AWOL and presumed dangerous due to a viral infection—nice code for werewolf transformation. If any student sees him or knows of his whereabouts, they're to stay away and call the school authorities. Dude went around the bend is what they should have said. All students are to be behind locked doors until sunrise—nobody can go to pre-sunrise or post-sunset detentions without an escort. The library—the frickin' library—is closed until further notice."

"Outdoor excursions are cancelled," Tami said. "This place is on total lockdown."

Sarah frantically waved her hands in front of her as though the other girls were a swarm of bees. "*Forget all o' that*—how are 'Cinth and the others? I just wanna hear about that!"

"Keep your voice down," Jessica warned as a teary-eyed Allie dashed forward and hugged Sarah.

"Ohmigod, Sarah. 'Cinth almost stopped breathing. She just fell on the floor and started turning gray. All the girls did. Uncle Richard and Aunt Marj—they're in ICU with 'Cinth now. Nana Marlene hit the school lockdown alarms, charging all the walls. We thought you might know if she's all right."

"What happened when you met with Nana?" Tami asked, talking with her hands.

In fits and starts between short bursts of sobs, Sarah relayed what had happened, what she'd told and what she hadn't. She didn't care if her friends were relieved that although the drug operation was common knowledge, their contraband services weren't. Nothing could stop the heartache of knowing Ayana was missing and Hyacinth was losing life force by the hour, and that Bebe, Darlene, Tina and Andrea were also at death's door.

None of the petty differences between her crew and Melissa's mattered anymore, only restoring everyone to full health, and finding Yaya and the others who were still missing.

As the group slowly dispersed and promptly got in trouble with Titan Troy for being out of their rooms without an escort, all Sarah could think about was how she would ever be able to live with herself if even one student died because they were trying to be junior detectives and get even with whatever evil had breached the school.

Life and death put things into context. Tami was lucky to still be her impulsive self. The girl had almost died, and there was something different in her eyes now, even though she'd talked tough in the group. Sarah could see beyond that, though—Tami was rattled to the bone. Just as she and her brother and Val had been. She'd never seen Alejandro so close to tears or heard such raw panic in his voice as when he'd thought Tami had drowned or seen Val step forward as when he'd captured her hand to pull her to safety.

Now the fear in people's voices, the fear in their eyes, the way they went to bed and then curled up in fetal position was what her dad had spoken of on the stage, the thing they hadn't really comprehended—how fragile life was, how insignificant most struggles between people were, but how deadly things could be if they went too far. And the aftermath, for the survivors, was a level of guilt so profound that there was no way to ever describe it to another human being.

She drifted in fitful sleep, those thoughts filling her brain as she wished she could find the PIUs, could help find Stefan so he could be purged and saved and helped…wishing that God wouldn't make this lesson about vengeance so hard and would heal her classmates—all of them—and just let bygones be bygones, chalking this up as a serious wake-up call.

But the Divine must have really been pissed, because when she looked over to Hyacinth's empty bed she knew the only thing that would wake her up this morning wouldn't be a miracle, just her three A.M. PIU alarm.

Chapter 27

There was no use lying in bed a moment longer. Her problems weren't just going to disappear on their own, anyway. Besides, sleep was impossible—all she'd been doing the whole night was tossing and turning, tears dampening her pillow.

Detention also wasn't going anywhere, and after what she'd been party to, she felt guilty enough to sign up for it all year long…if only that would guarantee a cure for her friends.

Moving as quietly as possible, Sarah pulled on her underwear and a pair of gray sweats and the hoodie that she'd left out on her desk chair to reduce any bumping around in the dark, then she stopped for a moment.

She could see in the dark—not just gray tones like she could before, but with total clarity and even a little color…Freaky.

It took her a moment to absorb that new reality. She closed her eyes for a moment and then opened them again. It was like she was seeing the room through a gray filter that stole most of the color from everything, but she could definitely see. Then, slowly but surely, full color crept into things.

And then the room became a jumble of white streaks, and she had to hold onto the back of her chair and do what Nana Marlene had told her: Concentrate on just one person at a time to see their shadow echo signature without being bombarded by too many at once.

She picked Allie's signature as a test and watched the white lines buzz around the room from the door to the bed and back to the door, then to the bed, the chair, the desk, the door and finally to the bed again. Sarah closed her eyes. She looked at that energy signature and understood exactly how upset Allie had been. Now all she had to do was breathe quietly for a moment and hopefully the signatures would recede until she called them forward.

Gift though it was, all of this was going to take some getting used to, and she didn't have time for it this morning.

Her PIU blinked from its spot on her desk. Quickly snatching it up, she saw Wil's sig and let out a sigh. It took her a moment to try reading the words backward, and then she just held her unit up to the mirror.

Gld UR ok. Hrd whts up.

She texted him back quickly.

Gld UR ok 2—GTG, CU at brkfst

She could only imagine the powwows that must have happened in the boys' dorm last night; no wonder she hadn't gotten a call from Wil then…or Val.

Sarah reached for her hiking boots—her sneakers were still damp—and quickly put them on over a pair of thick white tube socks. Remembering the apples in her backpack, which would probably be her breakfast, she shoved them into the hoodie's front pocket, found her toothbrush, toothpaste and a face towel, and grabbed her PIU. Allie and Tami were still asleep, fitfully twisting in their covers, just like she'd been doing all night.

Quietly opening the dorm room door, she slipped out and gave Titan Troy a little wave. He simply nodded, his expression unreadable. Sarah held up her toothbrush. He nodded again and followed her to the girls' bathroom, held up his hand for her to stop, entered and checked around, and then faced the wall, just as he'd done last night when she took a much-needed shower to get the sea water out of her hair.

Sarah let out a sigh. This was so icky—she had to pee. But no way could she do that when he'd *hear* her. She decided not to think of that while squeezing a glob of toothpaste onto her brush, but when she turned on the water, she had to wiggle and hum a little tune to distract herself.

She brushed more quickly than she'd ever done, followed by a cold splash of water on her face. Finally nature would not be put off for any man or woman, and she had to embarrass herself by leaving the faucet on, dashing into a stall and just doing what came naturally.

Too humiliated, she didn't say a word or look at Titan Troy as she exited the facilities and walked quickly down the hall to deposit her toiletries back in her dorm room. How could guys be so casual about such deeply personal things? But the giant's expression hadn't changed one bit when she glimpsed him from the corner of her eye.

Her PIU sounded, and he swung around so fast that she ducked, fearing decapitation.

"My apologies, Miss Rivera," he said in an expressionless voice. "My senses are tuned for battle."

"It was my PIU."

He nodded. "True, but we must be vigilant."

She didn't respond, just fell in double-step with his brisk pace while trying to read a backward text message from Val. The only way she knew it was him was that his PirateNet homepage pic came up. Concentrating hard, she could get the words to slowly reverse themselves. It was a sweet note, really thoughtful. It was the first thing that made her smile in what felt like forever.

Hrd wht hapnd. Got prayers for 'Cinth. Wntd u 2 C I was up. Didnt 4get2 call u, but Titan 2 big. C U l8tr.

A soft smile began in her heart and then made its way to her face. She hit the letter *K* and pushed send, and then jammed her PIU into her front pocket with the apples.

* * *

She felt like she'd been walking for two miles and was surprised when she and Titan Troy passed the gym. Surely they'd gone much further than that. Frowning Fae were touching up the mural and drying the floor with mops that seemed much too big for them to wield. As she passed, they gave her the evil eye and let out small grunts of annoyance.

Well past the boiler room, Titan Troy led her to a heavy, locked steel door that had a spinner handle like the old movie images she'd seen of bank vaults and submarine hatches. After entering a code on a side panel and waiting for huge tumblers to fall into place, he set down his sword and shield on the floor, then gripped the thick spindles and turned, straining the muscles in his massive back, arms and thighs.

Spellbound, Sarah just watched in awe. The amount of strength it required to open the door, even once unlocked, was incomprehensible. Finally the spinner moved clockwise. When the door opened, six feet of steel swung away from the wall, revealing a long iron staircase that seemed to extend without end in both directions.

"Let me lead the way into the darkness," Titan Troy said in a somber voice. "I must light a torch—as this beast we seek abhors fire, it may have taken refuge in the emergency exit tunnel."

Sarah watched mutely as he turned over his shield and revealed a cleverly attached length of wood that had been wrapped at one end with what looked like a tar-dipped sheet. Working quickly, he extracted a long stick match that had been bundled with it and struck it against his jaw stubble.

Oh, yeah, she definitely had to catalogue this experience to tell the gang. He'd lit a match off his face? OMG!

Torch in hand, he tossed her his shield as he picked up his sword. She caught the large metal disc and fell.

"Ow!"

The thing weighed what felt like a ton. He let out a hard breath, set down his sword and then came over to hoist his shield over his shoulder and yank her up off her butt before picking up his sword again.

She silently vowed not to lag too far behind him as the door slammed shut and the spinners automatically whirred back into a locked position. If she hadn't been able to see in the dark, she would have screamed for sure.

Five stories up at a Titan's pace, with only a small L-turn to break the upward trajectory, her thighs were burning, her chest felt like it was about to explode, and her eyes were watering from the fiery fumes of his torch. This was crazy.

Finally they stopped and he passed her the torch.

"Stand back," he ordered. "Entering the upworld from below is always dangerous." He punched in another code and grunted as he unlocked a round steel hatch, waited a moment as he readied his shield and blade, and then flung open the heavy hatch. Then he was gone.

Sarah froze, holding the torch out like it was a weapon. Cold mountain air rushed in and made her shudder. She listened hard, then slumped against the railing when she saw Titan Troy's face peering over the edge at her. He offered her a huge hand; she offered him the torch. He sighed and smiled, then simply lifted both her and the torch together with one quick pull of her forearm.

She landed on her feet, and he caught the torch before she set her hair ablaze, then locked the door.

"You will be strong one day, wee one," he said with a smile. "You come from good stock. Just remember, there are all kinds of strength—physical is just one kind."

He stood and looked off into the distance, and she followed his line of vision. On the other side of a football field and outdoor track, she could see what looked like a long barn surrounded by several smaller buildings, a grain silo and a large penned-in pasture area. Sarah whirled around, shivering.

There was nothing else as far as her eyes could see but green grass, plowed rows and haystacks.

"We must not keep Mr. Milton waiting. I believe you have five minutes, and then you will be late for detention, earning you another."

Titan Troy didn't have to tell her twice. In a flat-out dash behind him, she ignored the catch in her side, ignored the breath that wouldn't come, and just ran. The moment she passed the entrance gate, a pair of blue flannel-clad disembodied arms unfolded from the air, bringing her to a skidding, screaming halt.

"Whoa, young filly—hold your horses. You will have my stables in an uproar if you're not careful."

Titan Troy simply looked at the floating arms and chuckled. "This one is high-strung, Milt. I'll wait over on the house porch…let you take it from here."

"Help yourself, the missus is up—couldn't sleep. She's got breakfast going."

"None of us can rest until the contagion is resolved and the missing are found," Titan Troy said. "Mrs. Hogan will not be overburdened attempting to feed me this morning?"

"No, no trouble at all—for her, it's all magic."

"Thank you, I am honored," Titan Troy said with a deep bow.

Sarah placed a hand over her heart as a squat little man in a blue flannel shirt and denim overalls fully materialized, scratching his beard. Bushy red hair covered most of his round face. He chewed on a corncob pipe and wore a cap that partially covered his mostly bald scalp. Smiling, he looked up at Sarah and simply shook his head.

"I'd be Milton Hogan, but most students call me Mr. Milton. Hmmm, lemme see," he said, pulling out small scraps of paper from his overall pockets and creating colorful confetti as he simply let his notes fall to the ground. "Oh, I know you—you're Miss Tittle's homeroom tantrum." He clucked his tongue and did a little jig. "Three minutes late on the first day of homeroom and had the nerve, gall and unmitigated audacity to bear fangs. My, my, I like 'em feisty."

"Sir, the fangs were an accident…I can't really control them like I should yet. I'm a Blend and a Shadow and sometimes, well…I just don't have my act together yet."

"Ahhh, yes, a Shadow. I heard," he said with a wink. "Impressive." Then he waved off her explanation, beginning to walk and forcing her to follow him. "Ah, Miss Tittle, flaming old hen—she's enough to make a Regular bare fangs, no worries. Three minutes and detention. I get so tired of that dreadful shrew, but that's just between us." He looked over his shoulder and gave Sarah another wink. "Stables detail is far from the worst of it, if you can stand the smell. The beauty in here and the freedom of being outdoors would send more students my way, if they could only look through the manure to find the pot of gold buried in it."

Three feet from the barn the wind shifted, and Sarah covered her mouth and nose with her forearm. Her eyes watered, and her stomach lurched. "Ohhhh, maaan."

Mr. Milton just shook his head and opened the massive doors with a wave of his hand. "Kids today," he muttered, walking briskly into the center of the huge structure.

Proud as could be, he bowed and opened his arms. "Welcome to the Pegasus and Unicorn stables. This is a rare treat, even if you're shoveling manure. You will never see any finer creatures in all creation."

Soft whinnies and snorts greeted Sarah as she moved farther into the barn. Beautiful, curious, shining eyes and noses peered over wooden doors, and she laughed, dropping her arm, no longer focused on the pungent aroma.

"They are sooo pretty," she said, going from stall to stall. "Look at them!"

"I think they like you, too, lassie, which is a real fine thing indeed. They know good souls." Mr. Milton walked over to a stall and opened it, ushering out a gleaming white stallion with marble blue eyes and wings folded tightly against his body. "This would be Sir Brandon. Please, Sir, would you bow for milady?"

The horse whinnied and opened up its majestic thirty-foot wingspan, then went down on one knee.

Sarah gasped and covered her mouth as she started up at the impressive beast. "He's spectacular," she murmured in awe. "I've heard of them, but I never thought I'd get to see one."

"Aye, today you'll definitely have a gander at more than one," Mr. Milton said, rubbing the horse's nose and giving him a small sugar treat from his pocket. The horse stood, then reared on his hind legs and came down with a thud. "Look at his hooves—clad in pure silver…shod by the same blacksmith that crafted Excalibur. King Arthur commissioned him to us after the last war, and Merlin brought him to us himself. Now that was a very special day indeed!"

"Whoa…"

Mr. Milton walked the horse back to his stall. "Agreed. That is why me and me groomsmen place such honor in taking care of them." He opened his arms again, motioning toward the eager noses that whinnied for him with joy. "These are my babies. Each one was a Neteru King or Queen's favorite. Come," Mr. Milton urged. "This beauty belonged to Queen Aset, and this warhorse was the charger who bore King Ausar."

Sarah stepped back as Mr. Milton brought out two huge beasts with silver eyes and hooves set against snowy white, glistening coats. The sound of several stalls being kicked made him smile. "Yes, this is Neteru Damali and Neteru Carlos's daughter." Mr. Milton winked at Sarah. "They know you—you're a celebrity."

"How do they know me?" she asked, laughing and pleased.

"They will only allow a Neteru to mount them, and they know your smell. It's regal, carried in your blood. These animals have highly developed senses of smell and loyalties." He motioned toward her with a quick whistle, and both massive creatures strode up to her and sniffed, then nuzzled her. "Miss Tittle, for all her histrionics, did you a favor, lassie. You got to see something that most students don't." Waving his hands, he laughed and shooed away the curious creatures. "Back in your stalls, no fussing and that's that."

Once he had them put away, Mr. Milton turned around and smiled. "I have Queen Eve's mare and King Adam's stallion, too. Oh, my, my, my, there is no stable like this in all the world."

"But don't they get bored? Don't they like to fly?" Sarah asked, feeling suddenly and inexplicably sad for the magnificent creatures confined here.

"Aye, I do imagine they get bored sometimes, when once they would ride into Hades or into earthbound battles with a warrior of light on their backs to right wrongs and heal injustice, and now...they deliver vegetables."

"Deliver vegetables?" Sarah frowned as she considered what seemed like such a waste of potential.

"It is perilous business these days, to be sure."

"Huh?" Sarah scratched her head. "I don't get that part."

"Come," he said. "I'll help you understand."

He walked ahead of her quickly to the far end of the barn and then opened a stall. Inside was an opalescent white unicorn whose coat caught the barn light in pinks and blues and golds, depending on which direction she turned. A small golden pile sat in the far corner of her stall, and she darted back and forth nervously until Mr. Milton quieted her with soft clicks of his tongue and a bribe of sugar.

"They are so shy and so high-strung," he murmured, petting the animal's silky mane. "But they eat grass and return gold," he said with a nod. "Add that to compost and to what the Pegasus horses leave, and you can grow anything in any soil conditions. They bring dead soil back to fruitfulness to revive and resurrect the cycle of life. Our unicorns were the cornerstone of our ability to reestablish this hidden valley, and our Pegasus cavalry are trained warhorses. I'll show you Hannibal's stallion in a moment. He's a real monster—snorts fire, ready at all times for battle—and that's what we need. Strength like that that can fly in under the radar to the towns on the other side of the dead zone."

Mr. Milton backed out of the stall and closed the door behind him. "We glamour the Pegasus wagons so no one can see the wings, and we look like the Amish." He sighed when she gave him a blank stare. "You will learn about them in history, but they're peaceful people who never modernized, so they were able to live off the land without being connected to the power grid—so those who survived the war and floods, earthquakes and pestilence, had the skills to rebuild log cabins, sow and plow fields. Unlike most modern humans, they knew how to work with their hands.

"We use the Fae glamour to take what we cannot use at the Academy to help the local Regulars in the small towns below. Sometimes we take Upper Sphere students on field trips for good behavior. We also trade with the townsfolk—food for wool and linens and other goods. We're also occasionally called upon to send airlift support to dug-in Guardian units, and only a Pegasus is strong enough for that vital and dangerous work."

"That is very, very cool, Mr. Milton."

He beamed at her. "Yes, indeed, it is very cool, lassie. But I bet this is cooler." He hustled down the rows until he reached almost the end stall and tossed a large hunk of apple over the door. "Stand back," he warned, and then undid the latch. "This is one stall only me and the boys clean."

A gigantic, crimson warhorse burst out, standing eight feet at the withers and pawing the earth with golden hooves. Fire blasted from his nose, and his eyes glowed golden. Then he whinnied and reared on his hind legs, his sixty-foot wingspan casting a shadow inside the entire barn.

"Down, Sophocles!" Mr. Milton ordered. "Don't make me call King Hannibal—you act nice for this young lady."

The horse came down off his hind legs, snorted hard several times, and pranced back and forth, agitated.

"He can't help it. His sole purpose was to ride into battle, with or without a rider—that's how smart he is. This was Hannibal's favorite mount, and he rode this magnificent creature right into the second battle of Masada to battle the devil's wife, Lilith."

At the mention of the demon's name, the horse reared and blasted the barn floor with fire.

"No, no, she's vanquished and he's missing in action," Mr. Milton said, throwing another apple, which the giant beast caught in the air and swallowed whole. "Come on, back ye go." After several attempts, the red Pegasus finally relented. "They're all very sensitive and very attuned to environmental stress," Mr. Milton said, placing one finger to his lips. "The mention of certain entities that should go nameless just makes them ready for war."

Sarah signed that her lips were sealed, and Mr. Milton nodded approvingly.

"Normally, when a student comes in for detention, my groomsmen walk the animals all out to the pasture so they can fly a bit—they know not to venture far—and I feed and water them while the unlucky student gets a dolly and a shovel. That way, neither the student nor our babies get hurt. But today, given that there's something running wild that would love to get hold of one of our horses, we'll wait till the sun is up and the moon is down before we turn them loose in the pasture, so we'll see…maybe you caught a break. I need to think on that a spell."

He pointed to a long flatbed hand truck on wheels, which had a long manure trough and a big metal snow shovel on it. Somehow, just seeing that took a lot of the enthusiasm for the beautiful creatures out of Sarah's soul, but she tried to smile and be a good sport. What she'd just witnessed really had been totally awesome.

"Yeah, I know," Mr. Milton said, chuckling behind his unlit pipe. He stuffed it with aromatic cherry tobacco, but didn't light it and just drew on the flavor as he walked, motioning with his chin for Sarah to follow him.

"Ah…sense and sensibilities. Dung is so underrated and so reviled, but it's a vital part of the cycle of life, lassie. You will come to appreciate the lesson in being faced with a pile of crap one day. Makes you strong. "

"Horse doo-doo makes you strong? C'mon, Mr. Milton," she said, laughing as she followed him.

"The pot of gold at the end of our Fae rainbows was always unicorn puckey—because what foolish humans never seemed to understand was that gold is nothing but a conductive metal or a rate of exchange when you have a monetary system—but what happens when that is gone? What is of value is what makes the trees turn green and bear beautiful, succulent fruit, and the crops grow. In times of pestilence, clean, clear brooks and mountain streams are worth a king's ransom—you can't live off metal, but manure and good earth can save a man's life. Fertilized fields are mother earth's perfume," he said, drawing a deep breath. "Took three world wars, famine and the Armageddon for them to figure that out."

He stopped at a stall and leaned in. "This one, like her daddy, is a little different." He chuckled deeply when the animal inside objected by kicking the sides of the stall. "Littlest thing in the stable, as Pegasus horses go…and feisty, but she's my favorite."

As Sarah neared the stall to look in, a loud kick made her draw back.

"Go ahead. She's just testing you. This one is a wee bit scary, but she's smart as a whip, gifted."

Sarah swallowed hard and stepped up to the stall. Staring back at her was the prettiest chestnut mare she'd ever seen. A pair of big brown intelligent eyes studied her with curious disdain. But the horn really threw her for a loop.

"She has wings *and* a horn that changes colors under the light!" Sarah exclaimed, as the animal backed up to the far wall.

"Aye. She's a hybrid. A mix of old Sophocles—who we didn't realize still had a bit of young buck in him—and of one of our unicorn mares. Normally that doesn't happen, but I guess the old boy was too eager to resist. Most often the unicorn stallions give the Pegasus lads a run for their money with the mares, but none of 'em wanted to mess with Red."

"I can see why not," Sarah said, glancing down the row of stalls.

A loud bang farther up the aisle made Mr. Milton laugh. "Settle down, old boy," he called. "We know you've still got run of the pasture."

Sarah covered her mouth and laughed. The barn wasn't so different from the student caf.

"Come, take a good look," Mr. Milton said, opening the stall. "That's my Peggi in there. The Peg part of her name is in homage to her Pegasus father, and the little *I* at the end, instead of a *Y,* is for her unicorn mum. Leaves pure gold-spun manure in her stall, and she's a flier, too—just never allows anyone to mount her. Wild, she is. We can't let her out of the pen too often because if she ran away, we'd be heartbroken—not to mention she could lead disaster right to our door because she doesn't understand all the rules of concealment yet."

Timidly, Sarah entered the stall, and the skittery animal backed up again.

"Aw, I won't hurt you," Sarah said in a gentle voice. She dug in her hoodie pocket and held out an apple on a straight, flat palm. "They're pink ladies," she said, tempting the frightened mare.

"Ya hear that, Peggi girl? She just met you, and she knew pink ladies were your favorite kind."

The mare's ears were up and alert as she sniffed the air and came closer to Sarah, until finally, overwhelmed by temptation, she took the apple.

"Good, girl…" Sarah crooned, but didn't move from where she stood. "Nice to meet you. Want another one?" She produced the second apple and held it out, and Peggi swiped it the second Sarah extended it.

"She's awesome," Sarah said, watching the horse munch on her treat.

"She is indeed." Mr. Milton motioned with his head and placed a finger to his lips. He left the stall open, and bade Sarah to turn her back and walk out with him down the aisle. "She's a Unisus or Pega-uni or Peguni, depending on your predilection and leanings.

"So you see," he said, ignoring Peggi as she followed them, "we glamour this restored valley to keep it hidden from prying eyes, both human and dark forces. And we've enriched the barren earth so beautifully that our crops are like none you've ever seen. Our corn, summer squash, tomatoes, pumpkins, melons—oh. We export the manure to small Guardian outposts, too. That's how we get things in like untainted mangoes and citrus fruits. We are an unseen network within a network within a network, and—"

"Hey," Sarah said with a gentle laugh as Peggi nosed her, almost making her fall. "I only had two."

Peggi bobbed her head and then spread her wings, but didn't rear.

"Stroke her nose, lassie. See if she'll allow that while she's got her head down low."

Sarah timidly followed Mr. Milton's instructions and was rewarded by a gentle nuzzle.

"Ah…she likes you."

"You are so beautiful," Sarah said, continuing to stroke Peggi's nose. "You've got all the gifts wrapped up inside you—some from your dad, some from your mom, and who knows the long lines they came from. Don't worry if the other mares don't treat you nice. I'll come see you and bring you more apples, okay? Maybe one day, when it's safe, maybe I can teach you the rules so you'll be safe and Mr. Milton will let you fly around a little. Until then, you behave yourself." Sarah laughed as the mare shook her head no. "You remind me of me. Stubborn, but all that will get you is detention."

Peggi trotted away, swishing her tail, but then came right back to stand beside Sarah.

"Okay," Sarah said cheerfully. "What stall do I start in?"

Mr. Milton smiled as Peggi went down on one knee. "None, lassie," he murmured. "You won her over."

"What do you mean?" Sarah asked, turning from him to the mare.

"She's gonna let you ride, aren't you, Peggi?" He stroked the mare's shoulder as she bobbed her head.

"You serious?" Sarah whispered.

"Aye. Haven't you always wanted to feel what it'd be like to fly?"

"Yes," she murmured, then turned to Peggi. "Would you let me? I'd be honored."

"Maybe when dawn breaks," he said with a wink. "By five we should see a glimpse of sunlight."

The mare gave a friendly snort, then nuzzled Sarah.

"Oh, I just want to hug you," she said quietly.

"Then do that," Mr. Milton said in a tender voice. "She wants somebody to dote on her—all living things do." He rounded the mare and pushed Sarah forward gently. "First of all, you saw her magnificence, and she appreciated that. Then you showed how much you appreciated her by giving her a small treat, just because, and expecting nothing in return. The gift given for no reason is the purest gift of all. Then you asked her, respected her wishes, and said thank you in your own way. Now a hug seals it, lets her feel the love coming from within. They can sense it, animals can—so can humans, but sometimes they are so blind."

With a gentle stroke down Peggi's nose, Sarah hugged her, only to be surprised when the mare gave her a swift knock with her head that made her stumble backward.

"Hey," Sarah said, laughing. "What was that for?

"Her way of tendering an invitation. Climb up."

"Seriously? Like now?"

"Aye, it be now or never," Mr. Milton said, cupping his hands so Sarah could step into them and hoisting her up. "Some opportunities just fall in your lap, if you're blessed—and you'd be that, Miss Sarah Rivera. Hold onto her mane and don't let go."

He held the mare by her face and looked deeply into the animal's eyes. "No tricks or flips. She's never flown before, Peggi my girl. We want her back whole, no broken bones from a fall. One circle around the pyramid, then back—no shenanigans." He waited until the mare snorted an assent and bobbed her head, then he double-checked Sarah's grip. "You ready."

"Yes!" she said, laughing.

Mr. Milton watched the mare gallop down the barn aisle like a jumbo jet taxiing down a runway. As soon as she broke the plane of the barn threshold, Peggi pushed off the ground in a powerful leap and went airborne, wings spread.

A squeal of delight rushed from Sarah's mouth the moment they left the ground. Her stomach did teeny wheelies, and the sensation made her laugh yet again. Everything on the ground got smaller and smaller as Peggi took to the clouds. Cold morning air and rushing wind blew Sarah's hoodie back, lifting her ponytail and stinging her face. Exhilaration shot through her bloodstream, and she laughed and cried and held her face close to the wonderful mare's neck.

"Thank you, thank you, thank you—Peggi, I love you," Sarah said, holding on tightly as the capstone library came into view among the clouds.

Peggi whinnied and dove toward the lower section of pyramid, making Sarah's stomach drop and her spirits soar. Free had never felt so free. For a second she just closed her eyes, experiencing the rush, imagining it was her own wings taking them on this wondrous flight, her body alone sailing through the air against the purple-blue haze of breaking dawn, wondering if this was what Valencio felt when he spread his wings and became one with the air. When she opened her eyes, the sky was split in two, one part the purple-blue haze of night, the other the victorious pink-orange morn.

"This is so beautiful!" Sarah shouted. "Just like you, Peggi."

The mare snorted and circled the pyramid, allowing Sarah to see the valley, the protective ring of darkness that surrounded the school and the lush open fields before it—a perspective that couldn't be matched even from the platform where she and Razor had stood.

Fae field workers were out in the early light, cultivating crops that fed the entire school and much of the surrounding community. She had to find out who was abducting her fellow students and putting everyone at risk. This was a community, a diverse and beautiful community, and darkness was trying to ravage it.

Never again would she take anything—not what she ate or, especially, her family and the gifts she'd inherited—for granted. Nor would she take for granted the compound and the school her parents and grandparents had created—it just took a wonderfully high altitude to get perspective. Her friends, her family, this school…all of it was worth protecting.

She kissed Peggi's neck and held on tighter as the feisty mare followed the rules, just this one time, and took her back to the barn. Titan Troy, Mrs. Hogan and Mr. Milton were all in the yard when Peggi touched down for a graceful landing with only the slightest skid.

Excited, the mare pranced a bit before going down on one knee to let Sarah hop off, though she did give Mr. Milton a wee bit of trouble as he tried to confine her back in her stall. A little taste of freedom had obviously added to Peggi's penchant for rebellion, and everybody laughed.

"You've spoiled her rotten in one detention," he told Sarah with a wink, chasing the mare around the yard, while she whinnied as though laughing and dodged him.

"Peggi," Sarah said with a laugh, hands on hips. "You have to behave so we can go again."

Grudgingly, the mare trotted over to Mr. Milton and swished her tail; Mrs. Hogan doubled over with laughter.

Titan Troy smiled. "Quite impressive, Miss Rivera. Shall we now make haste to your gym detention? And I take it since you shoveled no manure this morning, you will be back again tomorrow to complete your assigned task?"

Sarah smiled. "Absolutely!"

CHAPTER 28

The moment the steel door closed behind her and she looked down the dark descending stairs, she felt like she was about to suffocate. All the problems that had flown out of her mind while flying with Peggi returned to her body, mind and spirit, making her feel heavy, weighted. Guilt stabbed at her; she'd had fun and her cousin was still missing. If she'd been brave or even knew where to look, she should have ridden Peggi out far and wide and come home with Ayana on her back. But she wasn't brave or wise or daring or anything she needed to be right now.

Instead, she was suddenly too warm, her boots too heavy, like walking in anvils—and then she realized …boots…gym, running…*uh-oh*! And when she saw the damp blue hallway and then the gym, the sight brought everything back in an emotional flood.

"It is time, Miss Rivera," Titan Troy said with a chivalrous bow. "I shall leave you safely inside the gym. Other students have arrived by Headmaster's escort. Amazon Aziza Akoben awaits. She is a fine and dedicated drill instructor, one who is always fair if she understands your plight." He looked over her sweats and hiking boots. "The unembellished truth always works. Good day."

"Thanks, Titan Troy," Sarah said softly, truly meaning it. "I wasn't so afraid, standing next to you."

She hadn't expected any reaction from him, just his normal Spartan farewell. But her genuine compliment made him pause, even stand a little taller, which she hadn't realized was possible.

"You have your mother's grace. One day you will make a fine queen, young Neteru."

"Thanks," Sarah said quietly, then followed him into the gym.

Students were already stretching and warming up. She could hear the gym teacher's shrill whistle cutting through the morning with precision. But at Titan Troy's presence, the teacher turned and smiled a very different kind of smile. He nodded a slow and very different kind of nod. Sarah discreetly looked from one to the other as she jogged over to the track and began stretching with the other students. Had she really seen what she thought she'd seen between the gym teacher and the security guard? Whoa. She must be tired or something, because that was just too crazy.

"Yo, sis," a tall jock said, motioning toward her boots. "You might wanna put on some lighter gear and definitely lose the cinder blocks. The Amazon is pushing us five miles this morning, and if this is your first time on our squad, you're gonna puke or pass out."

"Or both," a tall ripped female Tactical said. "Didn't you bring your sneakers? You've got, like, ten minutes before we finish with warm ups and start running."

Wil jogged over and looked at her in despair. "Oh, man, Sarah, I would have told you, but I figured you'd know. I'll keep stride with you, all right? Don't you have sneakers in a locker or something?"

Sarah shook her head. "This is detention number two today. Just came from the stables."

A lean, muscular kid next to her doing hamstring lunges smiled. "I wasn't gonna say anything, 'cause most of us smell like horses when we're done here anyway, so it's cool."

"Lay off, man," Wil said with a scowl.

It was a bit different, but a genuine way of welcoming her to the group all the same. Sarah chuckled. She was in too good a mood to be upset. "Guess I fit in, then?"

"Yeah, one of us will hang back with you and help pace you when you hit the wall." A tall girl with braids gave her a nod. "That's sorta the unspoken thing—we never leave our own. But if you show up again tomorrow, you've gotta have the right gear on or you can really overheat, even pull a muscle."

"Okay, thanks. I had to dress for stables detention—wasn't time to go all the way back to the dorm and get back here before the start whistle. And I definitely have to go back there tomorrow, since I didn't actually shovel what I was supposed to today."

"Man, that sucks…on a Friday, too," the friendly girl with braids said. "You'd think they'd let up with everything that's going on around here."

"Yeah, and you don't wanna be late," the lean boy said. "We run seven days a week, early mornings, to be on the team, so Coach Akoben will be here anyway, and she'll be expecting you if she says you haven't fulfilled your obligation." He looked down at Sarah's boots and shook his head. "Which you probably won't, so I'd plan to be here bright and early tomorrow with the right gear on, sis."

"If you give me your sneakers at lunch or something, I'll put 'em in my locker for you for tomorrow—since you'll still have detention, okay?" Wil looked so upset that he seemed ready to take detention himself for going up against the gym teacher on Sarah's behalf.

A long whistle sounded, and everyone got to their feet. Sarah looked up and realized that every person standing around her was at least a head and a half taller than she was. That meant her legs were way shorter, her stride would be much shorter, and to her mind, that made the track way longer.

"Didn't realize that we were going to run laps today, Miss Rivera?" Amazon Akoben placed her hands on her svelte hips.

"Yes, ma'am. I was at the stables, had to dress for that detail, plus my sneakers were, uhmmm, still kinda wet from the night before."

"Admirable that you were prepared for the stables and I do not want to hazard a guess about the sneakers or the depth of your involvement in what happened to my gym. But what about a backpack or a gym bag or borrowing a pair of sneakers from a fellow roommate? Preparedness is key for a warrior."

"She's going gangsta," one of the guys hollered from the back.

"We are doing five miles this morning," the teacher said, arching a shapely eyebrow. "But, before we pass judgment, maybe Sarah has a point. In real-life battles, unlike battle simulations, you will be running with combat boots, carrying heavy artillery and wearing thick flack jackets in adverse conditions. I have deep respect for a warrior who challenges him or herself. So, Sarah, this is about more than serving out a detention—are you ready to find out how deep you can go inside yourself to pull out that extra something you need to meet this challenge? Are you ready to push yourself today on my track?"

Sarah just nodded.

Wil gave her a sidelong glance.

"All right, we'll see, but my bet is that by the third mile you'll pass out in that outfit." Amazon Akoben shook her head. "Go as far as you can, and then you can come properly dressed tomorrow to do the miles you cannot complete today—and ask my team, I can count."

Again, Sarah just nodded, but Amazon Akoben's words about pushing oneself and what it felt like to be in a real battle, carrying real artillery, stuck in her mind and fused with the aerial view she'd enjoyed less than an hour ago. What if she became head of this compound one day? What if she had to protect the people within it, secure their safety and their way of life?

The whistle sounded, and the runners took off at a steady clip around the damp track. Amazon Akoben ran backward for the first lap, yelling instructions about form and speed, and watching Sarah's face. But soon everything around Sarah became blurry and distant, as heat and pain and heaviness cramped her legs. Air cut in and out of her lungs, rattling a rasp up her throat. Her face was on fire, her body wet as her sweats turned from light gray to charcoal. Her heart beat in her ears. It felt like a knife was stabbing her side, the blade turning as she struggled for air. One compound sister was missing…another was in critical condition. She would find the source, she would hunt it down, and she would find Yaya. And Hyacinth? Hyacinth had to get better. Everyone would be all right!

Sweat stung Sarah's eyes, and she blinked it away, finally lifting her forearm to wipe at the stinging, salty rivulets that had merged with her tears.

A whistle sounded, and she registered it somewhere in the back of her mind, and then slowly but surely the room came back into focus. Amazon Akoben was jogging beside her, calling her name as she slowed to a stop and then bent over with her hands on her knees, gulping air. After a moment she managed to straighten, thoroughly prepared to face the ridicule of having earned another detention.

"You went two extra miles," Amazon Akoben said loudly. "You see that!" She smiled broadly and slapped Sarah on the back, almost knocking her over. "In the time it took the rest of your sorry carcasses to run a five in running shorts and sneakers, Sarah was able to do seven while wearing hiking boots and sweats." She turned to Sarah and nodded, her forearms crossed over her chest. "Well done, young warrior, well done—welcome to track and field."

"But—"

"Varsity squad," Amazon Akoben said. "I should have expected nothing less from a Shadows division student. One day you will chase the dark side and be victorious. I will see you tomorrow at six A.M., and I will accept nothing less than yes—you are a role model and an example. Welcome."

Wil came over to her slowly, breathing hard. "That was…I've never seen anybody do anything like that, Sarah. Freakin' awesome."

She looked up but didn't have the energy to respond.

* * *

Her legs were aching and rubbery, but she still ran to the girls' dorm, arriving just in time to take a quick hot shower, find a clean uniform and yank it on, affix her pin to the collar, grab her backpack and head to the cafeteria. As she loaded up on apples for Peggi and some grapes she planned to hand peel later for Miss Tillie, she spotted her crew—but arranged in a very new configuration.

The walls had come down. Alejandro was at their table sitting beside Tami, while Val's backpack was reserving the chair next to him. Donnie was seated across from Allie, scarfing down French toast, with Miguel next to her. Wil was next, sitting with Jess and a tall quiet guy from the track team, Randall Chapman, one of Wil's buddies and an Upper Sphere Tactical. Sarah remembered him from that morning—he was a good runner with a nice stride, and kind, intense dark eyes—and released her breath. Why couldn't Ayana have given a guy like that a chance? she wondered, becoming sad all over again.

Famished, Sarah piled her plate with tofu scramble and French toast, then hurried to claim the open seat by Val.

"Hey, everybody," she said quietly, feeling oddly exhilarated physically, even though the prevailing mood was clearly somber. It was a difficult balance to manage. Part of her wanted to gush about the fantastic experience of riding Peggi and the awesome surprise stable duty had been, as well as shout to the rafters that she'd bested Amazon Akoben's track team *and* some of her special powers were starting to come in. But she glanced at Wil and thought about how Hyacinth and Ayana should have been sitting with them, then sat down and kept her head low. It didn't feel right that she was lucky enough to have so many things to celebrate when so many others were missing or fighting for their lives.

Quiet greetings met Sarah in return as everyone mumbled some form of hello. She picked up the strand of the morbid conversation and just pushed food around her plate, suddenly losing her appetite.

"I just wish we could go visit them, you know," Allie said in a quiet rush. "Like, couldn't we send them some love and light?"

"Take it to the chapel, kiddo," Jessica said in a sad voice. "They won't let any of us in there, and definitely don't want any telepathy going on. That could get a healthy student sick—that's why the quarantine. Dark consciousness energy spreads like wildfire."

"But I feel so helpless," Tami said, blowing out a breath and holding her head in her hands. "So utterly…freakin'…helpless. I hate feeling like there's nothing we can do but wait."

"Yeah, I know," Donnie muttered. "'Cinth is one of the sweetest kids—a real innocent."

Miguel nodded. "My pop used to talk about growing up in East LA before the war. He said street gangs would be going at it, somebody would pull out a piece or do a drive-by, and a bullet didn't have no name on it. Kids, old people…hell, your damned dog in the yard, could get mowed down as easy as breathing. This ain't no diff, the way I see it."

"It's fucked up is what it is," Alejandro said, brooding over his plate. "'Cinth, of all people."

"I feel you, bro, but whatcha gonna do?" Val said, digging into his pancakes. He was sitting in his chair the way he always did, wide-legged, with it turned around backward. He glanced at Sarah. "Hey."

"Hey," she said quietly.

"How was detention?" He gave her a half-smile.

She returned it, deeply appreciating that he'd even asked, given everything that was going on. "It was all right," she said, stuffing the butterflies down with a bite of tofu scramble. Now came the *real* balancing act, being sure to give equal attention to both guys who liked her. Damn, this was crazy. There were so many bigger issues at stake. "Tell you 'bout it later."

Val nodded and shoved a big bite of his pancakes into his mouth. "Cool."

"Yeah, we can talk about everything that ain't this problem later," Al said, clearly annoyed. "We've gotta address this, gotta stay focused."

"Thing is, though," Wil said in a solemn tone, "Patty Gray got sick this morning, too. She's in the infirmary. Far as I know, Patty didn't do drugs or go off on the Shady Path, and I feel like I'm to blame. I was trying to get her to help us, for old time's sake, and maybe she went in alone after everyone left." Wil let his head drop into his hands. "I found out about her sit after I got out of track. Melissa sent me a text from the infirmary."

"And what about Stefan?" Al said. "That dude is dangerous, and who knows who he's working with on the outside? All these people getting sick and going down because of that mofo contagion? He could be the one who booby trapped the Shady Path, or maybe he's been abducting students—maybe taking them to the Morrigan. I say if the Neteru Guardian squad doesn't come back with a pelt in the next twenty-four hours, we take matters into our own hands."

"You cannot be serious," Sarah said quietly, but her voice was gentle, lacking the sarcastic tone she normally used when speaking to her brother. She stared at him, and everyone at the table looked from her to Al. "Didn't we learn anything from what happened to 'Cinth and the others? They could be dying because we tried to handle things ourselves, force-to-force." She looked at Tami, then back to her brother when Tami looked away. "I know you heard about the plan we had and how it backfired, and now a bunch of kids—our friends—are on freakin' respirators, Al."

Fury kindled in her brother's eyes, but she could tell it wasn't directed at her; it was pure frustration.

"Yeah, I heard about it. But I don't blame you—the plan was sweet. You all went about it the only way you could. But that's the problem with all that devious female planning—it's just too complicated. Sometimes brute force is required, and I'm ready to throw down right now, especially if it'll help find Yaya."

She just stared at her brother and Val when they bumped fists, then got Miguel, Wil and Donnie in on the action.

"Okay," Sarah said, pushing back from her plate and folding her arms. "Just a question, so don't shoot the messenger." The last thing she wanted to do was go back to fighting with Alejandro, and she knew her twin well enough to know that if she stepped on his ego in public, she'd never rein him in from doing something stupid.

Sarah waited until Al lifted his hands in front of his chest. "Peace. Speak."

"Okay," she said after a moment. "I just want to know what on *earth* can we do, brute-forcewise against a dark forces virus? I'm not being critical, not trying to be a know-it-all. I just don't get it. Call me slow."

Alejandro let out a hard breath of impatience. "Sis…be real. What's probably letting in the virus is that sick bastard, Stefan. You know the buzz is that those two fliers who got eaten in the dead zone lost their PIUs, which are probably still broadcasting as we speak. Find the PIUs and we should have a recording of what went down, and maybe a solid way to track that loser. Even if we don't find him, getting those open channels shut down that are broadcasting from the dead zone is a key to all this, if you ask me."

"Yeah, and I can work with some of the other Blends to triangulate on the signal," Donnie said. "All we need is to get someone inside to be able to—"

"You all are *not* going into the dead zone. Tell me you aren't even remotely thinking about it!" Sarah glanced around frantically.

"Okay, okay," Donnie said in a defensive tone. "I can try to lock in from up on Mojo's platform, if the other guys mind stun him long enough."

Sarah leaned forward and looked at all the boys at the table, and then sat back horrified. "No! And by the way, if you were listening to anything Mr. Everett said in class, you cannot broadcast in or out of the dead zone. It's on demon vibration—totally different frequency from a white light channel. If it were that simple, don't you think they would already have done it?"

"Gotta do something," Al said, silver beginning to overtake his irises. "Plus, if it's werewolf virus that's booby trapped the Shady Path, there's only one cure if people are turning." He looked around the table and nodded. "You've gotta take the wolf's head off before the victims turn. I'm not just sitting here—"

"Wait! You aren't making any kind of sense. This isn't a werewolf virus, it's a dark energy virus—two completely separate things, even if Stefan is a—"

"All right, all right," Alejandro said, talking quickly and gesturing with his hands. "Maybe he's not turning people into werewolves, but his ass is contagious and is dark as hell. That's your source right there. If not, why is he missing? We find him or the PIUs, and we've got our problem solved." To end the subject, her brother folded his arms over his chest and lifted his chin, looking very much like their father in that moment.

"But don't you think the doctors and staff have already tried everything you're talking about?" Sarah looked around the table, incredulous. "I'm dead serious. Don't you think that trying to find those PIUs in order to stop a contagion leak into the school would have been the first thing they did? And are you actually going to hunt down a fellow student and behead him—*just in case*? Al, listen to yourself. I know we're all upset about Yaya, 'Cinth and the other girls, but come on. Be serious. You don't even know what's going on, what they've got."

Silence was her vindication.

"Aw'right," Al finally conceded, rubbing his jaw. "You've always been the best with the books, so maybe you've got a point about the science."

Sarah slumped back in her chair, relieved, but it was a short-lived victory as Al let out another hard breath and sat forward again.

"But we still need to go after wolf boy, even if it's just to drag him back to school so those in the know can deal with him." Al looked around the table as though counting Senate votes.

Sarah shot her brother a glare. "But then here comes my next stupid question." She returned her gaze to Al. "Are you ready to actually launch a wolf hunt against a fellow student and possibly actually kill him if he fights back—and you know he will?"

Alejandro rolled his shoulders. "Him or me. I ain't trying to go for the kill, and the plan as it stands is to only drag his mangy ass back here, but in the end, I gotta do what I gotta do."

"Oh, for crying out loud!" Sarah slapped her hand on the table, temporarily drawing looks from other tables. "First of all, until there's clear evidence that it was him—"

"I looked the SOB right in his eye," Al said, leaning forward. "I've got night vision, Val's got it, Tami's got it and—"

"Yeah, well, I've got it, too," Sarah said, hysteria escalating her voice. "And even though I think it was him, the fact is, I can't say for a hundred percent sure!"

"Well *I'm* sure," Al said through clenched teeth. "What I saw up close and personal was somebody who didn't have a problem with taking my life, so why should I have a problem taking his, if it comes to mortal combat?"

Sarah dug her fingers into her hair and pulled, exasperated. "Do you hear yourself, Al? Do you really want blood on your hands?"

"I know it's a hard concept," Val said calmly, then took a sip of his orange juice like he was talking about the weather. "But I, for one, am standing with Al on this. We can't let that predator hurt anybody else. I know Nana Marlene's got a problem with that, philosophically, but Pop 'Bazz don't. Why?" Val set down his juice glass. "Because he understands the law of the jungle—kill or be killed. Pop 'Bazz understands the mind of a predator. He's been one—kinda still is—been in lockup, seen things. Do you feel me?"

Sarah slowly lowered her hands and sat back. She'd never been so thoroughly disappointed in her life. Hurt constricted her throat. Val was siding with her brother on something so wrong that she was finding it hard to breathe.

"What's your father say, Tam?" Al said, pointing to Tami, not missing a beat.

"Don't blink or stutter when it's time to pull the trigger." She bobbed her head in an exaggerated nod. "Famous motto of Neteru Guardian Jack Rider."

"Handling your bizness with authority is a Rivera tradition," Al said with confidence. "You know our father doesn't have a problem with protecting the fam, and that was the one thing he told me to do—and if you ask me, his word overrides Headmistress Stone's any day, any time. And like Val says, I know Headmaster Shabazz ain't gonna have a problem if I bring in a werewolf pelt. And another thing, I'm the only one that can get up close to him, hand-to-hand, and not come away with any bug he's carrying, it's that Neteru blood."

"But how will you feel if you find out you were wrong?' Sarah searched the group frantically for someone to stand with her.

"You know, Sarah does have a point," Wil hedged. "Like, what if by some chance it wasn't Stefan who went after you guys? Or what if he didn't have squat to do with whatever came through the portal? There's a lot we still don't know, guys."

"It's true," Allie finally said. "Like, Jess, you said you were there when it all went down after they lost those two fliers, right? So you can tell us what it was like."

"It's true," Jessica said quickly, leaning in and keeping her head and voice low. "Headmistress Stone scanned every student, looking for who was making and selling." She looked around the table conspiratorially. "Students worked together to block her mental access. Like everybody in here has secrets, so everybody made a pact not to let her or any administration seer break us down, so all she got was the fact that there were drugs involved. People didn't want her to know about who'd been in the Shady Path, about any contraband operations, you know? Then her concern about drugs got sidelined as more people turned up missing. She has to be frantic at this point."

"Yeah, but what about Stefan? Didn't she scan him? Wasn't he questioned?" Sarah leaned forward so far that she almost got cold tofu scramble on her sweater.

"Yeah, and he had an alibi, just like everybody else. They couldn't pin the sell on him or pick up that he'd had anything to do with those fliers getting high," Wil said, dragging his fingers through his silky black curls. "Patty told me about it."

"But on the other hand," Donnie said quietly, making everyone listen harder to hear him, "based on stuff from Mr. Everett's class and stuff I've read, a demon doesn't have a consciousness to scan. It's just black, void."

Everyone there leaned farther forward, hanging on Donnie's every word. Sarah herself was stunned, listening to Donnie's rare display of leadership. The only problem was, he could be leading the group in the wrong direction—right into danger.

"Here's the thing," Donnie said, sending his gaze around the group. "If this kid is part werewolf, then he might be like those kids who are born without a conscience because their moms took drugs or drank too much while carrying them. You know, a part of their brain isn't like a normal person's brain. Right versus wrong doesn't mean anything to them. They function on sheer impulse. There've been a lot of studies on that. They look normal, but there's a part of them that's…off. In Stefan's case, when he goes rogue at the full moon, maybe a part of his psyche just shuts down. There could be no way to glean evidence from it, even if there wasn't a single kid in here willing to block for him to get him past Nana Mar."

"And that's my point," Al said, nodding firmly toward his sister and then sitting back with his arms folded, vindicated. "You know taking in strays is Nana's blind spot. She did that for our mother, and she turned out to be Neteru. She did that for our father and didn't off him while he was a mad-crazy vamp, and look who he turned out to be. So Nana can't bring herself to blow away some kid, even if he's too far gone. She just can't see it. So, come sundown, on this last night of the full moon, it's on. We'll give the Neteru squad an assist, but then, if they don't find him, we get more boots on the ground and try to find the guy. Okay, okay, Sarah, with the intention of bringing him in. Then dad can have at him for all I care. That's the for-real point is all I'm saying."

"And that is *my* point, Alejandro," Sarah said, gesturing wildly, she was so upset. "Nana didn't blow our dad away or back him in a corner where he felt so threatened he attacked her 'cuz he was running on survival instinct. What you're proposing is dangerous for both of you! She saw something in Dad, even before he could see it in himself." She looked at Val, unshed tears of frustration beginning to well in her eyes and make her voice tight. "Your father is a two-hundred-and-something-year-old vampire who hung with my father, his best *hombre* from their old days. Still my dad's right hand lieutenant, his best friend. Both of them had something redeeming inside. Both of them made it into the Light. Both of them ran Hell together for a while—the damned Vampire Council! But they changed. That's what Nana saw, what she sees in every student who comes here, good or so-called bad. That's why she can't just eliminate Stefan like he's nothing."

Sarah looked back to her brother, her impassioned plea fracturing her voice. "Our grandmother is not blind to human potential. She sees more than you think she can see and knows more than you think she knows, Al, but I guarantee you, you will break her if you kill a kid in this school over a personal vendetta. And I will not be a part of it."

Pushing away from the table as two big tears rolled down the bridge of her nose, Sarah stood and angrily wiped them away. "I'm so disappointed in you, Al, and you, too, Val…in all of you guys, and especially you, Tami, and I don't care what you think. All I know is, our nana didn't raise us like this. She never cared where a kid came from or blamed him for the circumstances of his birth. Every soul matters to her, so don't you do this Al. Don't any of you. It's not right!"

Breathing hard, she hoisted her backpack over one shoulder and rushed away from the table. She could hear Allie on her heels, but she just wanted to find a private place to let it all out. Her brother and his friends—Val, of all people—were plotting the unthinkable, a potentially deadly attack on a fellow student—something so wrong that she didn't know where to begin to stop it. Sure, Wil was hedging, but only because of her, not because of his own personal convictions.

Sarah ran down the corridor, feeling the need to escape, rounded the corner and pushed her way into a girl's room stall. She covered her eyes with her forearm, willing herself not to sob. They were forcing her hand, boxing her into a corner. If she couldn't get them to call off this wolf hunt by sundown, she was gonna have to out their dumb asses to the administration—

and that was the *last* thing she wanted to do. Val would never speak to her again. Her brother would never speak to her again. None of her friends would, but right was right.

"Sarah?" Allie called. "Come on, Sarah, it's me."

"Go away!" Sarah shouted. "Just go back with them!"

"Some of us think you're right. I don't wanna see anybody get hurt. Neither does Wil."

Sarah slammed out of the stall, making the door bounce and rounded on her friend. "Then why didn't you speak up? Why didn't you say anything!"

Silence met her, and Allie looked down. "What if they're right, though?" she finally said quietly.

"And what if they're not? Are you ready to live with that?" Sarah began to pace.

"We're gonna be late for homeroom," Allie said in a soft voice.

"Screw homeroom!" Sarah shrieked, losing all control as the tears came. "My brother and his crew are about to commit murder!"

"But what if…what if Stefan *is* part of what's going on?" Allie asked, her voice unsure.

"Then if any of us know where he is, we tell the school authorities, we lay low till they pick him up. And if he is connected to the contagion, we let them follow the lead from his dark consciousness energy back to the dead zone looking for the missing people and the PIUs! What about this don't you get? Al is only doing this because Stefan scared the crap out of him, and I know my brother—now that he knows how strong Stefan really is, he doesn't want to walk around looking over his shoulder all the time. He thinks this is the easy answer, the quick fix, so he isn't even rational right now, and Val is no better, I'm sorry to say. He's stupid loyal to Al, just like Miguel and Donnie are, and once Al gets them all fired up in ride-or-die mode, they're liable to do anything."

Sarah slumped against the wall. Defeat claimed her, disappointment burrowing into her heart like a tick.

"You gonna rat 'em out?" Allie asked softly, staring at Sarah.

Releasing a long sigh, Sarah closed her eyes. The end-of-breakfast gong sounded, and she straightened.

"Only if I have to."

* * *

It was the longest half hour of her life. Even Miss Tittle was subdued. No homework assignments would be collected until next week, given the shock all the students were experiencing. Only English, math and bio classes would be held, and the school would be dismissed for a half day—since the chemistry, history and specialty-section instructors were all engaged in holding vigil over the critically ill students or searching the grounds and surrounding area for the missing students, missing PIUs, open portals and Stefan.

Sarah didn't meet anyone's eyes. She kept her focus on Miss Tittle. It was too upsetting to look at her brother, too stabbingly painful to look at Val. Glancing at Wil just made her weary. Hyacinth's chair was empty, and when Sarah saw that out of the corner of her eye, she could have put her head down on the desk and wept.

"Classes will end at eleven-thirty," Miss Tittle said in a somber, gentle voice. "Amazon Akoben's gym will be open, as some may find it easier to relieve their stress with vigorous activity. The chapels will also be open, and Counselor Zehiradangra will be in the Great Hall until two P.M., available to any students who are having difficulties processing this. After that, she will be convening with Headmistress Stone and the rest of the administration. The library is off limits for now, but students are welcome to congregate in the lounges, game room, auditorium and cafeteria…though access to the outside, for now, is not permitted."

Miss Tittle looked around the classroom and sighed deeply. To all the students' surprise, a large, diamond tear rolled down her gaunt cheek, and as it did, gorgeous, multi-hued plumage began to overtake her dress and skin. Long, jewel-toned feathers in azure blue, emerald green, topaz, golden fuchsia, crimson and bronze sprouted from her skin. Her eyes became large, oval pools of beautiful onyx, and her pursed mouth stretched out to become an amazing golden beak.

Students gasped as her arms became majestic wings and her tail spilled out in a golden fan. She was the most beautiful creature Sarah had ever seen, next to Peggi.

"I share your pain," Miss Tittle warbled. "Oh, students…so much potential wasted, if any of these children die. I promised myself I wouldn't do this in front of you all, that I would remain composed, but…Forgive me, I am simply overwrought."

More teardrop-shaped diamonds fell from her eyes to bounce across the classroom floor as she broke down and openly wept. It started the girls in the class weeping, too—first someone in the back, then Allie, then, the next thing Sarah knew, everyone had gone there. The guys just looked away, sometimes sniffing, trying to act like they could deal. But a few wiped their faces openly, because they either didn't care or couldn't help themselves.

A girl in the front row stood, ready to go to Miss Tittle to console her, but another student wisely held her back.

"Stay back. She's gonna go," the second girl told her friend.

"Yes," Miss Tittle warned, hastening from the room, "but bless you, child."

An awful shriek and an influx of floating cinders made the students cringe where they sat. Sarah finally lowered her head to her desk. She could hear frantic elves scrambling about in the hall, and the sound of fire extinguishers discharging. Their chemical scent, along with the odor of burning bird flesh and feathers, made several students hurl.

That was Sarah's breaking point. She was out of there. She got up and headed for the door. Val was on her heels as she passed the awful sight of Miss Tittle's entrails frying. She ran harder and faster than she'd ever thought she could run. The outdoors was calling her. She had to get to fresh air and peace and beauty and hope, and rules be damned.

"Don't follow me!" she screamed, feeling Val closing on her. "Get away from me!"

Tears flowed down her face as she ran blindly toward the only portal to freedom she knew, past the gym, to the exit staircase. If Titan Troy would let her, she'd go clean the stables—that would be her excuse. She'd do it in daylight, moonlight, whenever. She'd clean horse shit until it soaked into her pores—anything but this!

When she rounded the bend she hit the steel door and started crying even more hysterically.

"Damn, damn, damn!" she shouted, sobbing. "I don't know the code. I'm not strong enough to open the door!" She turned around and looked at Val, who'd skidded to a halt behind her. "Why aren't I strong enough to fix the things I've messed up? Why can't I get my own brother not to do something terrible? This isn't how we were raised!"

"I'm not going to let him kill anybody," Val said, softly, coming to her quickly. He held her by both arms and then hugged her. "Al is a hothead—we all know that. If you go against him in public, he just digs in, gets blind. We talked about it at the table after you left. I don't think any of us wants innocent blood on our hands. Do you trust me?"

Sarah held his sweater to her face, clutching it in her fists as she nodded, breathing hard as he kept talking.

"We've got a senior Tactical with us, Wil; two senior Clavs; a couple more of Ayana's friends who can work with Donnie, plus a couple of

Shadows like Wil and his boys from track. They can rig something to triangulate on Stefan's PIU, not the missing ones in the dead zone. Nobody's gonna do anything messed up or put anybody at risk. You, Tami and Allie need to lie low. We're just gonna try to locate Stefan and bind him in white light, then call Headmaster Shabazz. Cool?"

She was almost too spent emotionally to answer; for a moment she could only nod and allow her heart rate to slow. Val's voice had petted her hair and scalp with comforting warmth, and his solid frame felt like safety, a haven, as his arms enfolded her. His heart beat a steady, calming rhythm against her cheek as she kept her eyes closed tightly against the world. Soon she became aware of his scent. It was nice, earthy, masculine, oddly comforting and unsettling at the same time. She relaxed, and she wiped her tears on her sleeve then finally looked up.

A pair of deep brown understanding eyes filled with patience—and something else she couldn't define—stared back at her.

"Thank you," she said with a sniff.

He didn't answer, just closed his own eyes, his long dark lashes dusting his cheeks, and lowered his mouth to hers.

It was the softest of sensations, the most tender of touches, and it sent a jag of heart-stopping electricity through her. She had to remember to breathe as she looked up at him when he pulled back a bit. He had only touched her lips. A hint of more to come that hadn't. He hadn't assumed, hadn't force his tongue into her mouth or pushed her against the wall. Now he just stood there, holding her in a friendship hug that held the promise of so much more. She could see the question in his eyes. He was waiting for her answer, waiting to see if it had been all right to coax her heart out to fly.

In that moment she felt so crazy, so skittery, yet so free, as her mind grappled with what had just happened. She felt strangely like Peggi must have—anxious and unsure, scared but curious, but not wanting to be rushed or made to do what she wasn't sure she wanted to. Someone caring had asked. Someone respectful hadn't assumed. Someone patient and with a different perspective had seen her beauty. Someone had cared. Every living being wanted to be cherished. In that moment, she knew that she was.

She lifted her chin to try the sensation again as he lowered his head. But then a booming voice made her freeze, and made Val jump away from her as though he'd been electrocuted.

"All students are to be in designated areas during this emergency lockdown!" Titan Troy thundered.

"I…we…I was just going to show him Peggi…since I was supposed to go back and shovel for Mr. Milton." Heart pounding fast, Sarah thrust out her backpack and unzipped it quickly, so she could show the appley contents to Titan Troy.

"You are supposed to request an escort so that we know where each student is at all times." He walked over to Val and leaned down to study him, his shadow falling intimidatingly over her friend as he lowered his blade. "Also, you do not have the door code."

"It's cool," Val said, holding his hands in front of his chest. "I was just walking her here so she could wait for you, and then I was—"

"Silence!" Titan Troy bellowed, and then punched in the code. He put his shoulder to the task of opening the door, then looked at Sarah. "For you, young queen…I will take you both to the Pegasus stables. But do not ever let me find you lingering here in the hallways alone—your father, my brother in arms, is *not* so understanding...And I don't care that this young suitor is the son of his best friend, Guardian Yolando. Friendship between those old vampires will perish if more than what I witnessed ever transpires before it is time, are we clear?"

She and Val just glanced at each other and nodded.

Chapter 29

"Aye, I see you've come back with a friend," Mr. Milton said in a cheerful tone.

Titan Troy glowered down on them as he shoved Val forward with the face of his shield. "Emotions are running high. Please give these two something constructive to do. They need to expend energy under a watchful eye."

"Aye, yes, and it's not even spring," Mr. Milton chuckled, rubbing his beard as he bit on his pipe.

"I will be back to collect them in a few hours, after rounds. Call me if they make trouble, and I shall come take them off your hands by lunch."

Mr. Milton gave the huge Titan a jaunty salute and began walking to the barn. Sarah's face burned and she kept her eyes on Mr. Milton's back, unable to even glance at Val.

"I thought you all had English, then math, followed by biology, if me memory serves," the little man called back at them. "Skipping three classes will levy a heck of a toll on your studies, don'tcha think? Little early in the semester to be playing hooky. Then again, nothing is going according to Hoyle now. I don't suspect teachers with a heart will be handing out assignments until all this tragedy has been resolved."

Mr. Milton didn't even turn around as he opened the barn doors.

"Miss Tittle was really upset," Val said, trying to offer an explanation for why they'd been in the hall. "Pretty nasty to see her explode like that, and Sarah—"

Mr. Milton nodded. "I know just what ye mean, laddie—witnessed me first phoenix rising during the Fae Spring Equinox Ball when I was just a boy. I had no idea it was so gruesome," he said, making a face. "So I guess a little fresh air after that is in order." He laughed and stepped through the open barn door. "Aye, at your age, when tensions run high and wild, fresh air is definitely a must."

Sarah glimpsed Val from the corner of her eye and swallowed a smile. The old man was talking in riddles, as old folks tended to do—seemingly talking about one thing while hinting at some other thing he secretly knew.

Friendly whinnies greeted Mr. Milton, but most of the stalls were empty. "My Pegasus fliers are already out to pasture. Only my unicorns who like to go about at night are being recalcitrant, so I gave them the option to stay in…and of course there's our Peggi."

Sarah took off running. "Val, I wanna introduce you to her. Come look!" She heard him running after her, then coming to a stop when she did. "Peggi, look what I brought you," Sarah said, extracting a juicy apple and holding out her hand.

Mr. Milton leaned against the wall nearby and smiled. "Careful. You've brought someone with a little demon in his blood. She might take exception."

"But she let me near her," Sarah said, turning to look at Mr. Milton.

"Aye, but Neteru blood overrides a bit of the vamp in your veins. Always does."

Peggi swiped the apple, then backed up with a loud snort and stomped the hay covered floor.

"Val is all right," Sarah said, laughing. "He's like me and you—a mutt."

"Hey," Val said, laughing. "Watch it. Do I call you names?"

"Well, we *are*," Sarah said, tossing him an apple. "Your Mom is a Valkyrie…and for a long time your dad was a vampire, until he became a daywalker and the Light granted him amnesty." She shot Mr. Milton a meaningful look.

He nodded, catching on. "It's as the lass states," he said to Val in a loud voice. "Peggi wouldn't be prejudiced against someone's pedigree, not after all the ridicule she's encountered."

"Of course not," Sarah said with a smile, slinging another apple toward the mare. "She let me ride her, and my dad was once a vamp, too. Peggi is no snob."

After devouring the apple, Peggi slowly walked forward, snorting. She peered over the low half-door of her stall and considered Val with a tilt of her head.

Sarah went to him and held his forearm, showing him how to lay his palm completely flat using touch, not words.

"Hey," he said softly, looking at the mare.

"He has gorgeous amber wings like yours…wanna see?" Sarah said, then smiled as Peggi took the apple from Val and came closer to allow him to rub her nose. After a moment she nuzzled him and then bumped the door, asking to be let out.

"She's curious," Mr. Milton said with a droll little chuckle. "So, laddie, show her what you've got."

"Right here? In the barn?" Val said, and then started laughing. "Show a horse?"

"She's a Peguni, or maybe a Unipeg," Mr. Milton corrected, drawing on his unlit pipe as he let Peggi out into the aisle.

The moment she was out, she began prancing and strutting as though in a parade. Sarah laughed and clapped as Peggi showed off for Val, spreading her magnificent wings and beating the air.

Val laughed, yanked his school sweater over his head and took off his button-down white shirt.

Sarah stood mesmerized for a moment just staring at Val's beautiful dark skin and the way the muscles in his chest, abdomen and back moved with fluid grace as he ran alongside Peggi. Wild and free and natural, his hair was a thick mane of unruly Afro, his arms were open wide, biceps flexing as his long strides kept up with Peggi's, pure joy on his face as the mare played with him. Then it happened, the moment when he could generate enough energy to let his gorgeous amber wings unfurl from his shoulder blades to spread and beat the air.

Peggi went up on her hind legs, rearing with an excited whinny. It seemed as though she knew something, sensed something, and she danced for Val before dropping down to all fours, snorting wildly.

"It's in 'er blood—to fly alongside the Valkyries in battle," Mr. Milton said, running to the front of the barn, as Peggi took off at a gallop. "Go to her, boy! She wants to show you to the other horses."

Sarah dropped her backpack and followed as Val ran full speed, his wings out, then was suddenly airborne. Peggi lifted off with him, staying at his side and leading him to the pasture. Initially Sophocles charged, but as soon as he saw Peggi by Val's side, he fell into formation, leading Peggi and Val, and the rest of the herd lining up behind them, in an impressive aerial display.

"They're magnificent," Sarah said quietly, standing beside Mr. Milton.

"To fly with the Valkyries is a magnificent thing indeed, child. You picked a good friend…dogs and horses know."

She stood quietly on the ground, gazing up, a smile on her face, her heart full enough to burst. One day they'd all come out there. She hoped it wouldn't have to be for battle but could be like this…flying for the sheer beauty of it, flying to rescue people, flying for peace. No matter what they said her destiny was, she didn't have the heart of a warrior, didn't have the blood lust for shadow battle…she had the heart of a loving soul. The battles she wanted to fight were different from the ones her parents had fought…were still fighting. Maybe one day someone else, like Val, would understand that.

"Whooo hoo!" Val shouted, coming to land in the barnyard with Peggi at his side.

"Did you see the big red one?" he asked, breathing hard.

"That'd be Sophocles, Peggi's Da," Mr. Milton said with a wink. "Breathes fire. All warhorse, he is…a formidable creature and not to be tested in the air or on the ground, laddie. We clear?"

Val nodded and wiped his brow with his forearm, wings still outstretched. "I hear you, sir."

"Good. It's an honor for them to fly with a Valkyrie—even a half-Valkyrie. They really like you…and I hope you know it was an honor for you to fly with them."

"Most definitely," Val said, petting Peggi's shoulder.

The mare went down on one knee and stared at Sarah, and then whinnied. Sarah ran to her, and Val laughed.

"She's gonna let Sarah ride?"

"That she is," Mr. Milton said with a smile. "The lassie earned her respect, didn't rush her, had patience…so when the time was right in Peggi's mind, she said okay. That is the way of the world. Respect, friendship, patience, trust."

"I hear you," Val said, his expression serious, as he watched Sarah climb up on Peggi's back.

"Aye," Mr. Milton said, as Val took off next to Sarah and Peggi. "That's what they all say."

Sarah pressed her face to Peggi's neck and looked at Val. He smiled at her and then did a fancy spiraling nosedive that sent Peggi after him, making Sarah scream as her mount followed his twirling path.

Laughter rang out as wind buffeted their faces. Life was so worth living in this moment, she thought. After a while, just watching Val, looking at him, hurt. It was the kind of glorious pain that too much joy causes, that split-second in time when a person feels like every cell membrane inside them will burst and melt together.

Val reached out but didn't get too close for fear of a collision, the tips of his fingers straining toward her like he wanted to touch her cheek and causing Peggi to whinny. His expression slowly changed from smiling to somber, his dark, intense eyes seeming haunted, and then he spun away as though unable to stand being in the air beside her any longer, to head back to the barnyard, where he landed hard before Peggi did.

"Quite a run there," Mr. Milton said, tossing Val his shirt as he folded his wings. "Go take a shower. Mrs. Hogan isn't home, and all the field hands are out. Go on now." He smiled. "House is empty, towels are in the linen closet. You're all sweaty. Can't put your uniform back on and walk the halls of the Academy escortin' a lady all dirty like that."

"Thanks," Val said without turning around, and took off running as Peggi landed behind him.

"Hey, where're you going?" Sarah called out, laughing as Val took the house steps two at a time.

"Oh, he's just a proud lad who's embarrassed because he's all sweaty—which he was," Mr. Milton said, holding his nose and grinning playfully. "So I sent him to the showers...How about me and you put away Miss Peggi here, and feed her some more of these apples you've got?"

* * *

Feeling much better after the break, Sarah didn't even mind Titan Troy scowling at them the whole way back. In fact, she was so bubbly, felt so alive, that she chattered poor Val's ear off the whole walk back to the cafeteria for lunch.

"Hey, you're awfully quiet," she said after a moment, stopping so he'd slow down.

When he kept going, she jogged and caught his arm, and finally got him to stop walking.

"You okay?" she asked, suddenly nervous. "You're not gonna get all weird on me, are you?"

Val shrugged and shook his head. "No. Like…why would I get weird?"

"Because you and I have always been tight, friends…then, in the hall, it was more than friends...And when we went riding it was really cool…but now, you haven't said two words since."

She stared at him, and he looked off down the hall. "Just got a lot on my mind."

"I understand," she said quietly, remembering that their problems hadn't gone away, even though they'd enjoyed life at its most free for those few brief hours.

"No, you don't."

"Hey," she said, pulling on his arm gently. "Don't say that. I do. Really. I do." She let out her breath hard. "Like, we both got away from it for a couple of hours, and nobody else got to do that…and we were laughing and having the best time…the best time I've ever had in my life, actually…but people are really sick…and Ayana's gone." She looked down and let her hand fall away from his arm. "But maybe that's just me. You've got every right to feel—"

"It was the best time of your life?' he said, his voice low and hoarse.

"In the air, just feeling free, soaring, tumbling, falling, laughing," she said, opening her arms and spinning around in the empty hallway. "Flying beside you…" She closed her eyes and stopped spinning. "It was the best time of my life," she whispered, closing her eyes.

His kiss grazed her mouth, making her eyes pop open in surprise. Val stepped away from her, gasping as though he couldn't catch his breath.

"It was the best time of my life, too," he said, staring at her for a moment before he turned his gaze down the hall. "That's what I had on my mind, and I can't shake it—but in there," he said, pointing toward the caf, "I've gotta. You follow me?"

She nodded, only half understanding, still stunned by his impassioned outburst. He strode away from her quickly, as though he didn't trust himself around her for one second more. She watched his retreat for a second, remembering how his back had looked naked under the sun, his magnificent wings spread, then closed her eyes. Her PIU sounded, and she read the message, still numb.

It took a few seconds and the ringing of the lunch bell for her to remember to breathe.

* * *

Professor Zachariah Raziel had called an emergency Shadows class. The PIU message said it would only be for a half hour, and the caf would stay open so his students could still eat. After that, classes were dismissed for the rest of the day, anyway. A half hour wasn't going to kill her, but she was so not in the mood.

Somehow, seeing life at its fullest while out with Val, and knowing that the entire school was teetering on the precipice of tragedy took away all her enthusiasm for exploring any hidden Shadows talents she had.

She raced down the hall, then opened the door to the Crematorium. Student desks and chairs had been arranged around the room, and she was glad to see a bunch of kids she already knew, including Wil. Everyone there was wearing a pin like hers. She selected the seat next to Wil, and they shared a look. Aaron Wu was sitting next to Jim Wilkerson, a tall, gangly almond-hued kid with a big red afro and wicked acne. There were still two empty seats.

The students glanced at one another but kept their focus on Professor Razor. He looked like he'd been up all night; his t-shirt was filthy. He paced in front of the long metal table with a mug of black coffee in his hand, and the air smelled like he hadn't bothered to go outside for a cigarette break. An ominous pile of ashes rested on the metal work table behind him, and all the students noticed it before returning their confused attention to Razor.

He took a long, slow swallow of coffee and gestured around the room with his mug. "I brought a few items from my old post: my scythe, an old Amanthra demon jaw bone—I fondly remember killing that sucker—the old angel breastplate from years gone by, a shield, the usual—oh, yeah, and my coffee mug just to keep me focused, and meanwhile, I want you all to know who will be in class with you."

Professor Razor looked back at the pile of ash. "Don't let that trouble you. It was going to be your first homework assignment," he said, moving toward it to scoop some of the sooty substance into his palm. He allowed it to filter through his fingers as he spoke. "I wanted to see if you could use your skills to separate out what part per billion were human remains versus demon remains." He let out a weary sigh as the last of the ash hit the table and then wiped his dirty palm on the back of his fatigues. "But I guess the point is moot until we get another Ollie in here. I swear, I hate delay as much as I hate demons."

The students shared worried glances that the professor didn't miss.

"That empty seat was for Josh Abrams. That young man would have been a wicked Ollie—he could have told me that the mix on the table was three parts human, one part messenger demon—albeit only after he puked up breakfast, but Josh could have done it. That young man is also one of the best special languages masters in this school—he's fluent in written Cuneiform. However, right now he's on the run for using his superior skills for something stupid. Drugs."

The huge Reaper folded his arms and looked at the stunned faces in the room. "Instead of using his extraordinary talent for something productive, he decided to use his nose to mix the right concentrations of Australian sea wasp venom with belladonna, which is Italian for beautiful woman, otherwise known as *atropa belladonna* or nightshade, hence the illegal's other name, *blue lady*—the same drug the dead fliers were on. It's unfortunately easy to make since night shade is common in the Americas near the Mexican border and on the East Coast. But, I digress.

"Mr. Abrams and his buddy Mr. Scheeler went one step further and taught this school a huge lesson in advanced chemistry—taking substances right out of our wall murals. What do you think you get when you take a sensation- and communication-carrier like pure quartz crystal, then infuse it with a minimal amount of venom that mildly shocks the heart and begins to paralyze or relax the central nervous system, and finally add trace elements of a poison that dilates pupils, blurs vision, increases your heart rate—literally makes your heart audible to others at a distance of several feet, that's how freakin' hard your heart is pounding—makes you aggressive, makes your skin hot, disorients you and gives you hallucinations?"

No one spoke. No one even breathed.

"You get a substance that can kill you while at the same time it opens your psyche to dark forces invasion, that's what you get." Professor Raziel walked across the room and kicked over Josh's empty chair. "There is nothing I hate more than wasted human potential!

"What, you thought our investigation wasn't going to turn up anything?" In an apparent fury, he whirled around and toppled the second empty desk. "That would have been Patty Gray's desk—now that she was finally strong enough to place into my division," he said, pacing away from it to lean against the metal table. "She is a Reverse Clav—a blinder," he said, shaking his head. "And then she got mixed up with the two of them."

Sarah could only stare at the man, still focused on the boys he'd mentioned. Ernie Scheeler and Josh Abrams, two Blends—guys who were the epitome of nerdy. They were the ones manufacturing drugs, not Stefan? And Patty, of all people, was helping them? Sarah felt like her world had tipped off its axis. Nothing was what it seemed to be, just like she'd been trying to tell her bone-headed brother. The only remaining question was what the heck had Melissa swiped from Stefan the night of the luau that had made him so mad? Or had he been as wrong to accuse her as they had been to accuse him of dealing drugs?

"Have you any idea how valuable a skill she has?" Professor Raziel railed as he looked around before taking a deep sip from his mug. "Of course you don't," he muttered. "Patty Gray could have blinded demons, Morrigan, you name it, all from the safety of a Guardian encampment out in the field. She was going to be a part of our field exercises in the woods before we moved up to the forbidden zone exercises. But instead she decided to help blind this administration to a drug ring so the guys could go into town and sell something that couldn't be easily manufactured anywhere but this school!" He shook his head. "Stupid! Their little profit center may have put everyone's life at risk by tipping off the Morrigan!"

Professor Raziel started pacing again, his hands clasped behind his back. "Now that poor girl is fighting for her life in ICU. What a waste." He stopped and stared out at the room, then resumed his slow pacing. "And all for a code of student honor. Code of student honor? Where's her honor now? Answer me that." He let out a harsh breath and stared challengingly at the class, suddenly flinging his mug into the furnace with a crash. "I don't know why I asked you to come here. Maybe after last night, flying high and low to no avail, I just needed to vent." His shoulders slumped as he wiped his broad palms down his face, then looked straight at Aaron Wu and pointed.

"This boy here is not only one of the school's best bio-chem students and a strong general Tactical, but Alan can throw his voice anywhere, can mimic any voice or sound with perfect pitch—and I would know. We in the angel legions know perfect pitch when we hear it. Show 'em, Alan."

"Uh…it's Aaron, sir," the boy said nervously.

"Okay, all right, my apologies. Aaron. Like I said, it's been a long night."

Aaron nodded and then flawlessly duplicated Professor Razor's voice, throwing it from behind the students, making them turn just to double-check no one else was there.

Everyone murmured in awe.

"Whoa, man…that is craaazy," Jim said, reaching across the aisle to slap Aaron five.

"I thought I'd be able to get an advanced Audio in my group this time, but it wasn't meant to be," said "Professor Razor" from behind them.

"Man, he sounds just like you," Wil said, shaking his head. "Freaky."

"That is a skill that could save all your lives one day," the real Professor Razor replied. "But beware. It's also something demons can do."

All eyes immediately went to Aaron, who looked shocked.

"Vampires can throw their voices to make it sound like it's your own dear momma calling you," the professor said, walking around the room again. "But there's always a slight warble, a slight distortion, in the copycat's electronic voice signature. We'll do blindfolded experiments in the field. If you're right and it's me, you get to advance. If you're wrong and it's Aaron, then you'll earn a black armband and you're dead."

He stopped at Jim's desk and looked down. "Jim is a Builder Tactical, not to be confused with a General Tactical, like Wil and Aaron." "Look around the room, Jim, and build me a shield—fast."

The professor stepped away from Jim's side, but Jim only looked up at him, seeming confused. "Sir…uh…I can use anything? And, uh, wood or metal?"

Professor Razor simply stared at the wall clock. "You are being pursued by a demon black bolt charge. In twenty seconds you will fry. Make up your mind and act, boy!"

The empty desks exploded; metal from knives on the wall and the metal table sheered down into a reinforced disc. A plume of ashes from the metal table billowed up as though hit with a mortar round. Thunderous blue-white light flash-bleached the room, making students cup their palms over their eyes as they peeked through. Razor's eyes simply became pure midnight. A handle made from a bent desk leg attached itself on one side of the huge shield, while spikes, chains and knife tips whirred around the edges.

Spent and sweating, Jim held his work up for the professor to inspect. The shield was still sparking as the professor grabbed it, biceps contracting as he lifted the heavy object.

"This is indeed a shield that would block an attack. Well done, young man, well done!" Professor Razor strutted around with it held in front of his chest. "Look at the edges, the blade work," he said, nodding, and then dragged it along the wall leaving deep gashes. "Creative. This is not just a shield but also a weapon. We just have to work on your decision-making skills and show you how to adjust for different Guardian strengths," he added, motioning for Sarah to come up to the front of the class, where he thrust the shield into her arms. "Here. Hold this."

Sarah tried to hold it but went down to the floor alongside it with a massive thud.

"See my point, Jim? You've gotta make something with a weight and density to protect your team members, but that's also something they can carry. We'll work on that." He turned to Wil. "Wil is a rescuer. A guy like Jim is necessary when you're low on artillery, but when you need a guy to throw you a line and pull you out of a hot spot, Wil's your man."

Sarah watched her classmates sit up taller at having been recognized. A sense of quiet defeat filled her as she abandoned the shield on the floor and slunk back to her desk. What did she have but crazy little shadow thingies and weird double vision?

"But that one…" Professor Razor said, pointing at her and causing her to turn. "She's the class leader."

All eyes were on Sarah, but her questioning gaze was on the professor.

"She has night-vision, courtesy of her father. Dormant healer and righteous indignation in her, courtesy of her mother. Sarah can not only see where there have been traces of life in the shadows, Headmaster Stone tells me that she is beginning to be able to see actual shadow echoes. Paired with a flier, she can look down into the dark and discern where on the target of a search-and-recovery mission has been. And I suspect she probably has some other very interesting talents beginning to bloom. Time will tell."

Sarah sat down slowly as the students in the room nodded at her, their eyes filled with a strange combination of skeptical acceptance and respect.

"Way cool, Sarah," Wil murmured for her ears only.

"Thanks," she replied in a shy voice.

"Myself, I'm a Reaper," Professor Razor said proudly. "I see death echoes—the place where the departed dropped their soul, and my job is to drag it down to Hell where it belongs, if it's going in that direction. We Reapers are always on the battlefield, just like Valkyries. The difference is, while our brethren fly to the light or rescue the injured, we go in the opposite direction, and if it's still moving and breathing and shouldn't be…" He smiled a sinister smile and shrugged. "We make sure it stops."

"So don't let that pretty face fool you, gentlemen." Professor Razor pointedly glanced at Wil, folded his arms over his chest and then stared at Sarah. "She's a Shadow Walker. She sees the pulse of life. Entire battalions of Reapers report to a trained Shadow Walker, as do their Collectors. That's why I'll be giving her practice leading this class when things get back to normal around here."

"Wait," Wil said, slack-jawed. "You're saying Sarah can lead Reapers? Guys like you?"

She wanted to die.

"Of course. We're a phylum of the angels, and all angels are meant to serve humankind. Haven't you read your cosmic history? That's what started the first big war. One angel in particular—the best of the best, aka Lucifer—had issues with taking a direct order from On High and had his ass fried for his trouble. Seems dude couldn't get it through his head that his orders from the Big Boss were to serve humans. Suffice to say that they didn't see eye-to-eye on the subject because old Lu didn't want to bow to mortals or serve them, and that led to that very prominent angel's fall. Stupid move, if you ask me. Who argues with the General? It was a pure violation of the chain of command, something any newbie angel learns the moment you get your wings. Anyway, from that point on, he's been a pure bitch to contend with—so listen up. His legions are no joke."

The professor walked back toward the furnace, stepping through the ashes on the floor, now that his metal desk was gone. He peered into the fire, speaking toward the flames as though talking to himself. "The Light Corps report to Neterus. Reapers report specifically to Shadow Walkers. The other Rivera kid will probably be this millennium's Light Neteru, which is why the little snot is so cocky—and why he's not in my class. I'd probably stomp him into a demon puddle, but that's a subject for another time. All I know for certain is that this one is my Shadow Walker. She is much stronger than her brother and doesn't even know it. That's the irony of it all."

"But I'm not some kind of superhero warrior angel or a battalion leader," Sarah said in a small voice. "Be serious."

"Only a mortal with a soul and human free will can direct angels—well, along with the One. Angels, by direct edict, report to humans and the Light. Everything in the heavens is very organized—it's called divine order." He closed the furnace door, turned and looked at the stunned faces before him.

"Now that you know who some of your classmates are and what talents they have, don't be stupid and squander them like some of your fellow students have. Study hard and brush up on your skills, because when you come back to class after the current crisis, you'll think you're doing drills in Hell."

He sent a withering gaze around the room. "I don't give a damn what they teach you in the other divisions you hail from. In Shadows, all my war games are live, and our search-and-rescue missions are real. It burns my ass that until this situation is resolved, I cannot begin to properly teach you. What the hell can you learn sitting behind a desk? We need to be out in the field!" He nodded toward the shield Jim had made. "Keep your noses clean, and don't wind up a foolish waste of resources."

The room was so quiet that the only sounds were the students breathing, the dull roar of the furnace and the ticking wall clock.

"Class dismissed."

All the students jumped up simultaneously, ready to bolt. But Professor Razor instantly intercepted Sarah like the supernatural he was, his gaze bearing down on hers.

"Stay," he commanded in a low rumble and then pointed to her seat. "Sit."

Wil gave her an empathy-filled glance and then left when the professor glared at him.

Razor circled her desk like a huge bird of prey, waiting for the heavy metal door to slam shut behind Wil.

"I heard you were out of your room with friends last night trying to hunt, trying to set up a sting," he said, walking and talking in a dizzying circle.

"Prof—"

"I know all about it," he said, cutting her off. "I'm not here to chastise you or to baby you like some of the other professors might." He stopped walking and stared down at her. "You are a Shadow Walker Neteru—one of the most elite Neteru there are. Your own mother, who is a Powers Angel Neteru, didn't even have what you have at your age. She manipulates the

Light the way you will soon learn to manipulate the shadows in service of the Light." He paused, then made her jump when he shouted, "You are supposed to hunt!"

She could only stare at him.

"The Dark Realms rue the day you were born," he said with eerie satisfaction gleaming in his supernatural eyes. "When you sense evil, you go after it. Your blood is impervious to contagion. You can call your Collectors to fend off an attacker. And if whatever you catch by the tail is stronger than you," he added with a sinister smile, "that's when you call me."

"You really don't care if I investigate?" she said in a rasp of disbelief.

"My teaching style vastly differs from this administration's preferred methodology. I just ask that you promise me one thing if your curiosity finally gets the better of you."

She stared up into his midnight-blue eyes, not sure she was ready to take the bait of freedom he was dangling before her. "What?" she finally murmured.

"No good leader takes the unprepared into battle with them. There's not a student in this school ready to do what you can do naturally. Got that?"

Sarah nodded. "But I'm not ready, either. I'm trying to get people not to do anything crazy."

"So I've heard, and yes, the walls do talk. We angels are a part of nature, so the murals speak to us." He let out a breath, shooing her away with a dismissive wave of his huge hand. "One day, Shadow Walker, you'll keep us busy, but maybe your grandmother and father are right. I could be pushing you too hard too soon. You may go."

* * *

She ran to her room, changed clothes after a quick shower, and made it to the caf just in time to catch up with her friends, who were dawdling and waiting for her return from Razor's class. The lunch tables were mostly back to their normal factional divisions. Wil had found a group of neutral guys, but had a somber expression each time he glanced at Sarah. The Neteru compound guys were off in their own war party huddle. There was a table of Blends that consisted of Jess and some girls Sarah didn't know. The compound girls sat together, minus Ayana and Hyacinth. The big difference was that Aaron and Jim had taken up residence in their normally all-female space.

She could feel something in the air. People smiled at her who normally acted like they didn't know she existed. Kids made way for her as she went to get her food. No one assumed she was going to sit with them, but everyone made it clear by their eager expressions that it was okay with them if she chose to sit at their table.

It was like she'd suddenly become a celebrity, and it felt weird. The word was obviously out about what had gone down in Razor's class. She just wanted to remain neutral about everything while she tried to process her very formidable destiny.

Sarah tried not to look in Val's direction, or Wil's. That was next to impossible, but she kept her gaze secretive and as unreadable as possible. She sat with her friends, which felt the safest and most familiar, but at the same time, that only made her miss Hyacinth and Ayana more.

Still, every now and then, in between bites of lunch, her mind would drift, and so would her gaze, and she'd catch a sidelong glimpse of Val, and he'd catch one of her. It was so crazy, so inopportune. Then she'd glance at Wil, and guilt would churn her insides.

"So where did you and Val go?" Allie leaned in and whispered.

"Where do ya think?" Tami said, scraping the sides of her yogurt container. "Don't be such a—"

"After Miss Tittle flamed, I had to get out of here," Sarah said firmly, ignoring Tami's knowing smile. "Val came after me to make sure I was okay, and we asked Titan Troy to let us out so I could show Val the stables. I wanted to show him the Pegasus horses—just get my head out of this place for a minute."

"Okaaay, if you say so," Tami drawled skeptically. "The Titan let you *and* Val out while the entire school is in emergency lockdown to see the Pegasus horses."

"Why are you like this all the time, Tami?" Sarah snapped. "That's what happened." She flung her wet ponytail over her shoulder. "Period!"

"Keep your voice down and don't be so touchy," Tami said with a smirk. "I understand, and your secret is safe with me."

Sarah stood up. "Why do you always have to make everything sound so, so…You're doing it again. Trying to bring me down a peg, right, Tam? Trying to make me feel awkward and silly and insignificant. The resentment you felt before what happened by the pool hasn't gone away—it's just morphed into this. Well, get over yourself, Tamara Rider! Even as your best friend, I can't keep making myself small so you can look big."

Sarah got up and walked away as words failed her. What happened out by the stables hadn't been anything like what Tami was making it out to be, and the fact that Tami's resentment of her was still so palpable, even with everything else that was going on, just tore her up inside.

"Why do you do stuff like this, Tami?" Allie said loudly enough for Sarah to hear, then ran after her.

"Hey, wait up!" Allie called. "You know how Tami is."

Sarah slammed her tray on the conveyor belt, then whirled on Allie. "It wasn't like she said! We went to the stables, then I had class with Wil—special Shadows class, called by Razor—and then I took a shower to get stable smell off me and came to eat."

"I know," Allie said in a soothing voice. "Okay? I know."

Sarah sighed hard. "She works my last nerve, just says stuff that turns everything that could be beautiful into something that feels grimy. I hate when she gets like that."

Allie set down her own tray calmly and threaded her arm around Sarah's waist. "Everybody knows that's Tami's defense mechanism—open mouth, insert foot disease—when she's feeling insecure. You're all of a sudden a school star, she's not. You have two fantastic hunks vying for your attention. She has Al, but also Stefan, an outlaw werewolf, so you've trumped her again."

"I wasn't trying to trump her," Sarah said, squeezing her eyes shut. "This isn't some kind of competition. Stuff just keeps happening—it's not like I'm trying to do anything to her. I'm just living my life!"

"I know…and that's what's making her eat her heart out," Allie said in a calm, quiet voice. "You've beaten her at everything that's important to her without even trying, and it's really hard for a competitive girl like Tami to live with that, even though she really does love you, Sarah."

Sarah let out a long breath and stared at Allie, knowing that what her friend said was true. She'd known that all her life about Tami, but when they were at home it was so much easier to endure her teasing, take Tami's digs and be the butt of Tami's jokes just to keep the peace. However, more often than not, at home, Tami showed her soft side to her best friend and turned the blade of her tongue against everyone else. Thinking about that made Sarah very sad. Maybe the pressures of school and Tami's insecurities were making her lash out. But this time, Sarah didn't feel like backing down to keep the peace. Why did she always have to take Tami's crap and apologize to keep their friendship alive? Here, at the Academy, that routine had gotten old.

Allie touched Sarah's arm. "You know how Tami is. Let it go. Plus, right now she's prone to saying all kinds of stupid stuff because she's quietly bugging out about things with your brother, especially after things got really close with Stefan, but not all the way, you follow? She doesn't have Ayana to turn to. She's feeling that loss, too, like we all are. Like, who else is she gonna tell about whatever went on with her and Al making out, you know?"

"TMI, TMI, waaay too much information," Sarah said, trying to rush away from Allie's side.

Allie gave chase down the hall. "Tami's just scared and she wants company, so she was trying to pull you into the same club. I'd be scared, too, if I was with Al—no offense, but your brother doesn't exactly treat girls nice all the time, you know? He's kind of self-centered and all. I feel sorry for her. Get past the words. Tami is a marshmallow inside, and you know it. Everything happened so fast because she was so upset about people saying she was getting played by Stefan to upset Melissa. People saw them leaving the hall together after the luau, and word travelled fast. Al probably told her what people were saying, if I know your brother, and worked that to his advantage. What happened definitely shouldn't have gone down the way it did—are you hearing me, Sarah?"

The question made Sarah stop and close her eyes. She hated this predicament, and what Allie said was true. Stefan had been alone with Melissa. She'd seen that with her own eyes and tried to tell Tami, but Tami wouldn't listen. Al had no doubt added his own spin to the story. Then again, Tami wielded more power over her brother than she realized, which meant Al could get hurt bad—which was the way it always worked, the biggest dogs, once they fell, they fell hard. But Tami was definitely hurting, and they hadn't been able to really talk because things had been so chaotic.

"I think you see my point," Allie said patiently when Sarah opened her eyes. "I'm pretty sure more happened with Al and Tami than—"

Sarah held up her hand. "I don't want to hear about that. I just can't process it in my mind." She shivered and closed her eyes, hugging herself. "That's my brother and my home girl, and I cannot hear all the details, all right?" Sarah stared at Allie. "The whole thing is beyond awkward. I just hope they treat each other right."

"And while she's with Al, you've lost her as a confidante because Al is Val's best friend, which I guess leaves me," Allie said and let out a sigh.

"Why would you say it like that, Allie?" Sarah held Allie's arm, forcing her friend to stop and meet her eyes.

"Because when it's a big adventure or some crazy thing's going to happen, normally you and Tami just shunt me and 'Cinth aside to rush in where angels fear to tread." Allie yanked her arm away from Sarah, her voice hitching. "Why do you think Hyacinth ran into the Shady Path with the other girls, even though she was scared to death that first time, huh? She wanted to impress you—for once not to be a third or fourth wheel, Sarah!"

"Oh, God, Allie…" Sarah hugged her, even though Allie stiffened. "Don't you understand that most of the time it's not like that?"

Sarah pulled back and stared at Allie. "Everybody has a role. I run after Tami because she's nuts." That comment drew a smile from Allie at last. "The last thing I want to do is drag you guys into some mess that Tami's rushed into. But who do I always come back to when it's time to share the serious stuff?"

Allie looked down sheepishly, and Sarah hugged her again.

"I can't say certain things to Tam," Sarah admitted. "She always makes me feel stupid for caring about the people I care about or the things I believe in. And 'Cinth, God bless her, she's the voice of fairness and reason when I forget about being rational."

"It's kinda crazy, isn't it?" Allie said with a sniff. "It's like Tami is your adrenaline partner, I'm your confessional, and 'Cinth is your inner voice of reason. But Yaya was all of our big sister seer."

"Yeah," Sara said, slinging her arm over Allie's shoulder and heading farther away from the cafeteria, the mention of Ayana making silence settle between them for a little while.

Then Allie stopped walking as they neared the lounge. "So confess me this," she said. "You like Val—a lot—don't you?"

Sarah looked down at her sneakers. “Yeah. A lot.”

“I knew it,” Allie softly squealed. “I think he likes you a lot, too.”

Sarah nodded. “But then there’s Wil….”

Allie’s eyes got big. “What are you going to do? Do they know about each other? And how you feel about each of them?”

Sarah hugged herself. “I don’t know—and I don’t know what I’m going to do. They’re both…”

“Spill!”

Sarah closed her eyes for a moment. “It was so…magical.”

“You did it?” Allie squeaked. “Ohmigod! With which one?”

“No!”

Allie clutched her chest, feigning a heart attack, and making them both laugh.

“Val went with me to the stables and I got to show him the horses.”

“You two got to go out unescorted?”

“No such luck,” Sarah said, waving her hand as they walked along arm and arm. “Titan Troy took us.”

“Oh, then I know nothing happened. Tami is tripping.”

“Right. And wrong,” Sarah said, finding a couple of free computers in the sparsely occupied lounge. She sat down and waited for Allie to settle herself beside her, bursting to share the wonderful experience that had been bottled up inside her.

“Soooo?” Allie asked, her eyes alight with excitement.

“Mr. Milton is the nicest man. He let us take Peggi—she’s half Pegasus, half unicorn—out for a flight…and Val…you should have seen him. He took off his shirt and went running in a circle with his arms stretched out like we’d do when we were kids, and the most magnificent wings came out of his shoulders. I’ve seen them before, but today, seeing him like that…it was different. Do you know what I mean?”

Sarah smiled, knowing Allie didn't fully understand, even when she said that she did, but that was okay. She also decided not to discuss her first real kiss with Wil, or the way the ones she'd shared with Val took her breath away, and she was glad that Allie didn't pry. Good sister-confessors were like that—they let you tell as much as you wanted and no more, and never leaked a thing about anything you'd said. There was something so personal and private about everything she and Val had shared that morning that Sarah only shared a little off the top and tucked the rest of the deliciously wonderful feeling way down deep in her soul for safe keeping.

She felt differently about the stables now, too. They were her oasis and Val's now. She didn't even want to share the place with her friends just yet. It was a place of light…and where she'd been in the alcove wasn't, and yet that was equally special. The best thing about it was Beep and Bop hadn't come out and scared her either time. It seemed they were willing to grant her some privacy, thank heavens.

Sarah fired up the computer and waited for it to boot up. She stared at the screen, unable to read a word without concentration, and then Allie interrupted her.

"I'm sooo excited about you two," Allie said, squeezing Sarah's arm. "And don't worry about the classes you missed. I've got all the notes, and you can just download them from my PIU—not that much happened this morning anyway. The teachers are all pretty freaked."

"I figured as much. That's why I didn't rush back. But now I want me and you to go on an adventure. This is something that's definitely not Tami's style."

"Really? You wanna go on an adventure with me? So, like, what can I do?"

Sarah looked hard at her friend. "Research."

CHAPTER 30

"I think it's real cool that your powers are coming in, Sarah," Allie said, scanning the PirateNet site.

"Yeah, I thought so, too, until I couldn't read without a headache and started seeing blue light lines that nauseated me to death." Sarah sighed. "I just know there's something there. Some kind of pattern we're missing." She squinted at the screen as Allie scrolled the online Class Book pages. "I want to know everything I can about Stefan—things he liked, people he hated, people who wrote on his Class Book page alley, because if we know that, maybe we can get a clue to where he's hiding out or who might be helping him. That way we can at least let Nana get to him before Al and his crazy posse do."

Sarah sat back and rubbed her palms down her face. They'd been at it for a couple of hours, trying to see who in school was linked up with whom. She sat forward suddenly. "I wonder if the two Upper Sphere students who died had pages and if they're still up. Maybe there'd be something there."

"Sure thing, Sarah," Allie said, clicking over. "But those kids, well, I don't know how much good their pages will be 'cuz, you know they're dead and can't friend us, so there's only so much we can see."

"Yeah, I know. But I also wanna look at the kids who've gone missing." Sarah stared at the screen, feeling the chill of Allie's words. Gregory Duncan and Peter Matthews had had everything to live for—everything. After seeing Valencio fly majestic and free, she could only imagine what the two Upper Sphere Valkyries must have looked like taking off from the main hall platform at dusk, gleaming white wings spread…soaring, laughing, doing air wheelies and spiraling nose dives for their clapping girlfriends. Then to see it all go so horribly wrong, right before your very eyes.

Sarah closed her own eyes for a moment, not wanting to picture the tragedy but unable to escape the images forming in her head. No wonder seers sometimes went blind. She wondered if that would ever happen to her.

"Man," Allie said quietly, stopping at one of the many tribute pages to the dead fliers. "Both those guys were so hot. Such a waste. Look at this guy. He has—had—green eyes and perfect blond hair, and look at this pic of him with his wings out—that's gotta be a five- or six-foot span on each side."

Sarah couldn't look as Allie prattled on with her nose practically touching the screen. All she could think about was what if something terrible like that happened to Val…or Wil…or her brother.

"And look at the other guy," Allie said with a soft sigh.

Sarah cringed and rubbed her arms, tightly shutting her eyes. "Those guys are dead, Allie. Don't talk about them like you're going to run into them walking around the school."

"Sorry," Allie said, sounding defensive. "But can I help it if I'm drawn to this guy's strong jaw and gray eyes and—"

"What color did you just say his eyes were?" Sarah leaned forward and squinted at the picture on the screen.

"Gray. But an unusual blue-gray…almost like a husky's eyes."

Sarah stood. "Can you come walk with me, Allie? Like…wherever I go, write it down?"

"Okaaay," Allie said, indulging her. "Why? And where to?"

Ignoring the first question, Sarah said, "To follow some shadow echoes and maybe a coupla shadows."

* * *

"I know I said I'm ready for any adventure," Allie wheezed, trying to keep up with Sarah. "But what are we doing?"

"I've been following Stefan's life force, his shadow echo—or as much of it as I can pick up. It's very faint, and sometimes my concentration gets messed up, but as far as I can tell, he never came back as far as the gym."

The girls rounded a corner and entered the room in question just in time to see Val, wings extended, leap and soar and dunk the ball into the basket at the far end of the court.

"Wow," Allie whispered. "I see what you mean. I never really looked at Val like that before."

Sarah's reply caught in her throat as Val swooped to retrieve the ball and stood, wiping sweat from his face.

"Hey," he said in a surly tone.

"Hey," Sarah said, and then realized that his jaw was slightly swollen, with a long blue bruise on it. "What happened to you?"

"Nothing. It's cool."

"You oughta put some ice on that," Allie said, frowning.

"I said it's cool!" Val shouted, stalking away toward the bleachers where his shirt and sweater were piled.

"Who did this to you, Val?" Sarah said quietly, going to him. "What happened?"

"Al happened, aw'right."

"My brother did this to you?" Incredulous, she reached out to touch Val's jaw, but he stepped away from her, although not soon enough.

The moment her fingers graced his swollen jaw, intense images stabbed into her mind like a hard, fast movie.

The boys from their compound had all been together. Val had been trying to get her brother to slow down. For a moment, she wasn't standing in the gym; she was in the hall, reliving snatches of conversation and distorted bits of time inside her head.

"Yo, hold up, man," Val had said, jogging behind Al, with Miguel and Donnie on his flank. "I told you, I'm not down with burnin' no dude without knowing for a fact that he's a killer."

Val then landed a firm hand on Alejandro's shoulder to stop him from walking away, and Alejandro swung and caught Val square in the jaw. Blood and spit flew as Val went down hard.

Miguel bent and grabbed Val's arm to help him up.

Donnie wheeled on Alejandro and pointed at him in a rare display of courage, yelling, "What the hell is wrong with you, man?" He moved to grab Val's other arm, but Val was already up and circling Al, furious.

"What is your problem?" Val shouted, drawing onlookers into the hall.

"You kissed my sister!" Al flung his backpack down and squared off, slapping the center of his chest. "I thought we supposed to be boyz?"

Sarah's mouth flew open, but the images careened inside her head as Val looked away from her.

Stunned, the image of Val gaped at her brother. "How the hell did you—"

"I felt it on contact!" Al yelled, dropping fang. "The bullshit came right through my shoulder, it was so recent, and you think we'd still be friends after that? Sarah's not like that, man. All these *chicas* up in this school but you—my *hombre*, you go after my sister. Break her heart, motherfucker, and it's on!"

Al was about to fight Val for her? Nooo way!

Sarah closed her eyes tightly and began to walk in a tight circle, trying to get the images to stop. Val began walking away, clearly too humiliated for words.

"Would somebody tell me what the heck is going on?" Allie shouted, trying to get Sarah to stop walking in a dizzying circle.

But it was no use, once Sarah had touched Val, whatever the emotional sequence was that she'd tapped was destined to run its course. Bewildered, Allie ran over to Val, blocking his exit from the gym.

What's happening to her? You can't just leave her like this!" Allie shrieked, grabbing his arm.

"She'll be okay," Val muttered. "Just mind your business for once, aw'ight!"

"No." Allie, said, jumping in front of him and pointing toward Sarah. "With all this freaky stuff going on around the school, we're not leaving her in here alone."

"It's okay, Allie," Sarah wheezed, blinking hard to try to get the images in her head to disconnect. But it was like she was plugged into Val at a psychic level now, and as she stopped and stared at him and he stared back at her, she could tell he could feel it, too.

"First of all," Val's image said inside Sarah's head, and then she watched him step up and get in Al's face, his fangs lowering to match Al's, "I don't think about her like that. I don't treat girls the way you do!" He stared at Al then spat blood. "I've got too much respect for her to do her like that, but the next time you take a swing at your best *amigo*, I'ma show you what your ex-sergeant-at-arms can do."

Donnie and Miguel jumped between Alejandro and Val as Val advanced on Al with a level of fury that had spiked way beyond Al's.

"Yeah, whatever, man," Al muttered and turned away.

"And for the record," Val shouted toward Al's back, pushing Miguel and Donnie off him, "if you treat Tami like shit, I'm coming for you! I promise I'll wax your ass up and down this hallway until they throw us both out!"

"Walk it off, man," Miguel said in the vision. "Walk it off. You know how Al is."

"I'm tired of understanding how Al is—Al needs to grow the hell up." Val spat out more blood and started walking toward the gym.

"You gonna be cool, dude?" Donnie asked, catching up to him.

Val kept his head high, his gaze forward, his chest heaving and his nostrils flaring. He couldn't answer Donnie; rage had a stranglehold on him.

"Can I ask just one question?" Donnie asked as Miguel joined them. "Did you really kiss Sarah?"

Miguel yanked Donnie out of the way of a hard elbow jab from Val that would have caught Donnie in the throat, then spun him around and began walking in the opposite direction. "Man, you are one stupid SOB."

Moments later, Sarah saw a furious Val enter the gym inside her mind. Sweat rolled down his temples, his chest and back as he ran the court bare-chested, shooting hoops alone. His backpack sat on the bleachers with his sweater and Oxford shirt flung over them. It was clear that he needed to move, had to move, and needed a distraction. Anger and hurt echoed through her soul. His boy had sucker-punched him, taking offense when none was warranted. There was no way to explain, nor should he have had to that she was someone he thought about in an entirely different way. The awareness kept their eyes on each other as the telepathic link ran its course. Val offered her a slight nod. She swallowed hard. Her mouth had gone dry from the intensity of his emotions.

Then within the vision, Val ran down the court, spread his wings and hovered over the basket with the ball and then slam dunked it, only to grab it and dribble in down the court at a six-foot altitude.

She looked away from Val as the vision ebbed.

"I said it was cool. So now you know." He began stuffing his sweater and shirt into his backpack and turned to leave in earnest this time.

"No, it's not cool for Al to do something like this to his best friend." She didn't know what else to say. The other things she'd felt within him were too deep and way too intense to name.

"Ex-best friend," Val said. "Man thinks I'm gonna hurt his sister, so hey…"

Eyes wide and fascinated, Allie plopped down on the bleachers nearby.

"Where did he get some off-the-wall idea like—"

"I touched his shoulder, just like you touched my jaw," Val said, frowning and turning away from her. "Didn't know you had the gift too…guess a lot of shit is different since we got to school. But I just wanted to tell him something, wanted to get him off this crazy wolf-hunt mission and back on target with the light-binding thing. You know how it is—all us Specs are empaths. Guess how I felt was right up near the surface, and he spun and cold-cocked me for kissing his sister, but what his tiny brain couldn't figure out was, it meant something. I wasn't playing you the way he plays girls, so he got pissed. At least you know your big brother has your back, as messed up as his thinking is."

"Stop!" Sarah shouted, rounding on Val. "Listen, I know you're angry, and I know there's other serious personal stuff going on," she added, trying to preserve their privacy in front of Allie and hoping Val caught her drift. "But I need your help. You've said a whole buncha stuff I need to absorb, but I can't right now—can you understand that?" She reached for him, needing to feel his acceptance.

"Yeah," he said flatly, sidestepping her outstretched arm. "That's exactly how I feel right now—too much filling my head. So…what do you need my help with?"

"Stefan never came this way that night the four of us were in the hallway!"

"How do you know?" Val looked from her to Allie, still sitting on the bleachers but leaning forward avidly.

"My talents are starting to come in. One of the things I'm starting to be able to do is shadow echo—see shadows, follow where people have gone."

"Really?" Val rubbed his jaw, then winced. "I hear that's really rare. They told us about it in Spec orientation. None of the professors here can do it, not even Nana Marlene. Al can't do it, either. That's deep."

"Well, I can do it," Sarah said proudly. "I can't fly, but I can read the ground—and Allie's been my scribe while we walked all over the school following Stefan's trail, but it never got to the gym."

"Trust me," Allie said, joining them and shaking her head. "We walked this whole school like three times."

"The night we got attacked, something came from back toward the boiler room, because Al and Tami were over there." Sarah started walking, with Val and Allie following her.

"Right, they were up in the alcove, doing whatever," Val said. "Me and you came into the hall from that way."

Allie started writing.

"Tell your girl not to write that part down," Val muttered. "She looks like she's a reporter for the school paper or something."

"Allie, chill," Sarah said, walking back down the hall in the direction she'd gone with Titan Troy. "In the morning I had to go to detention," she went on, picking up her earlier thread, "and that's when I found out that exit stair and the hatch to the outside. There's a lock code, but—"

"But somebody could get in, if they had the code," he said, cutting her off.

"Which senior fliers, getting ready to graduate, probably would."

"Valkyries?" Val said, nodding in agreement with Sarah's assessment. "Definitely. They probably flew with the stable on a regular basis, and I doubt Titan Troy was assigned to escort them every time they wanted to go out. They would've been buff—the kind of guys to protect other people, not need protection themselves."

"Gotta agree with you," Sarah said.

"Buff? Buff!" Allie exclaimed. "These guys were monsters—like on steroids or something."

"Calm down," Val said laughing, flexing. "All Valkyries fill out the more they fly and do airlift reps—got that crazy Viking thing going on. Have to be able to dead-weight lift a man off the battlefield at full velocity. Valkyries are the best athletes in the school." Val rolled his shoulders and strutted a bit. "By Upper Sphere, I'm gonna be cut like…ridiculous."

"Focus," Sarah said with a big smile, jettisoning the enticing image of an even buffer Val from her mind. "Okay…so what if the night the four of us got attacked someone came in from the outside, someone who knew the codes?"

"I could see that," Val said calmly, walking toward the boiler room. "But how'd he get away? Once the water rushed in, it would be impossible to open the door against the water pressure."

"Yeah, but look at the walls," Allie said, running her hand along a series of vertical metal tracks that marked the hall on the way to the boiler room. "They'd've thought of everything, so wouldn't they have some kind of safety doors between the ocean mural and the boiler room?"

"Hell yeah," Val said, running over to where Allie stood. "The doors leading in and out are built like nautical hatches, so before you get to them, there'd be a series of spinners sealed off the boiler room and preserve the heating and cooling systems."

"Which means that whoever attacked us had time to get to the hatch and then the drop-downs went back up automatically once the water receded." Sarah pulled out her scrunchie and walked back and forth, opening her mind, focusing on the face of the dead Valkyrie with the beautiful gray eyes.

But his wasn't the face she saw. The attacker's traces were faint echoes now, like visual whispers. What she did see made her hug the wall. It was huge, hunchbacked and feral—and it had definitely came through the back door. The moment the fear slammed her system, she saw Beep and Bop peek out of a corner.

"It's okay," she said to her Collectors, knowing that no one else could see.

"You okay?" Val asked hesitantly, watching her cringe against the wall like she'd seen a ghost and then walk over to the code pad.

"I'm sure they changed the code for security purposes once those kids got killed, Sarah," Allie said, though she sounded unsure. She hung back as Val hurried to Sarah's side.

When Sarah spoke, her voice sounded very far away. "But if you could hear like a dog, or a wolf…"

"I'm part vamp," Val said proudly. "I hear pretty good, like the best of the Audios, and no worse than Al and Miguel. Heard his fingers hit the pads and then did a little stealth to watch his movements."

"You saw the code pattern when Titan Troy put it in this morning?"

Val smiled. "That was gonna be my secret, but, yeah…I think I mighta seen a li'l somethin'."

"Put it in," Sarah said, looking at him.

Allie walked away. "All this sounds way too personal."

Val gave a low, sexy chuckle and punched in the code. Allie and Sarah stared in amazement as the tumblers clicked.

"Oh, you are dangerous," Allie said, impressed.

"Criminal," Val said with a wicked half-grin.

"Can you open the door?" Sarah looked at him. "No offense, but that thing that attacked Al looked really, really strong, like Titan Troy strong, and even he had to really try to get the thing open."

"I got it, no offense taken," Val said, but he definitely sounded like he'd taken offense anyway.

Straining, his sneakers sliding on the ground in fits and squeaks, he pushed against the hatch spinners.

"But somebody with werewolf strength could get that open, if they had the code, right?" Sarah asked.

"I said I got it," Val said between clenched teeth, and slowly but surely, the huge spinner began to turn as the door eerily creaked open. "See," he said between heavy breaths. "No problem."

* * *

"Look, man, it's almost dusk, and they're gonna be doing roll call right before dinner," Wil said, standing on the platform under the library with Alejandro, Donnie and Tami.

"I don't know if this is a good idea," Tami said, craning her neck and shielding her eyes against the last of the sun.

"Listen, just be cool," Al said, and then kissed her quickly before turning back toward Wil. "Plenty of time for me to make a reconnaissance flight as long as you and Donnie work together to try to get a beacon inside the perimeter, and Ayana's girls and Miguel go on keeping old Mojo mind stunned over there." He nodded in their direction.

"One flight only, on this side of the dead zone, and hurry up before the light goes and you lose visual," Wil warned.

"I've got night vision, dude. Don't worry. Just juice up Donnie's and my PIUs and see if you can get a pulse back from the ones that're out there."

"Be careful, okay?" Tami said in a worried voice.

"I got this, baby." Al gave her a dashing smile. "All Neteru warrior," he said, slapping his bare chest.

Wil stood next to Donnie. "Al, man, I hope you know what you're doing."

* * *

"Hey, guys, before you lock the hatch, could we go see 'em?" Allie's eyes searched Val's and Sarah's faces, her voice so plaintive that they both smiled.

"They are really beautiful," Sarah said, hoping Val would humor her friend. But as she stood there, and the more she thought about it, a crazy plan began to hatch in her mind. "What if we talked to Mr. Milton about taking the Pegasus out with his Peguni to do a fly over to look for—"

"Are you crazy?" Val said. "You're scaring me, because you're sounding too much like your brother."

"Come on, Sarah," Allie said, looking between her and Val, "Be serious. Like, that's why Aunt Valkyrie and your mom are out there covering the area from the air. Seasoned warriors, okaaay."

Sarah's shoulders slumped. "All right. Fine. It was just an idea. I hate feeling like we're all helpless, and the only person taking action—my brother—is taking the totally wrong action."

"If you're gonna do something insane, I'm out." Val folded his arms over his chest.

"Me, too," Allie said, stomping a foot. "The only way I'm going out there is if we're just going to look at the beautiful horses, not try to attempt a raid with them. Promise me, Sarah."

"Okay, okay," Sarah muttered. "It was just an idea, like I said."

Allie's shoulders relaxed. "I bet they are really pretty."

"They're magnificent," Sarah said, staring toward the door.

Val shrugged and looked up the steep steps. "Okay, but it's getting late, so it'd hafta be a quick run. And that door is really hard to open, so…I don't know. I don't have a flashlight, so when I shut the hatch behind us, it's lights out till we get to the top, and that's assuming I can get the hatch up there open—could take a while."

"Can't you just leave this one cracked while we run up, see the stables, then come right back." Allie's pleading gaze went from Sarah to Val.

"It would be easier," Val said, considering the battle he'd fought to open the door.

"That's a hell of a security risk," Sarah said. "I dunno."

"All right," Allie said, dejected. "Some other time, like five years from now, when they lift the outdoor ban."

"What could it hurt, Sarah?" Val said, letting out a long breath. "Right now, while every staff member and most of security is in emergency meetings or working round the clock on research, this is the emptiest I've seen the halls. No reason for any students to come here even without the place being on lockdown. If there was ever a time to go for it, it would be now, and I think Mr. Milton would be cool with us coming."

* * *

"Do you see anything?" Donnie yelled into his PIU, squinting toward the waning sun.

"No," Al radioed back, diving low enough to buzz the fields.

"Tell him to come on, call him back," Wil said in an urgent tone. "This was stupid, and it's not gonna work.

Donnie pointed at Al. "You see how strong he is? You see that wingspan? Like…those aren't Valkyrie wings, his mom is part Powers Angel. Those wings don't even get dirty."

"Call your buddy back before I do!" Wil said, then dropped the Tactical magnetic charge he was creating and that was arcing between his PIU and Donnie's. "I'm serious. Before he gets hurt."

"All right, fine," Donnie said, and then spoke into his unit. "Wil said to come back. He wants to stop—and if he convinces Ayana's girls to stop, Miguel won't be able to keep Mojo stunned by himself."

"Tell Wil to stop being a wuss," Al shouted back, squinting. "I see something moving, man. Something right near the edge of the dead zone."

"Tell your boy to get away from there!" Wil shouted. "It's demon distortion. The forest is crawling. If he gets too close, the negative magnetic pull will drag him in like a whirlpool! Get him outta there!"

* * *

"I know they say three times a charm, but three times in one day?" Mr. Milton smiled at Sarah even as he shook his head. "Well, your friend is in for a surprise—I just brought them all in, barn's full."

Delighted Allie ran behind Mr. Milton, but Sarah and Val hung back. Sarah wanted to ask him about potentially using the horses to help create a wider search party, but the look on Val's face made her temporarily hold her thoughts.

"That was nice, what you did for her. She really feels left out, with 'Cinth sick and everything. This means a lot to her." Sarah stepped in close to Val, glad he hadn't put his shirt back on, and touched the dark bruise on his face. This time he didn't pull away. "I'm so sorry. I wish I had healing powers like my mom so I could just erase what Al did. He was wrong."

"You do have healing powers," Val said quietly, staring down at her.

"I was gonna ask you about that, laddie—quite a shiner. Who gave it to ya?" Mr. Milton said, surprising them with his proximity and raising his eyebrows in a way that made Sarah and Val jump apart.

"Long story, sir," Val said, clearing his throat and walking down the barn's center aisle.

"Always is, laddie," Mr. Milton said thoughtfully.

"Oh, my goodness!" Allie exclaimed, running from one stall to another. "They're beautiful!"

"Watch out for—"

Allie's scream made every animal in the barn erupt in whinnies and start kicking their stall doors. She hit the ground butt first as Sophocles charged out of his pen, pawing the ground, clearly ready for war.

"What is it, boy?" Mr. Milton said, trying to calm the agitated stallion. "I haven't seen him like this since we lost those two fliers.

Allie covered her head, and suddenly Peggi was whinnying in such distress that Sarah ran and let her out of her stall to comfort her as Val dragged Allie to safety.

"Milton, Milton," Mrs. Hogan said, running into the barn, wand raised and sparking. "One of the first years, that Neteru boy Alejandro, went out on a stupid attempt to find those missing students and got sucked into the energy of the back forest—that poor boy is in the dead zone!"

"Find Titan Troy. He's the only one strong enough to hold Sophocles!" Mr. Milton yelled. "Call Professor Razor immediately!"

"No!" Sarah hollered as Val took off running and glided into flight.

"Call him back!" Mr. Milton said shouting.

"It's my brother!" Sarah yelled, running alongside Peggi. "Val's his best friend, a Valkyrie. He can't leave Al out there any more than I can!"

Mrs. Hogan, Mr. Milton and Allie ran into the barnyard as the huge red stallion broke free, not waiting on Titan Troy and went airborne in the war party.

"We've got to stop him!" Mrs. Hogan shouted, sending useless glamour sparks toward the red stallion.

"Give it up, love," her husband said. "That's Hannibal's charger, and the boy who went down is a Neteru heir. Sophocles will die looking for him. Call Headmistress Stone and Headmaster Shabazz," he ordered her. "Tell them the Neteru children and their friend are in imminent danger!"

Chapter 31

The images battering her mind were so horrible that Sarah pressed her face to Peggi's neck and squeezed her eyes shut. Her brother was in mortal danger. She not only felt it, but saw it all in a terrible, intense vision.

Brutal magnetic force clawed at his body like a riptide current, the tendrils of its dark energy tangling his body in their horrifying grip. He lost altitude at a breath-stealing velocity, making the gnarled twists of black tree limbs seem as though they were reaching for him, yearning for his body and blood. Unable to fight gravity, he slammed into a blackened oak. They both heard and felt his wing snap just like a dead branch.

Sarah cried out at the same time Alejandro released a long yell of agony that echoed as his body continued to careen from snapping branch to snapping branch before finally coming to rest in a heap on the dank forest floor.

Groaning, she felt the pain in his shoulder stabbing into his back and spine as he finally opened his eyes and turned to survey the damage, only to quickly shut them again. But she saw what was coming for him.

"Get up," she screamed, making Peggi fly faster.

She wanted to hurl as nausea roiled in Alejandro's stomach. One of his glorious wings was broken. Jagged bone had torn through the skin and bloodied the once-pristine white feathers, which were now gray and covered with filth.

Panting, her brother couldn't even drag himself to the base of the tree. "Oh, God, oh, God, oh God, this hurts," he whispered between his fangs, then let out another scream as the bone slid at an odd angle. "Oh, Jesus…" Blood and saliva mixed in his mouth until the pain finally made him hurl.

Two inches from his own vomit, all he wanted to do was die—until he heard the howls. Shuddering and clutching the Peguni's mane, tears wet Sarah's face as terror made her repeatedly call out to him, "Al, get up! Get up!"

Sudden adrenaline helped him lift his head. His keen hearing picked up the sound of snuffles in the distance, footfalls, snapping branches. Frantic, he glanced around for anything he could use as a weapon. The ground was barren. Gnarled roots were so thick and dug in so deeply that even if he'd been uninjured, they would have been impossible to break lose. The rocks that bit into his skin were the crests of boulders, mammoth and half buried.

Survival instinct told him that he had to move. He seemed to be straining toward Sarah's insistent calls. Something quiet and deadly inside his mind told him that, as much as the broken wing hurt, getting eaten alive by walkers would be horrific and a hundred times worse. As soon as the thought crossed his mind, Sarah screamed, almost feeling his pending death. Her brother had to get up! He'd lost himself momentarily to despair, until a lonely howl cut through his pain and brought him back to reason.

Alejandro clawed the ground and finally pushed himself up with one arm, then clambered to his feet, wincing, sweat pouring off his face and favoring the left wing as he stumbled forward. He tried to remain quiet, stopping every few feet to pant like he was giving birth, blood running from his mouth where his fangs had punctured his tongue. Revenge was far away from his mind now, seemed so pointless as he struggled to live. How many times had his mom told him that he couldn't bargain with God? How many times had Nana Marlene said the same thing? Sarah said a silent prayer—Dear God, please save my brother!

Al slumped against a tree trunk for a moment to spit blood and gasp for air. “I swear, God,” he rasped out, eyes closed, “I’ll change my ways. Just get me out of here in one piece.”

After a moment he opened his eyes and saw a drop of blood from his wound hit the top of his sneaker, then watched as the black earth slid over this shoe, as though licking it. When it receded, it left black, wriggling maggots in its wake, and as he turned back to look at his path, he saw that everywhere he’d bled there stood a small, gargoylelike demon with red gleaming eyes, savoring his life essence.

“Run!” Sarah shouted against the wind.

Run. His mind shouted the command. *Run*.

So he did.

A sea of thousands of glowing red eyes and tiny, slimy, deformed demon bodies gave chase. Branches slapped his face and jarred his injured wing, making him cry out, but he had to push on. Glowing golden eyes suddenly opened in a huge tree as he knocked into it in passing. Vicious vampire bats rose up like a dark cloud from its branches, coalesced into a black funnel and then bore down on him, tearing up trees by the roots with the splintering force of a tornado.

Al zigzagged as if he were running a football play, and the effort paid off as the bats saw the gargoyles chasing what they considered their meal. The two groups of predators collided in a vicious, snarling, high-pitched battle. Small black beetles and scorpions poured over the ridge in a nasty carpet, sending him in a different direction that he was sure was taking him farther into the darkness.

It was as though the darkness was corralling him like a farm animal to be butchered—exhausting him, sending him this way and that, until pain, blood loss and fatigue would win.

Heavy branches broke before him, all around him. He spun wildly, knowing he was surrounded, holding the injured wing. And then they stepped from behind the trees, eyes vacant, teeth yellow and twisted, mouths black holes…hands reaching.

Complete terror shot through Al's nervous system and connected to Sarah's as he looked around wildly and spotted a path that had the fewest of the circling walkers. He stared at one of them, determined to lower his good shoulder and take it out in a football rush, but suddenly it screamed and held its face as its head exploded. He looked at the one behind it, and the same thing happened, and then they all started coming at him.

Al leaped over the two shuddering bodies. His silver stare and his fangs were his only defense. Then something huge came out of the thicket and lunged. He didn't see it, just felt it coming and had only seconds to go down on one knee. The attacker hurtled over his head in a blur, then began to take out the walkers like bowling pins.

Sarah was glad he didn't wait to watch the carnage. Her voice was hoarse now from screaming into the whipping wind. Her brother's internal sense of direction was beginning to return, his Neteru homing sense. Together they could hear the bone-crunching battle going on between what they now knew from the growls was a werewolf and the walkers. The fight for food—human blood—was to the death, but Alejandro and Sarah couldn't count on it lasting for long.

A stabbing pain shot into his third eye. His sister's voice was screaming his name. Val, airborne, was yelling that he was on the way. Alejandro stopped for a second, coughing blood, getting his bearings, then headed off toward their voices and the light.

* * *

The huge red stallion crashed through the green fields just before the land turned black. Val glided to a running stop, and Peggi and Sarah alit beside him. She slid to the ground and saw that her Collectors were going wild, screeching and squealing and running between her and Sophocles. The warhorse reared and pranced, his loud vocal protest added to the stomping of his hooves.

"We can't take him in there, Sarah. He can't spread his wings, could break a leg. I've gotta go in on foot, find Al and bring him out, and then we'll all get out of here on the horses. You stay—"

"Not on your life! He's my brother, and you're…special. So hell no, I'm not staying out here in the dark just waiting to hear you eaten."

"Then what?" Val said, spreading his arms in question. "We don't even know where he is!"

"He'll find me," Sarah said. "I'm his twin…well, at least we shared the same womb. And I know this much about war horses—they go in where angels fear to tread. My parents flew them right into Hell, and that forest's a portal to Hell, so we ride."

Sophocles bowed to allow Val to mount him, and Peggi went down low and whinnied for Sarah to hop back on as Beep and Bop ran headlong into the darkness. At a breakneck gallop, Peggi led the way, her unicorn horn turning a hot glowing white and then discharging a laserlike blast that blasted away enough trees for Sophocles to spread his wings. Beep and Bop scampered up trees and leaped over boulders, keeping pace and slashing out with showy claws as they ran.

"This is how they said it was done!" Sarah shouted, feeling something new and indefinable snap to life inside her. Her brother's life was at stake; there was nothing scarier than that. If her shadows could help them now, so be it.

They had to get to Alejandro! It no longer mattered that she'd always been afraid of the dark, always scared of what might come crawling out from under the bed. But as Peggi white-lighted a flight path, Sophocles torched everything beneath him, and Beep and Bop scampered beside her, a sense of power rose within her, even as dark and threatening shadows closed in behind her. A war cry burst forth from her lungs, raced up her throat and cut through the night. Beep and Bop jetted in front of her, inking the passage and attacking anything that entered the path.

"Lelelelelelelele!" she shrieked, swooping over Harpies and gargoyles and thick-bodied black serpents, Sophocles left everything burning in their wake, and then—finally—she saw a small form huddled by a tree.

"Down there!" Sarah shouted, urging Peggi forward.

Sophocles landed behind her, prancing, nervous, alert for anything as Sarah jumped off her mount and ran to her brother. Val finally got Sophocles to stop dancing long enough for him to get down, and he followed Sarah to Al's side, but when they tried to hoist him up, he let out a blood-curdling scream.

"My wing, man! Not that side—don't touch me!"

Black beetles and maggots already covered the bloodied flesh where the broken bone protruded.

"Oh, God," Sarah said as Val helped her drag Al over to the horses.

He'd lost a sneaker, his clothes were bloody, dirty and torn, and more maggots infested his hair. Peggi backed up nervously at the sight and smell of him, and Sophocles reared.

"They won't carry him like this," Sarah said, staring at Val as her brother passed out in their arms.

"He ain't heavy, he's my brother," Val said, hoisting Al's entire dead weight in both arms. He held him around the waist, Al's back to his chest. "If I carry him like this, I can follow the horses in the air." Val closed his eyes as beetles scuttled from Al's body up Val's chest, one even crawling up the side of his face. "Let's go!"

But just as Sophocles opened his wings for takeoff, the huge, golden-eyed werewolf that had been chasing Alejandro barreled through the trees. Peggi and Sophocles charged side by side. Beep and Bop let out a simultaneous high-pitched shriek and attacked. Then a huge translucent entity with a cruel face, bat wings and a massive spade-shaped tail hurtled toward the werewolf. The small Collectors dashed away and threaded themselves between Sarah's legs.

"Sarah!" Val came down, clearly torn between airlifting his friend and going back for her.

The werewolf went airborne toward her in the fragile seconds while Val lowered Al's body. The demon lobbed a cinderblock punch that knocked the werewolf off course. Peggi leapt, spearing the beast through the temple, and Sophocles scorched the wolf's body the second Peggi yanked her horn free. The beast roared a final death call as the red stallion's massive golden hooves crushed its skull. Then Beep and Bop pounced on the carcass, wrangling it out of sight through a small fissure in the ground.

The huge demon saluted the horses, who both reared and pawed the air in triumph, then Peggi went down on one knee so Sarah could ride.

"You kids get out of here," Mr. Hubert shouted, taking human form again. "I'll keep the rest back while you all high-tail it!"

Sarah climbed onto the red stallion, waiting for Peggi to take off, reaching over to give the smaller horse a quick pat. She had to let the mare rest; she just wasn't as strong as Sophocles.

"Are you all right? Can you carry him?" Sarah shouted to Val as they took to the air.

He nodded, even as he strained to hold onto Alejandro. "I am a Valkyrie! This is what we do. We airlift the dead and wounded to safety. Our motto is 'Be valiant, be victorious!' We never drop a warrior!"

Peggi's shrill whinny made Sarah clutch Sophocles' muscular red neck more tightly. The small Peguni broke formation and dipped down into the green zone.

"Keep going!" Sarah called to Val. "Get Al to the hospital before he goes too far into shock!"

There was no time to argue, no *way* to argue. Peggi was spiraling down like a missile, with Sophocles right on her heels. Both animals touched down, and what Sarah saw in the dark was a boy just a bit older than her brother, curled up in a fetal position.

Stefan was naked, shivering, beginning to turn gray from the contagion; his lips were black, and there were dark circles under his eyes. His upper and lower canines were extended, and his tongue was swollen and beginning to turn black. He held out two gooey, stained PIUs to Sarah, showing her his prize, then clutched them tightly to his chest.

Sophocles and Peggi dashed forward, clearly intending to stomp Stefan to death. Sarah realized that they'd mistaken him for a demon that had slithered out of the dead zone and into the fields where the Fae farmers worked.

"No!" She jumped off the huge war horse and covered Stefan with her own body.

"You'll catch it," he croaked. "Get back."

She shook her head no. "I'm a Neteru, daughter of two Neterus. I'm immune, and so is my brother. If you knew the Shady Path was booby-trapped…then why?"

"I didn't do it," Stefan said shuddering. "I didn't know."

"Why'd you run, then?" She looked at him as tears filled his mysterious gray eyes.

"My whole life, just because of my blood, no one's ever believed in me," he said in a rasp. "They judge who I am before they ever get to know me. Even Headmistress Stone doesn't believe in me anymore, and I don't think Headmaster Shabazz ever did. But I swear, I didn't think those guys would get so high they'd kill themselves. It was supposed to be a party drug—fun, not dangerous. I just distributed what Ernie and Josh made. I'm not a monster. I mean, I guess I am, but not that kind. My mom got scratched by a werewolf when her Guardian team was on a hunt, and my dad couldn't bear to kill her. She was pregnant with me at the time. The moon was full the night I was born.

She had me just before moonrise, then transformed and killed my dad as well as half the compound, before they took her down. The people who lived raised me, watched me, then finally gave me to Headmistress Stone out of fear. My own compound rejected me. The headmistress, she's like my grandmom, too, so why would I do anything to hurt her or the Academy?"

"Okay, but what about the drugs? Those hurt the school," Sarah asked quietly. "And how about whatever Melissa took from you?"

"Yeah, okay, I was making a little profit on the side, running stuff into town and bringing back cool shit for the fellas that they could trade for favors, but I wasn't trying to get anybody killed, and I definitely didn't mastermind how to make blue lady. Melissa lifted some forgetmenot from my stash, and I think she was gonna use it to get back at you guys somehow, 'cause she was jealous of Tam. I didn't want her using it, not for anything. It's some wicked shit that Ernie cooked up. All you have to do is let it dry in a cup, and when somebody fills that cup and drinks, they forget everything. I don't have time for her games and didn't want to be involved. Look at the PIUs when we get back. They've recorded everything that happened out here. If a student gets downed, a PIU keeps taking data like one of the old airline black boxes. They'll prove I didn't hurt anybody."

Deep, resounding sorrow and empathy filled Sarah as she looked at Stefan. For some reason, she believed him. A measure of guilt threaded through her, as well, because she had thought he was involved in everything he'd mentioned. All she could do for a moment was hug herself as she stared at him.

Stefan's voice turned gravelly with emotion as tears rose in his eyes but didn't fall. "Sarah, I had to come out here and right this wrong. Those fliers crash landed, according to their PIUs. They went down hard, but they were strong and weren't hurt too bad. They could've made it out, but while they were trying to find a clearing where they could open their wings, Peter got scratched by a werewolf…and you know the deal. One scratch is all it takes, and then you become a werewolf, too."

He let his breath out hard. "In here, there's no incubation period for anything like that. If you get scratched or bitten, you don't even have to wait till the next full moon—there's an instant transformation, the darkness out here is so intense. Greg didn't even know that Pete had been nicked until suddenly Pete ripped out of his clothes and transformed. It's all on the PIU recordings. Pete got hold of one of Greg's legs and ripped that off first. And that was the least of it. The rest of what I saw on there was really sick, Sarah."

"Oh, my God," Sarah whispered.

"Yeah," Stefan said and then coughed. "Maybe you don't wanna watch the playback, but Pete ate his own best friend. Beetles and slugs covered both PIUs when Mr. Hubert and Professor Razor went looking. I guess they eventually found both guys' clothes and whatever was left of Greg, so they figured both guys were dead."

"That's so awful," Sarah whispered, wrapping her arms around her waist. "But I don't understand how the contagion got in the school."

"Neither do I, really. You said the Path was booby-trapped? I can't help you there. All I know is Peter knew the school inside and out. Was a Spec, a strong Valkyrie flier, plus a serious Clav. He was addicted to blue, and after he was supposedly dead, he couldn't just walk back into the Academy to get some, that's for sure. So I'm thinking he used the Shady Path to get in and feed his habit, while hiding in the green zone taking down livestock, and the more blue he did, the more he needed, until he needed it so bad that he came in that night—hungry for blue, hungry for human flesh. I felt him. I was in there. I did the Shady Path the night you guys got attacked. I was in there and about to take a hit when the hair on my neck stood up, and then I was out of there. You make sure Tami knows that. Make sure she knows that no matter what. And yeah, I supplied Brent, but I wasn't about to help him break your cousin down so he could get what he wanted from her. Hell no!"

"I thought you and Brent were tight," Sarah said cautiously.

"He's a business partner. Period. But he's got everything, you know? He's rich and spoiled and got both parents, and he was working on your cousin 'cuz he wanted to use her to expand his influence. But your cousin is strong. She didn't break, and it pissed him off. I loved it. Privileged SOB."

His story rendered Sarah mute for a moment, but then she pressed forward as panic bubbled up inside her. "I understand how the guys died, but Ayana and everyone else who's missing, like Art and Casey and Alexis, and Josh and Ernie. Do you think, Peter...?" The question was too horrible to voice, so she just hugged herself more tightly and practically held her breath waiting on Stefan's answer.

He stared at Sarah like a man who needed to purge his soul before he died, even if it was to someone he wasn't sure would even believe him. She waited and let him talk, hoping her eyes would convey trust and the fact that every fiber in her said he was telling the truth.

"I don't know. All I can tell you is that I left the Shady Path that night because I could feel something stalking me in there. Something way stronger and crazier than me. I admit it. Strengthwise, I'd be nothing to Pete. He was a fully transformed alpha. A wolf always knows when another wolf is present, and when an attack is going down," Stefan said in a low, raspy murmur. "So as soon as I felt Pete, I was out. Didn't wanna get blamed for something I didn't do or catch a silver slug because somebody didn't understand. I don't know why everybody got so sick so fast, but he was in the Shady Path and then came in the building. Maybe the energy he left behind is what everyone's calling a booby-trap. I don't know. But a demon-infected werewolf, one that's a flesh eater, is from the Dark Realm, and anything coming from Hell is dragging along nothing but pure contagion."

"But, you didn't get sick right away."

“Wolf genetics…already got the dirty strain in me, so my system isn’t gonna get shocked to hell as fast as a hundred-percent human, I guess. Anyway, after I heard he attacked you guys, I went after Tami to warn her, but I overheard that your brother and his boyz had a bounty on my head. Then everybody started getting sick, so I came out here thinking maybe I could get the PIUs and fix things somehow.”

“How’d you get out here, though?” She tried to help him up, but he was heavy, and so weak that they both fell.

“I stunned Mojo. I didn’t want anyone knowing where I was or what I was doing, ’til I could find the missing units. Needed to clear my name once and for all, or die trying—who wants to live with everyone thinking you’re a monster or even some exotic oddity…sexy but dangerous? That’s why I can’t stand Melissa—she just wanted to brag about doing a wolf. Tami’s not like that.” He coughed and wheezed and had to take a moment to catch his breath after his long confession.

“Anyway, I’m a good tracker—got that wolf nose. It’s how I could always harvest the right ingredients in the right concentrations for that crazy bastard Josh. I knew I could find the PIUs if I could put my nose to the ground. I knew I could, and I did.”

“But your clothes…you’re naked. It looks like you transformed out here, and that looks bad for you, Stefan. Like you wanted to go over to the other side or something.”

“If you go into the dead zone smelling human, you won’t last long.” Stefan motioned to a small, dark pile off in the distance. “I went in, rolled in the scent of the place…the place where Greg died, found the PIUs and was trying to get back to the school when I started to feel like crap. The searchers, even Mr. Hubert, didn’t know where to look. You have to know the wolf, be a part of the wolf, to know where to look.” He fell silent then, clearly weakening.

Feeling the pressure of time, Sarah stood. “We should get back.” She ran over to grab Stefan’s clothes and spoke to Sophocles as she passed. “I know he smells like walking death and werewolf dung, but he’s a student from the Academy. And as a Neteru, I’m asking you to take him home to Nana Marlene.” She glanced over at Beep and Bop the second they leaped out of the shadows and started heading for Stefan. “No!” she told them firmly. “He’s a friend.” She shook her head as they fussed and hid behind Peggi’s legs.

Sarah pulled out her PIU and thrust Stefan’s clothes at him. “Put on whatever you can so Sophocles will carry you. Pants would be nice. Hurry!” Punching in the alarm code, she called Sarina. “I need you to sync to the two PIUs Stefan is holding…and let Nana know we’ve got incoming wounded—Al broke his wing and Val will be there with him any minute, Stefan’s got the virus but he’s not the bad guy, Peter Matthews is. He turned, and he’s still alive.”

* * *

Titan Troy greeted her at the barnyard. A full Fae infantry was waiting, along with a complete medical staff. They collected Stefan’s nearly unconscious form and Mr. Milton pried the PIUs from his hand.

“What’d I tell you, lassie? Sometimes the gold is in the pile of manure. Once Headmistress Stone knew Peter was the one behind the sickness, she could see where the energy fabric on the Shady Path was ripped, and then she was able to set the exact calibration on the crystal pyramids over the patients’ beds.”

“But, Mr. Milton—did Val come in okay with my brother?”

“Aye, and he did a fine job carrying his first battlefield victim. A couple years of lifting weights and he’ll be able to carry Sophocles.

The two horses pranced, and Sarah hugged them both. “They were brave. We couldn’t have done it without them,” she said, watching as the Fae medics took Stefan away.

“You were brave, lassie. All you kids were. But we want you inside. Peter Matthews is still on the loose, and I’m afraid we can’t save him. He’s too far gone…he’s eaten human flesh.”

* * *

Sarah stood in the infirmary looking down at Hyacinth, Val by her side. Her friend’s face had begun to clear. Protected as she was by the dwennimmen ward Ayana had given them, she’d been the first to respond to the new energy treatment. Sarah brushed Hyacinth’s damp bangs back, glad to see natural color in her friend’s face.

“Nana Marlene said they’re all gonna recover,” Val murmured, squeezing Sarah’s hand. “You’ve got a lotta heart, girl,” he said, nodding approvingly.

“*You’ve* got a lot of heart, Val,” Sarah said quietly. She looked at him and then up to the large, slowly spinning transparent pyramid filled with green and turquoise and silvery light rotating above Hyacinth’s bed. “That was some airlift. All those things crawling on you, and you still didn’t drop my brother. Don’t know if I could have done it.”

“They blasted me with white light as soon as I touched down and the crawlers got off me. Medics took Al, then Mrs. Hogan sent me to her shower and bippity-boppity-booped me up some new clothes.”

Sarah smiled. “Me, too.”

“Let’s go check on Al,” he said, holding her hand and gently pulling her along.

Suddenly she stopped. “Where’s Tami?”

Val shrugged. "Probably with Donnie and Miguel and Wil, I guess…or back in the girls' dorm with Allie, Jess and the gang. Everybody is pretty stressed out. The guys are probably waiting to find out if they've been expelled for being up on the platform and going along with Al's crazy scheme. We're in trouble, too—even Allie—for leaving school and going to the stables."

Sarah nodded, but worry still tugged at her insides. With Hyacinth, Stefan *and* Al in the infirmary, it was hard to believe Tami wasn't there, standing vigil. But she started walking again; she needed to see with her own eyes that her brother was going to be all right.

Al was resting quietly on his stomach, his damaged wing folded in and bandaged. Sarah went to her brother and kissed his forehead.

He opened his eyes and groaned. "Thanks, sis…Val. Can't believe you're still talking to me."

"We're cool, bro," Val said.

"You know, Al," Sarah said, "Stefan wasn't the one who attacked you. In fact, he risked his life to save this school by going—"

Al held up his hand. "I know, I know. Nana Marlene sent all the images. She even kicked my ass mentally while I was unconscious."

Sarah laughed, releasing all the tension that had built up in her nervous system. "Serves your dumb…I mean, I love you. If you'd died out there, half of me would have died, too, so stop being so reckless. At least for a little while." She bent and kissed his forehead again as he slurred an apology and drifted off to sleep.

"Walk you back to your dorm?"

"Yeah, thanks," Sarah said quietly as Val's long fingers laced through hers.

They walked for a long time without talking, which was so nice…just companionable silence, lost in their own thoughts, lost in each other. But her prayer the entire time was insistent—*Please, God, let them find Ayana.*

Both she and Val glanced at the library as they passed and then looked away. Something new and different and exciting and forbidden and private had been opened within them outside the Shady Path, but it was much too fragile to contemplate right now.

Mr. Anansi scurried under the door and ran up the wall. The strangeness of that made both Sarah and Val stop and stare. Val tilted his head and listened hard.

"What?" Sarah whispered.

"Shhhh!" he said quickly. "I coulda sworn I heard Miss Tillie scream."

Sarah looked around, the open hatch doors leading from the school up to the field flashing in her mind, blue streaks of something not human covering the floor. Beep and Bop appeared and started jumping up and down. Suddenly she sucked in a huge breath, pulling Val forward. "Run!"

They were down the hall like a shot, and a split second later the library door exploded. Alarms went off, and heavy footfalls echoed behind them. Val glanced over his shoulder and started stripping off his shirt. Sarah turned to look and saw a half transformed werewolf bearing down on them, gray eyes gleaming. Val grabbed her by the waist and flew, gaining momentum as the beast gave chase, a dozen Collectors racing behind it. A blast from a pump shotgun left cordite residue in the air but the wolf kept coming. Sarah knew the security guards had to be careful not to cause a deadly ricochet that could hit her and Val.

Titan Troy's voice boomed from behind them, shouting for them to go to the Great Hall, and Headmaster Shabazz added, "Now!"

Doors opened magically as Val swooped through the corridors, catching up to more students running in the same direction. The goal was clear: draw the beast out of the building where it could be surrounded, and where Val had the aerial advantage and could help protect the fleeing students.

Sarah glanced back as Val flew up the stairs and saw the beast unfurl massive leathery wings marred by scraggly patches of fur. It was stronger, faster and wasn't carrying the weight of a passenger. Headmaster Shabazz was giving chase, fully transformed, but he couldn't catch the beast as it spiraled ahead of him onto the platform. The beast snapped at Sarah's feet, and she drew them up, screaming.

Tapestries lit, dragons awakened. Fae archers ran up the pyramid steps and took aim, but held their fire because of Val and Sarah's orbiting flight.

There was nothing for her to hold onto as Val clutched her in front of him, and she could feel his fatigue. His palms were sweaty, and she began to slide, kicking her screams up a notch. Then the center opening from the great pyramid platform up toward the floating library entrance above it belched out a long-bodied dragon streaming into battle, his form sinuous and seemingly neverending. Gongs sounded inside the Great Hall, vibrating the air and hitting both fliers like a sonic boom.

Thrown off his trajectory, Val plummeted, his grip on Sarah continuing to slip. At the last moment two lithe dragons wrapped them like brightly colored ribbons and deposited both students gently on the platform. Headmaster Shabazz paced protectively in panther form around them and Headmistress Stone raised her lightning-charged walking stick as though conducting a cosmic orchestra. Light shot from the tip of the staff. Mojo caught the charge and shocked the air, hitting the demon so hard that it stopped falling and actually hung in mid-air for a second.

Out of nowhere, Professor Razor appeared, hovering, black wings glistening, his silver scythe swooshing through the air as he severed the head of the beast. As the creature fell, Mojo gulped the flaming pieces, then belched.

Sarah looked at Val, who looked back at her. No words could come close.

CHAPTER 32

"Yo, hold up," Wil said, catching Tami by the arm. "I want to ask you something."

Tami yanked free of Wil's hold, tears streaming down her face. "I can't talk to you right now, okay? Whatever questions you have will just hafta wait." She wiped at her face angrily and then hugged herself. "It's all because of me, don't you get it? Stefan only went out there to prove he wasn't a monster and now he's half dead with the contagion. Al almost got eaten in the dead zone. Even this whole bullshit with Melissa Gray was from her being pissed at me…not Sarah, not any of them—*me*!"

Wil looked around the vacant hall and then at Mr. Everett's door. "So what are you planning to do? Go throw yourself into the portal and disappear? It's not even there, Tami. It got shut down, remember?"

She stopped walking, leaned her head back and closed her eyes. "Damn…Yeah, yeah, I remember." She opened her eyes and looked into Mr. Everett's abandoned classroom, then dragged her fingers through her hair in frustration. "I just wanted to get away from this school, maybe go rogue…go into town, blend in with the Regulars, just be away from all this pressure and everybody looking at me like *I'm* some kind of virus. Just for a while."

"Tami, it wasn't your fault," Wil said quietly.

She groaned and turned away, allowing her back to hit the wall, then new tears brimmed and fell. "Just my luck they closed up every ticket to town, huh?"

"C'mon…I know everybody is gonna be worried about you, looking for you. Maybe we can go to the infirmary and—"

"No! I can't go back there right now," she said wrapping her arms around her waist. "The guys are both messed up because of me." She bit her lip. "Stefan could die…and Christ, Al broke his wing—what if he can never fly again?"

"Look, I know it's awkward." Wil let out a long, weary sigh. "I don't want to run into Val holding Sarah's hand or some crap like that, either…him being the hero of the day and all. It sucks."

Tami pushed off the wall and began walking quickly, forcing Wil to jog to catch up to her.

"You…like…them both, don't you?" Wil said, catching up to her at the end of the hall.

"How can something like that happen?" she asked quietly, wiping her face with both hands.

"I was hoping you could tell me. That's what I wanted to ask you. Like…do you think Sarah is—"

"Playing you and Val like this bitch played my sister's boyfriend—or like you played me?" Patty stepped out of the shadows with a sneer, her complexion still gray.

"I never played you," Wil said, stepping in front of Tami, but she pushed her way around him, ready to fight.

"So what happened in Boston stays in Boston, huh?"

"It was over when you started acting crazy and helping Josh and Ernie distribute," Wil said, lifting his chin. "I tried to protect you—even lied for you and told everybody you didn't do that, hoping you'd get a clue and stop!" he shouted, his voice filled with disgust.

"I was your first, Wil," Patty said in a scornful hiss.

"And you would have been my last," Wil said, swallowing hard.

"I was there when your mother died, and you picked that flat-chested, skinny little nobody over me?" Patty shrieked.

"Go on! Call my girl something else, bitch!" Tami shouted, about to lunge forward, but Wil caught her arm.

"Stay out of this, Tami!" he commanded, holding Tami by both arms now and turning away from Patty to face her. "This is between me and Patty, and she needs to get it straight about how I feel about Sarah."

A high-pitched scream of rage was followed by crackling static, and then gale-force winds filled the hall. A dark vortex opened, all three combatants standing at the edge. Wil tried to send an electromagnetic Tactical charge to lasso anything that might anchor him and Tami, but there was nothing for it to hold onto. They fell, clawing the floor.

Centrifugal force simply pulled them in.

* * *

Sarah got up slowly, holding onto Val and her grandmother's hands.

"It's over," her grandmother announced.

Sarah stared up at Professor Raziel, fuming and confused. "Why didn't you come earlier, when we were in the forest?" She shrugged away from her grandmother and Val to get up in the Reaper's face. But to her surprise, he smiled.

"I wasn't late to the party, kiddo. I saw history in the making and just let you work." He turned to Val. "Nice job, flier."

"You didn't…?" Headmistress Stone said, glaring at him and gripping her staff so tightly that it began to spark.

"I told you, if I'm to be her mentor, we have different teaching styles. Tonight that young lady came into her own."

"So you almost let her die!" Val bumped Sarah out of the way to challenge the professor.

Razor lowered his scythe in Val's direction. "Watch it, son…let the adrenaline damp down. Don't go there."

"We almost died!" Sarah shouted, pushing Val out of the way.

"Yeah…quite a rush, isn't it?" Professor Raziel said in a blasé tone. "Taste it, remember it. It'll make you a stronger warrior next time. But the important fact is, you lived."

Sarah was so furious that she could only stare at the ground for a moment…and then she saw them. Tami's and Wil's shadow echoes. Seeing the traces of her friend's footsteps gave her pause. Surely the adrenaline rush and the intensity of it all had boosted her powers in a way she'd never imagined was possible. Beep and Bop came out of hiding from behind Professor Raziel's legs, so agitated that she knew something was horribly wrong. Her gaze shot to the professor and then to her grandmother's exhausted face.

Val grabbed Sarah's arm. "What's wrong?"

"Let her hunt," Professor Raziel said calmly, staring at Headmistress Stone but speaking to Val. "Let her go. This is what she was born to do."

Two seconds later, Nana Marlene's PIU sounded and alarm gongs went off all over the school.

Unable to speak, Sarah tore away from the group and began running, her shadowy little friends nipping at her heels.

"Sarah, wait!" Val yelled.

Nana Marlene, clutching her walking stick, ran behind Sarah, directing the dragons. "She is on a hunt. Val, stay with her!"

Professor Raziel just smiled.

Sound had become muffled. Sarah heard her grandmother call out something behind her, heard the timbre of Val's voice but not the words. Racing through the school corridors, she could see Tami's trail, the most recent one standing out strong and neon, like Wil's. Shadows pulled away from the structures that cast them, following her, running beside her, folding into the walls and out again as she rounded stairwells, jumping half flights to get to where she needed to go.

The moment she entered the purple classroom level, tornado-like winds began to drag her toward an open funnel. She saw the claw marks scratched into the floor and didn't even try to stop as the yawning entrance swallowed her whole.

Sliding, falling, twists and turns, she slipped down the tube as though on a giant water slide. She hit the ground on a pile of hay inside a dark barn, the scent of animals and manure reminiscent of the smells of the stables, and the shadows were everywhere.

* * *

"You brought my son here!" a disbelieving voice shrieked. A backhanded slap caught Patty in the mouth, sending her stumbling backward to hit the floor.

"Mom?" Wil slowly stood, his eyes on the woman wearing a hooded black robe and a huge, golden demonic pentagram swinging from a thick gold chain. "What's going on?" he said, his voice fracturing.

He looked around, holding onto Tami's hand, staring at the students—some of them unconscious, looking lifeless—chained to a wall next to several Fae held by iron shackles. Ernie Scheeler and Josh Abrams were crying but unchained. His gaze fastened on Ayana, who looked exhausted and about to pass out.

"Son, sometimes during war, there are sacrifices," his mother murmured, her sea-green eyes filled with conflict and pain. She waved off the demons that had stepped forward to guard her son and the young woman beside him. "I am now of the Morrigan. Do you know what the word means?"

"Terror, or phantom queen…from Irish mythology," Wil said in a dry rasp. "But…"

"I am a magus. My line is out of Medes, one of many destined to resurrect Lilith to fulfill the prophecy and secure the Antichrist his rightful place at the end of days. Join me, son. Your father took you away from me. He—"

"Told me you were dead!" Wil shouted, tears rising in his eyes. He let go of Tami's hand as if he'd forgotten she was there.

"You see what a liar he is, son," his mother said quietly and stepped forward.

But Wil stepped back. "What are all these people…these students…doing here? What have you done?"

"Draining their talents, that's all…Soon, at midnight during the autumn equinox, each one of them will die on this altar as a blood sacrifice, increasing its power to its fullest potential. The dark magic requires power, as does a resurrection …and the master has been bereft since he lost his beloved Lilith. We will gain his favor and bring Lilith back in time to make sure the heir is placed—"

"Mother, are you insane?" Veins stood out in Wil's neck as the demons hissed at his sides.

"It was your job to compromise him, your job to take his innocence," his mother said, turning on Patty. "But you have failed. He is not ready to step into his inheritance!" She swung out her arm, and a black charge blew the girl against the wall to drop in a crumpled heap. "Is this the Neteru heir?" she asked, pointing to Tami.

"No, Desmonda," Patty whimpered and covered her head. "It's her best friend, but she'll come for her. I know she will."

"You'd better hope so," Desmonda said, her green eyes flickering at the edges. "She was supposed to come for her mother seer," she murmured in a near growl, pointing at Ayana. "But that only brought the adults and could have jeopardized the larger coven! I had to send Peter Matthews back to the school to defend our borders and throw them off our trail! Do you know how much energy it takes to keep a werewolf on a short leash? What use have you been to me? More importantly, what have you done to earn a place at my side…at my son's side? Are you a real Morrigan, or just a pretender, Patty?"

"I have done everything I could for you. Everything. I booby-trapped the portals to keep any Guardians and school staff from following," Patty said quickly, instantly regaining her normal complexion. "I let them think I was sick so I could stay in the infirmary long enough to pick up on their plans while they thought I was unconscious, *and* I brought Ernie and Josh to you safely. I got my sister to swipe the forget-me-not from Stefan's stash, made her think I was going to help her and her stupid friends, without her knowing any of our real goals, just like you asked, and I put it on Ayana's toothbrush, so she could be taken. I did everything you asked."

Ernie looked up, cowering from where he sat on the floor. "Please don't be mad at us, even if you're angry at her. We did our part. We drugged them all just like you wanted so it was easy for Patty to lead them here." He motioned to the pile of bathroom cups and toothbrushes on the altar. "We tainted that stuff like you said and didn't even bury it on school grounds. We sent it back through to you so there'd be no evidence."

Josh nodded emphatically. "We'll keep making your stuff, anything you want—just don't kill us."

"It took us a long time to infiltrate the Guardians," Desmonda said in a near hiss as she turned toward her son, then smiled wickedly at Patty, completely ignoring the two boys. "For years we didn't know where their stronghold was, and their powers were too great for us to locate them, but every citadel has a weakness, and theirs is the children. We only needed one on our side so we could focus our energies to her beacon, then let curiosity and human nature take its course. That is the *only* reason you are still alive, Patricia Gray. Don't make me regret my decision."

"You used to be a Guardian, Mom," Wil sobbed. "You used to fight—"

"We were poor! Living in hostile barracks! Food was scarce, water was scarce—don't judge me for making a choice your father was too weak to make!" She swept away from the altar she'd been tending and drew herself up in front of her son.

"Since the moment I supposedly died, you have experienced nothing but abundance. Boston fell, the East Coast Guardian teams are holed up in tiny villages, like the one above us, or in hiding in big cities, unable to buy or trade because they foolishly resist the mark of the beast. But you had everything you ever wanted. Your stupid father never had a clue as to why he was practically showered by good fortune after I was gone." She held Wil's face. "But now *you* know."

She released him when he jerked his head back. "Why do you think I allowed you to go to the Academy?" She smiled an evil smile and walked back over to her bloody altar. "Because you needed to sharpen your skills, learn their ways, so when it is your turn to become Morrigan, as is your birthright—"

"Never!" Wil shouted. "Death before dishonor!"

"Either way," his mother said coolly. "We'd only bring you back to work with us."

* * *

This time, when the shadows coalesced, Sarah didn't run from them. Instead she followed them deeper into the barn, noting how they stopped at the wall, the same way faint traces of Wil's and Tami's shadow echoes did, then saw that they were joined by another.

Something whooshed past her head and made her jump back. Two red-glowing eyes came out of the nothingness, and she realized that the whoosh had been a shadow, pulling her safely away from a swinging scythe. More eyes appeared, and Beep and Bop leaped at the demons, stealing their attention away from her for a split second. Panic made her drop to the ground to avoid another blade, and she rolled hard, hitting the wall as yet another demon stepped out of nowhere. The moment she touched the wall a trap door opened and she was falling into the blackness of a stone tunnel. But there, in the darkness, a face rimmed in light leaned in and touched her, forehead to forehead.

"Awake," the floating face murmured.

Sarah hit the ground hard, knocking the wind out of her, but Tami's and Wil's collective yells put her instantly on her feet. She saw Ayana weakly reach out to her from the corner of her eye even as a haughty laugh and a chorus of growls filled her ears. Huge beasts with glowering eyes and dripping fangs were closing in on her, but even as she screamed, her attendant shadows swept between their legs. She felt a pulse of energy run down her arms as she reached out to block the demon trying to grab at her, and it exploded, sending soot and embers flying everywhere.

"Get her!" a woman yelled out.

"Mom, *no*!"

Sarah saw Wil send a blue-white Tactical charge toward a hooded woman, but it missed her and exploded a section of an altar dripping with gore instead. Tami's screams could have shattered glass, but when Patty rushed her, Tami's fangs dropped—and then it was Patty's turn to try to get away.

Tami's superior speed and fangs, as well as compound training, soon won out. Patty's lip was bleeding and she was screaming curses. Wil was grappling with a demon as he tried to get to his mother. Sarah sent another shadow pulse toward the altar, further decimating it, as Beep and Bop tore through the demon guards and were first to reach Desmonda.

"What have you done!" she shrieked as the Collectors clawed at her robe and face as the guard demons rushed to her aid, trying to fend off the relentless shadows.

Sarah struggled forward, unable to reach Yaya, chained to the wall with the others. Too many adversaries were coming at her, and coming too fast.

"Don't let the seer get away—we need her alive!" Desmonda shouted. "Her power is necessary! She must be a part of the sacrifice!"

Sarah ducked as bricks and mortar, stones and hay, began to fall. Huge white light streaks blew what was left of the altar into a thousand pieces, sending bits of rotting goats and chickens to splatter against the wall. She covered her head and heard her nana's war cry. A silver scythe moved like a blur, moved like a razor.

Hooves stampeded across the ground. Sarah made herself very small, covering her bleeding ears against demon screeches as the stench of sulfur choked her.

Suddenly a pair of familiar hands caressed her back, and she peered up into her grandmother's face. Half the faculty was there. Professor Raziel clutched his scythe, breathing hard, wings spread. Titan Troy had Desmonda in his grasp as she struggled against Mr. Everett's blue-white energy shackles. Patty Gray was sobbing in Amazon Akoben's custody. Headmaster Shabazz stood on a pile of demon ash, snarling at Ernie Scheeler and Josh Abrams. Sarah glanced around at the trapped students and barely conscious Fae.

The Morrigan was in custody. The captured students, faculty and Fae were talent-drained but alive. The demons that would have escorted Desmonda and Patty to safety had been exterminated, but from the vicious look in the older woman's eyes, she did not consider the battle over.

Sarah knew in her gut that there had to be more of them, more turncoat Guardians, more members of Desmonda's wicked coven. The woman herself had referred to a larger coven. One Morrigan and a bunch of students hadn't pulled this off alone. Desmonda was right. The battle *was* far from over. But as the wrongdoers were secured, Sarah's grandmother walked over to her and stroked her hair.

"C'mon, baby," her nana murmured, pulling her up into her arms. "Let's go home."

CHAPTER 33

Epilogue

Three Weeks Later…

Once again, the entire school sat in the Great Hall, but this time it was early evening. And this time Sarah wasn't embarrassed that all her crazy relatives had shown up to sit at the back of the hall to watch the award presentations. She also wouldn't dwell on her disappointment because her father had apparently refused to attend. He wouldn't ruin this for her; she was a Shadow and proud of it.

She looked around, smiling. It felt great to be alive, even though she had no idea what to expect for the Autumn Equinox dance.

Headmistress Stone was bedecked in silver flowing robes, while her husband stood proud and regal before the school in a midnight-blue African-inspired suit. The entire faculty graced the main stage, adorned in their finest—all except Mrs. Gillison, who, for obvious reasons, was listening over the school broadcast system from the pool where she swam with her husband.

Titan Troy looked uncomfortable in a suit, and Amazon Aziza Akoben looked like she couldn't wait for the ceremony to be over so everyone could party in the gym. She looked hot, though, in her tanned leather halter and miniskirt, sporting gold wrap-up-the-leg sandals.

Even Razor was there, and Sarah had to smile, because he looked like he was going to a funeral in his black shoes, black suit, black shirt and black tie—but of course she wouldn't dare laugh to his face.

Sarah sat next to Val in her first formal gown, praying that the color she'd chosen would be okay, all the while staving off belly butterflies that simply wouldn't go away. She was wearing jewel green for the Fae good luck Mr. Milton always talked about, the green pastures and the beauty of seeing green life from so high in the air above. Tonight she actually felt beautiful.

And Val…He looked so handsome in a navy suit. She adjusted her spaghetti straps and hoped she could dance in her brand-new high heels. Al was sitting on the other side of Val, and then came Tami, a knockout in red. Donnie and Miguel book-ended Akiba and Adele, pretty in pastel pink and lilac. Allie simply glowed, the deep berry she was wearing perfect for her, and Aaron Wu and Jim Wilkerson both cleaned up nice. But best of all was seeing Hyacinth looking radiant in turquoise on Jim's arm.

Ayana, too, looked happy, and for that, Sarah was glad. The tall, lanky kid from track, Randall Chapman, sat by her side in his black suit looking positively hot to death while Ayana was drop-dead gorgeous in gold silk. Maybe one day, Sarah thought, she'd be able to aspire to such fashion greatness. But until then, Jess and the gang kept things interesting. She was just glad to have a second chance…glad to have gotten her Yaya and 'Cinth back. If life could just stay this way…

But it was hard to be completely happy, thinking of Wil and all he'd lost. Even though a part of her heart would always belong to him, he'd even lost her—to Val.

Sarah looked down at her clasped hands. Worse than anything, Wil had lost his mother—again. She couldn't imagine losing her own mother once, let alone the trauma of losing her twice. Wil had also lost his first love twice, and she couldn't be to him what he wanted her to be. Sadness filled her, and she allowed it to settle in for a moment before trying to expel it with a deep cleansing breath as she briefly closed her eyes. Wil was a good person, but all of this was bound to change him. She just hoped he'd still like her as a friend when he came back to school. He had taken a leave of absence to join his father and return to their compound to grieve, before attending his mother's and Patty's trials. She said a little prayer for him and then returned her eyes to the stage as her thoughts went elsewhere.

She didn't even want to know what they did to the Morrigan. Treason was a capital offense, but these days, did that mean instant death or lifelong imprisonment? she wondered. Melissa's fate was also still up in the air, though guilt by association didn't seem fair, and Melissa and her friends really hadn't been involved in the whole nightmare Patty had conspired in. Sarah tried to think about the dance as the ceremony droned on, but assembly was always a pain, and she didn't have the patience.

The Gray sisters' groupies had told all. Freaked out, they gave up everybody by name and no doubt would have behaved, had they been allowed to attend the dance. But after the whole fiasco of swiping drugs, bullying some students and spell-casting against others, their privileges had been suspended for the rest of the year. Still, not getting expelled alongside Josh, Ernie and Brent—the masterminds—probably outweighed not coming to the dance.

Sarah glanced at Stefan, who sat alone but looked good. His charcoal-gray suit matched his eyes, and when he noticed her looking at him, he gave her a brief nod, which she returned. Yes, she'd save him a dance, and no, neither her brother nor Val had to understand why. She was sure Tami would dance with him, too. Time and truth healed a lot of wrongs. His heroism and attempt to right the things he'd done wrong had earned him a well-deserved pass, though if he was caught so much as blinking wrong now, he'd be ejected from school on his behind. Still, it was very cool to know she'd be training with him in Shadows this year.

The big thing everyone was waiting for was the award for heroism under fire. A field trip to town was up for grabs. Until then, Headmistress Stone's voice seemed so far away, when all Sarah wanted to do was laugh with her girlfriends and dance, especially to that one special slow song with Val. Everyone else was restless, too; not a soul was really listening as they all thought ahead to the celebration. Special food and magical treats would be courtesy of the Fae, whose music would be playing down in the repaired gym. Her mind drifted to the pretty blue lit corridor; she couldn't wait to see what the faeries had done with their special blue fireflies for the dance.

When they called her and Val forward to accept the award, she thought she'd have a heart attack!

Val helped her up by her elbow, and she stood on wobbly heels. "If you fall, I'll catch you and just fly you to the front," he murmured softly in her ear, and then began to walk her to the stage.

She smiled, so happy that she almost bit her bottom lip to keep from squealing, and then remembered that she was never supposed to do that while wearing lip gloss, per Ayana and Jess's orders.

Thunderous applause rocketed through the Great Hall. Sarah covered her mouth as her grandmother read out their achievements, wondering if she ought to pinch herself to be sure she was awake. Val gave her a wink. She returned it with a smile, then glanced around the Great Hall. One minute all the shadows looked normal, the next they did a little jig. Professor Razor gave her a nod from the stage. Jonathan Federman and Alexis Woodrow started a cheer. Yeah, this was real, and so much better than a dream. She didn't care that Razor said she had a ton more work to do. Tonight she felt like the prettiest flower, a flower that wasn't standing in anyone's shadow.

The moment Headmistress Stone announced the close of the ceremony, complete pandemonium broke out. Sarah and Val left the riser with their awards in hand. Their friends and compound crew swarmed them, with family pressing in closely, and then she heard a familiar voice in her head.

She turned to look past everyone to see his silhouette in the entrance of the Great Hall. Her mother pushed him forward, and for a moment she couldn't move.

Her dad waded through the crowd in a pair of military fatigues. Sarah bit her lip—lip gloss be damned—and her friends turned, making way for him as Val stepped back. Professor Raziel jumped down from the riser and quickly pushed through the sea of students headed toward the gym, as though coming to her aid. He had the glint of battle in his eyes, seemingly ready to fight her father for her.

"She did good, Rivera," Professor Raziel said firmly, lifting his chin and squaring his broad shoulders.

To Sarah's surprise, her father nodded and released a resigned sigh. "I heard…and I saw from the door. I was wrong." Her father extended a warrior's handshake, and Professor Raziel grudgingly accepted it.

Sarah looked up at her dad, and suddenly everything she'd stored up to argue with him about, to blame him for and to brandish before him, faded with his sad smile. Her mother stood behind him, looking as if she were holding her breath.

He turned away from her mentor and put both hands on her shoulders. "My baby girl is all grown up," he said quietly. "I'm really proud of you, Sarah."

Despite the din and confusion of the crowd, at that moment her dad was the only other person in the Great Hall.

Her father held her at arm's length and shook his head. "Look at her, Razor…she's beautiful. My princess…went into the forbidden zone and came out without a scratch—and my boy flew in there and got busted up, broke a wing. I'm just a dinosaur. Old school." He took her award away from her and read it, allowing his fingers to trace the engraving, then he looked at her and swallowed hard. "I'm proud of you, baby," he repeated, as though seeing her with brand-new eyes. "I hope you can forgive your old man for just not being ready."

She barreled into his arms and held him tight. "Papi, I love you."

Her father just hung his head and let out a huge sigh of relief. "What can I say to that? I love you, too. You've had me wrapped around your little finger since the day you took your first breath in this big, bad world and came out crying and fighting."

"I'm gonna push her hard, Rivera," Professor Raziel said. "Because she can do it, and because to keep her safe, I have to. There are still traitor cells out there, and we need her to put them down, even though her talents are still evolving."

Her father nodded and finally released her. "I know," he said, not looking at her professor. But then he cocked his head to the side as her uncle Yonnie and aunt Valkyrie came up to hug Val, who was hanging nearby. He glanced at Val and gave him a curt nod. "You did all right. You get a pass for escorting Sarah to safety and flying Al out under combat conditions…that was good work."

"Thanks, Uncle Carlos."

"Uncle Carlos, hell. Be clear, son, if you're taking my daughter to a dance, I'm Mr. Rivera from this point forward."

"Yes, sir," Val said, as the adults around them swallowed broad smiles. Then Val stepped away from his parents and shook her father's hand, his head high and his shoulders back. "I would never have let anything happen to her out there, sir."

"I ain't half as worried about the walkers in the woods as I am about what goes on up in the dorms." Carlos looked at Yonnie. "Man…me and you been boys a long time, vamps that go way back, and Val's got the fangs like me and you, so…so you better talk to your son."

Sarah just hugged her father as everybody else laughed.

"Y'all think it's funny, but I'm dead serious."

“Dad!”

“Carlos!” her mother said, pulling her father away as the rest of her big crazy family laughed even harder. Even Professor Raziel cracked a rare smile.

“For goodness’ sake!” her mother fussed, then leaned over to kiss Sarah. “Leave those kids alone and just let ’em dance!”

Neteru Compound Glossary of Terms

Neteru—Divine qualities present in all things (Kemetian, also known as Egyptian); The Vampire Huntress Legends, a Neteru was born every 1,000 years to fight the dark side—but at the dawn of the Armageddon the Light sent two (Damali Richards and Carlos Rivera).

Neteru Guardians—Special Forces Guardians of the Light that stand by the Neterus in battle against the dark side.

The Morrigan—Guardians of the Light that have turned to the dark side.

Valkyrie—A warrior angel being who lifts fallen soldiers of righteousness to Valhalla; also Sarah's aunt's name.

Daywalker—A Vampire made impervious to sunlight. (For example, Sarah's Uncle Yonnie.)

The Land of Nod—A place between dimensions (in the fourth realm) created at the dawn of time, where all mystical creatures and species were cloaked from human interaction. This banishment zone was to protect humans from the supernatural, but every now and then the veil between worlds would rip. There were good members and bad members of this community, just as is found in human society. During the Armageddon the veil was permanently damaged, and some good refugees fled persecution and sought safety with the Neterus at the Temt Tchaas Academy.

NETERU COMPOUND FAMILY TREE

NOTE: All of the Neteru Compound siblings, seven in all, were born during the same season and the same year after the first major clash of the Armageddon, except Ayana, who was four years old at the time.

PARENTS:

Carlos Rivera + Damali Richards-Rivera [Both are the Neteru Compound Leaders] = (parents of twins) **Sarah Rivera** and **Alejandro Rivera.** Their father was once a Daywalker and was brought into the Light as a Neteru. He married their mother, who was both a Powers Angel—a fearless warrior angel—and Neteru. Both siblings have a combination of their parents' seven supernatural gifts and physical makeup.

Tara Rider (ex-Vampire) + Jack Rider (Olfactory Sensor Guardian, a tracker with a supernatural ability to smell demon residue and sense danger before it manifests) = Tami Rider (Sarah's BFF, with a lot of Vampire traits)

Jasmine Berkfield (Dragon Painter) + Bobby Berkfield (White Light Wizard) = Hyacinth Berkfield (one of Sarah's non-blood–related compound sisters who is psychic)

Heather Weinstein (Stoneworker/White Lighter) + Dan Weinstein (Tactical Guardian) = Allie Weinstein (one of Sarah's non-blood–related compound sisters who is electromagnetic)

Valkyrie Johnson (a Warrior Valkyrie) + Yolando Johnson (Daywalker) = Valencio Johnson (one of Sarah's non-blood–related compound brothers who is a handsome combo of Valkyrie and Vampire)

Juanita Ciponte (psychic) + Jose Ciponte (Olfactory Guardian) = Miguel Ciponte (one of Sarah's non-blood–related compound brothers who is a strong tracker)

Krissy Berkfield-Leung (White lighter) + J.L. Leung (Tactical Guardian) = Donnie Leung (one of Sarah's non-blood–related compound brothers who is a burgeoning White Lighter computer geek)

Inez Porter-Roberts (Psychic) + "Big" Mike Roberts (stepfather) = parents of **Ayana Porter** (one of Sarah's non-blood–related compound sister who is older by four years and is destined to become the mother seer of a Guardian compound)

GRANDPARENTS:

Headmistress Marlene Stone = Mother seer to the Neteru Compound and called Nana by all. She is also the headmistress of the Temt Tchaas Academy.

Headmaster Baba Shabazz = House security for the Temt Tchaas academy, called grandfather by all in the Neteru compound, married to Marlene Stone, and a martial arts master. Baba Shabazz is also a Tactical Guardian and panther shape-shifter.

Ms. Delores Filgueiras and Mr. Monty Sinclair (neither possesses any special supernatural gift, but "Mom Delores's daughter, Inez, was born with a very strong third eye psychic supernatural ability) = Aunt Inez's mother and new stepfather; grandparents to Ayana. Ms. Delores runs the school cafeteria, and Mr. Monty is in charge of building maintenance.

Stella and Frank Weinstein (neither possesses any special supernatural talent, but their son has the Tactical gift) = Uncle Dan's parents; Allie's grandparents. They are dorm resident advisors at the school.

Marjorie (a White Lighter by birth) **and Richard Berkfield** (a healer by gift) = Aunt Krissy's and Uncle Bobby's parents; also Hyacinth's grandparents. The whole family fought evil in the compound together. They are also dorm resident advisors at the school and don't go out on campaigns against the dark side anymore.

GUARDIAN TALENTS/GIFTS

Olfactors—taste/smell superiority—destiny: trackers.

Audios—superior hearing—destiny: point walkers for a team.

Clair-Vs—superior second sight—destiny: team seers/psychics.

Tacticals—touch sensitivity—destiny: team security barriers, emit strong electromagnetic energy, can levitate items and power zap predators.

Stoneworkers—Can feel where someone has passed by a natural stone object or touch that object to supercharge it to gather information from it.

Dragon Painters—Can use organic material to paint with and bring that image to life.

White Lighters and White Wizards—Can use the natural energy found in organic material to ward off predators with white light zaps.

Neterus—Have all the above abilities, plus the gifts of healing and walking between dimensions in energy whirls.

TEEN READER'S GUIDE

Shadow Walker

By: L. A. Banks

ABOUT THIS GUIDE

The information, activities and discussion questions that follow are intended to enhance your reading of *Shadow Walker*. Please feel free to adapt these materials to suit your needs and interests.

WRITING AND RESEARCH ACTIVITIES

I. STRANGE PHENOMENA

A. There are many metaphysical principles discussed in the first section of the book—everything from auras to clairvoyance. See if you can come up with a list of extrasensory phenomena. Go to the library or online to find a definition of these different items. What does aura mean? What is a chakra system? What is clairsentient, clairvoyant, etc.?

B. Look up the word *cryptozoological*. With friends or classmates, make a list of creatures that might be subjects of cryptozoological examination, such as the unicorn, the mermaid, werewolves or Mojo the dragon. Individually or in small groups, research, prepare and present an oral report on one creature or one of the various skill types that the kids in Sarah's school are grouped into.

C. From the viewpoint of Sarah or another character, write a new chapter for the novel in which you describe your first encounter with any of the mysterious creatures. Where are you when the encounter begins? What do you see, hear, smell and experience when you meet the creature? How does the encounter end?

D. Brightly colored walls and murals in the hallways of the Temt Tchaas Academy create wonderful atmosphere for the events that take place within *Shadow Walker*. Images of flooding water are also in the text. Use pencils, watercolor paints or pens to draw your own scene inspired by a scene from the book.

E. Learn more about the Egyptian symbols and ancient Ghanaian symbols. Learn what they mean and then see if you can match up their meaning with different personality types in your class.

F. What is the strangest symbol or creature you have ever seen or the most unusual experience you have ever had? Write a short essay or story describing this, beginning with the phrase "I would never have imagined…"

G. Imagine the book as a movie—draw a movie poster for it to promote the best part of the story. (What was your favorite scene?)

II. LEADERS AND FOLLOWERS

A. What hints do we have that Sarah is becoming a group leader? What things does Sarah do that would make her a leader among her friends? What character traits do you feel make a good leader?

B. In what ways was Sarah a stronger leader than her brother? In what ways was she weaker?

C. Make a list of all the characters in the novel engaged in learning lessons. Beside each character name, note what they learned, what they needed to change about themselves and who, if anyone, helped them.

D. What role does Valencio play in the group? How is his personality important? What role does Wil play in the group? How is his personality important?

E. In the character of Tami Rider, write a monologue in which you talk to yourself about your best friend's request that you stop taking dares. Perform your monologue for friends and classmates.

F. Consider what we learn by the end of the book—that things are not always as they seem. Discuss stereotypes and how we sometimes inaccurately think things about others because of their clothes, people they hang around, maybe because of their religion or ethnic background. How was Stefan misjudged? Describe a time when you or a friend misjudged someone without getting to know them.

III. ARCHITECTURE

A. Name the pyramids located on the Giza plateau. Look them up online or in the library.

B. There was actually a bunker created beneath the Greenbriar Hotel in West Virginia by President Dwight Eisenhower. Look up information on the cold war and on President Eisenhower, and see if you can find out any information about fall-out shelters.

C. The teens briefly escape into a small Amish town. Learn about the Amish culture online or at your library. What do they believe about farming, about technology and self-sufficiency (define that word)?

QUESTIONS FOR DISCUSSION

1. The opening chapters of the novel describe Sarah's encounters with nightmares and with her family/friends. How do these chapters help readers better understand Sarah? How do the dark and other natural elements (like the landscape) described in these chapters become important motifs throughout the novel—especially the forest?

2. What do Sarah, Tami and the boys discover in the dark outside the family compound? How does their discovery relate to Sarah's ongoing fear?

3. Explain Sarah's long-held view of the compound as a safe and peaceful place. Is Sarah's sense of calm created by the family or her relationship to the place, if so how? Does everyone feel this way about their home—discuss the different perspectives amongst the students? Do you think the presence of something scary at the compound changes Sarah's perspective, if so how? Who or what can truly disrupt this serenity?

4. Once Sarah and her compound siblings get to school, things change. List all the new things they have to encounter and why this adjustment is so hard. What about fitting in is so difficult for them?

5. What major rule do the older students break, and is it dangerous to do that in any way? Why is Sarah so nervous about following the crowd?

6. Do you think Sarah was right to confess what she knew to her grandmother?

7. Who is Professor Raziel and what is he to Sarah? Look up the words *mentor* and *protégée* and write out the definitions. Do you think Sarah's dad was right or wrong to do what he did? (Even if you think he is wrong, can you make a case for why he might have acted the way he did?) How would you have felt if you were in Sarah's situation?

8. What do you think about Sarah's little shadows?

9. Do you think being a Shadow Walker is basically a good or bad thing? What other formal and informal groups or societies operate within the novel? Can *Shadow Walker* be read as a study of the dynamics and loyalties at play between individuals and groups? Why or why not?

10. What is your reaction to Tami's jealousy of her best friend? In the end, do you feel that each person who did something unfair should be forgiven? Why or why not? List who you can forgive and why, as well as who you could not trust in the future and why. Which teachers, too, would you forgive or trust, or not?

Look for book 2, *Shadow Seekers*, sometime in 2011…

www.NeteruAcademy.com

Author Bio: LA BANKS has written more than 42 novels and contributed to 23 novellas. She writes in the genres of romance, women's fiction, crime/suspense thrillers and paranormal lore. In addition to a busy writing schedule, she is a proud member of The Liars Club, is a board of trustee member for the Philadelphia Free Library and serves on the Mayor's Commission on Literacy. Ms. Banks is a graduate of The University of Pennsylvania Wharton undergraduate program with a master's in fine arts from Temple University. She is a full-time writer living and working in Philadelphia.

Look for book 2, *Shadow Seekers*, sometime in 2011…

www.NeteruAcademy.com

CPSIA information can be obtained
at www.ICGtesting.com
Printed in the USA
LVHW021359120921
697665LV00009B/726